THE AWAKENING

by Kate Chopin

CHAPTER I

A green and yellow parrot, which hung in a cage outside the door, kept repeating over and over:

"*Allez vous-en! Allez vous-en! Sapristi!* That's all right!"

He could speak a little Spanish, and also a language which nobody understood, unless it was the mocking-bird that hung on the other side of the door, whistling his fluty notes out upon the breeze with maddening persistence.

Mr. Pontellier, unable to read his newspaper with any degree of comfort, arose with an expression and an exclamation of disgust. He walked down the gallery and across the narrow "bridges" which connected the Lebrun cottages one with the other. He had been seated before the door of the main house. The parrot and the mocking-bird were the property of Madame Lebrun, and they had the right to make all the noise they wished. Mr. Pontellier had the privilege of quitting their society when they ceased to be entertaining.

He stopped before the door of his own cottage, which was the fourth one from the main building and next to the last. Seating himself in a wicker rocker which was there, he once more applied himself to the task of reading the newspaper. The day was Sunday; the paper was a day old. The Sunday papers had not yet reached Grand Isle. He was already acquainted with the market reports, and he glanced restlessly over the editorials and bits of news which he had not had time to read before quitting New Orleans the day before.

Mr. Pontellier wore eye-glasses. He was a man of forty, of medium height and rather slender build; he stooped a little. His hair was brown and straight, parted on one side. His beard was neatly and closely trimmed.

Once in a while he withdrew his glance from the newspaper and looked about him. There was more noise than ever over at the house. The main building was called "the house," to distinguish it from the cottages. The chattering and whistling birds were still at it. Two young girls, the Farival twins, were playing a duet from "Zampa" upon the piano. Madame Lebrun was bustling in and out, giving orders in a high key to a yard-boy whenever she got inside the house, and directions in an equally high voice to a dining-room servant whenever she got outside. She was a fresh, pretty woman, clad always in white with elbow sleeves. Her starched skirts crinkled as she came and went. Farther down, before one of the cottages, a lady in black was walking demurely up and down, telling her beads. A good many persons of the *pension* had gone over to the *Chênière Caminada* in Beaudelet's lugger to hear mass. Some young people were out under the water-oaks playing croquet. Mr. Pontellier's two children were there—sturdy little fellows of four and five. A quadroon nurse followed them about with a faraway, meditative air.

Mr. Pontellier finally lit a cigar and began to smoke, letting the paper drag idly from his hand. He fixed his gaze upon a white sunshade that was advancing at snail's pace from the beach. He could see it plainly between the gaunt trunks of the water-oaks and across the stretch of yellow camomile. The gulf looked far away, melting hazily into the blue of the horizon. The sunshade continued to approach slowly. Beneath its pink-lined shelter were his wife, Mrs. Pontellier, and young Robert Lebrun. When they reached the cottage, the two seated themselves with some appearance of fatigue upon the upper step of the porch, facing each other, each leaning against a supporting post.

"What folly! to bathe at such an hour in such heat!" exclaimed Mr. Pontellier. He himself had taken a plunge at daylight. That was why the morning seemed long to him.

"You are burnt beyond recognition," he added, looking at his wife as one looks at a valuable piece of personal property which has suffered some damage. She held up her hands, strong, shapely hands, and surveyed them critically, drawing up her lawn sleeves above the wrists. Looking at them reminded her of her rings, which she had given to her husband before leaving for the beach. She silently reached out to him, and he, understanding, took the rings from his vest pocket and dropped them into her open palm. She slipped them upon her fingers; then clasping her knees, she looked across at Robert and began to laugh. The rings sparkled upon her fingers. He sent back an answering smile.

"What is it?" asked Pontellier, looking lazily and amused from one to the other. It was some utter nonsense; some adventure out there in the water, and they both tried to relate it at once. It did not seem half so amusing when told. They realized this, and so did Mr. Pontellier. He yawned and stretched himself. Then he got up, saying he had half a mind to go over to Klein's hotel and play a game of billiards.

"Come go along, Lebrun," he proposed to Robert. But Robert admitted quite frankly that he preferred to stay where he was and talk to Mrs. Pontellier.

"Well, send him about his business when he bores you, Edna," instructed her husband as he prepared to leave.

"Here, take the umbrella," she exclaimed, holding it out to him. He accepted the sunshade, and lifting it over his head descended the steps and walked away.

"Coming back to dinner?" his wife called after him. He halted a moment and shrugged his shoulders. He felt in his vest pocket; there was a ten-dollar bill there. He did not know; perhaps he would return for the early dinner and perhaps he would not. It all depended upon the company which he found over at Klein's and the size of "the game." He did not say this, but she understood it, and laughed, nodding good-by to him.

Both children wanted to follow their father when they saw him starting out. He kissed them and promised to bring them back bonbons and peanuts.

CHAPTER II

Mrs. Pontellier's eyes were quick and bright; they were a yellowish brown, about the color of her hair. She had a way of turning them swiftly upon an object and holding them there as if lost in some inward maze of contemplation or thought.

Her eyebrows were a shade darker than her hair. They were thick and almost horizontal, emphasizing the depth of her eyes. She was rather handsome than beautiful. Her face was captivating by reason of a certain frankness of expression and a contradictory subtle play of features. Her manner was engaging.

Robert rolled a cigarette. He smoked cigarettes because he could not afford cigars, he said. He had a cigar in his pocket which Mr. Pontellier had presented him with, and he was saving it for his after-dinner smoke.

This seemed quite proper and natural on his part. In coloring he was not unlike his companion. A clean-shaved face made the resemblance more pronounced than it would otherwise have been. There rested no shadow of care upon his open countenance. His eyes gathered in and reflected the light and languor of the summer day.

Mrs. Pontellier reached over for a palm-leaf fan that lay on the porch and began to fan herself, while Robert sent between his lips light puffs from his cigarette. They chatted incessantly: about the things around them; their amusing adventure out in the water—it had again assumed its entertaining aspect; about the wind, the trees, the people who had gone to the *Chênière;* about the children playing croquet under the oaks, and the Farival twins, who were now performing the overture to "The Poet and the Peasant."

Robert talked a good deal about himself. He was very young, and did not know any better. Mrs. Pontellier talked a little about herself for the same reason. Each was interested in what the other said. Robert spoke of his intention to go to Mexico in the autumn, where fortune awaited him. He was always intending to go to Mexico, but some way never got there. Meanwhile he held on to his modest position in a mercantile house in New Orleans, where an equal familiarity with English, French and Spanish gave him no small value as a clerk and correspondent.

He was spending his summer vacation, as he always did, with his mother at Grand Isle. In former times, before Robert could remember, "the house" had been a summer luxury of the Lebruns. Now, flanked by its dozen or more cottages, which were always filled with exclusive visitors from the "*Quartier Français*," it enabled Madame Lebrun to maintain the easy and comfortable existence which appeared to be her birthright.

Mrs. Pontellier talked about her father's Mississippi plantation and her girlhood home in the old Kentucky blue-grass country. She was an American woman, with a small infusion of French which seemed to have been lost in dilution. She read a letter from her sister, who was away in the East, and who had engaged herself to be married. Robert was interested, and wanted to know what manner of girls the sisters were, what the father was like, and how long the mother had been dead.

When Mrs. Pontellier folded the letter it was time for her to dress for the early dinner.

"I see Léonce isn't coming back," she said, with a glance in the direction whence her husband had disappeared. Robert supposed he was not, as there were a good many New Orleans club men over at Klein's.

When Mrs. Pontellier left him to enter her room, the young man descended the steps and strolled over toward the croquet players, where, during the half-hour before dinner, he amused himself with the little Pontellier children, who were very fond of him.

CHAPTER III

It was eleven o'clock that night when Mr. Pontellier returned from Klein's hotel. He was in an excellent humor, in high spirits, and very talkative. His entrance awoke his wife, who was in bed and fast asleep when he came in. He talked to her while he undressed, telling her anecdotes and bits of news and gossip that he had gathered during the day. From his trousers pockets he took a fistful of crumpled bank notes and a good deal of silver coin, which he piled on the bureau indiscriminately with keys, knife, handkerchief, and whatever else happened to be in his pockets. She was overcome with sleep, and answered him with little half utterances.

He thought it very discouraging that his wife, who was the sole object of his existence, evinced so little interest in things which concerned him, and valued so little his conversation.

Mr. Pontellier had forgotten the bonbons and peanuts for the boys. Notwithstanding he loved them very much, and went into the adjoining room where they slept to take a look at them and make sure that they were resting comfortably. The result of his investigation was far from satisfactory. He turned and shifted the youngsters about in bed. One of them began to kick and talk about a basket full of crabs.

Mr. Pontellier returned to his wife with the information that Raoul had a high fever and needed looking after. Then he lit a cigar and went and sat near the open door to smoke it.

Mrs. Pontellier was quite sure Raoul had no fever. He had gone to bed perfectly well, she said, and nothing had ailed him all day. Mr. Pontellier was too well acquainted with fever symptoms to be mistaken. He assured her the child was consuming at that moment in the next room.

He reproached his wife with her inattention, her habitual neglect of the children. If it was not a mother's place to look after children, whose on earth was it? He himself had his hands full with his brokerage business. He could not be in two places at once; making a living for his family on the street, and staying at home to see that no harm befell them. He talked in a monotonous, insistent way.

Mrs. Pontellier sprang out of bed and went into the next room. She soon came back and sat on the edge of the bed, leaning her head down on the pillow. She said nothing, and refused to answer her husband when he questioned her. When his cigar was smoked out he went to bed, and in half a minute he was fast asleep.

Mrs. Pontellier was by that time thoroughly awake. She began to cry a little, and wiped her eyes on the sleeve of her *peignoir*. Blowing out the candle, which her husband had left burning, she slipped her bare feet into a pair of satin *mules* at the foot of the bed and went out on the porch, where she sat down in the wicker chair and began to rock gently to and fro.

It was then past midnight. The cottages were all dark. A single faint light gleamed out from the hallway of the house. There was no sound abroad except the hooting of an old owl in the top of a water-oak, and the everlasting voice of the sea, that was not uplifted at that soft hour. It broke like a mournful lullaby upon the night.

The tears came so fast to Mrs. Pontellier's eyes that the damp sleeve of her *peignoir* no longer served to dry them. She was holding the back of her chair with one hand; her loose sleeve had slipped almost to the shoulder of her uplifted arm. Turning, she thrust her face, steaming and wet, into the bend of her arm, and she went on crying there, not caring any longer to dry her face, her eyes, her arms. She could not have told why she was crying. Such experiences as the foregoing were not uncommon in her married life. They seemed never before to have weighed much against the abundance of her husband's kindness and a uniform devotion which had come to be tacit and self-understood.

An indescribable oppression, which seemed to generate in some unfamiliar part of her consciousness, filled her whole being with a vague anguish. It was like a shadow, like a mist passing across her soul's summer day. It was strange and unfamiliar; it was a mood. She did not sit there inwardly upbraiding her husband, lamenting at Fate, which had directed her footsteps to the path which they had taken. She was just having a good cry all to herself. The mosquitoes made merry over her, biting her firm, round arms and nipping at her bare insteps.

The little stinging, buzzing imps succeeded in dispelling a mood which might have held her there in the darkness half a night longer.

The following morning Mr. Pontellier was up in good time to take the rockaway which was to convey him to the steamer at the wharf. He was returning to the city to his business, and they would not see him again at the Island till the coming Saturday. He had regained his composure, which seemed to have been somewhat impaired the night before. He was eager to be gone, as he looked forward to a lively week in Carondelet Street.

Mr. Pontellier gave his wife half of the money which he had brought away from Klein's hotel the evening before. She liked money as well as most women, and accepted it with no little satisfaction.

"It will buy a handsome wedding present for Sister Janet!" she exclaimed, smoothing out the bills as she counted them one by one.

"Oh! we'll treat Sister Janet better than that, my dear," he laughed, as he prepared to kiss her good-by.

The boys were tumbling about, clinging to his legs, imploring that numerous things be brought back to them. Mr. Pontellier was a great favorite, and ladies, men, children, even nurses, were always on hand to say good-by to him. His wife stood smiling and waving, the boys shouting, as he disappeared in the old rockaway down the sandy road.

A few days later a box arrived for Mrs. Pontellier from New Orleans. It was from her husband. It was filled with *friandises*, with luscious and toothsome bits—the finest of fruits, *patés*, a rare bottle or two, delicious syrups, and bonbons in abundance.

Mrs. Pontellier was always very generous with the contents of such a box; she was quite used to receiving them when away from home. The *patés* and fruit were brought to the dining-room; the bonbons were passed around. And the ladies, selecting with dainty and discriminating fingers and a little greedily, all declared that Mr. Pontellier was the best husband in the world. Mrs. Pontellier was forced to admit that she knew of none better.

CHAPTER IV

It would have been a difficult matter for Mr. Pontellier to define to his own satisfaction or any one else's wherein his wife failed in her duty toward their children. It was something which he felt rather than perceived, and he never voiced the feeling without subsequent regret and ample atonement.

If one of the little Pontellier boys took a tumble whilst at play, he was not apt to rush crying to his mother's arms for comfort; he would more likely pick himself up, wipe the water out of his eyes and the sand out of his mouth, and go on playing. Tots as they were, they pulled together and stood their ground in childish battles with doubled fists and uplifted voices, which usually prevailed against the other mother-tots. The quadroon nurse was looked upon as a huge encumbrance, only good to button up waists and panties and to brush and part hair; since it seemed to be a law of society that hair must be parted and brushed.

In short, Mrs. Pontellier was not a mother-woman. The mother-women seemed to prevail that summer at Grand Isle. It was easy to know them, fluttering about with extended, protecting wings when any harm, real or imaginary, threatened their precious brood. They were women who idolized their children, worshiped their husbands, and esteemed it a holy privilege to efface themselves as individuals and grow wings as ministering angels.

Many of them were delicious in the rôle; one of them was the embodiment of every womanly grace and charm. If her husband did not adore her, he was a brute, deserving of death by slow torture. Her name was Adèle Ratignolle. There are no words to describe her save the old ones that have served so often to picture the bygone heroine of romance and the fair lady of our dreams. There was nothing subtle or hidden about her charms; her beauty was all there, flaming and apparent: the spun-gold hair that comb nor confining pin could restrain; the blue eyes that were like nothing but sapphires; two lips that pouted, that were so red one could only think of cherries or some other delicious crimson fruit in looking at them. She was growing a little stout, but it did not seem to detract an iota from the grace of every step, pose, gesture. One would not have wanted her white neck a mite less full or her beautiful arms more slender. Never were hands more exquisite than hers, and it was a joy to look at them when she threaded her needle or adjusted her gold thimble to her taper middle finger as she sewed away on the little night-drawers or fashioned a bodice or a bib.

Madame Ratignolle was very fond of Mrs. Pontellier, and often she took her sewing and went over to sit with her in the afternoons. She was sitting there the afternoon of the day the box arrived from New Orleans. She had possession of the rocker, and she was busily engaged in sewing upon a diminutive pair of night-drawers.

She had brought the pattern of the drawers for Mrs. Pontellier to cut out—a marvel of construction, fashioned to enclose a baby's body so effectually that only two small eyes might look out from the garment, like an Eskimo's. They were designed for winter wear, when treacherous drafts came down chimneys and insidious currents of deadly cold found their way through key-holes.

Mrs. Pontellier's mind was quite at rest concerning the present material needs of her children, and she could not see the use of anticipating and making winter night garments the subject of her summer meditations. But she did not want to appear unamiable and uninterested, so she had brought forth newspapers, which she spread upon the floor of the gallery, and under Madame Ratignolle's directions she had cut a pattern of the impervious garment.

Robert was there, seated as he had been the Sunday before, and Mrs. Pontellier also occupied her former position on the upper step, leaning listlessly against the post. Beside her was a box of bonbons, which she held out at intervals to Madame Ratignolle.

That lady seemed at a loss to make a selection, but finally settled upon a stick of nougat, wondering if it were not too rich; whether it could possibly hurt her. Madame Ratignolle had been married seven years. About every two years she had a baby. At that time she had three babies, and was beginning to think of a fourth one. She was always talking about her "condition." Her "condition" was in no way apparent, and no one would have known a thing about it but for her persistence in making it the subject of conversation.

Robert started to reassure her, asserting that he had known a lady who had subsisted upon nougat during the entire—but seeing the color mount into Mrs. Pontellier's face he checked himself and changed the subject.

Mrs. Pontellier, though she had married a Creole, was not thoroughly at home in the society of Creoles; never before had she been thrown so intimately among them. There were only Creoles that summer at Lebrun's. They all knew each other, and felt like one large family, among whom existed the most amicable relations. A characteristic which distinguished them and which impressed Mrs. Pontellier most forcibly was their entire absence of prudery. Their freedom of expression was at first incomprehensible to her, though she had no difficulty in reconciling it with a lofty chastity which in the Creole woman seems to be inborn and unmistakable.

Never would Edna Pontellier forget the shock with which she heard Madame Ratignolle relating to old Monsieur Farival the harrowing story of one of her *accouchements*, withholding no intimate detail. She was growing accustomed to like shocks, but she could not keep the mounting color back from her cheeks. Oftener than once her coming had interrupted the droll story with which Robert was entertaining some amused group of married women.

A book had gone the rounds of the *pension*. When it came her turn to read it, she did so with profound astonishment. She felt moved to read the book in secret and solitude, though none of the others had done so—to hide it from view at the sound of approaching footsteps. It was openly criticised and freely discussed at table. Mrs. Pontellier gave over being astonished, and concluded that wonders would never cease.

CHAPTER V

They formed a congenial group sitting there that summer afternoon—Madame Ratignolle sewing away, often stopping to relate a story or incident with much expressive gesture of her perfect hands; Robert and Mrs. Pontellier sitting idle, exchanging occasional words, glances or smiles which indicated a certain advanced stage of intimacy and *camaraderie*.

He had lived in her shadow during the past month. No one thought anything of it. Many had predicted that Robert would devote himself to Mrs. Pontellier when he arrived. Since the age of fifteen, which was eleven years before, Robert each summer at Grand Isle had constituted himself the devoted attendant of some fair dame or damsel. Sometimes it was a young girl, again a widow; but as often as not it was some interesting married woman.

For two consecutive seasons he lived in the sunlight of Mademoiselle Duvigné's presence. But she died between summers; then Robert posed as an inconsolable, prostrating himself at the feet of Madame Ratignolle for whatever crumbs of sympathy and comfort she might be pleased to vouchsafe.

Mrs. Pontellier liked to sit and gaze at her fair companion as she might look upon a faultless Madonna.

"Could any one fathom the cruelty beneath that fair exterior?" murmured Robert. "She knew that I adored her once, and she let me adore her. It was 'Robert, come; go; stand up; sit down; do this; do that; see if the baby sleeps; my thimble, please, that I left God knows where. Come and read Daudet to me while I sew.' "

"*Par exemple!* I never had to ask. You were always there under my feet, like a troublesome cat."

"You mean like an adoring dog. And just as soon as Ratignolle appeared on the scene, then it *was* like a dog. '*Passez! Adieu! Allez vous-en!*' "

"Perhaps I feared to make Alphonse jealous," she interjoined, with excessive naïveté. That made them all laugh. The right hand jealous of the left! The heart jealous of the soul! But for that matter, the Creole husband is never jealous; with him the gangrene passion is one which has become dwarfed by disuse.

Meanwhile Robert, addressing Mrs. Pontellier, continued to tell of his one time hopeless passion for Madame Ratignolle; of sleepless nights, of consuming flames till the very sea sizzled when he took his daily plunge. While the lady at the needle kept up a little running, contemptuous comment:

"*Blagueur—farceur—gros bête, va!*"

He never assumed this serio-comic tone when alone with Mrs. Pontellier. She never knew precisely what to make of it; at that moment it was impossible for her to guess how much of it was jest and what proportion was earnest. It was understood that he had often spoken words of love to Madame Ratignolle, without any thought of being taken seriously. Mrs. Pontellier was glad he had not assumed a similar rôle toward herself. It would have been unacceptable and annoying.

Mrs. Pontellier had brought her sketching materials, which she sometimes dabbled with in an unprofessional way. She liked the dabbling. She felt in it satisfaction of a kind which no other employment afforded her.

She had long wished to try herself on Madame Ratignolle. Never had that lady seemed a more tempting subject than at that moment, seated there like some sensuous Madonna, with the gleam of the fading day enriching her splendid color.

Robert crossed over and seated himself upon the step below Mrs. Pontellier, that he might watch her work. She handled her brushes with a certain ease and freedom which came, not from long and close acquaintance with them, but from a natural aptitude. Robert followed her work with close attention, giving forth little ejaculatory expressions of appreciation in French, which he addressed to Madame Ratignolle.

"Mais ce n'est pas mal! Elle s'y connait, elle a de la force, oui."

During his oblivious attention he once quietly rested his head against Mrs. Pontellier's arm. As gently she repulsed him. Once again he repeated the offense. She could not but believe it to be thoughtlessness on his part; yet that was no reason she should submit to it. She did not remonstrate, except again to repulse him quietly but firmly. He offered no apology.

The picture completed bore no resemblance to Madame Ratignolle. She was greatly disappointed to find that it did not look like her. But it was a fair enough piece of work, and in many respects satisfying.

Mrs. Pontellier evidently did not think so. After surveying the sketch critically she drew a broad smudge of paint across its surface, and crumpled the paper between her hands.

The youngsters came tumbling up the steps, the quadroon following at the respectful distance which they required her to observe. Mrs. Pontellier made them carry her paints and things into the house. She sought to detain them for a little talk and some pleasantry. But they were greatly in earnest. They had only come to investigate the contents of the bonbon box. They accepted without murmuring what she chose to give them, each holding out two chubby hands scoop-like, in the vain hope that they might be filled; and then away they went.

The sun was low in the west, and the breeze soft and languorous that came up from the south, charged with the seductive odor of the sea. Children freshly befurbelowed, were gathering for their games under the oaks. Their voices were high and penetrating.

Madame Ratignolle folded her sewing, placing thimble, scissors, and thread all neatly together in the roll, which she pinned securely. She complained of faintness. Mrs. Pontellier flew for the cologne water and a fan. She bathed Madame Ratignolle's face with cologne, while Robert plied the fan with unnecessary vigor.

The spell was soon over, and Mrs. Pontellier could not help wondering if there were not a little imagination responsible for its origin, for the rose tint had never faded from her friend's face.

She stood watching the fair woman walk down the long line of galleries with the grace and majesty which queens are sometimes supposed to possess. Her little ones ran to meet her. Two of them clung about her white skirts, the third she took from its nurse and with a thousand endearments bore it along in her own fond, encircling arms. Though, as everybody well knew, the doctor had forbidden her to lift so much as a pin!

"Are you going bathing?" asked Robert of Mrs. Pontellier. It was not so much a question as a reminder.

"Oh, no," she answered, with a tone of indecision. "I'm tired; I think not." Her glance wandered from his face away toward the Gulf, whose sonorous murmur reached her like a loving but imperative entreaty.

"Oh, come!" he insisted. "You mustn't miss your bath. Come on. The water must be delicious; it will not hurt you. Come."

He reached up for her big, rough straw hat that hung on a peg outside the door, and put it on her head. They descended the steps, and walked away together toward the beach. The sun was low in the west and the breeze was soft and warm.

CHAPTER VI

Edna Pontellier could not have told why, wishing to go to the beach with Robert, she should in the first place have declined, and in the second place have followed in obedience to one of the two contradictory impulses which impelled her.

A certain light was beginning to dawn dimly within her,—the light which, showing the way, forbids it.

At that early period it served but to bewilder her. It moved her to dreams, to thoughtfulness, to the shadowy anguish which had overcome her the midnight when she had abandoned herself to tears.

In short, Mrs. Pontellier was beginning to realize her position in the universe as a human being, and to recognize her relations as an individual to the world within and about her. This may seem like a ponderous weight of wisdom to descend upon the soul of a young woman of twenty-eight—perhaps more wisdom than the Holy Ghost is usually pleased to vouchsafe to any woman.

But the beginning of things, of a world especially, is necessarily vague, tangled, chaotic, and exceedingly disturbing. How few of us ever emerge from such beginning! How many souls perish in its tumult!

The voice of the sea is seductive; never ceasing, whispering, clamoring, murmuring, inviting the soul to wander for a spell in abysses of solitude; to lose itself in mazes of inward contemplation.

The voice of the sea speaks to the soul. The touch of the sea is sensuous, enfolding the body in its soft, close embrace.

CHAPTER VII

Mrs. Pontellier was not a woman given to confidences, a characteristic hitherto contrary to her nature. Even as a child she had lived her own small life all within herself. At a very early period she had apprehended instinctively the dual life—that outward existence which conforms, the inward life which questions.

That summer at Grand Isle she began to loosen a little the mantle of reserve that had always enveloped her. There may have been—there must have been—influences, both subtle and apparent, working in their several ways to induce her to do this; but the most obvious was the influence of Adèle Ratignolle. The excessive physical charm of the Creole had first attracted her, for Edna had a sensuous susceptibility to beauty. Then the candor of the woman's whole existence, which every one might read, and which formed so striking a contrast to her own habitual reserve—this might have furnished a link. Who can tell what metals the gods use in forging the subtle bond which we call sympathy, which we might as well call love.

The two women went away one morning to the beach together, arm in arm, under the huge white sunshade. Edna had prevailed upon Madame Ratignolle to leave the children behind, though she could not induce her to relinquish a diminutive roll of needlework, which Adèle begged to be allowed to slip into the depths of her pocket. In some unaccountable way they had escaped from Robert.

The walk to the beach was no inconsiderable one, consisting as it did of a long, sandy path, upon which a sporadic and tangled growth that bordered it on either side made frequent and unexpected inroads. There were acres of yellow camomile reaching out on either hand. Further away still, vegetable gardens abounded, with frequent small plantations of orange or lemon trees intervening. The dark green clusters glistened from afar in the sun.

The women were both of goodly height, Madame Ratignolle possessing the more feminine and matronly figure. The charm of Edna Pontellier's physique stole insensibly upon you. The lines of her body were long, clean and symmetrical; it was a body which occasionally fell into splendid poses; there was no suggestion of the trim, stereotyped fashion-plate about it. A casual and indiscriminating observer, in passing, might not cast a second glance upon the figure. But with more feeling and discernment he would have recognized the noble beauty of its modeling, and the graceful severity of poise and movement, which made Edna Pontellier different from the crowd.

She wore a cool muslin that morning—white, with a waving vertical line of brown running through it; also a white linen collar and the big straw hat which she had taken from the peg outside the door. The hat rested any way on her yellow-brown hair, that waved a little, was heavy, and clung close to her head.

Madame Ratignolle, more careful of her complexion, had twined a gauze veil about her head. She wore dogskin gloves, with gauntlets that protected her wrists. She was dressed in pure white, with a fluffiness of ruffles that became her. The draperies and fluttering things which she wore suited her rich, luxuriant beauty as a greater severity of line could not have done.

There were a number of bath-houses along the beach, of rough but solid construction, built with small, protecting galleries facing the water. Each house consisted of two compartments, and each family at Lebrun's possessed a compartment for itself, fitted out with all the essential paraphernalia of the bath and whatever other conveniences the owners might desire. The two women had no intention of bathing; they had just strolled down to the beach for a walk and to be alone and near the water. The Pontellier and Ratignolle compartments adjoined one another under the same roof.

Mrs. Pontellier had brought down her key through force of habit. Unlocking the door of her bath-room she went inside, and soon emerged, bringing a rug, which she spread upon the floor of the gallery, and two huge hair pillows covered with crash, which she placed against the front of the building.

The two seated themselves there in the shade of the porch, side by side, with their backs against the pillows and their feet extended. Madame Ratignolle removed her veil, wiped her face with a rather delicate handkerchief, and fanned herself with the fan which she always carried suspended somewhere about her person by a long, narrow ribbon. Edna removed her collar and opened her dress at the throat. She took the fan from Madame Ratignolle and began to fan both herself and her companion. It was very warm, and for a while they did nothing but exchange remarks about the heat, the sun, the glare. But there was a breeze blowing, a choppy, stiff wind that whipped the water into froth. It fluttered the skirts of the two women and kept them for a while engaged in adjusting, readjusting, tucking in, securing hair-pins and hat-pins. A few persons were sporting some distance away in the water. The beach was very still of human sound at that hour. The lady in black was reading her morning devotions on the porch of a neighboring bath-house. Two young lovers were exchanging their hearts' yearnings beneath the children's tent, which they had found unoccupied.

Edna Pontellier, casting her eyes about, had finally kept them at rest upon the sea. The day was clear and carried the gaze out as far as the blue sky went; there were a few white clouds suspended idly over the horizon. A lateen sail was visible in the direction of Cat Island, and others to the south seemed almost motionless in the far distance.

"Of whom—of what are you thinking?" asked Adèle of her companion, whose countenance she had been watching with a little amused attention, arrested by the absorbed expression which seemed to have seized and fixed every feature into a statuesque repose.

"Nothing," returned Mrs. Pontellier, with a start, adding at once: "How stupid! But it seems to me it is the reply we make instinctively to such a question. Let me see," she went on, throwing back her head and narrowing her fine eyes till they shone like two vivid points of light. "Let me see. I was really not conscious of thinking of anything; but perhaps I can retrace my thoughts."

"Oh! never mind!" laughed Madame Ratignolle. "I am not quite so exacting. I will let you off this time. It is really too hot to think, especially to think about thinking."

"But for the fun of it," persisted Edna. "First of all, the sight of the water stretching so far away, those motionless sails against the blue sky, made a delicious picture that I just wanted to sit and look at. The hot wind beating in my face made me think—without any connection that I can trace—of a summer day in Kentucky, of a meadow that seemed as big as the ocean to the very little girl walking through the grass, which was higher than her waist. She threw out her arms as if swimming when she walked, beating the tall grass as one strikes out in the water. Oh, I see the connection now!"

"Where were you going that day in Kentucky, walking through the grass?"

"I don't remember now. I was just walking diagonally across a big field. My sun-bonnet obstructed the view. I could see only the stretch of green before me, and I felt as if I must walk on forever, without coming to the end of it.

I don't remember whether I was frightened or pleased. I must have been entertained.

"Likely as not it was Sunday," she laughed; "and I was running away from prayers, from the Presbyterian service, read in a spirit of gloom by my father that chills me yet to think of."

"And have you been running away from prayers ever since, *ma chère?*" asked Madame Ratignolle, amused.

"No! oh, no!" Edna hastened to say. "I was a little unthinking child in those days, just following a misleading impulse without question. On the contrary, during one period of my life religion took a firm hold upon me; after I was twelve and until—until—why, I suppose until now, though I never thought much about it—just driven along by habit. But do you know," she broke off, turning her quick eyes upon Madame Ratignolle and leaning forward a little so as to bring her face quite close to that of her companion, "sometimes I feel this summer as if I were walking through the green meadow again; idly, aimlessly, unthinking and unguided."

Madame Ratignolle laid her hand over that of Mrs. Pontellier, which was near her. Seeing that the hand was not withdrawn, she clasped it firmly and warmly. She even stroked it a little, fondly, with the other hand, murmuring in an undertone, "*Pauvre chérie.*"

The action was at first a little confusing to Edna, but she soon lent herself readily to the Creole's gentle caress. She was not accustomed to an outward and spoken expression of affection, either in herself or in others. She and her younger sister, Janet, had quarreled a good deal through force of unfortunate habit. Her older sister, Margaret, was matronly and dignified, probably from having assumed matronly and housewifely responsibilities too early in life, their mother having died when they were quite young. Margaret was not effusive; she was practical. Edna had had an occasional girl friend, but whether accidentally or not, they seemed to have been all of one type—the self-contained. She never realized that the reserve of her own character had much, perhaps everything, to do with this. Her most intimate friend at school had been one of rather exceptional intellectual gifts, who wrote fine-sounding essays, which Edna admired and strove to imitate; and with her she talked and glowed over the English classics, and sometimes held religious and political controversies.

Edna often wondered at one propensity which sometimes had inwardly disturbed her without causing any outward show or manifestation on her part. At a very early age—perhaps it was when she traversed the ocean of waving grass—she remembered that she had been passionately enamored of a dignified and sad-eyed cavalry officer who visited her father in Kentucky. She could not leave his presence when he was there, nor remove her eyes from his face, which was something like Napoleon's, with a lock of black hair falling across the forehead. But the cavalry officer melted imperceptibly out of her existence.

At another time her affections were deeply engaged by a young gentleman who visited a lady on a neighboring plantation. It was after they went to Mississippi to live. The young man was engaged to be married to the young lady, and they sometimes called upon Margaret, driving over of afternoons in a buggy. Edna was a little miss, just merging into her teens; and the realization that she herself was nothing, nothing, nothing to the engaged young man was a bitter affliction to her. But he, too, went the way of dreams.

She was a grown young woman when she was overtaken by what she supposed to be the climax of her fate. It was when the face and figure of a great tragedian began to haunt her imagination and stir her senses. The persistence of the infatuation lent it an aspect of genuineness. The hopelessness of it colored it with the lofty tones of a great passion.

The picture of the tragedian stood enframed upon her desk. Any one may possess the portrait of a tragedian without exciting suspicion or comment. (This was a sinister reflection which she cherished.) In the presence of others she expressed admiration for his exalted gifts, as she handed the photograph around and dwelt upon the fidelity of the likeness. When alone she sometimes picked it up and kissed the cold glass passionately.

Her marriage to Léonce Pontellier was purely an accident, in this respect resembling many other marriages which masquerade as the decrees of Fate. It was in the midst of her secret great passion that she met him. He fell in love, as men are in the habit of doing, and pressed his suit with an earnestness and an ardor which left nothing to be desired. He pleased her; his absolute devotion flattered her. She fancied there was a sympathy of thought and taste between them, in which fancy she was mistaken. Add to this the violent opposition of her father and her sister Margaret to her marriage with a Catholic, and we need seek no further for the motives which led her to accept Monsieur Pontellier for her husband.

The acme of bliss, which would have been a marriage with the tragedian, was not for her in this world. As the devoted wife of a man who worshiped her, she felt she would take her place with a certain dignity in the world of reality, closing the portals forever behind her upon the realm of romance and dreams.

But it was not long before the tragedian had gone to join the cavalry officer and the engaged young man and a few others; and Edna found herself face to face with the realities. She grew fond of her husband, realizing with some unaccountable satisfaction that no trace of passion or excessive and fictitious warmth colored her affection, thereby threatening its dissolution.

She was fond of her children in an uneven, impulsive way. She would sometimes gather them passionately to her heart; she would sometimes forget them. The year before they had spent part of the summer with their grandmother Pontellier in Iberville. Feeling secure regarding their happiness and welfare, she did not miss them except with an occasional intense longing. Their absence was a sort of relief, though she did not admit this, even to herself. It seemed to free her of a responsibility which she had blindly assumed and for which Fate had not fitted her.

Edna did not reveal so much as all this to Madame Ratignolle that summer day when they sat with faces turned to the sea. But a good part of it escaped her. She had put her head down on Madame Ratignolle's shoulder. She was flushed and felt intoxicated with the sound of her own voice and the unaccustomed taste of candor. It muddled her like wine, or like a first breath of freedom.

There was the sound of approaching voices. It was Robert, surrounded by a troop of children, searching for them. The two little Pontelliers were with him, and he carried Madame Ratignolle's little girl in his arms. There were other children beside, and two nurse-maids followed, looking disagreeable and resigned.

The women at once rose and began to shake out their draperies and relax their muscles. Mrs. Pontellier threw the cushions and rug into the bath-house. The children all scampered off to the awning, and they stood there in a line, gazing upon the intruding lovers, still exchanging their vows and sighs. The lovers got up, with only a silent protest, and walked slowly away somewhere else.

The children possessed themselves of the tent, and Mrs. Pontellier went over to join them.

Madame Ratignolle begged Robert to accompany her to the house; she complained of cramp in her limbs and stiffness of the joints. She leaned draggingly upon his arm as they walked.

CHAPTER VIII

"Do me a favor, Robert," spoke the pretty woman at his side, almost as soon as she and Robert had started their slow, homeward way. She looked up in his face, leaning on his arm beneath the encircling shadow of the umbrella which he had lifted.

"Granted; as many as you like," he returned, glancing down into her eyes that were full of thoughtfulness and some speculation.

"I only ask for one; let Mrs. Pontellier alone."

"*Tiens!*" he exclaimed, with a sudden, boyish laugh. "*Voilà que Madame Ratignolle est jalouse!*"

"Nonsense! I'm in earnest; I mean what I say. Let Mrs. Pontellier alone."

"Why?" he asked; himself growing serious at his companion's solicitation.

"She is not one of us; she is not like us. She might make the unfortunate blunder of taking you seriously."

His face flushed with annoyance, and taking off his soft hat he began to beat it impatiently against his leg as he walked. "Why shouldn't she take me seriously?" he demanded sharply. "Am I a comedian, a clown, a jack-in-the-box? Why shouldn't she? You Creoles! I have no patience with you! Am I always to be regarded as a feature of an amusing programme? I hope Mrs. Pontellier does take me seriously. I hope she has discernment enough to find in me something besides the *blagueur*. If I thought there was any doubt—"

"Oh, enough, Robert!" she broke into his heated outburst. "You are not thinking of what you are saying. You speak with about as little reflection as we might expect from one of those children down there playing in the sand. If your attentions to any married women here were ever offered with any intention of being convincing, you would not be the gentleman we all know you to be, and you would be unfit to associate with the wives and daughters of the people who trust you."

Madame Ratignolle had spoken what she believed to be the law and the gospel. The young man shrugged his shoulders impatiently.

"Oh! well! That isn't it," slamming his hat down vehemently upon his head. "You ought to feel that such things are not flattering to say to a fellow."

"Should our whole intercourse consist of an exchange of compliments? *Ma foi!*"

"It isn't pleasant to have a woman tell you—" he went on, unheedingly, but breaking off suddenly: "Now if I were like Arobin—you remember Alcée Arobin and that story of the consul's wife at Biloxi?" And he related the story of Alcée Arobin and the consul's wife; and another about the tenor of the French Opera, who received letters which should never have been written; and still other stories, grave and gay, till Mrs. Pontellier and her possible propensity for taking young men seriously was apparently forgotten.

Madame Ratignolle, when they had regained her cottage, went in to take the hour's rest which she considered helpful. Before leaving her, Robert begged her pardon for the impatience—he called it rudeness—with which he had received her well-meant caution.

"You made one mistake, Adèle," he said, with a light smile; "there is no earthly possibility of Mrs. Pontellier ever taking me seriously. You should have warned me against taking myself seriously. Your advice might then have carried some weight and given me subject for some reflection. *Au revoir*. But you look tired," he added, solicitously. "Would you like a cup of bouillon? Shall I stir you a toddy? Let me mix you a toddy with a drop of Angostura."

She acceded to the suggestion of bouillon, which was grateful and acceptable. He went himself to the kitchen, which was a building apart from the cottages and lying to the rear of the house. And he himself brought her the golden-brown bouillon, in a dainty Sèvres cup, with a flaky cracker or two on the saucer.

She thrust a bare, white arm from the curtain which shielded her open door, and received the cup from his hands. She told him he was a *bon garçon*, and she meant it. Robert thanked her and turned away toward "the house."

The lovers were just entering the grounds of the *pension*. They were leaning toward each other as the water-oaks bent from the sea. There was not a particle of earth beneath their feet. Their heads might have been turned upside-down, so absolutely did they tread upon blue ether. The lady in black, creeping behind them, looked a trifle paler and more jaded than usual. There was no sign of Mrs. Pontellier and the children. Robert scanned the distance for any such apparition. They would doubtless remain away till the dinner hour. The young man ascended to his mother's room. It was situated at the top of the house, made up of odd angles and a queer, sloping ceiling. Two broad dormer windows looked out toward the Gulf, and as far across it as a man's eye might reach. The furnishings of the room were light, cool, and practical.

Madame Lebrun was busily engaged at the sewing-machine. A little black girl sat on the floor, and with her hands worked the treadle of the machine. The Creole woman does not take any chances which may be avoided of imperiling her health.

Robert went over and seated himself on the broad sill of one of the dormer windows. He took a book from his pocket and began energetically to read it, judging by the precision and frequency with which he turned the leaves. The sewing-machine made a resounding clatter in the room; it was of a ponderous, by-gone make. In the lulls, Robert and his mother exchanged bits of desultory conversation.

"Where is Mrs. Pontellier?"

"Down at the beach with the children."

"I promised to lend her the Goncourt. Don't forget to take it down when you go; it's there on the bookshelf over the small table." Clatter, clatter, clatter, bang! for the next five or eight minutes.

"Where is Victor going with the rockaway?"

"The rockaway? Victor?"

"Yes; down there in front. He seems to be getting ready to drive away somewhere."

"Call him." Clatter, clatter!

Robert uttered a shrill, piercing whistle which might have been heard back at the wharf.

"He won't look up."

Madame Lebrun flew to the window. She called "Victor!" She waved a handkerchief and called again. The young fellow below got into the vehicle and started the horse off at a gallop.

Madame Lebrun went back to the machine, crimson with annoyance. Victor was the younger son and brother—a *tête montée*, with a temper which invited violence and a will which no ax could break.

"Whenever you say the word I'm ready to thrash any amount of reason into him that he's able to hold."

"If your father had only lived!" Clatter, clatter, clatter, clatter, bang! It was a fixed belief with Madame Lebrun that the conduct of the universe and all things pertaining thereto would have been manifestly of a more intelligent and higher order had not Monsieur Lebrun been removed to other spheres during the early years of their married life.

"What do you hear from Montel?" Montel was a middle-aged gentleman whose vain ambition and desire for the past twenty years had been to fill the void which Monsieur Lebrun's taking off had left in the Lebrun household. Clatter, clatter, bang, clatter!

"I have a letter somewhere," looking in the machine drawer and finding the letter in the bottom of the work-basket. "He says to tell you he will be in Vera Cruz the beginning of next month"—clatter, clatter!—"and if you still have the intention of joining him"—bang! clatter, clatter, bang!

"Why didn't you tell me so before, mother? You know I wanted—" Clatter, clatter, clatter!

"Do you see Mrs. Pontellier starting back with the children? She will be in late to luncheon again. She never starts to get ready for luncheon till the last minute." Clatter, clatter! "Where are you going?"

"Where did you say the Goncourt was?"

CHAPTER IX

Every light in the hall was ablaze; every lamp turned as high as it could be without smoking the chimney or threatening explosion. The lamps were fixed at intervals against the wall, encircling the whole room. Some one had gathered orange and lemon branches, and with these fashioned graceful festoons between. The dark green of the branches stood out and glistened against the white muslin curtains which draped the windows, and which puffed, floated, and flapped at the capricious will of a stiff breeze that swept up from the Gulf.

It was Saturday night a few weeks after the intimate conversation held between Robert and Madame Ratignolle on their way from the beach. An unusual number of husbands, fathers, and friends had come down to stay over Sunday; and they were being suitably entertained by their families, with the material help of Madame Lebrun. The dining tables had all been removed to one end of the hall, and the chairs ranged about in rows and in clusters. Each little family group had had its say and exchanged its domestic gossip earlier in the evening. There was now an apparent disposition to relax; to widen the circle of confidences and give a more general tone to the conversation.

Many of the children had been permitted to sit up beyond their usual bedtime. A small band of them were lying on their stomachs on the floor looking at the colored sheets of the comic papers which Mr. Pontellier had brought down. The little Pontellier boys were permitting them to do so, and making their authority felt.

Music, dancing, and a recitation or two were the entertainments furnished, or rather, offered. But there was nothing systematic about the programme, no appearance of prearrangement nor even premeditation.

At an early hour in the evening the Farival twins were prevailed upon to play the piano. They were girls of fourteen, always clad in the Virgin's colors, blue and white, having been dedicated to the Blessed Virgin at their baptism. They played a duet from "Zampa," and at the earnest solicitation of every one present followed it with the overture to "The Poet and the Peasant."

"*Allez vous-en! Sapristi!*" shrieked the parrot outside the door. He was the only being present who possessed sufficient candor to admit that he was not listening to these gracious performances for the first time that summer. Old Monsieur Farival, grandfather of the twins, grew indignant over the interruption, and insisted upon having the bird removed and consigned to regions of darkness. Victor Lebrun objected; and his decrees were as immutable as those of Fate. The parrot fortunately offered no further interruption to the entertainment, the whole venom of his nature apparently having been cherished up and hurled against the twins in that one impetuous outburst.

Later a young brother and sister gave recitations, which every one present had heard many times at winter evening entertainments in the city.

A little girl performed a skirt dance in the center of the floor. The mother played her accompaniments and at the same time watched her daughter with greedy admiration and nervous apprehension. She need have had no apprehension. The child was mistress of the situation. She had been properly dressed for the occasion in black tulle and black silk tights. Her little neck and arms were bare, and her hair, artificially crimped, stood out like fluffy black plumes over her head. Her poses were full of grace, and her little black-shod toes twinkled as they shot out and upward with a rapidity and suddenness which were bewildering.

But there was no reason why every one should not dance. Madame Ratignolle could not, so it was she who gaily consented to play for the others. She played very well, keeping excellent waltz time and infusing an expression into the strains which was indeed inspiring. She was keeping up her music on account of the children, she said; because she and her husband both considered it a means of brightening the home and making it attractive.

Almost every one danced but the twins, who could not be induced to separate during the brief period when one or the other should be whirling around the room in the arms of a man. They might have danced together, but they did not think of it.

The children were sent to bed. Some went submissively; others with shrieks and protests as they were dragged away. They had been permitted to sit up till after the ice-cream, which naturally marked the limit of human indulgence.

The ice-cream was passed around with cake—gold and silver cake arranged on platters in alternate slices; it had been made and frozen during the afternoon back of the kitchen by two black women, under the supervision of Victor. It was pronounced a great success—excellent if it had only contained a little less vanilla or a little more sugar, if it had been frozen a degree harder, and if the salt might have been kept out of portions of it. Victor was proud of his achievement, and went about recommending it and urging every one to partake of it to excess.

After Mrs. Pontellier had danced twice with her husband, once with Robert, and once with Monsieur Ratignolle, who was thin and tall and swayed like a reed in the wind when he danced, she went out on the gallery and seated herself on the low window-sill, where she commanded a view of all that went on in the hall and could look out toward the Gulf. There was a soft effulgence in the east. The moon was coming up, and its mystic shimmer was casting a million lights across the distant, restless water.

"Would you like to hear Mademoiselle Reisz play?" asked Robert, coming out on the porch where she was. Of course Edna would like to hear Mademoiselle Reisz play; but she feared it would be useless to entreat her.

"I'll ask her," he said. "I'll tell her that you want to hear her. She likes you. She will come." He turned and hurried away to one of the far cottages, where Mademoiselle Reisz was shuffling away. She was dragging a chair in and out of her room, and at intervals objecting to the crying of a baby, which a nurse in the adjoining cottage was endeavoring to put to sleep. She was a disagreeable little woman, no longer young, who had quarreled with almost every one, owing to a temper which was self-assertive and a disposition to trample upon the rights of others. Robert prevailed upon her without any too great difficulty.

She entered the hall with him during a lull in the dance. She made an awkward, imperious little bow as she went in. She was a homely woman, with a small weazened face and body and eyes that glowed. She had absolutely no taste in dress, and wore a batch of rusty black lace with a bunch of artificial violets pinned to the side of her hair.

"Ask Mrs. Pontellier what she would like to hear me play," she requested of Robert. She sat perfectly still before the piano, not touching the keys, while Robert carried her message to Edna at the window. A general air of surprise and genuine satisfaction fell upon every one as they saw the pianist enter. There was a settling down, and a prevailing air of expectancy everywhere. Edna was a trifle embarrassed at being thus signaled out for the imperious little woman's favor. She would not dare to choose, and begged that Mademoiselle Reisz would please herself in her selections.

Edna was what she herself called very fond of music. Musical strains, well rendered, had a way of evoking pictures in her mind. She sometimes liked to sit in the room of mornings when Madame Ratignolle played or practiced. One piece which that lady played Edna had entitled "Solitude." It was a short, plaintive, minor strain. The name of the piece was something else, but she called it "Solitude." When she heard it there came before her imagination the figure of a man standing beside a desolate rock on the seashore. He was naked. His attitude was one of hopeless resignation as he looked toward a distant bird winging its flight away from him.

Another piece called to her mind a dainty young woman clad in an Empire gown, taking mincing dancing steps as she came down a long avenue between tall hedges. Again, another reminded her of children at play, and still another of nothing on earth but a demure lady stroking a cat.

The very first chords which Mademoiselle Reisz struck upon the piano sent a keen tremor down Mrs. Pontellier's spinal column. It was not the first time she had heard an artist at the piano. Perhaps it was the first time she was ready, perhaps the first time her being was tempered to take an impress of the abiding truth.

She waited for the material pictures which she thought would gather and blaze before her imagination. She waited in vain. She saw no pictures of solitude, of hope, of longing, or of despair. But the very passions themselves were aroused within her soul, swaying it, lashing it, as the waves daily beat upon her splendid body. She trembled, she was choking, and the tears blinded her.

Mademoiselle had finished. She arose, and bowing her stiff, lofty bow, she went away, stopping for neither thanks nor applause. As she passed along the gallery she patted Edna upon the shoulder.

"Well, how did you like my music?" she asked. The young woman was unable to answer; she pressed the hand of the pianist convulsively. Mademoiselle Reisz perceived her agitation and even her tears. She patted her again upon the shoulder as she said:

"You are the only one worth playing for. Those others? Bah!" and she went shuffling and sidling on down the gallery toward her room.

But she was mistaken about "those others." Her playing had aroused a fever of enthusiasm. "What passion!" "What an artist!" "I have always said no one could play Chopin like Mademoiselle Reisz!" "That last prelude! Bon Dieu! It shakes a man!"

It was growing late, and there was a general disposition to disband. But some one, perhaps it was Robert, thought of a bath at that mystic hour and under that mystic moon.

CHAPTER X

At all events Robert proposed it, and there was not a dissenting voice. There was not one but was ready to follow when he led the way. He did not lead the way, however, he directed the way; and he himself loitered behind with the lovers, who had betrayed a disposition to linger and hold themselves apart. He walked between them, whether with malicious or mischievous intent was not wholly clear, even to himself.

The Pontelliers and Ratignolles walked ahead; the women leaning upon the arms of their husbands. Edna could hear Robert's voice behind them, and could sometimes hear what he said. She wondered why he did not join them. It was unlike him not to. Of late he had sometimes held away from her for an entire day, redoubling his devotion upon the next and the next, as though to make up for hours that had been lost. She missed him the days when some pretext served to take him away from her, just as one misses the sun on a cloudy day without having thought much about the sun when it was shining.

The people walked in little groups toward the beach. They talked and laughed; some of them sang. There was a band playing down at Klein's hotel, and the strains reached them faintly, tempered by the distance. There were strange, rare odors abroad—a tangle of the sea smell and of weeds and damp, new-plowed earth, mingled with the heavy perfume of a field of white blossoms somewhere near. But the night sat lightly upon the sea and the land. There was no weight of darkness; there were no shadows. The white light of the moon had fallen upon the world like the mystery and the softness of sleep.

Most of them walked into the water as though into a native element. The sea was quiet now, and swelled lazily in broad billows that melted into one another and did not break except upon the beach in little foamy crests that coiled back like slow, white serpents.

Edna had attempted all summer to learn to swim. She had received instructions from both the men and women; in some instances from the children. Robert had pursued a system of lessons almost daily; and he was nearly at the point of discouragement in realizing the futility of his efforts. A certain ungovernable dread hung about her when in the water, unless there was a hand near by that might reach out and reassure her.

But that night she was like the little tottering, stumbling, clutching child, who of a sudden realizes its powers, and walks for the first time alone, boldly and with over-confidence. She could have shouted for joy. She did shout for joy, as with a sweeping stroke or two she lifted her body to the surface of the water.

A feeling of exultation overtook her, as if some power of significant import had been given her to control the working of her body and her soul. She grew daring and reckless, overestimating her strength. She wanted to swim far out, where no woman had swum before.

Her unlooked-for achievement was the subject of wonder, applause, and admiration. Each one congratulated himself that his special teachings had accomplished this desired end.

"How easy it is!" she thought. "It is nothing," she said aloud; "why did I not discover before that it was nothing. Think of the time I have lost splashing about like a baby!" She would not join the groups in their sports and bouts, but intoxicated with her newly conquered power, she swam out alone.

She turned her face seaward to gather in an impression of space and solitude, which the vast expanse of water, meeting and melting with the moonlit sky, conveyed to her excited fancy. As she swam she seemed to be reaching out for the unlimited in which to lose herself.

Once she turned and looked toward the shore, toward the people she had left there. She had not gone any great distance—that is, what would have been a great distance for an experienced swimmer. But to her unaccustomed vision the stretch of water behind her assumed the aspect of a barrier which her unaided strength would never be able to overcome.

A quick vision of death smote her soul, and for a second of time appalled and enfeebled her senses. But by an effort she rallied her staggering faculties and managed to regain the land.

She made no mention of her encounter with death and her flash of terror, except to say to her husband, "I thought I should have perished out there alone."

"You were not so very far, my dear; I was watching you," he told her.

Edna went at once to the bath-house, and she had put on her dry clothes and was ready to return home before the others had left the water. She started to walk away alone. They all called to her and shouted to her. She waved a dissenting hand, and went on, paying no further heed to their renewed cries which sought to detain her.

"Sometimes I am tempted to think that Mrs. Pontellier is capricious," said Madame Lebrun, who was amusing herself immensely and feared that Edna's abrupt departure might put an end to the pleasure.

"I know she is," assented Mr. Pontellier; "sometimes, not often."

Edna had not traversed a quarter of the distance on her way home before she was overtaken by Robert.

"Did you think I was afraid?" she asked him, without a shade of annoyance.

"No; I knew you weren't afraid."

"Then why did you come? Why didn't you stay out there with the others?"

"I never thought of it."

"Thought of what?"

"Of anything. What difference does it make?"

"I'm very tired," she uttered, complainingly.

"I know you are."

"You don't know anything about it. Why should you

know? I never was so exhausted in my life. But it isn't unpleasant. A thousand emotions have swept through me to-night. I don't comprehend half of them. Don't mind what I'm saying; I am just thinking aloud. I wonder if I shall ever be stirred again as Mademoiselle Reisz's playing moved me to-night. I wonder if any night on earth will ever again be like this one. It is like a night in a dream. The people about me are like some uncanny, half-human beings. There must be spirits abroad to-night."

"There are," whispered Robert. "Didn't you know this was the twenty-eighth of August?"

"The twenty-eighth of August?"

"Yes. On the twenty-eighth of August, at the hour of midnight, and if the moon is shining—the moon must be shining—a spirit that has haunted these shores for ages rises up from the Gulf. With its own penetrating vision the spirit seeks some one mortal worthy to hold him company, worthy of being exalted for a few hours into realms of the semi-celestials. His search has always hitherto been fruitless, and he has sunk back, disheartened, into the sea. But to-night he found Mrs. Pontellier. Perhaps he will never wholly release her from the spell. Perhaps she will never again suffer a poor, unworthy earthling to walk in the shadow of her divine presence."

"Don't banter me," she said, wounded at what appeared to be his flippancy. He did not mind the entreaty, but the tone with its delicate note of pathos was like a reproach. He could not explain; he could not tell her that he had penetrated her mood and understood. He said nothing except to offer her his arm, for, by her own admission, she was exhausted. She had been walking alone with her arms hanging limp, letting her white skirts trail along the dewy path. She took his arm, but she did not lean upon it. She let her hand lie listlessly, as though her thoughts were elsewhere—somewhere in advance of her body, and she was striving to overtake them.

Robert assisted her into the hammock which swung from the post before her door out to the trunk of a tree.

"Will you stay out here and wait for Mr. Pontellier?" he asked.

"I'll stay out here. Good-night."

"Shall I get you a pillow?"

"There's one here," she said, feeling about, for they were in the shadow.

"It must be soiled; the children have been tumbling it about."

"No matter." And having discovered the pillow, she adjusted it beneath her head. She extended herself in the hammock with a deep breath of relief. She was not a supercilious or an over-dainty woman. She was not much given to reclining in the hammock, and when she did so it was with no cat-like suggestion of voluptuous ease, but with a beneficent repose which seemed to invade her whole body.

"Shall I stay with you till Mr. Pontellier comes?" asked Robert, seating himself on the outer edge of one of the steps and taking hold of the hammock rope which was fastened to the post.

"If you wish. Don't swing the hammock. Will you get my white shawl which I left on the window-sill over at the house?"

"Are you chilly?"

"No; but I shall be presently."

"Presently?" he laughed. "Do you know what time it is? How long are you going to stay out here?"

"I don't know. Will you get the shawl?"

"Of course I will," he said, rising. He went over to the house, walking along the grass. She watched his figure pass in and out of the strips of moonlight. It was past midnight. It was very quiet.

When he returned with the shawl she took it and kept it in her hand. She did not put it around her.

"Did you say I should stay till Mr. Pontellier came back?"

"I said you might if you wished to."

He seated himself again and rolled a cigarette, which he smoked in silence. Neither did Mrs. Pontellier speak. No multitude of words could have been more significant than those moments of silence, or more pregnant with the first-felt throbbings of desire.

When the voices of the bathers were heard approaching, Robert said good-night. She did not answer him. He thought she was asleep. Again she watched his figure pass in and out of the strips of moonlight as he walked away.

CHAPTER XI

"What are you doing out here, Edna? I thought I should find you in bed," said her husband, when he discovered her lying there. He had walked up with Madame Lebrun and left her at the house. His wife did not reply.

"Are you asleep?" he asked, bending down close to look at her.

"No." Her eyes gleamed bright and intense, with no sleepy shadows, as they looked into his.

"Do you know it is past one o'clock? Come on," and he mounted the steps and went into their room.

"Edna!" called Mr. Pontellier from within, after a few moments had gone by.

"Don't wait for me," she answered. He thrust his head through the door.

"You will take cold out there," he said, irritably. "What folly is this? Why don't you come in?"

"It isn't cold; I have my shawl."

"The mosquitoes will devour you."

"There are no mosquitoes."

She heard him moving about the room; every sound indicating impatience and irritation. Another time she would have gone in at his request. She would, through habit, have yielded to his desire; not with any sense of submission or obedience to his compelling wishes, but unthinkingly, as we walk, move, sit, stand, go through the daily treadmill of the life which has been portioned out to us.

"Edna, dear, are you not coming in soon?" he asked again, this time fondly, with a note of entreaty.

"No; I am going to stay out here."

"This is more than folly," he blurted out. "I can't permit you to stay out there all night. You must come in the house instantly."

With a writhing motion she settled herself more securely in the hammock. She perceived that her will had blazed up, stubborn and resistant. She could not at that moment have done other than denied and resisted. She wondered if her husband had ever spoken to her like that before, and if she had submitted to his command. Of course she had; she remembered that she had. But she could not realize why or how she should have yielded, feeling as she then did.

"Léonce, go to bed," she said. "I mean to stay out here. I don't wish to go in, and I don't intend to. Don't speak to me like that again; I shall not answer you."

Mr. Pontellier had prepared for bed, but he slipped on an extra garment. He opened a bottle of wine, of which he kept a small and select supply in a buffet of his own. He drank a glass of the wine and went out on the gallery and offered a glass to his wife. She did not wish any. He drew up the rocker, hoisted his slippered feet on the rail, and proceeded to smoke a cigar. He smoked two cigars; then he went inside and drank another glass of wine. Mrs. Pontellier again declined to accept a glass when it was offered to her. Mr. Pontellier once more seated himself with elevated feet, and after a reasonable interval of time smoked some more cigars.

Edna began to feel like one who awakens gradually out of a dream, a delicious, grotesque, impossible dream, to feel again the realities pressing into her soul. The physical need for sleep began to overtake her; the exuberance which had sustained and exalted her spirit left her helpless and yielding to the conditions which crowded her in.

The stillest hour of the night had come, the hour before dawn, when the world seems to hold its breath. The moon hung low, and had turned from silver to copper in the sleeping sky. The old owl no longer hooted, and the water-oaks had ceased to moan as they bent their heads.

Edna arose, cramped from lying so long and still in the hammock. [She tottered up the steps, clutching feebly at the post before passing into the house.] Weakness after being so bold/strong/independent

"Are you coming in, Léonce?" she asked, turning her face toward her husband.

"Yes, dear," he answered, with a glance following a misty puff of smoke. "Just as soon as I have finished my cigar."

CHAPTER XII

She slept but a few hours. They were troubled and feverish hours, disturbed with dreams that were intangible, that eluded her, leaving only an impression upon her half-awakened senses of something unattainable. She was up and dressed in the cool of the early morning. The air was invigorating and steadied somewhat her faculties. However, she was not seeking refreshment or help from any source, either external or from within. She was blindly following whatever impulse moved her, as if she had placed herself in alien hands for direction, and freed her soul of responsibility.

Most of the people at that early hour were still in bed and asleep. A few, who intended to go over to the *Chênière* for mass, were moving about. The lovers, who had laid their plans the night before, were already strolling toward the wharf. The lady in black, with her Sunday prayer-book, velvet and gold-clasped, and her Sunday silver beads, was following them at no great distance. Old Monsieur Farival was up, and was more than half inclined to do anything that suggested itself. He put on his big straw hat, and taking his umbrella from the stand in the hall, followed the lady in black, never overtaking her.

The little negro girl who worked Madame Lebrun's sewing-machine was sweeping the galleries with long, absent-minded strokes of the broom. Edna sent her up into the house to awaken Robert.

"Tell him I am going to the *Chênière*. The boat is ready; tell him to hurry."

He had soon joined her. She had never sent for him before. She had never asked for him. She had never seemed to want him before. She did not appear conscious that she had done anything unusual in commanding his presence. He was apparently equally unconscious of anything extraordinary in the situation. But his face was suffused with a quiet glow when he met her.

They went together back to the kitchen to drink coffee. There was no time to wait for any nicety of service. They stood outside the window and the cook passed them their coffee and a roll, which they drank and ate from the window-sill. Edna said it tasted good. She had not thought of coffee nor of anything. He told her he had often noticed that she lacked forethought.

"Wasn't it enough to think of going to the *Chênière* and waking you up?" she laughed. "Do I have to think of everything?—as Léonce says when he's in a bad humor. I don't blame him; he'd never be in a bad humor if it weren't for me."

They took a short cut across the sands. At a distance they could see the curious procession moving toward the wharf—the lovers, shoulder to shoulder, creeping; the lady in black, gaining steadily upon them; old Monsieur Farival, losing ground inch by inch, and a young bare-footed Spanish girl, with a red kerchief on her head and a basket on her arm, bringing up the rear.

Robert knew the girl, and he talked to her a little in the boat. No one present understood what they said. Her name was Mariequita. She had a round, sly, piquant face and pretty black eyes. Her hands were small, and she kept them folded over the handle of her basket. Her feet were broad and coarse. She did not strive to hide them. Edna looked at her feet, and noticed the sand and slime between her brown toes.

Beaudelet grumbled because Mariequita was there, taking up so much room. In reality he was annoyed at having old Monsieur Farival, who considered himself the better sailor of the two. But he would not quarrel with so old a man as Monsieur Farival, so he quarreled with Mariequita. The girl was deprecatory at one moment, appealing to Robert. She was saucy the next, moving her head up and down, making "eyes" at Robert and making "mouths" at Beaudelet.

The lovers were all alone. They saw nothing, they heard nothing. The lady in black was counting her beads for the third time. Old Monsieur Farival talked incessantly of what he knew about handling a boat, and of what Beaudelet did not know on the same subject.

Edna liked it all. She looked Mariequita up and down, from her ugly brown toes to her pretty black eyes, and back again.

"Why does she look at me like that?" inquired the girl of Robert.

"Maybe she thinks you are pretty. Shall I ask her?"

"No. Is she your sweetheart?"

"She's a married lady, and has two children."

"Oh! well! Francisco ran away with Sylvano's wife, who had four children. They took all his money and one of the children and stole his boat."

"Shut up!"

"Does she understand?"

"Oh, hush!"

"Are those two married over there—leaning on each other?"

"Of course not," laughed Robert.

"Of course not," echoed Mariequita, with a serious, confirmatory bob of the head.

The sun was high up and beginning to bite. The swift breeze seemed to Edna to bury the sting of it into the pores of her face and hands. Robert held his umbrella over her.

As they went cutting sidewise through the water, the sails bellied taut, with the wind filling and overflowing them. Old Monsieur Farival laughed sardonically at something as he looked at the sails, and Beaudelet swore at the old man under his breath.

Sailing across the bay to the *Chênière Caminada*, Edna felt as if she were being borne away from some anchorage which had held her fast, whose chains had been loosening—had snapped the night before when the mystic spirit was abroad, leaving her free to drift whithersoever she chose to set her sails. Robert spoke to her incessantly; he no longer noticed Mariequita. The girl had shrimps in her bamboo basket. They were covered with Spanish moss. She beat the moss down impatiently, and muttered to herself sullenly.

"Let us go to Grande Terre to-morrow?" said Robert in a low voice.

"What shall we do there?"

"Climb up the hill to the old fort and look at the little wriggling gold snakes, and watch the lizards sun themselves."

She gazed away toward Grande Terre and thought she would like to be alone there with Robert, in the sun, listening to the ocean's roar and watching the slimy lizards writhe in and out among the ruins of the old fort.

"And the next day or the next we can sail to the Bayou Brulow," he went on.

"What shall we do there?"

"Anything—cast bait for fish."

"No; we'll go back to Grande Terre. Let the fish alone."

"We'll go wherever you like," he said. "I'll have Tonie come over and help me patch and trim my boat. We shall not need Beaudelet nor any one. Are you afraid of the pirogue?"

"Oh, no."

"Then I'll take you some night in the pirogue when the moon shines. Maybe your Gulf spirit will whisper to you in which of these islands the treasures are hidden—direct you to the very spot, perhaps."

"And in a day we should be rich!" she laughed. "I'd give it all to you, the pirate gold and every bit of treasure we could dig up. I think you would know how to spend it. Pirate gold isn't a thing to be hoarded or utilized. It is something to squander and throw to the four winds, for the fun of seeing the golden specks fly."

"We'd share it, and scatter it together," he said. His face flushed.

They all went together up to the quaint little Gothic church of Our Lady of Lourdes, gleaming all brown and yellow with paint in the sun's glare.

Only Beaudelet remained behind, tinkering at his boat, and Mariequita walked away with her basket of shrimps, casting a look of childish ill humor and reproach at Robert from the corner of her eye.

CHAPTER XIII

A feeling of oppression and drowsiness overcame Edna during the service. Her head began to ache, and the lights on the altar swayed before her eyes. Another time she might have made an effort to regain her composure; but her one thought was to quit the stifling atmosphere of the church and reach the open air. She arose, climbing over Robert's feet with a muttered apology. Old Monsieur Farival, flurried, curious, stood up, but upon seeing that Robert had followed Mrs. Pontellier, he sank back into his seat. He whispered an anxious inquiry of the lady in black, who did not notice him or reply, but kept her eyes fastened upon the pages of her velvet prayer-book.

"I felt giddy and almost overcome," Edna said, lifting her hands instinctively to her head and pushing her straw hat up from her forehead. "I couldn't have stayed through the service." They were outside in the shadow of the church. Robert was full of solicitude.

"It was folly to have thought of going in the first place, let alone staying. Come over to Madame Antoine's; you can rest there." He took her arm and led her away, looking anxiously and continuously down into her face.

How still it was, with only the voice of the sea whispering through the reeds that grew in the salt-water pools! The long line of little gray, weather-beaten houses nestled peacefully among the orange trees. It must always have been God's day on that low, drowsy island, Edna thought. They stopped, leaning over a jagged fence made of sea-drift, to ask for water. A youth, a mild-faced Acadian, was drawing water from the cistern, which was nothing more than a rusty buoy, with an opening on one side, sunk in the ground. The water which the youth handed to them in a tin pail was not cold to taste, but it was cool to her heated face, and it greatly revived and refreshed her.

Madame Antoine's cot was at the far end of the village. She welcomed them with all the native hospitality, as she would have opened her door to let the sunlight in. She was fat, and walked heavily and clumsily across the floor. She could speak no English, but when Robert made her understand that the lady who accompanied him was ill and desired to rest, she was all eagerness to make Edna feel at home and to dispose of her comfortably.

The whole place was immaculately clean, and the big, four-posted bed, snow-white, invited one to repose. It stood in a small side room which looked out across a narrow grass plot toward the shed, where there was a disabled boat lying keel upward.

Madame Antoine had not gone to mass. Her son Tonie had, but she supposed he would soon be back, and she invited Robert to be seated and wait for him. But he went and sat outside the door and smoked. Madame Antoine busied herself in the large front room preparing dinner. She was boiling mullets over a few red coals in the huge fireplace.

Edna, left alone in the little side room, loosened her clothes, removing the greater part of them. She bathed her face, her neck and arms in the basin that stood between the windows. She took off her shoes and stockings and stretched herself in the very center of the high, white bed. How luxurious it felt to rest thus in a strange, quaint bed, with its sweet country odor of laurel lingering about the sheets and mattress! She stretched her strong limbs that ached a little. She ran her fingers through her loosened hair for a while. She looked at her round arms as she held them straight up and rubbed them one after the other, observing closely, as if it were something she saw for the first time, the fine, firm quality and texture of her flesh. She clasped her hands easily above her head, and it was thus she fell asleep.

She slept lightly at first, half awake and drowsily attentive to the things about her. She could hear Madame Antoine's heavy, scraping tread as she walked back and forth on the sanded floor. Some chickens were clucking outside the windows, scratching for bits of gravel in the grass. Later she half heard the voices of Robert and Tonie talking under the shed. She did not stir. Even her eyelids rested numb and heavily over her sleepy eyes. The voices went on—Tonie's slow, Acadian drawl, Robert's quick, soft, smooth French. She understood French imperfectly unless directly addressed, and the voices were only part of the other drowsy, muffled sounds lulling her senses.

When Edna awoke it was with the conviction that she had slept long and soundly. The voices were hushed under the shed. Madame Antoine's step was no longer to be heard in the adjoining room. Even the chickens had gone elsewhere to scratch and cluck. The mosquito bar was drawn over her; the old woman had come in while she slept and let down the bar. Edna arose quietly from the bed, and looking between the curtains of the window, she saw by the slanting rays of the sun that the afternoon was far advanced. Robert was out there under the shed, reclining in the shade against the sloping keel of the overturned boat. He was reading from a book. Tonie was no longer with him. She wondered what had become of the rest of the party. She peeped out at him two or three times as she stood washing herself in the little basin between the windows.

Madame Antoine had laid some coarse, clean towels upon a chair, and had placed a box of *poudre de riz* within easy reach. Edna dabbed the powder upon her nose and cheeks as she looked at herself closely in the little distorted mirror which hung on the wall above the basin. Her eyes were bright and wide awake and her face glowed.

When she had completed her toilet she walked into the adjoining room. She was very hungry. No one was there. But there was a cloth spread upon the table that stood against the wall, and a cover was laid for one, with a crusty brown loaf and a bottle of wine beside the plate. Edna bit a piece from the brown loaf, tearing it with her strong, white teeth. She poured some of the wine into the glass and drank it down. Then she went softly out of doors, and plucking an orange from the low-hanging bough of a tree, threw it at Robert, who did not know she was awake and up.

An illumination broke over his whole face when he saw her and joined her under the orange tree.

"How many years have I slept?" she inquired. "The whole island seems changed. A new race of beings must have sprung up, leaving only you and me as past relics. How many ages ago did Madame Antoine and Tonie die? and when did our people from Grand Isle disappear from the earth?"

He familiarly adjusted a ruffle upon her shoulder.

"You have slept precisely one hundred years. I was left here to guard your slumbers; and for one hundred years I have been out under the shed reading a book. The only evil I couldn't prevent was to keep a broiled fowl from drying up."

"If it has turned to stone, still will I eat it," said Edna, moving with him into the house. "But really, what has become of Monsieur Farival and the others?"

"Gone hours ago. When they found that you were sleeping they thought it best not to awake you. Any way, I wouldn't have let them. What was I here for?"

"I wonder if Léonce will be uneasy!" she speculated, as she seated herself at table.

"Of course not; he knows you are with me," Robert replied, as he busied himself among sundry pans and covered dishes which had been left standing on the hearth.

"Where are Madame Antoine and her son?" asked Edna.

"Gone to Vespers, and to visit some friends, I believe. I am to take you back in Tonie's boat whenever you are ready to go."

He stirred the smoldering ashes till the broiled fowl began to sizzle afresh. He served her with no mean repast, dripping the coffee anew and sharing it with her. Madame Antoine had cooked little else than the mullets, but while Edna slept Robert had foraged the island. He was childishly gratified to discover her appetite, and to see the relish with which she ate the food which he had procured for her.

"Shall we go right away?" she asked, after draining her glass and brushing together the crumbs of the crusty loaf.

"The sun isn't as low as it will be in two hours," he answered.

"The sun will be gone in two hours."

"Well, let it go; who cares!"

They waited a good while under the orange trees, till

Madame Antoine came back, panting, waddling, with a thousand apologies to explain her absence. Tonie did not dare to return. He was shy, and would not willingly face any woman except his mother.

It was very pleasant to stay there under the orange trees, while the sun dipped lower and lower, turning the western sky to flaming copper and gold. The shadows lengthened and crept out like stealthy, grotesque monsters across the grass.

Edna and Robert both sat upon the ground—that is, he lay upon the ground beside her, occasionally picking at the hem of her muslin gown.

Madame Antoine seated her fat body, broad and squat, upon a bench beside the door. She had been talking all the afternoon, and had wound herself up to the story-telling pitch.

And what stories she told them! But twice in her life she had left the *Chênière Caminada,* and then for the briefest span. All her years she had squatted and waddled there upon the island, gathering legends of the Baratarians and the sea. The night came on, with the moon to lighten it. Edna could hear the whispering voices of dead men and the click of muffled gold.

When she and Robert stepped into Tonie's boat, with the red lateen sail, misty spirit forms were prowling in the shadows and among the reeds, and upon the water were phantom ships, speeding to cover.

CHAPTER XIV

The youngest boy, Etienne, had been very naughty, Madame Ratignolle said, as she delivered him into the hands of his mother. He had been unwilling to go to bed and had made a scene; whereupon she had taken charge of him and pacified him as well as she could. Raoul had been in bed and asleep for two hours.

The youngster was in his long white nightgown, that kept tripping him up as Madame Ratignolle led him along by the hand. With the other chubby fist he rubbed his eyes, which were heavy with sleep and ill humor. Edna took him in her arms, and seating herself in the rocker, began to coddle and caress him, calling him all manner of tender names, soothing him to sleep.

It was not more than nine o'clock. No one had yet gone to bed but the children.

Léonce had been very uneasy at first, Madame Ratignolle said, and had wanted to start at once for the *Chênière*. But Monsieur Farival had assured him that his wife was only overcome with sleep and fatigue, that Tonie would bring her safely back later in the day; and he had thus been dissuaded from crossing the bay. He had gone over to Klein's, looking up some cotton broker whom he wished to see in regard to securities, exchanges, stocks, bonds, or something of the sort, Madame Ratignolle did not remember what. He said he would not remain away late. She herself was suffering from heat and oppression, she said. She carried a bottle of salts and a large fan. She would not consent to remain with Edna, for Monsieur Ratignolle was alone, and he detested above all things to be left alone.

When Etienne had fallen asleep Edna bore him into the back room, and Robert went and lifted the mosquito bar that she might lay the child comfortably in his bed. The quadroon had vanished. When they emerged from the cottage Robert bade Edna good-night.

"Do you know we have been together the whole livelong day, Robert—since early this morning?" she said at parting.

"All but the hundred years when you were sleeping. Good-night."

He pressed her hand and went away in the direction of the beach. He did not join any of the others, but walked alone toward the Gulf.

Edna stayed outside, awaiting her husband's return. She had no desire to sleep or to retire; nor did she feel like going over to sit with the Ratignolles, or to join Madame Lebrun and a group whose animated voices reached her as they sat in conversation before the house. She let her mind wander back over her stay at Grand Isle; and she tried to discover wherein this summer had been different from any and every other summer of her life. She could only realize that she herself—her present self—was in some way different from the other self. That she was seeing with different eyes and making the acquaintance of new conditions in herself that colored and changed her environment, she did not yet suspect.

She wondered why Robert had gone away and left her. It did not occur to her to think he might have grown tired of being with her the livelong day. She was not tired, and she felt that he was not. She regretted that he had gone. It was so much more natural to have him stay when he was not absolutely required to leave her.

As Edna waited for her husband she sang low a little song that Robert had sung as they crossed the bay. It began with "Ah! *Si tu savais*," and every verse ended with "*si tu savais.*"

Robert's voice was not pretentious. It was musical and true. The voice, the notes, the whole refrain haunted her memory.

CHAPTER XV

When Edna entered the dining-room one evening a little late, as was her habit, an unusually animated conversation seemed to be going on. Several persons were talking at once, and Victor's voice was predominating, even over that of his mother. Edna had returned late from her bath, had dressed in some haste, and her face was flushed. Her head, set off by her dainty white gown, suggested a rich, rare blossom. She took her seat at table between old Monsieur Farival and Madame Ratignolle.

As she seated herself and was about to begin to eat her soup, which had been served when she entered the room, several persons informed her simultaneously that Robert was going to Mexico. She laid her spoon down and looked about her bewildered. He had been with her, reading to her all the morning, and had never even mentioned such a place as Mexico. She had not seen him during the afternoon; she had heard some one say he was at the house, upstairs with his mother. This she had thought nothing of, though she was surprised when he did not join her later in the afternoon, when she went down to the beach.

She looked across at him, where he sat beside Madame Lebrun, who presided. Edna's face was a blank picture of bewilderment, which she never thought of disguising. He lifted his eyebrows with the pretext of a smile as he returned her glance. He looked embarrassed and uneasy.

"When is he going?" she asked of everybody in general, as if Robert were not there to answer for himself.

"To-night!" "This very evening!" "Did you ever!" "What possesses him!" were some of the replies she gathered, uttered simultaneously in French and English.

"Impossible!" she exclaimed. "How can a person start off from Grand Isle to Mexico at a moment's notice, as if he were going over to Klein's or to the wharf or down to the beach?"

"I said all along I was going to Mexico; I've been saying so for years!" cried Robert, in an excited and irritable tone, with the air of a man defending himself against a swarm of stinging insects.

Madame Lebrun knocked on the table with her knife handle.

"Please let Robert explain why he is going, and why he is going to-night," she called out. "Really, this table is getting to be more and more like Bedlam every day, with everybody talking at once. Sometimes—I hope God will forgive me—but positively, sometimes I wish Victor would lose the power of speech."

Victor laughed sardonically as he thanked his mother for her holy wish, of which he failed to see the benefit to anybody, except that it might afford her a more ample opportunity and license to talk herself.

Monsieur Farival thought that Victor should have been taken out in mid-ocean in his earliest youth and drowned. Victor thought there would be more logic in thus disposing of old people with an established claim for making themselves universally obnoxious. Madame Lebrun grew a trifle hysterical; Robert called his brother some sharp, hard names.

"There's nothing much to explain, mother," he said;

though he explained, nevertheless—looking chiefly at Edna—that he could only meet the gentleman whom he intended to join at Vera Cruz by taking such and such a steamer, which left New Orleans on such a day; that Beaudelet was going out with his lugger-load of vegetables that night, which gave him an opportunity of reaching the city and making his vessel in time.

"But when did you make up your mind to all this?" demanded Monsieur Farival.

"This afternoon," returned Robert, with a shade of annoyance.

"At what time this afternoon?" persisted the old gentleman, with nagging determination, as if he were cross-questioning a criminal in a court of justice.

"At four o'clock this afternoon, Monsieur Farival," Robert replied, in a high voice and with a lofty air, which reminded Edna of some gentleman on the stage.

She had forced herself to eat most of her soup, and now she was picking the flaky bits of a *court bouillon* with her fork.

The lovers were profiting by the general conversation on Mexico to speak in whispers of matters which they rightly considered were interesting to no one but themselves. The lady in black had once received a pair of prayer-beads of curious workmanship from Mexico, with very special indulgence attached to them, but she had never been able to ascertain whether the indulgence extended outside the Mexican border. Father Fochel of the Cathedral had attempted to explain it; but he had not done so to her satisfaction. And she begged that Robert would interest himself, and discover, if possible, whether she was entitled to the indulgence accompanying the remarkably curious Mexican prayer-beads.

Madame Ratignolle hoped that Robert would exercise extreme caution in dealing with the Mexicans, who, she considered, were a treacherous people, unscrupulous and revengeful. She trusted she did them no injustice in thus condemning them as a race. She had known personally but one Mexican, who made and sold excellent tamales, and whom she would have trusted implicitly, so soft-spoken was he. One day he was arrested for stabbing his wife. She never knew whether he had been hanged or not.

Victor had grown hilarious, and was attempting to tell an anecdote about a Mexican girl who served chocolate one winter in a restaurant in Dauphine Street. No one would listen to him but old Monsieur Farival, who went into convulsions over the droll story.

Edna wondered if they had all gone mad, to be talking and clamoring at that rate. She herself could think of nothing to say about Mexico or the Mexicans.

"At what time do you leave?" she asked Robert.

"At ten," he told her. "Beaudelet wants to wait for the moon."

"Are you all ready to go?"

"Quite ready. I shall only take a hand-bag, and shall pack my trunk in the city."

He turned to answer some question put to him by his mother, and Edna, having finished her black coffee, left the table.

She went directly to her room. The little cottage was close and stuffy after leaving the outer air. But she did not mind; there appeared to be a hundred different things demanding her attention indoors. She began to set the toilet-stand to rights, grumbling at the negligence of the quadroon, who was in the adjoining room putting the children to bed. She gathered together stray garments that were hanging on the backs of chairs, and put each where it belonged in closet or bureau drawer. She changed her gown for a more comfortable and commodious wrapper. She rearranged her hair, combing and brushing it with unusual energy. Then she went in and assisted the quadroon in getting the boys to bed.

They were very playful and inclined to talk—to do anything but lie quiet and go to sleep. Edna sent the quadroon away to her supper and told her she need not return. Then she sat and told the children a story. Instead of soothing it excited them, and added to their wakefulness. She left them in heated argument, speculating about the conclusion of the tale which their mother promised to finish the following night.

The little black girl came in to say that Madame Lebrun

would like to have Mrs. Pontellier go and sit with them over at the house till Mr. Robert went away. Edna returned answer that she had already undressed, that she did not feel quite well, but perhaps she would go over to the house later. She started to dress again, and got as far advanced as to remove her *peignoir*. But changing her mind once more she resumed the *peignoir*, and went outside and sat down before her door. She was overheated and irritable, and fanned herself energetically for a while. Madame Ratignolle came down to discover what was the matter.

"All that noise and confusion at the table must have upset me," replied Edna, "and moreover, I hate shocks and surprises. The idea of Robert starting off in such a ridiculously sudden and dramatic way! As if it were a matter of life and death! Never saying a word about it all morning when he was with me."

"Yes," agreed Madame Ratignolle. "I think it was showing us all—you especially—very little consideration. It wouldn't have surprised me in any of the others; those Lebruns are all given to heroics. But I must say I should never have expected such a thing from Robert. Are you not coming down? Come on, dear; it doesn't look friendly."

"No," said Edna, a little sullenly. "I can't go to the trouble of dressing again; I don't feel like it."

"You needn't dress; you look all right; fasten a belt around your waist. Just look at me!"

"No," persisted Edna; "but you go on. Madame Lebrun might be offended if we both stayed away."

Madame Ratignolle kissed Edna good-night, and went away, being in truth rather desirous of joining in the general and animated conversation which was still in progress concerning Mexico and the Mexicans.

Somewhat later Robert came up, carrying his hand-bag.

"Aren't you feeling well?" he asked.

"Oh, well enough. Are you going right away?"

He lit a match and looked at his watch. "In twenty minutes," he said. The sudden and brief flare of the match emphasized the darkness for a while. He sat down upon a stool which the children had left out on the porch.

"Get a chair," said Edna.

"This will do," he replied. He put on his soft hat and nervously took it off again, and wiping his face with his handkerchief, complained of the heat.

"Take the fan," said Edna, offering it to him.

"Oh, no! Thank you. It does no good; you have to stop fanning some time, and feel all the more uncomfortable afterward."

"That's one of the ridiculous things which men always say. I have never known one to speak otherwise of fanning. How long will you be gone?"

"Forever, perhaps. I don't know. It depends upon a good many things."

"Well, in case it shouldn't be forever, how long will it be?"

"I don't know."

"This seems to me perfectly preposterous and uncalled for. I don't like it. I don't understand your motive for silence and mystery, never saying a word to me about it this morning." He remained silent, not offering to defend himself. He only said, after a moment:

"Don't part from me in any ill humor. I never knew you to be out of patience with me before."

"I don't want to part in any ill humor," she said. "But can't you understand? I've grown used to seeing you, to having you with me all the time, and your action seems unfriendly, even unkind. You don't even offer an excuse for it. Why, I was planning to be together, thinking of how pleasant it would be to see you in the city next winter."

"So was I," he blurted. "Perhaps that's the—" He stood up suddenly and held out his hand. "Good-by, my dear Mrs. Pontellier; good-by. You won't—I hope you won't completely forget me." She clung to his hand, striving to detain him.

"Write to me when you get there, won't you, Robert?" she entreated.

"I will, thank you. Good-by."

How unlike Robert! The merest acquaintance would have said something more emphatic than "I will, thank you; good-by," to such a request.

He had evidently already taken leave of the people over at the house, for he descended the steps and went to join Beaudelet, who was out there with an oar across his shoulder waiting for Robert. They walked away in the darkness. She could only hear Beaudelet's voice; Robert had apparently not even spoken a word of greeting to his companion.

Edna bit her handkerchief convulsively, striving to hold back and to hide, even from herself as she would have hidden from another, the emotion which was troubling—tearing—her. Her eyes were brimming with tears.

For the first time she recognized the symptoms of infatuation which she had felt incipiently as a child, as a girl in her earliest teens, and later as a young woman. The recognition did not lessen the reality, the poignancy of the revelation by any suggestion or promise of instability. The past was nothing to her; offered no lesson which she was willing to heed. The future was a mystery which she never attempted to penetrate. The present alone was significant; was hers, to torture her as it was doing then with the biting conviction that she had lost that which she had held, that she had been denied that which her impassioned, newly awakened being demanded.

CHAPTER XVI

"Do you miss your friend greatly?" asked Mademoiselle Reisz one morning as she came creeping up behind Edna, who had just left her cottage on her way to the beach. She spent much of her time in the water since she had acquired finally the art of swimming. As their stay at Grand Isle drew near its close, she felt that she could not give too much time to a diversion which afforded her the only real pleasurable moments that she knew. When Mademoiselle Reisz came and touched her upon the shoulder and spoke to her, the woman seemed to echo the thought which was ever in Edna's mind; or, better, the feeling which constantly possessed her.

Robert's going had some way taken the brightness, the color, the meaning out of everything. The conditions of her life were in no way changed, but her whole existence was dulled, like a faded garment which seems to be no longer worth wearing. She sought him everywhere—in others whom she induced to talk about him. She went up in the mornings to Madame Lebrun's room, braving the clatter of the old sewing-machine. She sat there and chatted at intervals as Robert had done. She gazed around the room at the pictures and photographs hanging upon the wall, and discovered in some corner an old family album, which she examined with the keenest interest, appealing to Madame Lebrun for enlightenment concerning the many figures and faces which she discovered between its pages.

There was a picture of Madame Lebrun with Robert as a baby, seated in her lap, a round-faced infant with a fist in his mouth. The eyes alone in the baby suggested the man. And that was he also in kilts, at the age of five, wearing long curls and holding a whip in his hand. It made Edna laugh, and she laughed, too, at the portrait in his first long trousers; while another interested her, taken when he left for college, looking thin, long-faced, with eyes full of fire, ambition and great intentions. But there was no recent picture, none which suggested the Robert who had gone away five days ago, leaving a void and wilderness behind him.

"Oh, Robert stopped having his pictures taken when he had to pay for them himself! He found wiser use for his money, he says," explained Madame Lebrun. She had a letter from him, written before he left New Orleans. Edna wished to see the letter, and Madame Lebrun told her to look for it either on the table or the dresser, or perhaps it was on the mantelpiece.

The letter was on the bookshelf. It possessed the greatest interest and attraction for Edna; the envelope, its size and shape, the post-mark, the handwriting. She examined every detail of the outside before opening it. There were only a few lines, setting forth that he would leave the city that afternoon, that he had packed his trunk in good shape, that he was well, and sent her his love and begged to be affectionately remembered to all. There was no special message to Edna except a postscript saying that if Mrs. Pontellier desired to finish the book which he had been reading to her, his mother would find it in his room, among other books there on the table. Edna experienced a pang of jealousy because he had written to his mother rather than to her.

Every one seemed to take for granted that she missed him. Even her husband, when he came down the Saturday following Robert's departure, expressed regret that he had gone.

"How do you get on without him, Edna?" he asked.

"It's very dull without him," she admitted. Mr. Pontellier had seen Robert in the city, and Edna asked him a dozen questions or more. Where had they met? On Carondelet Street, in the morning. They had gone "in" and had a drink and a cigar together. What had they talked about? Chiefly about his prospects in Mexico, which Mr. Pontellier thought were promising. How did he look? How did he seem—grave, or gay, or how? Quite cheerful, and wholly taken up with the idea of his trip, which Mr. Pontellier found altogether natural in a young fellow about to seek fortune and adventure in a strange, queer country.

Edna tapped her foot impatiently, and wondered why the children persisted in playing in the sun when they might be under the trees. She went down and led them out of the sun, scolding the quadroon for not being more attentive.

It did not strike her as in the least grotesque that she should be making of Robert the object of conversation and leading her husband to speak of him. The sentiment which she entertained for Robert in no way resembled that which she felt for her husband, or had ever felt, or ever expected to feel. She had all her life long been accustomed to harbor thoughts and emotions which never voiced themselves. They had never taken the form of struggles. They belonged to her and were her own, and she entertained the conviction that she had a right to them and that they concerned no one but herself. Edna had once told Madame Ratignolle that she would never sacrifice herself for her children, or for any one. Then had followed a rather heated argument; the two women did not appear to understand each other or to be talking the same language. Edna tried to appease her friend, to explain.

"I would give up the unessential; I would give my money, I would give my life for my children; but I wouldn't give myself. I can't make it more clear; it's only something which I am beginning to comprehend, which is revealing itself to me."

"I don't know what you would call the essential, or what you mean by the unessential," said Madame Ratignolle, cheerfully; "but a woman who would give her life for her children could do no more than that—your Bible tells you so. I'm sure I couldn't do more than that."

"Oh, yes you could!" laughed Edna.

She was not surprised at Mademoiselle Reisz's question the morning that lady, following her to the beach, tapped her on the shoulder and asked if she did not greatly miss her young friend.

"Oh, good morning, Mademoiselle; is it you? Why, of course I miss Robert. Are you going down to bathe?"

"Why should I go down to bathe at the very end of the season when I haven't been in the surf all summer," replied the woman, disagreeably.

"I beg your pardon," offered Edna, in some embarrassment, for she should have remembered that Mademoiselle Reisz's avoidance of the water had furnished a theme for much pleasantry. Some among them thought it was on account of her false hair, or the dread of getting the violets wet, while others attributed it to the natural aversion for water sometimes believed to accompany the artistic temperament. Mademoiselle offered Edna some chocolates in a paper bag, which she took from her pocket, by way of showing that she bore no ill feeling. She habitually ate chocolates for their sustaining quality; they contained much nutriment in small compass, she said. They saved her from starvation, as Madame Lebrun's table was utterly impossible; and no one save so impertinent a woman as Madame Lebrun could think of offering such food to people and requiring them to pay for it.

"She must feel very lonely without her son," said Edna, desiring to change the subject. "Her favorite son, too. It must have been quite hard to let him go."

Mademoiselle laughed maliciously.

"Her favorite son! Oh, dear! Who could have been

imposing such a tale upon you? Aline Lebrun lives for Victor, and for Victor alone. She has spoiled him into the worthless creature he is. She worships him and the ground he walks on. Robert is very well in a way, to give up all the money he can earn to the family, and keep the barest pittance for himself. Favorite son, indeed! I miss the poor fellow myself, my dear. I liked to see him and to hear him about the place—the only Lebrun who is worth a pinch of salt. He comes to see me often in the city. I like to play to him. That Victor! hanging would be too good for him. It's a wonder Robert hasn't beaten him to death long ago."

"I thought he had great patience with his brother," offered Edna, glad to be talking about Robert, no matter what was said.

"Oh! he thrashed him well enough a year or two ago," said Mademoiselle. "It was about a Spanish girl, whom Victor considered that he had some sort of claim upon. He met Robert one day talking to the girl, or walking with her, or bathing with her, or carrying her basket—I don't remember what;—and he became so insulting and abusive that Robert gave him a thrashing on the spot that has kept him comparatively in order for a good while. It's about time he was getting another."

"Was her name Mariequita?" asked Edna.

"Mariequita—yes, that was it; Mariequita. I had forgotten. Oh, she's a sly one, and a bad one, that Mariequita!"

Edna looked down at Mademoiselle Reisz and wondered how she could have listened to her venom so long. For some reason she felt depressed, almost unhappy. She had not intended to go into the water; but she donned her bathing suit, and left Mademoiselle alone, seated under the shade of the children's tent. The water was growing cooler as the season advanced. Edna plunged and swam about with an abandon that thrilled and invigorated her. She remained a long time in the water, half hoping that Mademoiselle Reisz would not wait for her.

But Mademoiselle waited. She was very amiable during the walk back, and raved much over Edna's appearance in her bathing suit. She talked about music. She hoped that Edna would go to see her in the city, and wrote her address with the stub of a pencil on a piece of card which she found in her pocket.

"When do you leave?" asked Edna.

"Next Monday; and you?"

"The following week," answered Edna, adding, "It has been a pleasant summer, hasn't it, Mademoiselle?"

"Well," agreed Mademoiselle Reisz, with a shrug, "rather pleasant, if it hadn't been for the mosquitoes and the Farival twins."

CHAPTER XVII

The Pontelliers possessed a very charming home on Esplanade Street in New Orleans. It was a large, double cottage, with a broad front veranda, whose round, fluted columns supported the sloping roof. The house was painted a dazzling white; the outside shutters, or jalousies, were green. In the yard, which was kept scrupulously neat, were flowers and plants of every description which flourishes in South Louisiana. Within doors the appointments were perfect after the conventional type. The softest carpets and rugs covered the floors; rich and tasteful draperies hung at doors and windows. There were paintings, selected with judgment and discrimination, upon the walls. The cut glass, the silver, the heavy damask which daily appeared upon the table were the envy of many women whose husbands were less generous than Mr. Pontellier.

Mr. Pontellier was very fond of walking about his house examining its various appointments and details, to see that nothing was amiss. He greatly valued his possessions, chiefly because they were his, and derived genuine pleasure from contemplating a painting, a statuette, a rare lace curtain—no matter what—after he had bought it and placed it among his household gods.

On Tuesday afternoons—Tuesday being Mrs. Pontellier's reception day—there was a constant stream of callers—women who came in carriages or in the street cars, or walked when the air was soft and distance permitted. A light-colored mulatto boy, in dress coat and bearing a diminutive silver tray for the reception of cards, admitted them. A maid, in white fluted cap, offered the callers liqueur, coffee, or chocolate, as they might desire. Mrs. Pontellier, attired in a handsome reception gown, remained in the drawing-room the entire afternoon receiving her visitors. Men sometimes called in the evening with their wives.

This had been the programme which Mrs. Pontellier had religiously followed since her marriage, six years before. Certain evenings during the week she and her husband attended the opera or sometimes the play.

Mr. Pontellier left his home in the mornings between nine and ten o'clock, and rarely returned before half-past six or seven in the evening—dinner being served at half-past seven.

He and his wife seated themselves at table one Tuesday evening, a few weeks after their return from Grand Isle. They were alone together. The boys were being put to bed; the patter of their bare, escaping feet could be heard occasionally, as well as the pursuing voice of the quadroon, lifted in mild protest and entreaty. Mrs. Pontellier did not wear her usual Tuesday reception gown; she was in ordinary house dress. Mr. Pontellier, who was observant about such things, noticed it, as he served the soup and handed it to the boy in waiting.

"Tired out, Edna? Whom did you have? Many callers?" he asked. He tasted his soup and began to season it with pepper, salt, vinegar, mustard—everything within reach.

"There were a good many," replied Edna, who was eating her soup with evident satisfaction. "I found their cards when I got home; I was out."

"Out!" exclaimed her husband, with something like genuine consternation in his voice as he laid down the vinegar cruet and looked at her through his glasses. "Why, what could have taken you out on Tuesday? What did you have to do?"

"Nothing. I simply felt like going out, and I went out."

"Well, I hope you left some suitable excuse," said her

husband, somewhat appeased, as he added a dash of cayenne pepper to the soup.

"No, I left no excuse. I told Joe to say I was out, that was all."

"Why, my dear, I should think you'd understand by this time that people don't do such things; we've got to observe *les convenances* if we ever expect to get on and keep up with the procession. If you felt that you had to leave home this afternoon, you should have left some suitable explanation for your absence.

"This soup is really impossible; it's strange that woman hasn't learned yet to make a decent soup. Any free-lunch stand in town serves a better one. Was Mrs. Belthrop here?"

"Bring the tray with the cards, Joe. I don't remember who was here."

The boy retired and returned after a moment, bringing the tiny silver tray, which was covered with ladies' visiting cards. He handed it to Mrs. Pontellier.

"Give it to Mr. Pontellier," she said.

Joe offered the tray to Mr. Pontellier, and removed the soup.

Mr. Pontellier scanned the names of his wife's callers, reading some of them aloud, with comments as he read.

" 'The Misses Delasidas.' I worked a big deal in futures for their father this morning; nice girls; it's time they were getting married. 'Mrs. Belthrop.' I tell you what it is, Edna; you can't afford to snub Mrs. Belthrop. Why, Belthrop could buy and sell us ten times over. His business is worth a good, round sum to me. You'd better write her a note. 'Mrs. James Highcamp.' Hugh! the less you have to do with Mrs. Highcamp, the better. 'Madame Laforcé.' Came all the way from Carrolton, too, poor old soul. 'Miss Wiggs,' 'Mrs. Eleanor Boltons.' " He pushed the cards aside.

"Mercy!" exclaimed Edna, who had been fuming. "Why are you taking the thing so seriously and making such a fuss over it?"

"I'm not making any fuss over it. But it's just such seeming trifles that we've got to take seriously; such things count."

The fish was scorched. Mr. Pontellier would not touch it. Edna said she did not mind a little scorched taste. The roast was in some way not to his fancy, and he did not like the manner in which the vegetables were served.

"It seems to me," he said, "we spend money enough in this house to procure at least one meal a day which a man could eat and retain his self-respect."

"You used to think the cook was a treasure," returned Edna, indifferently.

"Perhaps she was when she first came; but cooks are only human. They need looking after, like any other class of persons that you employ. Suppose I didn't look after the clerks in my office, just let them run things their own way; they'd soon make a nice mess of me and my business."

"Where are you going?" asked Edna, seeing that her husband arose from table without having eaten a morsel except a taste of the highly-seasoned soup.

"I'm going to get my dinner at the club. Good night." He went into the hall, took his hat and stick from the stand, and left the house.

She was somewhat familiar with such scenes. They had often made her very unhappy. On a few previous occasions she had been completely deprived of any desire to finish her dinner. Sometimes she had gone into the kitchen to administer a tardy rebuke to the cook. Once she went to her room and studied the cookbook during an entire evening, finally writing out a menu for the week, which left her harassed with a feeling that, after all, she had accomplished no good that was worth the name.

But that evening Edna finished her dinner alone, with forced deliberation. Her face was flushed and her eyes flamed with some inward fire that lighted them. After finishing her dinner she went to her room, having instructed the boy to tell any other callers that she was indisposed.

It was a large, beautiful room, rich and picturesque in the soft, dim light which the maid had turned low. She went and stood at an open window and looked out upon the deep tangle of the garden below. All the mystery and witchery of the night seemed to have gathered there amid the perfumes and the dusky and tortuous outlines of flowers and foliage. She was seeking herself and finding herself in just such sweet, half-darkness which met her moods. But the voices were not soothing that came to her from the darkness and the sky above and the stars. They jeered and sounded mournful notes without promise, devoid even of hope. She turned back into the room and began to walk to and fro down its whole length, without stopping, without resting. She carried in her hands a thin handkerchief, which she tore into ribbons, rolled into a ball, and flung from her. Once she stopped, and taking off her wedding ring, flung it upon the carpet. When she saw it lying there, she stamped her heel upon it, striving to crush it. But her small boot heel did not make an indenture, not a mark upon the little glittering circlet.

In a sweeping passion she seized a glass vase from the table and flung it upon the tiles of the hearth. She wanted to destroy something. The crash and clatter were what she wanted to hear.

A maid, alarmed at the din of breaking glass, entered the room to discover what was the matter.

"A vase fell upon the hearth," said Edna. "Never mind; leave it till morning."

"Oh! you might get some of the glass in your feet, ma'am," insisted the young woman, picking up bits of the broken vase that were scattered upon the carpet. "And here's your ring, ma'am, under the chair."

Edna held out her hand, and taking the ring, slipped it upon her finger.

CHAPTER XVIII

The following morning Mr. Pontellier, upon leaving for his office, asked Edna if she would not meet him in town in order to look at some new fixtures for the library.

"I hardly think we need new fixtures, Léonce. Don't let us get anything new; you are too extravagant. I don't believe you ever think of saving or putting by."

"The way to become rich is to make money, my dear

Edna, not to save it," he said. He regretted that she did not feel inclined to go with him and select new fixtures. He kissed her good-by, and told her she was not looking well and must take care of herself. She was unusually pale and very quiet.

She stood on the front veranda as he quitted the house, and absently picked a few sprays of jessamine that grew upon a trellis near by. She inhaled the odor of the blossoms and thrust them into the bosom of her white morning gown. The boys were dragging along the banquette a small "express wagon," which they had filled with blocks and sticks. The quadroon was following them with little quick steps, having assumed a fictitious animation and alacrity for the occasion. A fruit vender was crying his wares in the street.

Edna looked straight before her with a self-absorbed expression upon her face. She felt no interest in anything about her. The street, the children, the fruit vender, the flowers growing there under her eyes, were all part and parcel of an alien world which had suddenly become antagonistic.

She went back into the house. She had thought of speaking to the cook concerning her blunders of the previous night; but Mr. Pontellier had saved her that disagreeable mission, for which she was so poorly fitted. Mr. Pontellier's arguments were usually convincing with those whom he employed. He left home feeling quite sure that he and Edna would sit down that evening, and possibly a few subsequent evenings, to a dinner deserving of the name.

Edna spent an hour or two in looking over some of her old sketches. She could see their shortcomings and defects, which were glaring in her eyes. She tried to work a little, but found she was not in the humor. Finally she gathered together a few of the sketches—those which she considered the least discreditable; and she carried them with her when, a little later, she dressed and left the house. She looked handsome and distinguished in her street gown. The tan of the seashore had left her face, and her forehead was smooth, white, and polished beneath her heavy, yellow-brown hair. There were a few freckles on her face, and a small, dark mole near the under lip and one on the temple, half-hidden in her hair.

As Edna walked along the street she was thinking of Robert. She was still under the spell of her infatuation. She had tried to forget him, realizing the inutility of remembering. But the thought of him was like an obsession, ever pressing itself upon her. It was not that she dwelt upon details of their acquaintance, or recalled in any special or peculiar way his personality; it was his being, his existence, which dominated her thought, fading sometimes as if it would melt into the mist of the forgotten, reviving again with an intensity which filled her with an incomprehensible longing.

Edna was on her way to Madame Ratignolle's. Their intimacy, begun at Grand Isle, had not declined, and they had seen each other with some frequency since their return to the city. The Ratignolles lived at no great distance from Edna's home, on the corner of a side street, where Monsieur Ratignolle owned and conducted a drug store which enjoyed a steady and prosperous trade. His father had been in the business before him, and Monsieur Ratignolle stood well in the community and bore an enviable reputation for integrity and clear-headedness. His family lived in commodious apartments over the store, having an entrance on the side within the *porte cochère*. There was something which Edna thought very French, very foreign, about their whole manner of living. In the large and pleasant salon which extended across the width of the house, the Ratignolles entertained their friends once a fortnight with a *soirée musicale*, sometimes diversified by card-playing. There was a friend who played upon the 'cello. One brought his flute and another his violin, while there were some who sang and a number who performed upon the piano with various degrees of taste and agility. The Ratignolles' *soirées musicales* were widely known, and it was considered a privilege to be invited to them.

Edna found her friend engaged in assorting the clothes which had returned that morning from the laundry. She at once abandoned her occupation upon seeing Edna, who had been ushered without ceremony into her presence.

" 'Cité can do it as well as I; it is really her business," she explained to Edna, who apologized for interrupting her. And she summoned a young black woman, whom she instructed, in French, to be very careful in checking off the list which she handed her. She told her to notice particularly if a fine linen handkerchief of Monsieur Ratignolle's, which was missing last week, had been returned; and to be sure to set to one side such pieces as required mending and darning.

Then placing an arm around Edna's waist, she led her to the front of the house, to the salon, where it was cool and sweet with the odor of great roses that stood upon the hearth in jars.

Madame Ratignolle looked more beautiful than ever there at home, in a negligé which left her arms almost wholly bare and exposed the rich, melting curves of her white throat.

"Perhaps I shall be able to paint your picture some day," said Edna with a smile when they were seated. She produced the roll of sketches and started to unfold them. "I believe I ought to work again. I feel as if I wanted to be doing something. What do you think of them? Do you think it worth while to take it up again and study some more? I might study for a while with Laidpore."

She knew that Madame Ratignolle's opinion in such a matter would be next to valueless, that she herself had not alone decided, but determined; but she sought the words of praise and encouragement that would help her to put heart into her venture.

"Your talent is immense, dear!"

"Nonsense!" protested Edna, well pleased.

"Immense, I tell you," persisted Madame Ratignolle, surveying the sketches one by one, at close range, then holding them at arm's length, narrowing her eyes, and dropping her head on one side. "Surely, this Bavarian peasant is worthy of framing; and this basket of apples! never have I seen anything more lifelike. One might almost be tempted to reach out a hand and take one."

Edna could not control a feeling which bordered upon complacency at her friend's praise, even realizing, as she did, its true worth. She retained a few of the sketches, and gave all the rest to Madame Ratignolle, who appreciated the gift far beyond its value and proudly exhibited the pictures to her husband when he came up from the store a little later for his midday dinner.

Mr. Ratignolle was one of those men who are called the salt of the earth. His cheerfulness was unbounded, and it was matched by his goodness of heart, his broad charity, and common sense. He and his wife spoke English with an accent which was only discernible through its un-English emphasis and a certain carefulness and deliberation. Edna's husband spoke English with no accent whatever. The Ratignolles understood each other perfectly. If ever the fusion of two human beings into one has been accomplished on this sphere it was surely in their union.

As Edna seated herself at table with them she thought, "Better a dinner of herbs," though it did not take her long to discover that it was no dinner of herbs, but a delicious repast, simple, choice, and in every way satisfying.

Monsieur Ratignolle was delighted to see her, though he found her looking not so well as at Grand Isle, and he advised a tonic. He talked a good deal on various topics, a little politics, some city news and neighborhood gossip. He spoke with an animation and earnestness that gave an exaggerated importance to every syllable he uttered. His wife was keenly interested in everything he said, laying down her fork the better to listen, chiming in, taking the words out of his mouth.

Edna felt depressed rather than soothed after leaving them. The little glimpse of domestic harmony which had been offered her, gave her no regret, no longing. It was not a condition of life which fitted her, and she could see in it but an appalling and hopeless ennui. She was moved by a kind of commiseration for Madame Ratignolle,—a pity for that colorless existence which never uplifted its possessor beyond the region of blind contentment, in which no moment of anguish ever visited her soul, in which she would never have the taste of life's delirium. Edna vaguely wondered what she meant by "life's delirium." It had crossed her thought like some unsought, extraneous impression.

CHAPTER XIX

Edna could not help but think that it was very foolish, very childish, to have stamped upon her wedding ring and smashed the crystal vase upon the tiles. She was visited by no more outbursts, moving her to such futile expedients. She began to do as she liked and to feel as she liked. She completely abandoned her Tuesdays at home, and did not return the visits of those who had called upon her. She made no ineffectual efforts to conduct her household *en bonne ménagère*, going and coming as it suited her fancy, and, so far as she was able, lending herself to any passing caprice.

Mr. Pontellier had been a rather courteous husband so long as he met a certain tacit submissiveness in his wife. But her new and unexpected line of conduct completely bewildered him. It shocked him. Then her absolute disregard for her duties as a wife angered him. When Mr. Pontellier became rude, Edna grew insolent. She had resolved never to take another step backward.

"It seems to me the utmost folly for a woman at the head of a household, and the mother of children, to spend in an atelier days which would be better employed contriving for the comfort of her family."

"I feel like painting," answered Edna. "Perhaps I shan't always feel like it." Sense of Edna vs. Madame Ratignolle

"Then in God's name paint! but don't let the family go to the devil. There's Madame Ratignolle; because she keeps up her music, she doesn't let everything else go to chaos. And she's more of a musician than you are a painter."

"She isn't a musician, and I'm not a painter. It isn't on account of painting that I let things go."

"On account of what, then?"

"Oh! I don't know. Let me alone; you bother me."

It sometimes entered Mr. Pontellier's mind to wonder if his wife were not growing a little unbalanced mentally. He could see plainly that she was not herself. That is, he could not see that she was becoming herself and daily casting aside that fictitious self which we assume like a garment with which to appear before the world.

Her husband let her alone as she requested, and went away to his office. Edna went up to her atelier—a bright room in the top of the house. She was working with great energy and interest, without accomplishing anything, however, which satisfied her even in the smallest degree. For a time she had the whole household enrolled in the service of art. The boys posed for her. They thought it amusing at first, but the occupation soon lost its attractiveness when they discovered that it was not a game arranged especially for their entertainment. The quadroon sat for hours before Edna's palette, patient as a savage, while the house-maid took charge of the children, and the drawing-room went undusted. But the house-maid, too, served her term as model when Edna perceived that the young woman's back and shoulders were molded on classic lines, and that her hair, loosened from its confining cap, became an inspiration. While Edna worked she sometimes sang low the little air, "*Ah! si tu savais!*"

It moved her with recollections. She could hear again the ripple of the water, the flapping sail. She could see the glint of the moon upon the bay, and could feel the soft, gusty beating of the hot south wind. A subtle current of desire passed through her body, weakening her hold upon the brushes and making her eyes burn.

There were days when she was very happy without knowing why. She was happy to be alive and breathing, when her whole being seemed to be one with the sunlight, the color, the odors, the luxuriant warmth of some perfect Southern day. She liked then to wander alone into strange and unfamiliar places. She discovered many a sunny, sleepy corner, fashioned to dream in. And she found it good to dream and to be alone and unmolested.

There were days when she was unhappy, she did not know why,—when it did not seem worth while to be glad or sorry, to be alive or dead; when life appeared to her like a grotesque pandemonium and humanity like worms struggling blindly toward inevitable annihilation. She could not work on such a day, nor weave fancies to stir her pulses and warm her blood.

CHAPTER XX

It was during such a mood that Edna hunted up Mademoiselle Reisz. She had not forgotten the rather disagreeable impression left upon her by their last interview; but she nevertheless felt a desire to see her—above all, to listen while she played upon the piano. Quite early in the afternoon she started upon her quest for the pianist. Unfortunately she had mislaid or lost Mademoiselle Reisz's card, and looking up her address in the city directory, she found that the woman lived on Bienville Street, some distance away. The directory which fell into her hands was a year or more old, however, and upon reaching the number indicated, Edna discovered that the house was occupied by a respectable family of mulattoes who had *chambres garnies* to let. They had been living there for six months, and knew absolutely nothing of a Mademoiselle Reisz. In fact, they knew nothing of any of their neighbors; their lodgers were all people of the highest distinction, they assured Edna. She did not linger to discuss class distinctions with Madame Pouponne, but hastened to a neighboring grocery store, feeling sure that Mademoiselle would have left her address with the proprietor.

He knew Mademoiselle Reisz a good deal better than he wanted to know her, he informed his questioner. In truth, he did not want to know her at all, or anything concerning her—the most disagreeable and unpopular woman who ever lived in Bienville Street. He thanked heaven she had left the neighborhood, and was equally thankful that he did not know where she had gone.

Edna's desire to see Mademoiselle Reisz had increased tenfold since these unlooked-for obstacles had arisen to thwart it. She was wondering who could give her the information she sought, when it suddenly occurred to her that Madame Lebrun would be the one most likely to do so. She knew it was useless to ask Madame Ratignolle, who was on the most distant terms with the musician, and preferred to know nothing concerning her. She had once been almost as emphatic in expressing herself upon the subject as the corner grocer.

Edna knew that Madame Lebrun had returned to the city, for it was the middle of November. And she also knew where the Lebruns lived, on Chartres Street.

Their home from the outside looked like a prison, with iron bars before the door and lower windows. The iron bars were a relic of the old *régime*, and no one had ever thought of dislodging them. At the side was a high fence enclosing the garden. A gate or door opening upon the street was locked. Edna rang the bell at this side garden gate, and stood upon the banquette, waiting to be admitted.

It was Victor who opened the gate for her. A black woman, wiping her hands upon her apron, was close at his heels. Before she saw them Edna could hear them in altercation, the woman—plainly an anomaly—claiming the right to be allowed to perform her duties, one of which was to answer the bell.

Victor was surprised and delighted to see Mrs. Pontellier, and he made no attempt to conceal either his astonishment or his delight. He was a dark-browed, good-looking youngster of nineteen, greatly resembling his mother, but with ten times her impetuosity. He instructed the black woman to go at once and inform Madame Lebrun that Mrs. Pontellier desired to see her. The woman grumbled a refusal to do part of her duty when she had not been permitted to do it all, and started back to her interrupted task of weeding the garden. Whereupon Victor administered a rebuke in the form of a volley of abuse, which, owing to its rapidity and incoherence, was all but incomprehensible to Edna. Whatever it was, the rebuke was convincing, for the woman dropped her hoe and went mumbling into the house.

Edna did not wish to enter. It was very pleasant there on the side porch, where there were chairs, a wicker lounge, and a small table. She seated herself, for she was tired from her long tramp; and she began to rock gently and smooth out the folds of her silk parasol. Victor drew up his chair beside her. He at once explained that the black woman's offensive conduct was all due to imperfect training, as he was not there to take her in hand. He had only come up from the island the morning before, and expected to return next day. He stayed all winter at the island; he lived there, and kept the place in order and got things ready for the summer visitors.

But a man needed occasional relaxation, he informed Mrs. Pontellier, and every now and again he drummed up a pretext to bring him to the city. My! but he had had a time of it the evening before! He wouldn't want his mother to know, and he began to talk in a whisper. He was scintillant with recollections. Of course, he couldn't think of telling Mrs. Pontellier all about it, she being a woman and not comprehending such things. But it all began with a girl peeping and smiling at him through the shutters as he passed by. Oh! but she was a beauty! Certainly he smiled back, and went up and talked to her. Mrs. Pontellier did not know him if she supposed he was one to let an opportunity like that escape him. Despite herself, the youngster amused her. She must have betrayed in her look some degree of interest or entertainment. The boy grew more daring, and Mrs. Pontellier might have found herself, in a little while, listening to a highly colored story but for the timely appearance of Madame Lebrun.

That lady was still clad in white, according to her custom of the summer. Her eyes beamed an effusive welcome. Would not Mrs. Pontellier go inside? Would she partake of some refreshment? Why had she not been there before? How was that dear Mr. Pontellier and how were those sweet children? Had Mrs. Pontellier ever known such a warm November?

Victor went and reclined on the wicker lounge behind his mother's chair, where he commanded a view of Edna's face. He had taken her parasol from her hands while he spoke to her, and he now lifted it and twirled it above him as he lay on his back. When Madame Lebrun complained that it was *so* dull coming back to the city; that she saw *so* few people now; that even Victor, when he came up from the island for a day or two, had *so* much to occupy him and engage his time; then it was that the youth went into contortions on the lounge and winked mischievously at

Edna. She somehow felt like a confederate in crime, and tried to look severe and disapproving.

There had been but two letters from Robert, with little in them, they told her. Victor said it was really not worth while to go inside for the letters, when his mother entreated him to go in search of them. He remembered the contents, which in truth he rattled off very glibly when put to the test.

One letter was written from Vera Cruz and the other from the City of Mexico. He had met Montel, who was doing everything toward his advancement. So far, the financial situation was no improvement over the one he had left in New Orleans, but of course the prospects were vastly better. He wrote of the City of Mexico, the buildings, the people and their habits, the conditions of life which he found there. He sent his love to the family. He inclosed a check to his mother, and hoped she would affectionately remember him to all his friends. That was about the substance of the two letters. Edna felt that if there had been a message for her, she would have received it. The despondent frame of mind in which she had left home began again to overtake her, and she remembered that she wished to find Mademoiselle Reisz.

Madame Lebrun knew where Mademoiselle Reisz lived. She gave Edna the address, regretting that she would not consent to stay and spend the remainder of the afternoon, and pay a visit to Mademoiselle Reisz some other day. The afternoon was already well advanced.

Victor escorted her out upon the banquette, lifted her parasol, and held it over her while he walked to the car with her. He entreated her to bear in mind that the disclosures of the afternoon were strictly confidential. She laughed and bantered him a little, remembering too late that she should have been dignified and reserved.

"How handsome Mrs. Pontellier looked!" said Madame Lebrun to her son.

"Ravishing!" he admitted. "The city atmosphere has improved her. Some way she doesn't seem like the same woman."

CHAPTER XXI

Some people contended that the reason Mademoiselle Reisz always chose apartments up under the roof was to discourage the approach of beggars, peddlars and callers. There were plenty of windows in her little front room. They were for the most part dingy, but as they were nearly always open it did not make so much difference. They often admitted into the room a good deal of smoke and soot; but at the same time all the light and air that there was came through them. From her windows could be seen the crescent of the river, the masts of ships and the big chimneys of the Mississippi steamers. A magnificent piano crowded the apartment. In the next room she slept, and in the third and last she harbored a gasoline stove on which she cooked her meals when disinclined to descend to the neighboring restaurant. It was there also that she ate, keeping her belongings in a rare old buffet, dingy and battered from a hundred years of use.

When Edna knocked at Mademoiselle Reisz's front room door and entered, she discovered that person standing beside the window, engaged in mending or patching an old prunella gaiter. The little musician laughed all over when she saw Edna. Her laugh consisted of a contortion of the face and all the muscles of the body. She seemed strikingly homely, standing there in the afternoon light. She still wore the shabby lace and the artificial bunch of violets on the side of her head.

"So you remembered me at last," said Mademoiselle. "I had said to myself, 'Ah, bah! she will never come.' "

"Did you want me to come?" asked Edna with a smile.

"I had not thought much about it," answered Mademoiselle. The two had seated themselves on a little bumpy sofa which stood against the wall. "I am glad, however, that you came. I have the water boiling back there, and was just about to make some coffee. You will drink a cup with me. And how is *la belle dame*? Always handsome!

always healthy! always contented!" She took Edna's hand between her strong wiry fingers, holding it loosely without warmth, and executing a sort of double theme upon the back and palm.

"Yes," she went on; "I sometimes thought: 'She will never come. She promised as those women in society always do, without meaning it. She will not come.' For I really don't believe you like me, Mrs. Pontellier."

"I don't know whether I like you or not," replied Edna, gazing down at the little woman with a quizzical look.

The candor of Mrs. Pontellier's admission greatly pleased Mademoiselle Reisz. She expressed her gratification by repairing forthwith to the region of the gasoline stove and rewarding her guest with the promised cup of coffee. The coffee and the biscuit accompanying it proved very acceptable to Edna, who had declined refreshment at Madame Lebrun's and was now beginning to feel hungry. Mademoiselle set the tray which she brought in upon a small table near at hand, and seated herself once again on the lumpy sofa.

"I have had a letter from your friend," she remarked, as she poured a little cream into Edna's cup and handed it to her.

"My friend?"

"Yes, your friend Robert. He wrote to me from the City of Mexico."

"Wrote to *you*?" repeated Edna in amazement, stirring her coffee absently.

"Yes, to me. Why not? Don't stir all the warmth out of your coffee; drink it. Though the letter might as well have been sent to you; it was nothing but Mrs. Pontellier from beginning to end."

"Let me see it," requested the young woman, entreatingly.

"No; a letter concerns no one but the person who writes it and the one to whom it is written."

"Haven't you just said it concerned me from beginning to end?"

"It was written about you, not to you. 'Have you seen Mrs. Pontellier? How is she looking?' he asks. 'As Mrs.

Pontellier says,' or 'as Mrs. Pontellier once said.' 'If Mrs. Pontellier should call upon you, play for her that Impromptu of Chopin's, my favorite. I heard it here a day or two ago, but not as you play it. I should like to know how it affects her,' and so on, as if he supposed we were constantly in each other's society."

"Let me see the letter."

"Oh, no."

"Have you answered it?"

"No."

"Let me see the letter."

"No, and again, no."

"Then play the Impromptu for me."

"It is growing late; what time do you have to be home?"

"Time doesn't concern me. Your question seems a little rude. Play the Impromptu."

"But you have told me nothing of yourself. What are you doing?"

"Painting!" laughed Edna. "I am becoming an artist. Think of it!"

"Ah! an artist! You have pretensions, Madame."

"Why pretensions? Do you think I could not become an artist?"

"I do not know you well enough to say. I do not know your talent or your temperament. To be an artist includes much; one must possess many gifts—absolute gifts—which have not been acquired by one's own effort. And, moreover, to succeed, the artist must possess the courageous soul."

"What do you mean by the courageous soul?"

"Courageous, *ma foi*! The brave soul. The soul that dares and defies."

"Show me the letter and play for me the Impromptu. You see that I have persistence. Does that quality count for anything in art?"

"It counts with a foolish old woman whom you have captivated," replied Mademoiselle, with her wriggling laugh.

The letter was right there at hand in the drawer of the little table upon which Edna had just placed her coffee cup. Mademoiselle opened the drawer and drew forth the letter, the topmost one. She placed it in Edna's hands, and without further comment arose and went to the piano.

Mademoiselle played a soft interlude. It was an improvisation. She sat low at the instrument, and the lines of her body settled into ungraceful curves and angles that gave it an appearance of deformity. Gradually and imperceptibly the interlude melted into the soft opening minor chords of the Chopin Impromptu.

Edna did not know when the Impromptu began or ended. She sat in the sofa corner reading Robert's letter by the fading light. Mademoiselle had glided from the Chopin into the quivering love-notes of Isolde's song, and back again to the Impromptu with its soulful and poignant longing.

The shadows deepened in the little room. The music grew strange and fantastic—turbulent, insistent, plaintive and soft with entreaty. The shadows grew deeper. The music filled the room. It floated out upon the night, over the housetops, the crescent of the river, losing itself in the silence of the upper air.

Edna was sobbing, just as she had wept one midnight at Grand Isle when strange, new voices awoke in her. She arose in some agitation to take her departure. "May I come again, Mademoiselle?" she asked at the threshold.

"Come whenever you feel like it. Be careful; the stairs and landings are dark; don't stumble."

Mademoiselle reëntered and lit a candle. Robert's letter was on the floor. She stooped and picked it up. It was crumpled and damp with tears. Mademoiselle smoothed the letter out, restored it to the envelope, and replaced it in the table drawer.

CHAPTER XXII

One morning on his way into town Mr. Pontellier stopped at the house of his old friend and family physician, Doctor Mandelet. The Doctor was a semi-retired physician, resting, as the saying is, upon his laurels. He bore a reputation for wisdom rather than skill—leaving the active practice of medicine to his assistants and younger contemporaries—and was much sought for in matters of consultation. A few families, united to him by bonds of friendship, he still attended when they required the services of a physician. The Pontelliers were among these.

Mr. Pontellier found the Doctor reading at the open window of his study. His house stood rather far back from the street, in the center of a delightful garden, so that it was quiet and peaceful at the old gentleman's study window. He was a great reader. He stared up disapprovingly over his eye-glasses as Mr. Pontellier entered, wondering who had the temerity to disturb him at that hour of the morning.

"Ah, Pontellier! Not sick, I hope. Come and have a seat. What news do you bring this morning?" He was quite portly, with a profusion of gray hair, and small blue eyes which age had robbed of much of their brightness but none of their penetration.

"Oh! I'm never sick, Doctor. You know that I come of tough fiber—of that old Creole race of Pontelliers that dry up and finally blow away. I came to consult—no, not precisely to consult—to talk to you about Edna. I don't know what ails her."

"Madame Pontellier not well?" marveled the Doctor. "Why, I saw her—I think it was a week ago—walking along Canal Street, the picture of health, it seemed to me."

"Yes, yes; she seems quite well," said Mr. Pontellier, leaning forward and whirling his stick between his two hands; "but she doesn't act well. She's odd, she's not like herself. I can't make her out, and I thought perhaps you'd help me."

"How does she act?" inquired the Doctor.

"Well, it isn't easy to explain," said Mr. Pontellier, throwing himself back in his chair. "She lets the housekeeping go to the dickens."

"Well, well; women are not all alike, my dear Pontellier. We've got to consider—"

"I know that; I told you I couldn't explain. Her whole attitude—toward me and everybody and everything—has changed. You know I have a quick temper, but I don't want to quarrel or be rude to a woman, especially my wife; yet I'm driven to it, and feel like ten thousand devils after I've made a fool of myself. She's making it devilishly uncomfortable for me," he went on nervously. "She's got some sort of notion in her head concerning the eternal rights of women; and—you understand—we meet in the morning at the breakfast table."

The old gentleman lifted his shaggy eyebrows, protruded his thick nether lip, and tapped the arms of his chair with his cushioned fingertips.

"What have you been doing to her, Pontellier?"

"Doing! *Parbleu!*"

"Has she," asked the Doctor, with a smile, "has she been associating of late with a circle of pseudo-intellectual women—super-spiritual superior beings? My wife has been telling me about them."

"That's the trouble," broke in Mr. Pontellier, "she hasn't been associating with any one. She has abandoned her Tuesdays at home, has thrown over all her acquaintances, and goes tramping about by herself, moping in the street-cars, getting in after dark. I tell you she's peculiar. I don't like it; I feel a little worried over it."

This was a new aspect for the Doctor. "Nothing hereditary?" he asked, seriously. "Nothing peculiar about her family antecedents, is there?"

"Oh, no, indeed! She comes of sound old Presbyterian Kentucky stock. The old gentleman, her father, I have heard, used to atone for his weekday sins with his Sunday devotions. I know for a fact, that his race horses literally ran away with the prettiest bit of Kentucky farming land I ever laid eyes upon. Margaret—you know Margaret—she has all the Presbyterianism undiluted. And the youngest is something of a vixen. By the way, she gets married in a couple of weeks from now."

"Send your wife up to the wedding," exclaimed the Doctor, foreseeing a happy solution. "Let her stay among her own people for a while; it will do her good."

"That's what I want her to do. She won't go to the marriage. She says a wedding is one of the most lamentable spectacles on earth. Nice thing for a woman to say to her husband!" exclaimed Mr. Pontellier, fuming anew at the recollection.

"Pontellier," said the Doctor, after a moment's reflection, "let your wife alone for a while. Don't bother her, and don't let her bother you. Woman, my dear friend, is a very peculiar and delicate organism—a sensitive and highly organized woman, such as I know Mrs. Pontellier to be, is especially peculiar. It would require an inspired psychologist to deal successfully with them. And when ordinary fellows like you and me attempt to cope with their idiosyncrasies the result is bungling. Most women are moody and whimsical. This is some passing whim of your wife, due to some cause or causes which you and I needn't try to fathom. But it will pass happily over, especially if you let her alone. Send her around to see me."

"Oh! I couldn't do that; there'd be no reason for it," objected Mr. Pontellier.

"Then I'll go around and see her," said the Doctor. "I'll drop in to dinner some evening *en bon ami.*"

"Do! by all means," urged Mr. Pontellier. "What evening will you come? Say Thursday. Will you come Thursday?" he asked, rising to take his leave.

"Very well; Thursday. My wife may possibly have some engagement for me Thursday. In case she has, I shall let you know. Otherwise, you may expect me."

Mr. Pontellier turned before leaving to say:

"I am going to New York on business very soon. I have a big scheme on hand, and want to be on the field proper to pull the ropes and handle the ribbons. We'll let you in on the inside if you say so, Doctor," he laughed.

"No, I thank you, my dear sir," returned the Doctor. "I leave such ventures to you younger men with the fever of life still in your blood."

"What I wanted to say," continued Mr. Pontellier, with his hand on the knob; "I may have to be absent a good while. Would you advise me to take Edna along?"

"By all means, if she wishes to go. If not, leave her here. Don't contradict her. The mood will pass, I assure you. It may take a month, two, three months—possibly longer, but it will pass; have patience."

"Well, good-by, *à jeudi*," said Mr. Pontellier, as he let himself out.

The Doctor would have liked during the course of conversation to ask, "Is there any man in the case?" but he knew his Creole too well to make such a blunder as that.

He did not resume his book immediately, but sat for a while meditatively looking out into the garden.

CHAPTER XXIII

Edna's father was in the city, and had been with them several days. She was not very warmly or deeply attached to him, but they had certain tastes in common, and when together they were companionable. His coming was in the nature of a welcome disturbance; it seemed to furnish a new direction for her emotions.

He had come to purchase a wedding gift for his daughter, Janet, and an outfit for himself in which he might make a creditable appearance at her marriage. Mr. Pontellier had selected the bridal gift, as every one immediately connected with him always deferred to his taste in such matters. And his suggestions on the question of dress—which too often assumes the nature of a problem—were of inestimable value to his father-in-law. But for the past few days the old gentleman had been upon Edna's hands, and in his society she was becoming acquainted with a new set of sensations. He had been a colonel in the Confederate army, and still maintained, with the title, the military bearing which had always accompanied it. His hair and mustache were white and silky, emphasizing the rugged bronze of his face. He was tall and thin, and wore his coats padded, which gave a fictitious breadth and depth to his shoulders and chest. Edna and her father looked very distinguished together, and excited a good deal of notice during their perambulations. Upon his arrival she began by introducing him to her atelier and making a sketch of him. He took the whole matter very seriously. If her talent had been ten-fold greater than it was, it would not have surprised him, convinced as he was that he had bequeathed to all of his daughters the germs of a masterful capability, which only depended upon their own efforts to be directed toward successful achievement.

Before her pencil he sat rigid and unflinching, as he had faced the cannon's mouth in days gone by. He resented the intrusion of the children, who gaped with wondering eyes at him, sitting so stiff up there in their mother's bright atelier. When they drew near he motioned them away with an expressive action of the foot, loath to disturb the fixed lines of his countenance, his arms, or his rigid shoulders.

Edna, anxious to entertain him, invited Mademoiselle Reisz to meet him, having promised him a treat in her piano playing; but Mademoiselle declined the invitation. So together they attended a *soirée musicale* at the Ratignolles'. Monsieur and Madame Ratignolle made much of the Colonel, installing him as the guest of honor and engaging him at once to dine with them the following Sunday, or any day which he might select. Madame coquetted with him in the most captivating and naïve manner, with eyes, gestures, and a profusion of compliments, till the Colonel's old head felt thirty years younger on his padded shoulders. Edna marveled, not comprehending. She herself was almost devoid of coquetry.

There were one or two men whom she observed at the *soirée musicale;* but she would never have felt moved to any kittenish display to attract their notice—to any feline or feminine wiles to express herself toward them. Their personality attracted her in an agreeable way. Her fancy selected them, and she was glad when a lull in the music gave them an opportunity to meet her and talk with her. Often on the street the glance of strange eyes had lingered in her memory, and sometimes had disturbed her.

Mr. Pontellier did not attend these *soirées musicales*. He considered them *bourgeois*, and found more diversion at the club. To Madame Ratignolle he said the music dispensed at her *soirées* was too "heavy," too far beyond his untrained comprehension. His excuse flattered her. But she disapproved of Mr. Pontellier's club, and she was frank enough to tell Edna so.

"It's a pity Mr. Pontellier doesn't stay home more in the evenings. I think you would be more—well, if you don't mind my saying it—more united, if he did."

"Oh! dear no!" said Edna, with a blank look in her eyes. "What should I do if he stayed home? We wouldn't have anything to say to each other."

She had not much of anything to say to her father, for that matter; but he did not antagonize her. She discovered that he interested her, though she realized that he might not interest her long; and for the first time in her life she felt as if she were thoroughly acquainted with him. He kept her busy serving him and ministering to his wants. It amused her to do so. She would not permit a servant or one of the children to do anything for him which she might do herself. Her husband noticed, and thought it was the expression of a deep filial attachment which he had never suspected.

The Colonel drank numerous "toddies" during the course of the day, which left him, however, imperturbed. He was an expert at concocting strong drinks. He had even invented some, to which he had given fantastic names, and for whose manufacture he required diverse ingredients that it devolved upon Edna to procure for him.

When Doctor Mandelet dined with the Pontelliers on Thursday he could discern in Mrs. Pontellier no trace of that morbid condition which her husband had reported to him. She was excited and in a manner radiant. She and her father had been to the race course, and their thoughts when they seated themselves at table were still occupied with the events of the afternoon, and their talk was still of the track. The Doctor had not kept pace with turf affairs. He had certain recollections of racing in what he called "the good old times" when the Lecompte stables flourished, and he drew upon this fund of memories so that he might not be left out and seem wholly devoid of the modern spirit. But he failed to impose upon the Colonel, and was even far from impressing him with this trumped-up knowledge of bygone days. Edna had staked her father on his last venture, with the most gratifying results to both of them. Besides, they had met some very charming people, according to the Colonel's impressions. Mrs. Mortimer

Merriman and Mrs. James Highcamp, who were there with Alcée Arobin, had joined them and had enlivened the hours in a fashion that warmed him to think of.

Mr. Pontellier himself had no particular leaning toward horse-racing, and was even rather inclined to discourage it as a pastime, especially when he considered the fate of that blue-grass farm in Kentucky. He endeavored, in a general way, to express a particular disapproval, and only succeeded in arousing the ire and opposition of his father-in-law. A pretty dispute followed, in which Edna warmly espoused her father's cause and the Doctor remained neutral.

He observed his hostess attentively from under his shaggy brows, and noted a subtle change which had transformed her from the listless woman he had known into a being who, for the moment, seemed palpitant with the forces of life. Her speech was warm and energetic. There was no repression in her glance or gesture. She reminded him of some beautiful, sleek animal waking up in the sun.

The dinner was excellent. The claret was warm and the champagne was cold, and under their beneficent influence the threatened unpleasantness melted and vanished with the fumes of the wine.

Mr. Pontellier warmed up and grew reminiscent. He told some amusing plantation experiences, recollections of old Iberville and his youth, when he hunted 'possum in company with some friendly darky; thrashed the pecan trees, shot the grosbec, and roamed the woods and fields in mischievous idleness.

The Colonel, with little sense of humor and of the fitness of things, related a somber episode of those dark and bitter days, in which he had acted a conspicuous part and always formed a central figure. Nor was the Doctor happier in his selection, when he told the old, ever new and curious story of the waning of a woman's love, seeking strange, new channels, only to return to its legitimate source after days of fierce unrest. It was one of the many little human documents which had been unfolded to him during his long career as a physician. The story did not seem especially to impress Edna. She had one of her own to tell, of a woman who paddled away with her lover one night in a pirogue and never came back. They were lost amid the Baratarian Islands, and no one ever heard of them or found trace of them from that day to this. It was a pure invention. She said that Madame Antoine had related it to her. That, also, was an invention. Perhaps it was a dream she had had. But every glowing word seemed real to those who listened. They could feel the hot breath of the Southern night; they could hear the long sweep of the pirogue through the glistening moonlit water, the beating of birds' wings, rising startled from among the reeds in the salt-water pools; they could see the faces of the lovers, pale, close together, rapt in oblivious forgetfulness, drifting into the unknown.

The champagne was cold, and its subtle fumes played fantastic tricks with Edna's memory that night.

Outside, away from the glow of the fire and the soft lamplight, the night was chill and murky. The Doctor doubled his old-fashioned cloak across his breast as he strode home through the darkness. He knew his fellow-creatures better than most men; knew that inner life which so seldom unfolds itself to unanointed eyes. He was sorry he had accepted Pontellier's invitation. He was growing old, and beginning to need rest and an imperturbed spirit. He did not want the secrets of other lives thrust upon him.

"I hope it isn't Arobin," he muttered to himself as he walked. "I hope to heaven it isn't Alcée Arobin."

CHAPTER XXIV

Edna and her father had a warm, and almost violent dispute upon the subject of her refusal to attend her sister's wedding. Mr. Pontellier declined to interfere, to interpose either his influence or his authority. He was following Doctor Mandelet's advice, and letting her do as she liked. The Colonel reproached his daughter for her lack of filial kindness and respect, her want of sisterly affection and womanly consideration. His arguments were labored and unconvincing. He doubted if Janet would accept any excuse—forgetting that Edna had offered none. He doubted if Janet would ever speak to her again, and he was sure Margaret would not.

Edna was glad to be rid of her father when he finally took himself off with his wedding garments and his bridal gifts, with his padded shoulders, his Bible reading, his "toddies" and ponderous oaths.

Mr. Pontellier followed him closely. He meant to stop at the wedding on his way to New York and endeavor by every means which money and love could devise to atone somewhat for Edna's incomprehensible action.

"You are too lenient, too lenient by far, Léonce," asserted the Colonel. "Authority, coercion are what is needed. Put your foot down good and hard; the only way to manage a wife. Take my word for it."

The Colonel was perhaps unaware that he had coerced his own wife into her grave. Mr. Pontellier had a vague suspicion of it which he thought it needless to mention at that late day.

Edna was not so consciously gratified at her husband's leaving home as she had been over the departure of her father. As the day approached when he was to leave her for a comparatively long stay, she grew melting and affectionate, remembering his many acts of consideration and his repeated expressions of an ardent attachment. She was solicitous about his health and his welfare. She bustled around, looking after his clothing, thinking about heavy underwear, quite as Madame Ratignolle would have done under similar circumstances. She cried when he went away, calling him her dear, good friend, and she was quite certain she would grow lonely before very long and go to join him in New York.

But after all, a radiant peace settled upon her when she at last found herself alone. Even the children were gone. Old Madame Pontellier had come herself and carried them off to Iberville with their quadroon. The old madame did not venture to say she was afraid they would be neglected during Léonce's absence; she hardly ventured to think so. She was hungry for them—even a little fierce in her attachment. She did not want them to be wholly "children of the pavement," she always said when begging to have them for a space. She wished them to know the country, with its streams, its fields, its woods, its freedom, so delicious to the young. She wished them to taste something of the life their father had lived and known and loved when he, too, was a little child.

When Edna was at last alone, she breathed a big, genuine sigh of relief. A feeling that was unfamiliar but very delicious came over her. She walked all through the house, from one room to another, as if inspecting it for the first time. She tried the various chairs and lounges, as if she had never sat and reclined upon them before. And she perambulated around the outside of the house, investigating, looking to see if windows and shutters were secure and in order. The flowers were like new acquaintances; she approached them in a familiar spirit, and made herself at home among them. The garden walks were damp, and Edna called to the maid to bring out her rubber sandals. And there she stayed, and stooped, digging around the plants, trimming, picking dead, dry leaves. The children's little dog came out, interfering, getting in her way. She scolded him, laughed at him, played with him. The garden smelled so good and looked so pretty in the afternoon sunlight. Edna plucked all the bright flowers she could find, and went into the house with them, she and the little dog.

Even the kitchen assumed a sudden interesting character which she had never before perceived. She went in to give directions to the cook, to say that the butcher would have to bring much less meat, that they would require only half their usual quantity of bread, of milk and groceries. She told the cook that she herself would be greatly occupied during Mr. Pontellier's absence, and she begged her to take all thought and responsibility of the larder upon her own shoulders.

That night Edna dined alone. The candelabra, with a few candles in the center of the table, gave all the light she needed. Outside the circle of light in which she sat, the large dining-room looked solemn and shadowy. The cook, placed upon her mettle, served a delicious repast—a luscious tenderloin broiled *à point*. The wine tasted good;

the *marron glacé* seemed to be just what she wanted. It was so pleasant, too, to dine in a comfortable *peignoir*.

She thought a little sentimentally about Léonce and the children, and wondered what they were doing. As she gave a dainty scrap or two to the doggie, she talked intimately to him about Etienne and Raoul. He was beside himself with astonishment and delight over these companionable advances, and showed his appreciation by his little quick, snappy barks and a lively agitation.

Then Edna sat in the library after dinner and read Emerson until she grew sleepy. She realized that she had neglected her reading, and determined to start anew upon a course of improving studies, now that her time was completely her own to do with as she liked.

After a refreshing bath, Edna went to bed. And as she snuggled comfortably beneath the eiderdown a sense of restfulness invaded her, such as she had not known before.

CHAPTER XXV

When the weather was dark and cloudy Edna could not work. She needed the sun to mellow and temper her mood to the sticking point. She had reached a stage when she seemed to be no longer feeling her way, working, when in the humor, with sureness and ease. And being devoid of ambition, and striving not toward accomplishment, she drew satisfaction from the work in itself.

On rainy or melancholy days Edna went out and sought the society of the friends she had made at Grand Isle. Or else she stayed indoors and nursed a mood with which she was becoming too familiar for her own comfort and peace of mind. It was not despair; but it seemed to her as if life were passing by, leaving its promise broken and unfulfilled. Yet there were other days when she listened, was led on and deceived by fresh promises which her youth held out to her.

She went again to the races, and again. Alcée Arobin and Mrs. Highcamp called for her one bright afternoon in

Arobin's drag. Mrs. Highcamp was a worldly but unaffected, intelligent, slim, tall blonde woman in the forties, with an indifferent manner and blue eyes that stared. She had a daughter who served her as a pretext for cultivating the society of young men of fashion. Alcée Arobin was one of them. He was a familiar figure at the race course, the opera, the fashionable clubs. There was a perpetual smile in his eyes, which seldom failed to awaken a corresponding cheerfulness in any one who looked into them and listened to his good-humored voice. His manner was quiet, and at times a little insolent. He possessed a good figure, a pleasing face, not overburdened with depth of thought or feeling; and his dress was that of the conventional man of fashion.

He admired Edna extravagantly, after meeting her at the races with her father. He had met her before on other occasions, but she had seemed to him unapproachable until that day. It was at his instigation that Mrs. Highcamp called to ask her to go with them to the Jockey Club to witness the turf event of the season.

There were possibly a few track men out there who knew the race horse as well as Edna, but there was certainly none who knew it better. She sat between her two companions as one having authority to speak. She laughed at Arobin's pretensions, and deplored Mrs. Highcamp's ignorance. The race horse was a friend and intimate associate of her childhood. The atmosphere of the stables and the breath of the blue grass paddock revived in her memory and lingered in her nostrils. She did not perceive that she was talking like her father as the sleek geldings ambled in review before them. She played for very high stakes, and fortune favored her. The fever of the game flamed in her cheeks and eyes, and it got into her blood and into her brain like an intoxicant. People turned their heads to look at her, and more than one lent an attentive ear to her utterances, hoping thereby to secure the elusive but ever-desired "tip." Arobin caught the contagion of excitement which drew him to Edna like a magnet. Mrs. Highcamp remained, as usual, unmoved, with her indifferent stare and uplifted eyebrows.

Edna stayed and dined with Mrs. Highcamp upon

being urged to do so. Arobin also remained and sent away his drag.

The dinner was quiet and uninteresting, save for the cheerful efforts of Arobin to enliven things. Mrs. Highcamp deplored the absence of her daughter from the races, and tried to convey to her what she had missed by going to the "Dante reading" instead of joining them. The girl held a geranium leaf up to her nose and said nothing, but looked knowing and noncommittal. Mr. Highcamp was a plain, bald-headed man, who only talked under compulsion. He was unresponsive. Mrs. Highcamp was full of delicate courtesy and consideration toward her husband. She addressed most of her conversation to him at table. They sat in the library after dinner and read the evening papers together under the droplight; while the younger people went into the drawing-room near by and talked. Miss Highcamp played some selections from Grieg upon the piano. She seemed to have apprehended all of the composer's coldness and none of his poetry. While Edna listened she could not help wondering if she had lost her taste for music.

When the time came for her to go home, Mr. Highcamp grunted a lame offer to escort her, looking down at his slippered feet with tactless concern. It was Arobin who took her home. The car ride was long, and it was late when they reached Esplanade Street. Arobin asked permission to enter for a second to light his cigarette—his match safe was empty. He filled his match safe, but did not light his cigarette until he left her, after she had expressed her willingness to go to the races with him again.

Edna was neither tired nor sleepy. She was hungry again, for the Highcamp dinner, though of excellent quality, had lacked abundance. She rummaged in the larder and brought forth a slice of Gruyère and some crackers. She opened a bottle of beer which she found in the icebox. Edna felt extremely restless and excited. She vacantly hummed a fantastic tune as she poked at the wood embers on the hearth and munched a cracker.

She wanted something to happen—something, anything; she did not know what. She regretted that she had not made Arobin stay a half hour to talk over the horses with her. She counted the money she had won. But there was nothing else to do, so she went to bed, and tossed there for hours in a sort of monotonous agitation.

In the middle of the night she remembered that she had forgotten to write her regular letter to her husband; and she decided to do so next day and tell him about her afternoon at the Jockey Club. She lay wide awake composing a letter which was nothing like the one which she wrote next day. When the maid awoke her in the morning Edna was dreaming of Mr. Highcamp playing the piano at the entrance of a music store on Canal Street, while his wife was saying to Alcée Arobin, as they boarded an Esplanade Street car:

"What a pity that so much talent has been neglected! but I must go."

When, a few days later, Alcée Arobin again called for Edna in his drag, Mrs. Highcamp was not with him. He said they would pick her up. But as that lady had not been apprised of his intention of picking her up, she was not at home. The daughter was just leaving the house to attend the meeting of a branch Folk Lore Society, and regretted that she could not accompany them. Arobin appeared nonplused, and asked Edna if there were any one else she cared to ask.

She did not deem it worth while to go in search of any of the fashionable acquaintances from whom she had withdrawn herself. She thought of Madame Ratignolle, but knew that her fair friend did not leave the house, except to take a languid walk around the block with her husband after nightfall. Mademoiselle Reisz would have laughed at such a request from Edna. Madame Lebrun might have enjoyed the outing, but for some reason Edna did not want her. So they went alone, she and Arobin.

The afternoon was intensely interesting to her. The excitement came back upon her like a remittent fever. Her talk grew familiar and confidential. It was no labor to become intimate with Arobin. His manner invited easy confidence. The preliminary stage of becoming acquainted was one which he always endeavored to ignore when a pretty and engaging woman was concerned.

He stayed and dined with Edna. He stayed and sat beside the wood fire. They laughed and talked; and before it was time to go he was telling her how different life might have been if he had known her years before. With ingenuous frankness he spoke of what a wicked, ill-disciplined boy he had been, and impulsively drew up his cuff to exhibit upon his wrist the scar from a saber cut which he had received in a duel outside of Paris when he was nineteen. She touched his hand as she scanned the red cicatrice on the inside of his white wrist. A quick impulse that was somewhat spasmodic impelled her fingers to close in a sort of clutch upon his hand. He felt the pressure of her pointed nails in the flesh of his palm.

She arose hastily and walked toward the mantel.

"The sight of a wound or scar always agitates and sickens me," she said. "I shouldn't have looked at it."

"I beg your pardon," he entreated, following her; "it never occurred to me that it might be repulsive."

He stood close to her, and the effrontery in his eyes repelled the old, vanishing self in her, yet drew all her awakening sensuousness. He saw enough in her face to impel him to take her hand and hold it while he said his lingering good night.

"Will you go to the races again?" he asked.

"No," she said. "I've had enough of the races. I don't want to lose all the money I've won, and I've got to work when the weather is bright, instead of—"

"Yes; work; to be sure. You promised to show me your work. What morning may I come up to your atelier? To-morrow?"

"No!"

"Day after?"

"No, no."

"Oh, please don't refuse me! I know something of such things. I might help you with a stray suggestion or two."

"No. Good night. Why don't you go after you have said good night? I don't like you," she went on in a high, excited pitch, attempting to draw away her hand. She felt that her words lacked dignity and sincerity, and she knew that he felt it.

"I'm sorry you don't like me. I'm sorry I offended you. How have I offended you? What have I done? Can't you forgive me?" And he bent and pressed his lips upon her hand as if he wished never more to withdraw them.

"Mr. Arobin," she complained, "I'm greatly upset by the excitement of the afternoon; I'm not myself. My manner must have misled you in some way. I wish you to go, please." She spoke in a monotonous, dull tone. He took his hat from the table, and stood with eyes turned from her, looking into the dying fire. For a moment or two he kept an impressive silence.

"Your manner has not misled me, Mrs. Pontellier," he said finally. "My own emotions have done that. I couldn't help it. When I'm near you, how could I help it? Don't think anything of it, don't bother, please. You see, I go when you command me. If you wish me to stay away, I shall do so. If you let me come back, I—oh! you will let me come back?"

He cast one appealing glance at her, to which she made no response. Alcée Arobin's manner was so genuine that it often deceived even himself.

Edna did not care or think whether it were genuine or not. When she was alone she looked mechanically at the back of her hand which he had kissed so warmly. Then she leaned her head down on the mantelpiece. She felt somewhat like a woman who in a moment of passion is betrayed into an act of infidelity, and realizes the significance of the act without being wholly awakened from its glamour. The thought was passing vaguely through her mind, "What would he think?"

She did not mean her husband; she was thinking of Robert Lebrun. Her husband seemed to her now like a person whom she had married without love as an excuse.

She lit a candle and went up to her room. Alcée Arobin was absolutely nothing to her. Yet his presence, his manners, the warmth of his glances, and above all the touch of his lips upon her hand had acted like a narcotic upon her.

She slept a languorous sleep, interwoven with vanishing dreams.

CHAPTER XXVI

Alcée Arobin wrote Edna an elaborate note of apology, palpitant with sincerity. It embarrassed her; for in a cooler, quieter moment it appeared to her absurd that she should have taken his action so seriously, so dramatically. She felt sure that the significance of the whole occurrence had lain in her own self-consciousness. If she ignored his note it would give undue importance to a trivial affair. If she replied to it in a serious spirit it would still leave in his mind the impression that she had in a susceptible moment yielded to his influence. After all, it was no great matter to have one's hand kissed. She was provoked at his having written the apology. She answered in as light and bantering a spirit as she fancied it deserved, and said she would be glad to have him look in upon her at work whenever he felt the inclination and his business gave him the opportunity.

He responded at once by presenting himself at her home with all his disarming naïveté. And then there was scarcely a day which followed that she did not see him or was not reminded of him. He was prolific in pretexts. His attitude became one of good-humored subservience and tacit adoration. He was ready at all times to submit to her moods, which were as often kind as they were cold. She grew accustomed to him. They became intimate and friendly by imperceptible degrees, and then by leaps. He sometimes talked in a way that astonished her at first and brought the crimson into her face; in a way that pleased her at last, appealing to the animalism that stirred impatiently within her.

There was nothing which so quieted the turmoil of Edna's senses as a visit to Mademoiselle Reisz. It was then, in the presence of that personality which was offensive to her, that the woman, by her divine art, seemed to reach Edna's spirit and set it free.

It was misty, with heavy, lowering atmosphere, one afternoon, when Edna climbed the stairs to the pianist's apartments under the roof. Her clothes were dripping with moisture. She felt chilled and pinched as she entered the room. Mademoiselle was poking at a rusty stove that smoked a little and warmed the room indifferently. She was endeavoring to heat a pot of chocolate on the stove. The room looked cheerless and dingy to Edna as she entered. A bust of Beethoven, covered with a hood of dust, scowled at her from the mantelpiece.

"Ah! here comes the sunlight!" exclaimed Mademoiselle, rising from her knees before the stove. "Now it will be warm and bright enough; I can let the fire alone."

She closed the stove door with a bang, and approaching, assisted in removing Edna's dripping mackintosh.

"You are cold; you look miserable. The chocolate will soon be hot. But would you rather have a taste of brandy? I have scarcely touched the bottle which you brought me for my cold." A piece of red flannel was wrapped around Mademoiselle's throat; a stiff neck compelled her to hold her head on one side.

"I will take some brandy," said Edna, shivering as she removed her gloves and overshoes. She drank the liquor from the glass as a man would have done. Then flinging herself upon the uncomfortable sofa she said, "Mademoiselle, I am going to move away from my house on Esplanade Street."

"Ah!" ejaculated the musician, neither surprised nor especially interested. Nothing ever seemed to astonish her very much. She was endeavoring to adjust the bunch of violets which had become loose from its fastening in her hair. Edna drew her down upon the sofa, and taking a pin from her own hair, secured the shabby artificial flowers in their accustomed place.

"Aren't you astonished?"

"Passably. Where are you going? to New York? to Iberville? to your father in Mississippi? where?"

"Just two steps away," laughed Edna, "in a little four-room house around the corner. It looks so cozy, so inviting and restful, whenever I pass by; and it's for rent. I'm tired looking after that big house. It never seemed like mine, anyway—like home. It's too much trouble. I have to keep too many servants. I am tired bothering with them."

"That is not your true reason, *ma belle*. There is no use in telling me lies. I don't know your reason, but you have not told me the truth." Edna did not protest or endeavor to justify herself.

"The house, the money that provides for it, are not mine. Isn't that enough reason?"

"They are your husband's," returned Mademoiselle, with a shrug and a malicious elevation of the eyebrows.

"Oh! I see there is no deceiving you. Then let me tell you: It is a caprice. I have a little money of my own from my mother's estate, which my father sends me by driblets. I won a large sum this winter on the races, and I am beginning to sell my sketches. Laidpore is more and more pleased with my work; he says it grows in force and individuality. I cannot judge of that myself, but I feel that I have gained in ease and confidence. However, as I said, I have sold a good many through Laidpore. I can live in the tiny house for little or nothing, with one servant. Old Celestine, who works occasionally for me, says she will come stay with me and do my work. I know I shall like it, like the feeling of freedom and independence."

"What does your husband say?"

"I have not told him yet. I only thought of it this morning. He will think I am demented, no doubt. Perhaps you think so."

Mademoiselle shook her head slowly. "Your reason is not yet clear to me," she said.

Neither was it quite clear to Edna herself; but it unfolded itself as she sat for a while in silence. Instinct had prompted her to put away her husband's bounty in casting off her allegiance. She did not know how it would be when he returned. There would have to be an understanding, an explanation. Conditions would some way adjust themselves, she felt; but whatever came, she had resolved never again to belong to another than herself.

"I shall give a grand dinner before I leave the old house!" Edna exclaimed. "You will have to come to it,

Mademoiselle. I will give you everything that you like to eat and to drink. We shall sing and laugh and be merry for once." And she uttered a sigh that came from the very depths of her being.

If Mademoiselle happened to have received a letter from Robert during the interval of Edna's visits, she would give her the letter unsolicited. And she would seat herself at the piano and play as her humor prompted her while the young woman read the letter.

The little stove was roaring; it was red-hot, and the chocolate in the tin sizzled and sputtered. Edna went forward and opened the stove door, and Mademoiselle rising, took a letter from under the bust of Beethoven and handed it to Edna.

"Another! so soon!" she exclaimed, her eyes filled with delight. "Tell me, Mademoiselle, does he know that I see his letters?"

"Never in the world! He would be angry and would never write to me again if he thought so. Does he write to you? Never a line. Does he send you a message? Never a word. It is because he loves you, poor fool, and is trying to forget you, since you are not free to listen to him or to belong to him."

"Why do you show me his letters, then?"

"Haven't you begged for them? Can I refuse you anything? Oh! you cannot deceive me," and Mademoiselle approached her beloved instrument and began to play. Edna did not at once read the letter. She sat holding it in her hand, while the music penetrated her whole being like an effulgence, warming and brightening the dark places of her soul. It prepared her for joy and exultation.

"Oh!" she exclaimed, letting the letter fall to the floor. "Why did you not tell me?" She went and grasped Mademoiselle's hands up from the keys. "Oh! unkind! malicious! Why did you not tell me?"

"That he was coming back? No great news, *ma foi.* I wonder he did not come long ago."

"But when, when?" cried Edna, impatiently. "He does not say when."

"He says 'very soon.' You know as much about it as I do; it is all in the letter."

"But why? Why is he coming? Oh, if I thought—" and she snatched the letter from the floor and turned the pages this way and that way, looking for the reason, which was left untold.

"If I were young and in love with a man," said Mademoiselle, turning on the stool and pressing her wiry hands between her knees as she looked down at Edna, who sat on the floor holding the letter, "it seems to me he would have to be some *grand esprit;* a man with lofty aims and ability to reach them; one who stood high enough to attract the notice of his fellow-men. It seems to me if I were young and in love I should never deem a man of ordinary caliber worthy of my devotion."

"Now it is you who are telling lies and seeking to deceive me, Mademoiselle; or else you have never been in love, and know nothing about it. Why," went on Edna, clasping her knees and looking up into Mademoiselle's twisted face, "do you suppose a woman knows why she loves? Does she select? Does she say to herself: 'Go to! Here is a distinguished statesman with presidential possibilities; I shall proceed to fall in love with him.' Or, 'I shall set my heart upon this musician, whose fame is on every tongue?' Or, 'This financier, who controls the world's money markets?' "

"You are purposely misunderstanding me, *ma reine.* Are you in love with Robert?"

"Yes," said Edna. It was the first time she had admitted it, and a glow overspread her face, blotching it with red spots.

"Why?" asked her companion. "Why do you love him when you ought not to?"

Edna, with a motion or two, dragged herself on her knees before Mademoiselle Reisz, who took the glowing face between her two hands.

"Why? Because his hair is brown and grows away from his temples; because he opens and shuts his eyes, and his nose is a little out of drawing; because he has two lips and a square chin, and a little finger which he can't straighten from having played baseball too energetically in his youth. Because—"

"Because you do, in short," laughed Mademoiselle. "What will you do when he comes back?" she asked.

"Do? Nothing, except feel glad and happy to be alive."

She was already glad and happy to be alive at the mere thought of his return. The murky, lowering sky, which had depressed her a few hours before, seemed bracing and invigorating as she splashed through the streets on her way home.

She stopped at a confectioner's and ordered a huge box of bonbons for the children in Iberville. She slipped a card in the box, on which she scribbled a tender message and sent an abundance of kisses.

Before dinner in the evening Edna wrote a charming letter to her husband, telling him of her intention to move for a while into the little house around the block, and to give a farewell dinner before leaving, regretting that he was not there to share it, to help out with the menu and assist her in entertaining the guests. Her letter was brilliant and brimming with cheerfulness.

CHAPTER XXVII

"What is the matter with you?" asked Arobin that evening. "I never found you in such a happy mood." Edna was tired by that time, and was reclining on the lounge before the fire.

"Don't you know the weather prophet has told us we shall see the sun pretty soon?"

"Well, that ought to be reason enough," he acquiesced. "You wouldn't give me another if I sat here all night imploring you." He sat close to her on a low tabouret, and as he spoke his fingers lightly touched the hair that fell a little over her forehead. She liked the touch of his fingers through her hair, and closed her eyes sensitively.

"One of these days," she said, "I'm going to pull myself together for a while and think—try to determine what character of a woman I am; for, candidly, I don't know. By all the codes which I am acquainted with, I am a devilishly wicked specimen of the sex. But some way I can't convince myself that I am. I must think about it."

"Don't. What's the use? Why should you bother thinking about it when I can tell you what manner of woman you are." His fingers strayed occasionally down to her warm, smooth cheeks and firm chin, which was growing a little full and double.

"Oh, yes! You will tell me that I am adorable; everything that is captivating. Spare yourself the effort."

"No; I shan't tell you anything of the sort, though I shouldn't be lying if I did."

"Do you know Mademoiselle Reisz?" she asked irrelevantly.

"The pianist? I know her by sight. I've heard her play."

"She says queer things sometimes in a bantering way that you don't notice at the time and you find yourself thinking about afterward."

"For instance?"

"Well, for instance, when I left her to-day, she put her arms around me and felt my shoulder blades, to see if my wings were strong, she said. 'The bird that would soar above the level plain of tradition and prejudice must have strong wings. It is a sad spectacle to see the weaklings bruised, exhausted, fluttering back to earth.' "

"Whither would you soar?"

"I'm not thinking of any extraordinary flights. I only half comprehend her."

"I've heard she's partially demented," said Arobin.

"She seems to me wonderfully sane," Edna replied.

"I'm told she's extremely disagreeable and unpleasant. Why have you introduced her at a moment when I desired to talk of you?"

"Oh! talk of me if you like," cried Edna, clasping her hands beneath her head; "but let me think of something else while you do."

"I'm jealous of your thoughts to-night. They're making you a little kinder than usual; but some way I feel as if they were wandering, as if they were not here with me." She only looked at him and smiled. His eyes were very near. He leaned upon the lounge with an arm extended across her, while the other hand still rested upon her hair. They continued silently to look into each other's eyes. When he leaned forward and kissed her, she clasped his head, holding his lips to hers.

It was the first kiss of her life to which her nature had really responded. It was a flaming torch that kindled desire.

CHAPTER XXVIII

Edna cried a little that night after Arobin left her. It was only one phase of the multitudinous emotions which had assailed her. There was with her an overwhelming feeling of irresponsibility. There was the shock of the unexpected and the unaccustomed. There was her husband's reproach looking at her from the external things around her which he had provided for her external existence. There was Robert's reproach making itself felt by a quicker, fiercer, more overpowering love, which had awakened within her toward him. Above all, there was understanding. She felt as if a mist had been lifted from her eyes, enabling her to look upon and comprehend the significance of life, that monster made up of beauty and brutality. But among the conflicting sensations which assailed her, there was neither shame nor remorse. There was a dull pang of regret because it was not the kiss of love which had inflamed her, because it was not love which had held this cup of life to her lips.

CHAPTER XXIX

Without even waiting for an answer from her husband regarding his opinion or wishes in the matter, Edna hastened her preparations for quitting her home on Esplanade Street and moving into the little house around the block. A feverish anxiety attended her every action in that direction. There was no moment of deliberation, no interval of repose between the thought and its fulfillment. Early upon the morning following those hours passed in Arobin's society, Edna set about securing her new abode and hurrying her arrangements for occupying it. Within the precincts of her home she felt like one who has entered and lingered within the portals of some forbidden temple in which a thousand muffled voices bade her begone.

Whatever was her own in the house, everything which she had acquired aside from her husband's bounty, she caused to be transported to the other house, supplying simple and meager deficiencies from her own resources.

Arobin found her with rolled sleeves, working in company with the house-maid when he looked in during the afternoon. She was splendid and robust, and had never appeared handsomer than in the old blue gown, with a red silk handkerchief knotted at random around her head to protect her hair from the dust. She was mounted upon a high stepladder, unhooking a picture from the wall when he entered. He had found the front door open, and had followed his ring by walking in unceremoniously.

"Come down!" he said. "Do you want to kill yourself?" She greeted him with affected carelessness, and appeared absorbed in her occupation.

If he had expected to find her languishing, reproachful, or indulging in sentimental tears, he must have been greatly surprised.

He was no doubt prepared for any emergency, ready for any one of the foregoing attitudes, just as he bent himself easily and naturally to the situation which confronted him.

"Please come down," he insisted, holding the ladder and looking up at her.

"No," she answered; "Ellen is afraid to mount the ladder. Joe is working over at the 'pigeon house'—that's the name Ellen gives it, because it's so small and looks like a pigeon house—and some one has to do this."

Arobin pulled off his coat, and expressed himself ready and willing to tempt fate in her place. Ellen brought him one of her dust-caps, and went into contortions of mirth, which she found it impossible to control, when she saw him put it on before the mirror as grotesquely as he could. Edna herself could not refrain from smiling when she fastened it at his request. So it was he who in turn mounted the ladder, unhooking pictures and curtains, and dislodging ornaments as Edna directed. When he had finished he took off his dust-cap and went out to wash his hands.

Edna was sitting on the tabouret, idly brushing the tips of a feather duster along the carpet when he came in again.

"Is there anything more you will let me do?" he asked.

"That is all," she answered. "Ellen can manage the rest." She kept the young woman occupied in the drawing-room, unwilling to be left alone with Arobin.

"What about the dinner?" he asked; "the grand event, the *coup d'état*?"

"It will be day after to-morrow. Why do you call it the '*coup d'état*?' Oh! it will be very fine; all my best of everything—crystal, silver and gold, Sèvres, flowers, music, and champagne to swim in. I'll let Léonce pay the bills. I wonder what he'll say when he sees the bills."

"And you ask me why I call it a *coup d'état*?" Arobin had put on his coat, and he stood before her and asked if his cravat was plumb. She told him it was, looking no higher than the tip of his collar.

"When do you go to the 'pigeon house?'—with all due acknowledgment to Ellen."

"Day after to-morrow, after the dinner. I shall sleep there."

"Ellen, will you very kindly get me a glass of water?" asked Arobin. "The dust in the curtains, if you will pardon me for hinting such a thing, has parched my throat to a crisp."

"While Ellen gets the water," said Edna, rising, "I will say good-by and let you go. I must get rid of this grime, and I have a million things to do and think of."

"When shall I see you?" asked Arobin, seeking to detain her, the maid having left the room.

"At the dinner, of course. You are invited."

"Not before?—not to-night or to-morrow morning or to-morrow noon or night? or the day after morning or noon? Can't you see yourself, without my telling you, what an eternity it is?"

He had followed her into the hall and to the foot of the stairway, looking up at her as she mounted with her face half turned to him.

"Not an instant sooner," she said. But she laughed and looked at him with eyes that at once gave him courage to wait and made it torture to wait.

CHAPTER XXX

Though Edna had spoken of the dinner as a very grand affair, it was in truth a very small affair and very select, in so much as the guests invited were few and were selected with discrimination. She had counted upon an even dozen seating themselves at her round mahogany board, forgetting for the moment that Madame Ratignolle was to the last degree *souffrante* and unpresentable, and not foreseeing that Madame Lebrun would send a thousand regrets at the last moment. So there were only ten, after all, which made a cozy, comfortable number.

There were Mr. and Mrs. Merriman, a pretty, vivacious little woman in the thirties; her husband, a jovial fellow, something of a shallow-pate, who laughed a good deal at other people's witticisms, and had thereby made himself extremely popular. Mrs. Highcamp had accompanied them. Of course, there was Alcée Arobin; and Mademoiselle Reisz had consented to come. Edna had sent her a fresh bunch of violets with black lace trimmings for her hair. Monsieur Ratignolle brought himself and his wife's excuses. Victor Lebrun, who happened to be in the city, bent upon relaxation, had accepted with alacrity. There was a Miss Mayblunt, no longer in her teens, who looked at the world through lorgnettes and with the keenest interest. It was thought and said that she was intellectual; it was suspected of her that she wrote under a *nom de guerre*. She had come with a gentleman by the name of Gouvernail, connected with one of the daily papers, of whom nothing special could be said, except that he was observant and seemed quiet and inoffensive. Edna herself made the tenth, and at half-past eight they seated themselves at table, Arobin and Monsieur Ratignolle on either side of their hostess.

Mrs. Highcamp sat between Arobin and Victor Lebrun. Then came Mrs. Merriman, Mr. Gouvernail, Miss Mayblunt, Mr. Merriman, and Mademoiselle Reisz next to Monsieur Ratignolle.

There was something extremely gorgeous about the appearance of the table, an effect of splendor conveyed by a cover of pale yellow satin under strips of lace-work. There were wax candles, in massive brass candelabra, burning softly under yellow silk shades; full, fragrant roses, yellow and red, abounded. There were silver and gold, as she had said there would be, and crystal which glittered like the gems which the women wore.

The ordinary stiff dining chairs had been discarded for the occasion and replaced by the most commodious and luxurious which could be collected throughout the house. Mademoiselle Reisz, being exceedingly diminutive, was elevated upon cushions, as small children are sometimes hoisted at table upon bulky volumes.

"Something new, Edna?" exclaimed Miss Mayblunt, with lorgnette directed toward a magnificent cluster of diamonds that sparkled, that almost sputtered, in Edna's hair, just over the center of her forehead.

"Quite new; 'brand' new, in fact; a present from my husband. It arrived this morning from New York. I may as well admit that this is my birthday, and that I am twenty-nine. In good time I expect you to drink my health. Meanwhile, I shall ask you to begin with this cocktail, composed—would you say 'composed?' " with an appeal to

Miss Mayblunt—"composed by my father in honor of Sister Janet's wedding."

Before each guest stood a tiny glass that looked and sparkled like a garnet gem.

"Then, all things considered," spoke Arobin, "it might not be amiss to start out by drinking the Colonel's health in the cocktail which he composed, on the birthday of the most charming of women—the daughter whom he invented."

Mr. Merriman's laugh at this sally was such a genuine outburst and so contagious that it started the dinner with an agreeable swing that never slackened.

Miss Mayblunt begged to be allowed to keep her cocktail untouched before her, just to look at. The color was marvelous! She could compare it to nothing she had ever seen, and the garnet lights which it emitted were unspeakably rare. She pronounced the Colonel an artist, and stuck to it.

Monsieur Ratignolle was prepared to take things seriously; the *mets*, the *entre-mets*, the service, the decorations, even the people. He looked up from his pompano and inquired of Arobin if he were related to the gentleman of that name who formed one of the firm of Laitner and Arobin, lawyers. The young man admitted that Laitner was a warm personal friend, who permitted Arobin's name to decorate the firm's letterheads and to appear upon a shingle that graced Perdido Street.

"There are so many inquisitive people and institutions abounding," said Arobin, "that one is really forced as a matter of convenience these days to assume the virtue of an occupation if he has it not."

Monsieur Ratignolle stared a little, and turned to ask Mademoiselle Reisz if she considered the symphony concerts up to the standard which had been set the previous winter. Mademoiselle Reisz answered Monsieur Ratignolle in French, which Edna thought a little rude, under the circumstances, but characteristic. Mademoiselle had only disagreeable things to say of the symphony concerts, and insulting remarks to make of all the musicians of New Orleans, singly and collectively. All her interest seemed to be centered upon the delicacies placed before her.

Mr. Merriman said that Mr. Arobin's remark about

inquisitive people reminded him of a man from Waco the other day at the St. Charles Hotel—but as Mr. Merriman's stories were always lame and lacking point, his wife seldom permitted him to complete them. She interrupted him to ask if he remembered the name of the author whose book she had bought the week before to send to a friend in Geneva. She was talking "books" with Mr. Gouvernail and trying to draw from him his opinion upon current literary topics. Her husband told the story of the Waco man privately to Miss Mayblunt, who pretended to be greatly amused and to think it extremely clever.

Mrs. Highcamp hung with languid but unaffected interest upon the warm and impetuous volubility of her left-hand neighbor, Victor Lebrun. Her attention was never for a moment withdrawn from him after seating herself at table; and when he turned to Mrs. Merriman, who was prettier and more vivacious than Mrs. Highcamp, she waited with easy indifference for an opportunity to reclaim his attention. There was the occasional sound of music, of mandolins, sufficiently removed to be an agreeable accompaniment rather than an interruption to the conversation. Outside the soft, monotonous splash of a fountain could be heard; the sound penetrated into the room with the heavy odor of jessamine that came through the open windows.

The golden shimmer of Edna's satin gown spread in rich folds on either side of her. There was a soft fall of lace encircling her shoulders. It was the color of her skin, without the glow, the myriad living tints that one may sometimes discover in vibrant flesh. There was something in her attitude, in her whole appearance when she leaned her head against the high-backed chair and spread her arms, which suggested the regal woman, the one who rules, who looks on, who stands alone.

But as she sat there amid her guests, she felt the old ennui overtaking her; the hopelessness which so often assailed her, which came upon her like an obsession, like something extraneous, independent of volition. It was something which announced itself; a chill breath that seemed to issue from some vast cavern wherein discords wailed. There came over her the acute longing which always summoned into her spiritual vision the presence of the beloved one, overpowering her at once with a sense of the unattainable.

The moments glided on, while a feeling of good fellowship passed around the circle like a mystic cord, holding and binding these people together with jest and laughter. Monsieur Ratignolle was the first to break the pleasant charm. At ten o'clock he excused himself. Madame Ratignolle was waiting for him at home. She was *bien souffrante*, and she was filled with vague dread, which only her husband's presence could allay.

Mademoiselle Reisz arose with Monsieur Ratignolle, who offered to escort her to the car. She had eaten well; she had tasted the good, rich wines, and they must have turned her head, for she bowed pleasantly to all as she withdrew from table. She kissed Edna upon the shoulder, and whispered: "*Bonne nuit, ma reine; soyez sage.*" She had been a little bewildered upon rising, or rather, descending from her cushions, and Monsieur Ratignolle gallantly took her arm and led her away.

Mrs. Highcamp was weaving a garland of roses, yellow and red. When she had finished the garland, she laid it lightly upon Victor's black curls. He was reclining far back in the luxurious chair, holding a glass of champagne to the light.

As if a magician's wand had touched him, the garland of roses transformed him into a vision of Oriental beauty. His cheeks were the color of crushed grapes, and his dusky eyes glowed with a languishing fire.

"*Sapristi!*" exclaimed Arobin.

But Mrs. Highcamp had one more touch to add to the picture. She took from the back of her chair a white silken scarf, with which she had covered her shoulders in the early part of the evening. She draped it across the boy in graceful folds, and in a way to conceal his black, conventional evening dress. He did not seem to mind what she did to him, only smiled, showing a faint gleam of white teeth, while he continued to gaze with narrowing eyes at the light through his glass of champagne.

"Oh! to be able to paint in color rather than in words!" exclaimed Miss Mayblunt, losing herself in a rhapsodic dream as she looked at him.

" 'There was a graven image of Desire
Painted with red blood on a ground of gold.' "

murmured Gouvernail, under his breath.

The effect of the wine upon Victor was to change his accustomed volubility into silence. He seemed to have abandoned himself to a reverie, and to be seeing pleasing visions in the amber bead.

"Sing," entreated Mrs. Highcamp. "Won't you sing to us?"

"Let him alone," said Arobin.

"He's posing," offered Mr. Merriman; "let him have it out."

"I believe he's paralyzed," laughed Mrs. Merriman. And leaning over the youth's chair, she took the glass from his hand and held it to his lips. He sipped the wine slowly, and when he had drained the glass she laid it upon the table and wiped his lips with her little filmy handkerchief.

"Yes, I'll sing for you," he said, turning in his chair toward Mrs. Highcamp. He clasped his hands behind his head, and looking up at the ceiling began to hum a little, trying his voice like a musician tuning an instrument. Then, looking at Edna, he began to sing:

"Ah! si tu savais!"

"Stop!" she cried, "don't sing that. I don't want you to sing it," and she laid her glass so impetuously and blindly upon the table as to shatter it against a carafe. The wine spilled over Arobin's legs and some of it trickled down upon Mrs. Highcamp's black gauze gown. Victor had lost all idea of courtesy, or else he thought his hostess was not in earnest, for he laughed and went on:

"Ah! si tu savais
Ce que tes yeux me disent"—

"Oh! you mustn't! you mustn't," exclaimed Edna, and pushing back her chair she got up, and going behind him placed her hand over his mouth. He kissed the soft palm that pressed upon his lips.

"No, no, I won't, Mrs. Pontellier. I didn't know you meant it," looking up at her with caressing eyes. The touch of his lips was like a pleasing sting to her hand. She lifted the garland of roses from his head and flung it across the room.

"Come, Victor; you've posed long enough. Give Mrs. Highcamp her scarf."

Mrs. Highcamp undraped the scarf from about him with her own hands. Miss Mayblunt and Mr. Gouvernail suddenly conceived the notion that it was time to say good night. And Mr. and Mrs. Merriman wondered how it could be so late.

Before parting from Victor, Mrs. Highcamp invited him to call upon her daughter, who she knew would be charmed to meet him and talk French and sing French songs with him. Victor expressed his desire and intention to call upon Miss Highcamp at the first opportunity which presented itself. He asked if Arobin were going his way. Arobin was not.

The mandolin players had long since stolen away. A profound stillness had fallen upon the broad, beautiful street. The voices of Edna's disbanding guests jarred like a discordant note upon the quiet harmony of the night.

CHAPTER XXXI

"Well?" questioned Arobin, who had remained with Edna after the others had departed.

"Well," she reiterated, and stood up, stretching her arms, and feeling the need to relax her muscles after having been so long seated.

"What next?" he asked.

"The servants are all gone. They left when the musicians did. I have dismissed them. The house has to be closed and locked, and I shall trot around to the pigeon house, and shall send Celestine over in the morning to straighten things up."

He looked around, and began to turn out some of the lights.

"What about upstairs?" he inquired.

"I think it is all right; but there may be a window or two unlatched. We had better look; you might take a candle and see. And bring me my wrap and hat on the foot of the bed in the middle room."

He went up with the light, and Edna began closing doors and windows. She hated to shut in the smoke and the fumes of the wine. Arobin found her cape and hat, which he brought down and helped her to put on.

When everything was secured and the lights put out, they left through the front door, Arobin locking it and taking the key, which he carried for Edna. He helped her down the steps.

"Will you have a spray of jessamine?" he asked, breaking off a few blossoms as he passed.

"No; I don't want anything."

She seemed disheartened, and had nothing to say. She took his arm, which he offered her, holding up the weight of her satin train with the other hand. She looked down, noticing the black line of his leg moving in and out so close to her against the yellow shimmer of her gown. There was the whistle of a railway train somewhere in the distance, and the midnight bells were ringing. They met no one in their short walk.

The "pigeon house" stood behind a locked gate, and a shallow *parterre* that had been somewhat neglected. There was a small front porch, upon which a long window and the front door opened. The door opened directly into the parlor; there was no side entry. Back in the yard was a room for servants, in which old Celestine had been ensconced.

Edna had left a lamp burning low upon the table. She had succeeded in making the room look habitable and homelike. There were some books on the table and a lounge near at hand. On the floor was a fresh matting, covered with a rug or two; and on the walls hung a few tasteful pictures. But the room was filled with flowers. These were a surprise to her. Arobin had sent them, and had had Celestine distribute them during Edna's absence.

Her bedroom was adjoining, and across a small passage were the dining-room and kitchen.

Edna seated herself with every appearance of discomfort.

"Are you tired?" he asked.

"Yes, and chilled, and miserable. I feel as if I had been wound up to a certain pitch—too tight—and something inside of me had snapped." She rested her head against the table upon her bare arm.

"You want to rest," he said, "and to be quiet. I'll go; I'll leave you and let you rest."

"Yes," she replied.

He stood up beside her and smoothed her hair with his soft, magnetic hand. His touch conveyed to her a certain physical comfort. She could have fallen quietly asleep there if he had continued to pass his hand over her hair. He brushed the hair upward from the nape of her neck.

"I hope you will feel better and happier in the morning," he said. "You have tried to do too much in the past few days. The dinner was the last straw; you might have dispensed with it."

"Yes," she admitted; "it was stupid."

"No, it was delightful; but it has worn you out." His hand had strayed to her beautiful shoulders, and he could feel the response of her flesh to his touch. He seated himself beside her and kissed her lightly upon the shoulder.

"I thought you were going away," she said, in an uneven voice.

"I am, after I have said good night."

"Good night," she murmured.

He did not answer, except to continue to caress her. He did not say good night until she had become supple to his gentle, seductive entreaties.

CHAPTER XXXII

When Mr. Pontellier learned of his wife's intention to abandon her home and take up her residence elsewhere, he immediately wrote her a letter of unqualified disapproval and remonstrance. She had given reasons which he was unwilling to acknowledge as adequate. He hoped she had not acted upon her rash impulse; and he begged her to consider first, foremost, and above all else, what people would say. He was not dreaming of scandal when he uttered this warning; that was a thing which would never have entered into his mind to consider in connection with his wife's name or his own. He was simply thinking of his financial integrity. It might get noised about that the Pontelliers had met with reverses, and were forced to conduct their *ménage* on a humbler scale than heretofore. It might do incalculable mischief to his business prospects.

But remembering Edna's whimsical turn of mind of late, and foreseeing that she had immediately acted upon her impetuous determination, he grasped the situation with his usual promptness and handled it with his well-known business tact and cleverness.

The same mail which brought to Edna his letter of disapproval carried instructions—the most minute instructions—to a well-known architect concerning the remodeling of his home, changes which he had long contemplated, and which he desired carried forward during his temporary absence.

Expert and reliable packers and movers were engaged to convey the furniture, carpets, pictures—everything movable, in short—to places of security. And in an incredibly short time the Pontellier house was turned over to the artisans. There was to be an addition—a small snuggery; there was to be frescoing, and hardwood flooring was to be put into such rooms as had not yet been subjected to this improvement.

Furthermore, in one of the daily papers appeared a brief notice to the effect that Mr. and Mrs. Pontellier were contemplating a summer sojourn abroad, and that their handsome residence on Esplanade Street was undergoing sumptuous alterations, and would not be ready for occupancy until their return. Mr. Pontellier had saved appearances!

Edna admired the skill of his maneuver, and avoided any occasion to balk his intentions. When the situation as set forth by Mr. Pontellier was accepted and taken for granted, she was apparently satisfied that it should be so.

The pigeon house pleased her. It at once assumed the intimate character of a home, while she herself invested it with a charm which it reflected like a warm glow. There was with her a feeling of having descended in the social scale, with a corresponding sense of having risen in the spiritual. Every step which she took toward relieving herself from obligations added to her strength and expansion as an individual. She began to look with her own eyes; to see and to apprehend the deeper undercurrents of life. No longer was she content to "feed upon opinion" when her own soul had invited her.

After a little while, a few days, in fact, Edna went up and spent a week with her children in Iberville. They were delicious February days, with all the summer's promise hovering in the air.

How glad she was to see the children! She wept for very pleasure when she felt their little arms clasping her; their hard, ruddy cheeks pressed against her own glowing cheeks. She looked into their faces with hungry eyes that could not be satisfied with looking. And what stories they had to tell their mother! About the pigs, the cows, the mules! About riding to the mill behind Gluglu; fishing back in the lake with their Uncle Jasper; picking pecans with Lidie's little black brood, and hauling chips in their express wagon. It was a thousand times more fun to haul real chips for old lame Susie's real fire than to drag painted blocks along the banquette on Esplanade Street!

She went with them herself to see the pigs and the cows, to look at the darkies laying the cane, to thrash the pecan trees, and catch fish in the back lake. She lived with them a whole week long, giving them all of herself, and gathering and filling herself with their young existence. They listened, breathless, when she told them the house in Esplanade Street was crowded with workmen, hammering, nailing, sawing, and filling the place with clatter. They wanted to know where their bed was; what had been done with their rocking-horse; and where did Joe sleep, and where had Ellen gone, and the cook? But, above all, they were fired with a desire to see the little house around the block. Was there any place to play? Were there any boys next door? Raoul, with pessimistic foreboding, was convinced that there were only girls next door. Where would they sleep, and where would papa sleep? She told them the fairies would fix it all right.

The old Madame was charmed with Edna's visit, and showered all manner of delicate attentions upon her. She was delighted to know that the Esplanade Street house was in a dismantled condition. It gave her the promise and pretext to keep the children indefinitely.

It was with a wrench and a pang that Edna left her children. She carried away with her the sound of their voices and the touch of their cheeks. All along the journey homeward their presence lingered with her like the memory of a delicious song. But by the time she had regained the city the song no longer echoed in her soul. She was again alone.

CHAPTER XXXIII

It happened sometimes when Edna went to see Mademoiselle Reisz that the little musician was absent, giving a lesson or making some small necessary household purchase. The key was always left in a secret hiding-place in the entry, which Edna knew. If Mademoiselle happened to be away, Edna would usually enter and wait for her return.

When she knocked at Mademoiselle Reisz's door one afternoon there was no response; so unlocking the door, as usual, she entered and found the apartment deserted, as she had expected. Her day had been quite filled up, and it was for a rest, for a refuge, and to talk about Robert, that she sought out her friend.

She had worked at her canvas—a young Italian character study—all the morning, completing the work without the model; but there had been many interruptions, some incident to her modest housekeeping, and others of a social nature.

Madame Ratignolle had dragged herself over, avoiding the too public thoroughfares, she said. She complained that Edna had neglected her much of late. Besides, she was consumed with curiosity to see the little house and the manner in which it was conducted. She wanted to hear all about the dinner party; Monsieur Ratignolle had left *so* early. What had happened after he left? The champagne and grapes which Edna sent over were *too* delicious. She had so little appetite; they had refreshed and toned her stomach. Where on earth was she going to put Mr. Pontellier in that little house, and the boys? And then she made Edna promise to go to her when her hour of trial overtook her.

"At any time—any time of the day or night, dear," Edna assured her.

Before leaving Madame Ratignolle said:

"In some way you seem to me like a child, Edna. You seem to act without a certain amount of reflection which is necessary in this life. That is the reason I want to say you mustn't mind if I advise you to be a little careful while you are living here alone. Why don't you have some one come and stay with you? Wouldn't Mademoiselle Reisz come?"

"No; she wouldn't wish to come, and I shouldn't want her always with me."

"Well, the reason—you know how evil-minded the world is—some one was talking of Alcée Arobin visiting you. Of course, it wouldn't matter if Mr. Arobin had not such a dreadful reputation. Monsieur Ratignolle was telling me that his attentions alone are considered enough to ruin a woman's name."

"Does he boast of his successes?" asked Edna, indifferently, squinting at her picture.

"No, I think not. I believe he is a decent fellow as far as that goes. But his character is so well known among the men. I shan't be able to come back and see you; it was very, very imprudent to-day."

"Mind the step!" cried Edna.

"Don't neglect me," entreated Madame Ratignolle; "and don't mind what I said about Arobin, or having some one to stay with you."

"Of course not," Edna laughed. "You may say anything you like to me." They kissed each other good-by. Madame

Ratignolle had not far to go, and Edna stood on the porch a while watching her walk down the street.

Then in the afternoon Mrs. Merriman and Mrs. Highcamp had made their "party call." Edna felt that they might have dispensed with the formality. They had also come to invite her to play *vingt-et-un* one evening at Mrs. Merriman's. She was asked to go early, to dinner, and Mr. Merriman or Mr. Arobin would take her home. Edna accepted in a half-hearted way. She sometimes felt very tired of Mrs. Highcamp and Mrs. Merriman.

Late in the afternoon she sought refuge with Mademoiselle Reisz, and stayed there alone, waiting for her, feeling a kind of repose invade her with the very atmosphere of the shabby, unpretentious little room.

Edna sat at the window, which looked out over the house-tops and across the river. The window frame was filled with pots of flowers, and she sat and picked the dry leaves from a rose geranium. The day was warm, and the breeze which blew from the river was very pleasant. She removed her hat and laid it on the piano. She went on picking the leaves and digging around the plants with her hat pin. Once she thought she heard Mademoiselle Reisz approaching. But it was a young black girl, who came in, bringing a small bundle of laundry, which she deposited in the adjoining room, and went away.

Edna seated herself at the piano, and softly picked out with one hand the bars of a piece of music which lay open before her. A half-hour went by. There was the occasional sound of people going and coming in the lower hall. She was growing interested in her occupation of picking out the aria, when there was a second rap at the door. She vaguely wondered what these people did when they found Mademoiselle's door locked.

"Come in," she called, turning her face toward the door. And this time it was Robert Lebrun who presented himself. She attempted to rise; she could not have done so without betraying the agitation which mastered her at sight of him, so she fell back upon the stool, only exclaiming, "Why, Robert!"

He came and clasped her hand, seemingly without knowing what he was saying or doing.

"Mrs. Pontellier! How do you happen—oh! how well you look! Is Mademoiselle Reisz not here? I never expected to see you."

"When did you come back?" asked Edna in an unsteady voice, wiping her face with her handkerchief. She seemed ill at ease on the piano stool, and he begged her to take the chair by the window. She did so, mechanically, while he seated himself on the stool.

"I returned day before yesterday," he answered, while he leaned his arm on the keys, bringing forth a crash of discordant sound.

"Day before yesterday!" she repeated, aloud; and went on thinking to herself, "day before yesterday," in a sort of an uncomprehending way. She had pictured him seeking her at the very first hour, and he had lived under the same sky since day before yesterday; while only by accident had he stumbled upon her. Mademoiselle must have lied when she said, "Poor fool, he loves you."

"Day before yesterday," she repeated, breaking off a spray of Mademoiselle's geranium; "then if you had not met me here to-day you wouldn't—when—that is, didn't you mean to come and see me?"

"Of course, I should have gone to see you. There have been so many things—" he turned the leaves of Mademoiselle's music nervously. "I started in at once yesterday with the old firm. After all there is as much chance for me here as there was there—that is, I might find it profitable some day. The Mexicans were not very congenial."

So he had come back because the Mexicans were not congenial; because business was as profitable here as there; because of any reason, and not because he cared to be near her. She remembered the day she sat on the floor, turning the pages of his letter, seeking the reason which was left untold.

She had not noticed how he looked—only feeling his presence; but she turned deliberately and observed him. After all, he had been absent but a few months, and was not changed. His hair—the color of hers—waved back from his temples in the same way as before. His skin was not more burned than it had been at Grand Isle. She found in his eyes, when he looked at her for one silent moment, the same tender caress, with an added warmth and entreaty which had not been there before—the same glance which had penetrated to the sleeping places of her soul and awakened them.

A hundred times Edna had pictured Robert's return, and imagined their first meeting. It was usually at her home, whither he had sought her out at once. She always fancied him expressing or betraying in some way his love for her. And here, the reality was that they sat ten feet apart, she at the window, crushing geranium leaves in her hand and smelling them, he twirling around on the piano stool, saying:

"I was very much surprised to hear of Mr. Pontellier's absence; it's a wonder Mademoiselle Reisz did not tell me; and your moving—mother told me yesterday. I should think you would have gone to New York with him, or to Iberville with the children, rather than be bothered here with housekeeping. And you are going abroad, too, I hear. We shan't have you at Grand Isle next summer; it won't seem—do you see much of Mademoiselle Reisz? She often spoke of you in the few letters she wrote."

"Do you remember that you promised to write to me when you went away?" A flush overspread his whole face.

"I couldn't believe that my letters would be of any interest to you."

"That is an excuse; it isn't the truth." Edna reached for her hat on the piano. She adjusted it, sticking the hat pin through the heavy coil of hair with some deliberation.

"Are you not going to wait for Mademoiselle Reisz?" asked Robert.

"No; I have found when she is absent this long, she is liable not to come back till late." She drew on her gloves, and Robert picked up his hat.

"Won't you wait for her?" asked Edna.

"Not if you think she will not be back till late," adding, as if suddenly aware of some discourtesy in his speech, "and I should miss the pleasure of walking home with you." Edna locked the door and put the key back in its hiding-place.

They went together, picking their way across muddy streets and sidewalks encumbered with the cheap display of small tradesmen. Part of the distance they rode in the car, and after disembarking, passed the Pontellier mansion, which looked broken and half torn asunder. Robert had never known the house, and looked at it with interest.

"I never knew you in your home," he remarked.

"I am glad you did not."

"Why?" She did not answer. They went on around the corner, and it seemed as if her dreams were coming true after all, when he followed her into the little house.

"You must stay and dine with me, Robert. You see I am all alone, and it is so long since I have seen you. There is so much I want to ask you."

She took off her hat and gloves. He stood irresolute, making some excuse about his mother who expected him; he even muttered something about an engagement. She struck a match and lit the lamp on the table; it was growing dusk. When he saw her face in the lamp-light, looking pained, with all the soft lines gone out of it, he threw his hat aside and seated himself.

"Oh! you know I want to stay if you will let me!" he exclaimed. All the softness came back. She laughed, and went and put her hand on his shoulder.

"This is the first moment you have seemed like the old Robert. I'll go tell Celestine." She hurried away to tell Celestine to set an extra place. She even sent her off in search of some added delicacy which she had not thought of for herself. And she recommended great care in dripping the coffee and having the omelet done to a proper turn.

When she reëntered, Robert was turning over magazines, sketches, and things that lay upon the table in great disorder. He picked up a photograph, and exclaimed:

"Alcée Arobin! What on earth is his picture doing here?"

"I tried to make a sketch of his head one day," answered Edna, "and he thought the photograph might help me. It was at the other house. I thought it had been left there. I must have packed it up with my drawing materials."

"I should think you would give it back to him if you have finished with it."

"Oh! I have a great many such photographs. I never

think of returning them. They don't amount to anything." Robert kept on looking at the picture.

"It seems to me—do you think his head worth drawing? Is he a friend of Mr. Pontellier's? You never said you knew him."

"He isn't a friend of Mr. Pontellier's; he's a friend of mine. I always knew him—that is, it is only of late that I know him pretty well. But I'd rather talk about you, and know what you have been seeing and doing and feeling out there in Mexico." Robert threw aside the picture.

"I've been seeing the waves and the white beach of Grand Isle; the quiet, grassy street of the *Chênière;* the old fort at Grande Terre. I've been working like a machine, and feeling like a lost soul. There was nothing interesting."

She leaned her head upon her hand to shade her eyes from the light.

"And what have you been seeing and doing and feeling all these days?" he asked.

"I've been seeing the waves and the white beach of Grand Isle; the quiet, grassy street of the *Chênière Caminada;* the old sunny fort at Grande Terre. I've been working with a little more comprehension than a machine, and still feeling like a lost soul. There was nothing interesting."

"Mrs. Pontellier, you are cruel," he said, with feeling, closing his eyes and resting his head back in his chair. They remained in silence till old Celestine announced dinner.

CHAPTER XXXIV

The dining-room was very small. Edna's round mahogany would have almost filled it. As it was there was but a step or two from the little table to the kitchen, to the mantel, the small buffet, and the side door that opened out on the narrow brick-paved yard.

A certain degree of ceremony settled upon them with

the announcement of dinner. There was no return to personalities. Robert related incidents of his sojourn in Mexico, and Edna talked of events likely to interest him, which had occurred during his absence. The dinner was of ordinary quality, except for the few delicacies which she had sent out to purchase. Old Celestine, with a bandana *tignon* twisted about her head, hobbled in and out, taking a personal interest in everything; and she lingered occasionally to talk patois with Robert, whom she had known as a boy.

He went out to a neighboring cigar stand to purchase cigarette papers, and when he came back he found that Celestine had served the black coffee in the parlor.

"Perhaps I shouldn't have come back," he said. "When you are tired of me, tell me to go."

"You never tire me. You must have forgotten the hours and hours at Grand Isle in which we grew accustomed to each other and used to being together."

"I have forgotten nothing at Grand Isle," he said, not looking at her, but rolling a cigarette. His tobacco pouch, which he laid upon the table, was a fantastic embroidered silk affair, evidently the handiwork of a woman.

"You used to carry your tobacco in a rubber pouch," said Edna, picking up the pouch and examining the needlework.

"Yes; it was lost."

"Where did you buy this one? In Mexico?"

"It was given to me by a Vera Cruz girl; they are very generous," he replied, striking a match and lighting his cigarette.

"They are very handsome, I suppose, those Mexican women; very picturesque, with their black eyes and their lace scarfs."

"Some are; others are hideous. Just as you find women everywhere."

"What was she like—the one who gave you the pouch? You must have known her very well."

"She was very ordinary. She wasn't of the slightest importance. I knew her well enough."

"Did you visit at her house? Was it interesting? I should like to know and hear about the people you met, and the impressions they made on you."

"There are some people who leave impressions not so lasting as the imprint of an oar upon the water."

"Was she such a one?"

"It would be ungenerous for me to admit that she was of that order and kind." He thrust the pouch back in his pocket, as if to put away the subject with the trifle which had brought it up.

Arobin dropped in with a message from Mrs. Merriman, to say that the card party was postponed on account of the illness of one of her children.

"How do you do, Arobin?" said Robert, rising from the obscurity.

"Oh! Lebrun. To be sure! I heard yesterday you were back. How did they treat you down in Mexique?"

"Fairly well."

"But not well enough to keep you there. Stunning girls, though, in Mexico. I thought I should never get away from Vera Cruz when I was down there a couple of years ago."

"Did they embroider slippers and tobacco pouches and hat-bands and things for you?" asked Edna.

"Oh! my! no! I didn't get so deep in their regard. I fear they made more impression on me than I made on them."

"You were less fortunate than Robert, then."

"I am always less fortunate than Robert. Has he been imparting tender confidences?"

"I've been imposing myself long enough," said Robert, rising, and shaking hands with Edna. "Please convey my regards to Mr. Pontellier when you write."

He shook hands with Arobin and went away.

"Fine fellow, that Lebrun," said Arobin when Robert had gone. "I never heard you speak of him."

"I knew him last summer at Grand Isle," she replied. "Here is that photograph of yours. Don't you want it?"

"What do I want with it? Throw it away." She threw it back on the table.

"I'm not going to Mrs. Merriman's," she said. "If you see her, tell her so. But perhaps I had better write. I think I shall write now, and say that I am sorry her child is sick, and tell her not to count on me."

"It would be a good scheme," acquiesced Arobin. "I don't blame you; stupid lot!"

Edna opened the blotter, and having procured paper and pen, began to write the note. Arobin lit a cigar and read the evening paper, which he had in his pocket.

"What is the date?" she asked. He told her.

"Will you mail this for me when you go out?"

"Certainly." He read to her little bits out of the newspaper, while she straightened things on the table.

"What do you want to do?" he asked, throwing aside the paper. "Do you want to go out for a walk or a drive or anything? It would be a fine night to drive."

"No; I don't want to do anything but just be quiet. You go away and amuse yourself. Don't stay."

"I'll go away if I must; but I shan't amuse myself. You know that I only live when I am near you."

He stood up to bid her good night.

"Is that one of the things you always say to women?"

"I have said it before, but I don't think I ever came so near meaning it," he answered with a smile. There were no warm lights in her eyes; only a dreamy, absent look.

"Good night. I adore you. Sleep well," he said, and he kissed her hand and went away.

She stayed alone in a kind of reverie—a sort of stupor. Step by step she lived over every instant of the time she had been with Robert after he had entered Mademoiselle Reisz's door. She recalled his words, his looks. How few and meager they had been for her hungry heart! A vision—a transcendently seductive vision of a Mexican girl arose before her. She writhed with a jealous pang. She wondered when he would come back. He had not said he would come back. She had been with him, had heard his voice and touched his hand. But some way he had seemed nearer to her off there in Mexico.

CHAPTER XXXV

The morning was full of sunlight and hope. Edna could see before her no denial—only the promise of excessive joy. She lay in bed awake, with bright eyes full of speculation. "He loves you, poor fool." If she could but get that conviction firmly fixed in her mind, what mattered about the rest? She felt she had been childish and unwise the night before in giving herself over to despondency. She recapitulated the motives which no doubt explained Robert's reserve. They were not insurmountable; they would not hold if he really loved her; they could not hold against her own passion, which he must come to realize in time. She pictured him going to his business that morning. She even saw how he was dressed; how he walked down one street, and turned the corner of another; saw him bending over his desk, talking to people who entered the office, going to his lunch, and perhaps watching for her on the street. He would come to her in the afternoon or evening, sit and roll his cigarette, talk a little, and go away as he had done the night before. But how delicious it would be to have him there with her! She would have no regrets, nor seek to penetrate his reserve if he still chose to wear it.

Edna ate her breakfast only half dressed. The maid brought her a delicious printed scrawl from Raoul, expressing his love, asking her to send him some bonbons, and telling her they had found that morning ten tiny white pigs all lying in a row beside Lidie's big white pig.

A letter also came from her husband, saying he hoped to be back early in March, and then they would get ready for that journey abroad which he had promised her so long, which he felt now fully able to afford; he felt able to travel as people should, without any thought of small economies—thanks to his recent speculations in Wall Street.

Much to her surprise she received a note from Arobin, written at midnight from the club. It was to say good morning to her, to hope she had slept well, to assure her of his devotion, which he trusted she in some faintest manner returned.

All these letters were pleasing to her. She answered the children in a cheerful frame of mind, promising them bonbons, and congratulating them upon their happy find of the little pigs.

She answered her husband with friendly evasiveness, —not with any fixed design to mislead him, only because all sense of reality had gone out of her life; she had abandoned herself to Fate, and awaited the consequences with indifference.

To Arobin's note she made no reply. She put it under Celestine's stove-lid.

Edna worked several hours with much spirit. She saw no one but a picture dealer, who asked her if it were true that she was going abroad to study in Paris.

She said possibly she might, and he negotiated with her for some Parisian studies to reach him in time for the holiday trade in December.

Robert did not come that day. She was keenly disappointed. He did not come the following day, nor the next. Each morning she awoke with hope, and each night she was a prey to despondency. She was tempted to seek him out. But far from yielding to the impulse, she avoided any occasion which might throw her in his way. She did not go to Mademoiselle Reisz's nor pass by Madame Lebrun's, as she might have done if he had still been in Mexico.

When Arobin, one night, urged her to drive with him, she went—out to the lake, on the Shell Road. His horses were full of mettle, and even a little unmanageable. She liked the rapid gait at which they spun along, and the quick, sharp sound of the horses' hoofs on the hard road. They did not stop anywhere to eat or to drink. Arobin was not needlessly imprudent. But they ate and they drank when they regained Edna's little dining-room—which was comparatively early in the evening.

It was late when he left her. It was getting to be more than a passing whim with Arobin to see her and be with her. He had detected the latent sensuality, which unfolded under his delicate sense of her nature's requirements like a torpid, torrid, sensitive blossom.

There was no despondency when she fell asleep that night; nor was there hope when she awoke in the morning.

CHAPTER XXXVI

There was a garden out in the suburbs; a small, leafy corner, with a few green tables under the orange trees. An old cat slept all day on the stone step in the sun, and an old *mulatresse* slept her idle hours away in her chair at the open window, till some one happened to knock on one of the green tables. She had milk and cream cheese to sell, and bread and butter. There was no one who could make such excellent coffee or fry a chicken so golden brown as she.

The place was too modest to attract the attention of people of fashion, and so quiet as to have escaped the notice of those in search of pleasure and dissipation. Edna had discovered it accidentally one day when the high-board gate stood ajar. She caught sight of a little green table, blotched with the checkered sunlight that filtered through the quivering leaves overhead. Within she had found the slumbering *mulatresse*, the drowsy cat, and a glass of milk which reminded her of the milk she had tasted in Iberville.

She often stopped there during her perambulations; sometimes taking a book with her, and sitting an hour or two under the trees when she found the place deserted. Once or twice she took a quiet dinner there alone, having instructed Celestine beforehand to prepare no dinner at home. It was the last place in the city where she would have expected to meet any one she knew.

Still she was not astonished when, as she was partaking of a modest dinner late in the afternoon, looking into an open book, stroking the cat, which had made friends with her—she was not greatly astonished to see Robert come in at the tall garden gate.

"I am destined to see you only by accident," she said, shoving the cat off the chair beside her. He was surprised, ill at ease, almost embarrassed at meeting her thus so unexpectedly.

"Do you come here often?" he asked.

"I almost live here," she said.

"I used to drop in very often for a cup of Catiche's good coffee. This is the first time since I came back."

"She'll bring you a plate, and you will share my dinner. There's always enough for two—even three." Edna had intended to be indifferent and as reserved as he when she met him; she had reached the determination by a laborious train of reasoning, incident to one of her despondent moods. But her resolve melted when she saw him before her, seated there beside her in the little garden, as if a designing Providence had led him into her path.

"Why have you kept away from me, Robert?" she asked, closing the book that lay open upon the table.

"Why are you so personal, Mrs. Pontellier? Why do you force me to idiotic subterfuges?" he exclaimed with sudden warmth. "I suppose there's no use telling you I've been very busy, or that I've been sick, or that I've been to see you and not found you at home. Please let me off with any one of these excuses."

"You are the embodiment of selfishness," she said. "You save yourself something—I don't know what—but there is some selfish motive, and in sparing yourself you never consider for a moment what I think, or how I feel your neglect and indifference. I suppose this is what you would call unwomanly; but I have got into a habit of expressing myself. It doesn't matter to me, and you may think me unwomanly if you like."

"No; I only think you cruel, as I said the other day. Maybe not intentionally cruel; but you seem to be forcing me into disclosures which can result in nothing; as if you would have me bare a wound for the pleasure of looking at it, without the intention or power of healing it."

"I'm spoiling your dinner, Robert; never mind what I say. You haven't eaten a morsel."

"I only came in for a cup of coffee." His sensitive face was all disfigured with excitement.

"Isn't this a delightful place?" she remarked. "I am so glad it has never actually been discovered. It is so quiet, so sweet, here. Do you notice there is scarcely a sound to be heard? It's so out of the way; and a good walk from the car. However, I don't mind walking. I always feel so sorry for women who don't like to walk; they miss so much—so many rare little glimpses of life; and we women learn so little of life on the whole.

"Catiche's coffee is always hot. I don't know how she manages it, here in the open air. Celestine's coffee gets cold bringing it from the kitchen to the dining-room. Three lumps! How can you drink it so sweet? Take some of the cress with your chop; it's so biting and crisp. Then there's the advantage of being able to smoke with your coffee out here. Now, in the city—aren't you going to smoke?"

"After a while," he said, laying a cigar on the table.

"Who gave it to you?" she laughed.

"I bought it. I suppose I'm getting reckless; I bought a whole box." She was determined not to be personal again and make him uncomfortable.

The cat made friends with him, and climbed into his lap when he smoked his cigar. He stroked her silky fur, and talked a little about her. He looked at Edna's book, which he had read; and he told her the end, to save her the trouble of wading through it, he said.

Again he accompanied her back to her home; and it was after dusk when they reached the little "pigeon-house." She did not ask him to remain, which he was grateful for, as it permitted him to stay without the discomfort of blundering through an excuse which he had no intention of considering. He helped her to light the lamp; then she went into her room to take off her hat and to bathe her face and hands.

When she came back Robert was not examining the pictures and magazines as before; he sat off in the shadow, leaning his head back on the chair as if in a reverie. Edna lingered a moment beside the table, arranging the books there. Then she went across the room to where he sat. She bent over the arm of his chair and called his name.

"Robert," she said, "are you asleep?"

"No," he answered, looking up at her.

She leaned over and kissed him—a soft, cool, delicate kiss, whose voluptuous sting penetrated his whole being—then she moved away from him. He followed, and took her in his arms, just holding her close to him. She put her hand up to his face and pressed his cheek against her own. The action was full of love and tenderness. He sought her lips again. Then he drew her down upon the sofa beside him and held her hand in both of his.

"Now you know," he said, "now you know what I have been fighting against since last summer at Grand Isle; what drove me away and drove me back again."

"Why have you been fighting against it?" she asked. Her face glowed with soft lights.

"Why? Because you were not free; you were Léonce Pontellier's wife. I couldn't help loving you if you were ten times his wife; but so long as I went away from you and kept away I could help telling you so." She put her free hand up to his shoulder, and then against his cheek, rubbing it softly. He kissed her again. His face was warm and flushed.

"There in Mexico I was thinking of you all the time, and longing for you."

"But not writing to me," she interrupted.

"Something put into my head that you cared for me; and I lost my senses. I forgot everything but a wild dream of your some way becoming my wife."

"Your wife!"

"Religion, loyalty, everything would give way if only you cared."

"Then you must have forgotten that I was Léonce Pontellier's wife."

"Oh! I was demented, dreaming of wild, impossible things, recalling men who had set their wives free, we have heard of such things."

"Yes, we have heard of such things."

"I came back full of vague, mad intentions. And when I got here—"

"When you got here you never came near me!" She was still caressing his cheek.

"I realized what a cur I was to dream of such a thing, even if you had been willing."

She took his face between her hands and looked into it as if she would never withdraw her eyes more. She kissed him on the forehead, the eyes, the cheeks, and the lips.

"You have been a very, very foolish boy, wasting your time dreaming of impossible things when you speak of Mr. Pontellier setting me free! I am no longer one of Mr. Pontellier's possessions to dispose of or not. I give myself where I choose. If he were to say, 'Here, Robert, take her and be happy; she is yours,' I should laugh at you both."

His face grew a little white. "What do you mean?" he asked.

There was a knock at the door. Old Celestine came in to say that Madame Ratignolle's servant had come around the back way with a message that Madame had been taken sick and begged Mrs. Pontellier to go to her immediately.

"Yes, yes," said Edna, rising; "I promised. Tell her yes—to wait for me. I'll go back with her."

"Let me walk over with you," offered Robert.

"No," she said; "I will go with the servant." She went into her room to put on her hat, and when she came in again she sat once more upon the sofa beside him. He had not stirred. She put her arms about his neck.

"Good-by, my sweet Robert. Tell me good-by." He kissed her with a degree of passion which had not before entered into his caress, and strained her to him.

"I love you," she whispered, "only you; no one but you. It was you who awoke me last summer out of a life-long, stupid dream. Oh! you have made me so unhappy with your indifference. Oh! I have suffered, suffered! Now you are here we shall love each other, my Robert. We shall be everything to each other. Nothing else in the world is of any consequence. I must go to my friend; but you will wait for me? No matter how late; you will wait for me, Robert?"

"Don't go; don't go! Oh! Edna, stay with me," he pleaded. "Why should you go? Stay with me, stay with me."

"I shall come back as soon as I can; I shall find you here." She buried her face in his neck, and said good-by again. Her seductive voice, together with his great love for her, had enthralled his senses, had deprived him of every impulse but the longing to hold her and keep her.

CHAPTER XXXVII

Edna looked in at the drug store. Monsieur Ratignolle was putting up a mixture himself, very carefully, dropping a red liquid into a tiny glass. He was grateful to Edna for having come; her presence would be a comfort to his wife. Madame Ratignolle's sister, who had always been with her at such trying times, had not been able to come up from the plantation, and Adèle had been inconsolable until Mrs. Pontellier so kindly promised to come to her. The nurse had been with them at night for the past week, as she lived a great distance away. And Dr. Mandelet had been coming and going all the afternoon. They were then looking for him any moment.

Edna hastened upstairs by a private stairway that led from the rear of the store to the apartments above. The children were all sleeping in a back room. Madame Ratignolle was in the salon, whither she had strayed in her suffering impatience. She sat on the sofa, clad in an ample white *peignoir*, holding a handkerchief tight in her hand with a nervous clutch. Her face was drawn and pinched, her sweet blue eyes haggard and unnatural. All her beautiful hair had been drawn back and plaited. It lay in a long braid on the sofa pillow, coiled like a golden serpent. The nurse, a comfortable looking *Griffe* woman in white apron and cap, was urging her to return to her bedroom.

"There is no use, there is no use," she said at once to Edna. "We must get rid of Mandelet; he is getting too old and careless. He said he would be here at half-past seven; now it must be eight. See what time it is, Joséphine."

The woman was possessed of a cheerful nature, and refused to take any situation too seriously, especially a situation with which she was so familiar. She urged Madame to have courage and patience. But Madame only set her teeth hard into her under lip, and Edna saw the sweat gather in beads on her white forehead. After a moment or two she uttered a profound sigh and wiped her face with the handkerchief rolled in a ball. She appeared exhausted. The nurse gave her a fresh handkerchief, sprinkled with cologne water.

"This is too much!" she cried. "Mandelet ought to be killed! Where is Alphonse? Is it possible I am to be abandoned like this—neglected by every one?"

"Neglected, indeed!" exclaimed the nurse. Wasn't she there? And here was Mrs. Pontellier leaving, no doubt, a pleasant evening at home to devote to her? And wasn't Monsieur Ratignolle coming that very instant through the hall? And Joséphine was quite sure she had heard Doctor Mandelet's coupé. Yes, there it was, down at the door.

Adèle consented to go back to her room. She sat on the edge of a little low couch next to her bed.

Doctor Mandelet paid no attention to Madame Ratignolle's upbraidings. He was accustomed to them at such times, and was too well convinced of her loyalty to doubt it.

He was glad to see Edna, and wanted her to go with him into the salon and entertain him. But Madame Ratignolle would not consent that Edna should leave her for an instant. Between agonizing moments, she chatted a little, and said it took her mind off her sufferings.

Edna began to feel uneasy. She was seized with a vague dread. Her own like experiences seemed far away, unreal, and only half remembered. She recalled faintly an ecstasy of pain, the heavy odor of chloroform, a stupor which had deadened sensation, and an awakening to find a little new life to which she had given being, added to the great unnumbered multitude of souls that come and go.

She began to wish she had not come; her presence was not necessary. She might have invented a pretext for staying away; she might even invent a pretext now for going. But Edna did not go. With an inward agony, with a flaming, outspoken revolt against the ways of Nature, she witnessed the scene of torture.

She was still stunned and speechless with emotion

when later she leaned over her friend to kiss her and softly say good-by. Adèle, pressing her cheek, whispered in an exhausted voice: "Think of the children, Edna. Oh think of the children! Remember them!"

CHAPTER XXXVIII

Edna still felt dazed when she got outside in the open air. The Doctor's coupé had returned for him and stood before the *porte cochère*. She did not wish to enter the coupé, and told Doctor Mandelet she would walk; she was not afraid, and would go alone. He directed his carriage to meet him at Mrs. Pontellier's, and he started to walk home with her.

Up—away up, over the narrow street between the tall houses, the stars were blazing. The air was mild and caressing, but cool with the breath of spring and the night. They walked slowly, the Doctor with a heavy, measured tread and his hands behind him; Edna, in an absent-minded way, as she had walked one night at Grand Isle, as if her thoughts had gone ahead of her and she was striving to overtake them.

"You shouldn't have been there, Mrs. Pontellier," he said. "That was no place for you. Adèle is full of whims at such times. There were a dozen women she might have had with her, unimpressionable women. I felt that it was cruel, cruel. You shouldn't have gone."

"Oh, well!" she answered, indifferently. "I don't know that it matters after all. One has to think of the children some time or other; the sooner the better."

"When is Léonce coming back?"

"Quite soon. Some time in March."

"And you are going abroad?"

"Perhaps—no, I am not going. I'm not going to be forced into doing things. I don't want to go abroad. I want to be let alone. Nobody has any right—except children, perhaps—and even then, it seems to me—or it did seem—"

She felt that her speech was voicing the incoherency of her thoughts, and stopped abruptly.

"The trouble is," sighed the Doctor, grasping her meaning intuitively, "that youth is given up to illusions. It seems to be a provision of Nature; a decoy to secure mothers for the race. And Nature takes no account of moral consequences, of arbitrary conditions which we create, and which we feel obliged to maintain at any cost."

"Yes," she said. "The years that are gone seem like dreams—if one might go on sleeping and dreaming—but to wake up and find—oh! well! perhaps it is better to wake up after all, even to suffer, rather than to remain a dupe to illusions all one's life."

"It seems to me, my dear child," said the Doctor at parting, holding her hand, "you seem to me to be in trouble. I am not going to ask for your confidence. I will only say that if ever you feel moved to give it to me, perhaps I might help you. I know I would understand, and I tell you there are not many who would—not many, my dear."

"Some way I don't feel moved to speak of things that trouble me. Don't think I am ungrateful or that I don't appreciate your sympathy. There are periods of despondency and suffering which take possession of me. But I don't want anything but my own way. That is wanting a good deal, of course, when you have to trample upon the lives, the hearts, the prejudices of others—but no matter—still, I shouldn't want to trample upon the little lives. Oh! I don't know what I'm saying, Doctor. Good night. Don't blame me for anything."

"Yes, I will blame you if you don't come and see me soon. We will talk of things you never have dreamt of talking about before. It will do us both good. I don't want you to blame yourself, whatever comes. Good night, my child."

She let herself in at the gate, but instead of entering she sat upon the step of the porch. The night was quiet and soothing. All the tearing emotion of the last few hours seemed to fall away from her like a somber, uncomfortable garment, which she had but to loosen to be rid of. She went back to that hour before Adèle had sent for her; and her senses kindled afresh in thinking of Robert's words, the pressure of his arms, and the feeling of his lips upon her own. She could picture at that moment no greater bliss on earth than possession of the beloved one. His expression of love had already given him to her in part. When she thought that he was there at hand, waiting for her, she grew numb with the intoxication of expectancy. It was so late; he would be asleep perhaps. She would awaken him with a kiss. She hoped he would be asleep that she might arouse him with her caresses.

Still, she remembered Adèle's voice whispering, "Think of the children; think of them." She meant to think of them; that determination had driven into her soul like a death wound—but not to-night. To-morrow would be time to think of everything.

Robert was not waiting for her in the little parlor. He was nowhere at hand. The house was empty. But he had scrawled on a piece of paper that lay in the lamplight:

"I love you. Good-by—because I love you."

Edna grew faint when she read the words. She went and sat on the sofa. Then she stretched herself out there, never uttering a sound. She did not sleep. She did not go to bed. The lamp sputtered and went out. She was still awake in the morning, when Celestine unlocked the kitchen door and came in to light the fire.

CHAPTER XXXIX

Victor, with hammer and nails and scraps of scantling, was patching a corner of one of the galleries. Mariequita sat near by, dangling her legs, watching him work, and handing him nails from the tool-box. The sun was beating down upon them. The girl had covered her head with her apron folded into a square pad. They had been talking for an hour or more. She was never tired of hearing Victor describe the dinner at Mrs. Pontellier's. He exaggerated every detail, making it appear a veritable Lucullean feast. The flowers were in tubs, he said. The champagne was quaffed from huge golden goblets. Venus rising from the foam could have presented no more entrancing a spectacle than Mrs. Pontellier, blazing with beauty and diamonds at the head of the board, while the other women were all of them youthful houris, possessed of incomparable charms.

She got it into her head that Victor was in love with Mrs. Pontellier, and he gave her evasive answers, framed so as to confirm her belief. She grew sullen and cried a little, threatening to go off and leave him to his fine ladies. There were a dozen men crazy about her at the *Chênière;* and since it was the fashion to be in love with married people, why, she could run away any time she liked to New Orleans with Célina's husband.

Célina's husband was a fool, a coward, and a pig, and to prove it to her, Victor intended to hammer his head into a jelly the next time he encountered him. This assurance was very consoling to Mariequita. She dried her eyes, and grew cheerful at the prospect.

They were still talking of the dinner and the allurements of city life when Mrs. Pontellier herself slipped around the corner of the house. The two youngsters stayed dumb with amazement before what they considered to be an apparition. But it was really she in flesh and blood, looking tired and a little travel-stained.

"I walked up from the wharf," she said, "and heard the hammering. I supposed it was you, mending the porch. It's a good thing. I was always tripping over those loose planks last summer. How dreary and deserted everything looks!"

It took Victor some little time to comprehend that she had come in Beaudelet's lugger, that she had come alone, and for no purpose but to rest.

"There's nothing fixed up yet, you see. I'll give you my room; it's the only place."

"Any corner will do," she assured him.

"And if you can stand Philomel's cooking," he went on, "though I might try to get her mother while you are here. Do you think she would come?" turning to Mariequita.

Mariequita thought that perhaps Philomel's mother might come for a few days, and money enough.

Beholding Mrs. Pontellier make her appearance, the

girl had at once suspected a lovers' rendezvous. But Victor's astonishment was so genuine, and Mrs. Pontellier's indifference so apparent, that the disturbing notion did not lodge long in her brain. She contemplated with the greatest interest this woman who gave the most sumptuous dinners in America, and who had all the men in New Orleans at her feet.

"What time will you have dinner?" asked Edna. "I'm very hungry; but don't get anything extra."

"I'll have it ready in little or no time," he said, bustling and packing away his tools. "You may go to my room to brush up and rest yourself. Mariequita will show you."

"Thank you," said Edna. "But, do you know, I have a notion to go down to the beach and take a good wash and even a little swim, before dinner?"

"The water is too cold!" they both exclaimed. "Don't think of it."

"Well, I might go down and try—dip my toes in. Why, it seems to me the sun is hot enough to have warmed the very depths of the ocean. Could you get me a couple of towels? I'd better go right away, so as to be back in time. It would be a little too chilly if I waited till this afternoon."

Mariequita ran over to Victor's room, and returned with some towels, which she gave to Edna.

"I hope you have fish for dinner," said Edna, as she started to walk away; "but don't do anything extra if you haven't."

"Run and find Philomel's mother," Victor instructed the girl. "I'll go to the kitchen and see what I can do. By Gimminy! Women have no consideration! She might have sent me word."

Edna walked on down to the beach rather mechanically, not noticing anything special except that the sun was hot. She was not dwelling upon any particular train of thought. She had done all the thinking which was necessary after Robert went away, when she lay awake upon the sofa till morning.

She had said over and over to herself: "To-day it is Arobin; to-morrow it will be some one else. It makes no difference to me, it doesn't matter about Léonce Pontellier—but Raoul and Etienne!" She understood now clearly what she had meant long ago when she said to Adèle Ratignolle that she would give up the unessential, but she would never sacrifice herself for her children.

Despondency had come upon her there in the wakeful night, and had never lifted. There was no one thing in the world that she desired. There was no human being whom she wanted near her except Robert; and she even realized that the day would come when he, too, and the thought of him would melt out of her existence, leaving her alone. The children appeared before her like antagonists who had overcome her; who had overpowered and sought to drag her into the soul's slavery for the rest of her days. But she knew a way to elude them. She was not thinking of these things when she walked down to the beach.

The water of the Gulf stretched out before her, gleaming with the million lights of the sun. The voice of the sea is seductive, never ceasing, whispering, clamoring, murmuring, inviting the soul to wander in abysses of solitude. All along the white beach, up and down, there was no living thing in sight. A bird with a broken wing was beating the air above, reeling, fluttering, circling disabled down, down to the water.

Edna had found her old bathing suit still hanging, faded, upon its accustomed peg.

She put it on, leaving her clothing in the bath-house. But when she was there beside the sea, absolutely alone, she cast the unpleasant, pricking garments from her, and for the first time in her life she stood naked in the open air, at the mercy of the sun, the breeze that beat upon her, and the waves that invited her.

How strange and awful it seemed to stand naked under the sky! how delicious! She felt like some new-born creature, opening its eyes in a familiar world that it had never known.

The foamy wavelets curled up to her white feet, and coiled like serpents about her ankles. She walked out. The water was chill, but she walked on. The water was deep, but she lifted her white body and reached out with a long, sweeping stroke. The touch of the sea is sensuous, enfolding the body in its soft, close embrace.

She went on and on. She remembered the night she

swam far out, and recalled the terror that seized her at the fear of being unable to regain the shore. She did not look back now, but went on and on, thinking of the blue-grass meadow that she had traversed when a little child, believing that it had no beginning and no end.

Her arms and legs were growing tired.

She thought of Léonce and the children. They were a part of her life. But they need not have thought that they could possess her, body and soul. How Mademoiselle Reisz would have laughed, perhaps sneered, if she knew! "And you call yourself an artist! What pretensions, Madame! The artist must possess the courageous soul that dares and defies."

Exhaustion was pressing upon and overpowering her.

"Good-by—because I love you." He did not know; he did not understand. He would never understand. Perhaps Doctor Mandelet would have understood if she had seen him—but it was too late; the shore was far behind her, and her strength was gone.

She looked into the distance, and the old terror flamed up for an instant, then sank again. Edna heard her father's voice and her sister Margaret's. She heard the barking of an old dog that was chained to the sycamore tree. The spurs of the cavalry officer clanged as he walked across the porch. There was the hum of bees, and the musky odor of pinks filled the air.

ETHAN FROME

by Edith Wharton

I had the story, bit by bit, from various people, and, as generally happens in such cases, each time it was a different story.

If you know Starkfield, Massachusetts, you know the post-office. If you know the post-office you must have seen Ethan Frome drive up to it, drop the reins on his hollow-backed bay and drag himself across the brick pavement to the white colonnade: and you must have asked who he was.

It was there that, several years ago, I saw him for the first time; and the sight pulled me up sharp. Even then he was the most striking figure in Starkfield, though he was but the ruin of a man. It was not so much his great height that marked him, for the "natives" were easily singled out by their lank longitude from the stockier foreign breed: it was the careless powerful look he had, in spite of a lameness checking each step like the jerk of a chain. There was something bleak and unapproachable in his face, and he was so stiffened and grizzled that I took him for an old man and was surprised to hear that he was not more than fifty-two. I had this from Harmon Gow, who had driven the stage from Bettsbridge to Starkfield in pre-trolley days and knew the chronicle of all the families on his line.

"He's looked that way ever since he had his smash-up; and that's twenty-four years ago come next February," Harmon threw out between reminiscent pauses.

The "smash-up" it was—I gathered from the same informant—which, besides drawing the red gash across Ethan Frome's forehead, had so shortened and warped his right side that it cost him a visible effort to take the few steps from his buggy to the post-office window. He used to drive in from his farm every day at about noon, and as that was my own hour for fetching my mail I often passed him in the porch or stood beside him while we waited on the motions of the distributing hand behind the grating. I noticed that, though he came so punctually, he seldom received anything but a copy of the *Bettsbridge Eagle*, which he put without a glance into his sagging pocket. At intervals, however, the post-master would hand him an envelope addressed to Mrs. Zenobia—or Mrs. Zeena—Frome, and usually bearing conspicuously in the upper left-hand corner the address of some manufacturer of patent medicine and the name of his specific. These documents my neighbour would also pocket without a glance, as if too much used to them to wonder at their number and variety, and would then turn away with a silent nod to the post-master.

Every one in Starkfield knew him and gave him a greeting tempered to his own grave mien; but his taciturnity was respected and it was only on rare occasions that one of the older men of the place detained him for a word. When this happened he would listen quietly, his blue eyes on the speaker's face, and answer in so low a tone that his words never reached me; then he would climb stiffly into his buggy, gather up the reins in his left hand and drive slowly away in the direction of his farm.

"It was a pretty bad smash-up?" I questioned Harmon, looking after Frome's retreating figure, and thinking how gallantly his lean brown head, with its shock of light hair, must have sat on his strong shoulders before they were bent out of shape.

"Wust kind," my informant assented. "More'n enough to kill most men. But the Fromes are tough. Ethan'll likely touch a hundred."

"Good God!" I exclaimed. At the moment Ethan Frome, after climbing to his seat, had leaned over to assure himself of the security of a wooden box—also with a druggist's label on it—which he had placed in the back of the buggy, and I saw his face as it probably looked when he thought himself alone. "*That* man touch a hundred? He looks as if he was dead and in hell now!"

Harmon drew a slab of tobacco from his pocket, cut off a wedge and pressed it into the leather pouch of his cheek. "Guess he's been in Starkfield too many winters. Most of the smart ones get away."

"Why didn't *he*?"

"Somebody had to stay and care for the folks. There warn't ever anybody but Ethan. Fust his father—then his mother—then his wife."

"And then the smash-up?"

Harmon chuckled sardonically. "That's so. He *had* to stay then."

"I see. And since then they've had to care for him?"

Harmon thoughtfully passed his tobacco to the other cheek. "Oh, as to that: I guess it's always Ethan done the caring."

Though Harmon Gow developed the tale as far as his mental and moral reach permitted there were perceptible gaps between his facts, and I had the sense that the deeper meaning of the story was in the gaps. But one phrase stuck in my memory and served as the nucleus about which I grouped my subsequent inferences: "Guess he's been in Starkfield too many winters."

Before my own time there was up I had learned to know what that meant. Yet I had come in the degenerate day of trolley, bicycle and rural delivery, when communication was easy between the scattered mountain villages, and the bigger towns in the valleys, such as Bettsbridge and Shadd's Falls, had libraries, theatres and Y. M. C. A. halls to which the youth of the hills could descend for recreation. But when winter shut down on Starkfield, and the village lay under a sheet of snow perpetually renewed from the pale skies, I began to see what life there—or rather its negation—must have been in Ethan Frome's young manhood.

I had been sent up by my employers on a job connected with the big power-house at Corbury Junction, and a long-drawn carpenters' strike had so delayed the work that I found myself anchored at Starkfield—the nearest habitable spot—for the best part of the winter. I chafed at first, and then, under the hypnotising effect of routine, gradually began to find a grim satisfaction in the life. During the early part of my stay I had been struck by the contrast between the vitality of the climate and the deadness of the community. Day by day, after the December snows were over, a blazing blue sky poured down torrents of light and air on the white landscape, which gave them back in an intenser glitter. One would have supposed that such an atmosphere must quicken the emotions as well as the blood; but it seemed to produce no change except that of retarding still more the sluggish pulse of Starkfield. When I had been there a little longer, and had seen this phase of crystal clearness followed by long stretches of sunless cold; when the storms of February had pitched their white tents about the devoted village and the wild cavalry of March winds had charged down to their support; I began to understand why Starkfield emerged from its six months' siege like a starved garrison capitulating without quarter. Twenty years earlier the means of resistance must have been far fewer, and the enemy in command of almost all the lines of access between the beleaguered villages; and, considering these things, I felt the sinister force of Harmon's phrase: "Most of the smart ones get away." But if that were the case, how could any combination of obstacles have hindered the flight of a man like Ethan Frome?

During my stay at Starkfield I lodged with a middle-aged widow colloquially known as Mrs. Ned Hale. Mrs. Hale's father had been the village lawyer of the previous generation, and "lawyer Varnum's house," where my landlady still lived with her mother, was the most considerable mansion in the village. It stood at one end of the main street, its classic portico and small-paned windows looking down a flagged path between Norway spruces to the slim white steeple of the Congregational church. It was clear that the Varnum fortunes were at the ebb, but the two women did what they could to preserve a decent dignity; and Mrs. Hale, in particular, had a certain wan refinement not out of keeping with her pale old-fashioned house.

In the "best parlour," with its black horse-hair and mahogany weakly illuminated by a gurgling Carcel lamp, I listened every evening to another and more delicately shaded version of the Starkfield chronicle. It was not that Mrs. Ned Hale felt, or affected, any social superiority to the people about her; it was only that the accident of a finer sensibility and a little more education had put just enough distance between herself and her neighbours to enable her to judge them with detachment. She was not unwilling to exercise this faculty, and I had great hopes of getting from her the missing facts of Ethan Frome's story, or rather such a key to his character as should co-ordinate the facts I knew. Her mind was a store-house of innocuous anecdote and any question about her acquaintances brought forth a volume of detail; but on the subject of Ethan Frome I found her unexpectedly reticent. There was no hint of disapproval in her reserve; I merely felt in her an insurmountable reluctance to speak of him or his affairs, a low "Yes, I knew them both . . . it was awful . . ." seeming to be the utmost concession that her distress could make to my curiosity.

So marked was the change in her manner, such depths of sad initiation did it imply, that, with some doubts as to my delicacy, I put the case anew to my village oracle, Harmon Gow; but got for my pains only an uncomprehending grunt.

"Ruth Varnum was always as nervous as a rat; and, come to think of it, she was the first one to see 'em after they was picked up. It happened right below lawyer Varnum's, down at the bend of the Corbury road, just round about the time that Ruth got engaged to Ned Hale. The young folks was all friends, and I guess she just can't bear to talk about it. She's had troubles enough of her own."

All the dwellers in Starkfield, as in more notable communities, had had troubles enough of their own to make them comparatively indifferent to those of their neighbours; and though all conceded that Ethan Frome's had been beyond the common measure, no one gave me an explanation of the look in his face which, as I persisted in thinking, neither poverty nor physical suffering could have put there. Nevertheless, I might have contented myself with the story pieced together from these hints had it not been for the provocation of Mrs. Hale's silence, and—a little later—for the accident of personal contact with the man.

On my arrival at Starkfield, Denis Eady, the rich Irish grocer, who was the proprietor of Starkfield's nearest approach to a livery stable, had entered into an agreement to send me over daily to Corbury Flats, where I had to pick up my train for the Junction. But about the middle of the winter Eady's horses fell ill of a local epidemic. The illness spread to the other Starkfield stables and for a day or two I was put to it to find a means of transport. Then Harmon Gow suggested that Ethan Frome's bay was still on his legs and that his owner might be glad to drive me over.

I stared at the suggestion. "Ethan Frome? But I've never even spoken to him. Why on earth should he put himself out for me?"

Harmon's answer surprised me still more. "I don't know as he would; but I know he wouldn't be sorry to earn a dollar."

I had been told that Frome was poor, and that the saw-mill and the arid acres of his farm yielded scarcely enough to keep his household through the winter; but I had not supposed him to be in such want as Harmon's words implied, and I expressed my wonder.

"Well, matters ain't gone any too well with him," Harmon said. "When a man's been setting round like a hulk for twenty years or more, seeing things that want doing, it eats inter him, and he loses his grit. That Frome farm was always 'bout as bare's a milkpan when the cat's been round; and you know what one of them old water-mills is wuth nowadays. When Ethan could sweat over 'em both from sun-up to dark he kinder choked a living out of 'em; but his folks ate up most everything, even then, and I don't see how he makes out now. Fust his father got a kick, out haying, and went soft in the brain, and gave away money like Bible texts afore he died. Then his mother got queer and dragged along for years as weak as a baby; and his wife Zeena, she's always been the greatest hand at doctoring in the county. Sickness and trouble: that's what Ethan's had his plate full up with, ever since the very first helping."

The next morning, when I looked out, I saw the hollow-backed bay between the Varnum spruces, and Ethan Frome, throwing back his worn bearskin, made room for me in the sleigh at his side. After that, for a week, he drove me over every morning to Corbury Flats, and on my return in the afternoon met me again and carried me back through the icy night to Starkfield. The distance each way was barely three miles, but the old bay's pace was slow, and even with firm snow under the runners we were nearly an hour on the way. Ethan Frome drove in silence, the reins loosely held in his left hand, his brown seamed profile, under the helmet-like peak of the cap, relieved against the banks of snow like the bronze image of a hero. He never turned his face to mine, or answered, except in monosyllables, the questions I put, or such slight pleasantries as I ventured. He seemed a part of the mute melancholy landscape, an incarnation of its frozen woe, with all that was warm and sentient in him fast bound below the surface; but there was nothing unfriendly in his silence. I simply felt that he lived in a depth of moral isolation too remote for casual access, and I had the sense that his loneliness was not merely the result of his personal plight, tragic as I guessed that to be, but had in it, as Harmon Gow had hinted, the profound accumulated cold of many Starkfield winters.

Only once or twice was the distance between us bridged for a moment; and the glimpses thus gained confirmed my desire to know more. Once I happened to speak of an engineering job I had been on the previous year in Florida, and of the contrast between the winter landscape about us and that in which I had found myself the year before; and to my surprise Frome said suddenly: "Yes: I was down there once, and for a good while afterward I could call up the sight of it in winter. But now it's all snowed under."

He said no more, and I had to guess the rest from the inflection of his voice and his sharp relapse into silence.

Another day, on getting into my train at the Flats, I missed a volume of popular science—I think it was on some recent discoveries in bio-chemistry—which I had carried with me to read on the way. I thought no more about it till I got into the sleigh again that evening, and saw the book in Frome's hand.

"I found it after you were gone," he said.

I put the volume into my pocket and we dropped back into our usual silence; but as we began to crawl up the long hill from Corbury Flats to the Starkfield ridge I became aware in the dusk that he had turned his face to mine.

"There are things in that book that I didn't know the first word about," he said.

I wondered less at his words than at the queer note of resentment in his voice. He was evidently surprised and slightly aggrieved at his own ignorance.

"Does that sort of thing interest you?" I asked.

"It used to."

"There are one or two rather new things in the book: there have been some big strides lately in that particular line of research." I waited a moment for an answer that did not come; then I said: "If you'd like to look the book through I'd be glad to leave it with you."

He hesitated, and I had the impression that he felt himself about to yield to a stealing tide of inertia; then, "Thank you—I'll take it," he answered shortly.

I hoped that this incident might set up some more direct communication between us. Frome was so simple and straightforward that I was sure his curiosity about the book was based on a genuine interest in its subject. Such tastes and acquirements in a man of his condition made the contrast more poignant between his outer situation and his inner needs, and I hoped that the chance of giving expression to the latter might at least unseal his lips. But something in his past history, or in his present way of living, had apparently driven him too deeply into himself for any casual impulse to draw him back to his kind. At our next meeting he made no allusion to the book, and our intercourse seemed fated to remain as negative and one-sided as if there had been no break in his reserve.

Frome had been driving me over to the Flats for about a week when one morning I looked out of my window into a thick snow-fall. The height of the white waves massed against the garden-fence and along the wall of the church showed that the storm must have been going on all night, and that the drifts were likely to be heavy in the open. I thought it probable that my train would be delayed; but I had to be at the power-house for an hour or two that afternoon, and I decided, if Frome turned up, to push through to the Flats and wait there till my train came in. I don't know why I put it in the conditional, however, for I never doubted that Frome would appear. He was not the kind of man to be turned from his business by any commotion of the elements; and at the appointed hour his sleigh glided up through the snow like a stage-apparition behind thickening veils of gauze.

I was getting to know him too well to express either wonder or gratitude at his keeping his appointment; but I exclaimed in surprise as I saw him turn his horse in a direction opposite to that of the Corbury road.

"The railroad's blocked by a freight-train that got stuck in a drift below the Flats," he explained, as we jogged off into the stinging whiteness.

"But look here—where are you taking me, then?"

"Straight to the Junction, by the shortest way," he answered, pointing up School House Hill with his whip.

"To the Junction—in this storm? Why, it's a good ten miles!"

"The bay'll do it if you give him time. You said you had some business there this afternoon. I'll see you get there."

He said it so quietly that I could only answer: "You're doing me the biggest kind of a favour."

"That's all right," he rejoined.

Abreast of the schoolhouse the road forked, and we dipped down a lane to the left, between hemlock boughs bent inward to their trunks by the weight of the snow. I had often walked that way on Sundays, and knew that the solitary roof showing through bare branches near the bottom of the hill was that of Frome's saw-mill. It looked exanimate enough, with its idle wheel looming above the black stream dashed with yellow-white spume, and its cluster of sheds sagging under their white load. Frome did not even turn his head as we drove by, and still in silence we began to mount the next slope. About a mile farther, on a road I had never travelled, we came to an orchard of starved apple-trees writhing over a hillside among outcroppings of slate that nuzzled up through the snow like animals pushing out their noses to breathe. Beyond the orchard lay a field or two, their boundaries lost under drifts; and above the fields, huddled against the white immensities of land and sky, one of those lonely New England farm-houses that make the landscape lonelier.

"That's my place," said Frome, with a sideway jerk of

his lame elbow; and in the distress and oppression of the scene I did not know what to answer. The snow had ceased, and a flash of watery sunlight exposed the house on the slope above us in all its plaintive ugliness. The black wraith of a deciduous creeper flapped from the porch, and the thin wooden walls, under their worn coat of paint, seemed to shiver in the wind that had risen with the ceasing of the snow.

"The house was bigger in my father's time: I had to take down the 'L,' a while back," Frome continued, checking with a twitch of the left rein the bay's evident intention of turning in through the broken-down gate.

I saw then that the unusually forlorn and stunted look of the house was partly due to the loss of what is known in New England as the "L": that long deep-roofed adjunct usually built at right angles to the main house, and connecting it, by way of storerooms and tool-house, with the wood-shed and cowbarn. Whether because of its symbolic sense, the image it presents of a life linked with the soil, and enclosing in itself the chief sources of warmth and nourishment, or whether merely because of the consolatory thought that it enables the dwellers in that harsh climate to get to their morning's work without facing the weather, it is certain that the "L" rather than the house itself seems to be the centre, the actual hearth-stone of the New England farm. Perhaps this connection of ideas, which had often occurred to me in my rambles about Starkfield, caused me to hear a wistful note in Frome's words, and to see in the diminished dwelling the image of his own shrunken body.

"We're kinder side-tracked here now," he added, "but there was considerable passing before the railroad was carried through to the Flats." He roused the lagging bay with another twitch; then, as if the mere sight of the house had let me too deeply into his confidence for any farther pretence of reserve, he went on slowly: "I've always set down the worst of mother's trouble to that. When she got the rheumatism so bad she couldn't move around she used to sit up there and watch the road by the hour; and one year, when they was six months mending the Bettsbridge pike after the floods, and Harmon Gow had to bring his stage round this way, she picked up so that she used to get down to the gate most days to see him. But after the trains begun running nobody ever come by here to speak of, and mother never could get it through her head what had happened, and it preyed on her right along till she died."

As we turned into the Corbury road the snow began to fall again, cutting off our last glimpse of the house; and Frome's silence fell with it, letting down between us the old veil of reticence. This time the wind did not cease with the return of the snow. Instead, it sprang up to a gale which now and then, from a tattered sky, flung pale sweeps of sunlight over a landscape chaotically tossed. But the bay was as good as Frome's word, and we pushed on to the Junction through the wild white scene.

In the afternoon the storm held off, and the clearness in the west seemed to my inexperienced eye the pledge of a fair evening. I finished my business as quickly as possible, and we set out for Starkfield with a good chance of getting there for supper. But at sunset the clouds gathered again, bringing an earlier night, and the snow began to fall straight and steadily from a sky without wind, in a soft universal diffusion more confusing than the gusts and eddies of the morning. It seemed to be a part of the thickening darkness, to be the winter night itself descending on us layer by layer.

The small ray of Frome's lantern was soon lost in this smothering medium, in which even his sense of direction, and the bay's homing instinct, finally ceased to serve us. Two or three times some ghostly landmark sprang up to warn us that we were astray, and then was sucked back into the mist; and when we finally regained our road the old horse began to show signs of exhaustion. I felt myself to blame for having accepted Frome's offer, and after a short discussion I persuaded him to let me get out of the sleigh and walk along through the snow at the bay's side. In this way we struggled on for another mile or two, and at last reached a point where Frome, peering into what seemed to me formless night, said: "That's my gate down yonder."

The last stretch had been the hardest part of the way. The bitter cold and the heavy going had nearly knocked the wind out of me, and I could feel the horse's side ticking like a clock under my hand.

"Look here, Frome," I began, "there's no earthly use in your going any farther—" but he interrupted me: "Nor you neither. There's been about enough of this for anybody."

I understood that he was offering me a night's shelter at the farm, and without answering I turned into the gate at his side, and followed him to the barn, where I helped him to unharness and bed down the tired horse. When this was done he unhooked the lantern from the sleigh, stepped out again into the night, and called to me over his shoulder: "This way."

Far off above us a square of light trembled through the screen of snow. Staggering along in Frome's wake I floundered toward it, and in the darkness almost fell into one of the deep drifts against the front of the house. Frome scrambled up the slippery steps of the porch, digging a way through the snow with his heavily booted foot. Then he lifted his lantern, found the latch, and led the way into the house. I went after him into a low unlit passage, at the back of which a ladder-like staircase rose into obscurity. On our right a line of light marked the door of the room which had sent its ray across the night; and behind the door I heard a woman's voice droning querulously.

Frome stamped on the worn oil-cloth to shake the snow from his boots, and set down his lantern on a kitchen chair which was the only piece of furniture in the hall. Then he opened the door.

"Come in," he said; and as he spoke the droning voice grew still . . .

It was that night that I found the clue to Ethan Frome, and began to put together this vision of his story.

CHAPTER I

The village lay under two feet of snow, with drifts at the windy corners. In a sky of iron the points of the Dipper hung like icicles and Orion flashed his cold fires. The moon had set, but the night was so transparent that the white house-fronts between the elms looked grey against the snow, clumps of bushes made black stains on it, and the basement windows of the church sent shafts of yellow light far across the endless undulations.

Young Ethan Frome walked at a quick pace along the deserted street, past the bank and Michael Eady's new brick store and Lawyer Varnum's house with the two black Norway spruces at the gate. Opposite the Varnum gate, where the road fell away toward the Corbury valley, the church reared its slim white steeple and narrow peristyle. As the young man walked toward it the upper windows drew a black arcade along the side wall of the building, but from the lower openings, on the side where the ground sloped steeply down to the Corbury road, the light shot its long bars, illuminating many fresh furrows in the track leading to the basement door, and showing, under an adjoining shed, a line of sleighs with heavily blanketed horses.

The night was perfectly still, and the air so dry and pure that it gave little sensation of cold. The effect produced on Frome was rather of a complete absence of atmosphere, as though nothing less tenuous than ether intervened between the white earth under his feet and the metallic dome overhead. "It's like being in an exhausted receiver," he thought. Four or five years earlier he had taken a year's course at a technological college at Worcester, and dabbled in the laboratory with a friendly professor of physics; and the images supplied by that experience still cropped up, at unexpected moments, through the totally different associations of thought in which he had since been living. His father's death, and the misfortunes following it, had put a premature end to Ethan's studies; but though they had not gone far enough to be of much practical use they had fed his fancy and made him aware of huge cloudy meanings behind the daily face of things.

As he strode along through the snow the sense of such meanings glowed in his brain and mingled with the bodily flush produced by his sharp tramp. At the end of the village he paused before the darkened front of the church. He stood there a moment, breathing quickly, and looking up and down the street, in which not another figure moved. The pitch of the Corbury road, below lawyer Varnum's spruces, was the favourite coasting-ground of Starksfield, and on clear evenings the church corner rang till late with the shouts of the coasters; but to-night not a sled darkened the whiteness of the long declivity. The hush of midnight lay on the village, and all its waking life was gathered behind the church windows, from which strains of dance-music flowed with the broad bands of yellow light.

The young man, skirting the side of the building, went down the slope toward the basement door. To keep out of range of the revealing rays from within he made a circuit through the untrodden snow and gradually approached the farther angle of the basement wall. Thence, still hugging the shadow, he edged his way cautiously forward to the nearest window, holding back his straight spare body and craning his neck till he got a glimpse of the room.

Seen thus, from the pure and frosty darkness in which he stood, it seemed to be seething in a mist of heat. The metal reflectors of the gas-jets sent crude waves of light against the whitewashed walls, and the iron flanks of the stove at the end of the hall looked as though they were heaving with volcanic fires. The floor was thronged with girls and young men. Down the side wall facing the window stood a row of kitchen chairs from which the older women had just risen. By this time the music had stopped, and the musicians—a fiddler, and the young lady who played the harmonium on Sundays—were hastily refreshing themselves at one corner of the supper-table which aligned its devastated pie-dishes and ice-cream saucers on the platform at the end of the hall. The guests were preparing to leave, and the tide had already set toward the passage where coats and wraps were hung, when a young man with a sprightly foot and a shock of black hair shot into the middle of the floor and clapped his hands. The signal took instant effect. The musicians hurried to their instruments, the dancers—some already half-muffled for departure—fell into line down each side of the room, the older spectators slipped back to their chairs, and the lively young man, after diving about here and there in the throng, drew forth a girl who had already wound a cherry-coloured "fascinator" about her head, and, leading her up to the end of the floor, whirled her down its length to the bounding tune of a Virginia reel.

Frome's heart was beating fast. He had been straining for a glimpse of the dark head under the cherry-coloured scarf and it vexed him that another eye should have been quicker than his. The leader of the reel, who looked as if he had Irish blood in his veins, danced well, and his partner caught his fire. As she passed down the line, her light figure swinging from hand to hand in circles of increasing swiftness, the scarf flew off her head and stood out behind her shoulders, and Frome, at each turn, caught sight of her laughing panting lips, the cloud of dark hair about her forehead, and the dark eyes which seemed the only fixed points in a maze of flying lines.

The dancers were going faster and faster, and the musicians, to keep up with them, belaboured their instruments like jockeys lashing their mounts on the home-stretch; yet it seemed to the young man at the window that the reel would never end. Now and then he turned his eyes from the girl's face to that of her partner, which, in the exhilaration of the dance, had taken on a look of almost impudent ownership. Denis Eady was the son of Michael Eady, the ambitious Irish grocer, whose suppleness and effrontery had given Starkfield its first notion of "smart" business methods, and whose new brick store testified to the success of the attempt. His son seemed likely to follow in his steps, and was meanwhile applying the same arts to the conquest of the Starkfield maidenhood. Hitherto Ethan Frome had been content to think him a mean fellow; but now he positively invited a horse-whipping. It was strange that the girl did not seem aware of it: that she could lift her rapt face to her dancer's, and drop her hands into his, without appearing to feel the offence of his look and touch.

Frome was in the habit of walking into Starkfield to fetch home his wife's cousin, Mattie Silver, on the rare evenings when some chance of amusement drew her to the village. It was his wife who had suggested, when the girl came to live with them, that such opportunities should be put in her way. Mattie Silver came from Stamford, and when she entered the Fromes' household to act as her cousin Zeena's aid it was thought best, as she came without pay, not to let her feel too sharp a contrast between the life she had left and the isolation of a Starkfield farm. But for this—as Frome sardonically reflected—it would hardly have occurred to Zeena to take any thought for the girl's amusement.

When his wife first proposed that they should give Mattie an occasional evening out he had inwardly demurred at having to do the extra two miles to the village and back after his hard day on the farm; but not long afterward he had reached the point of wishing that Starkfield might give all its nights to revelry.

Mattie Silver had lived under his roof for a year, and from early morning till they met at supper he had frequent chances of seeing her; but no moments in her company were comparable to those when, her arm in his, and her light step flying to keep time with his long stride, they walked back through the night to the farm. He had taken to the girl from the first day, when he had driven over to the Flats to meet her, and she had smiled and waved to him from the train, crying out, "You must be Ethan!" as she jumped down with her bundles, while he reflected, looking over her slight person: "She don't look much on housework, but she ain't a fretter, anyhow." But it was not only that the coming to his house of a bit of hopeful young life was like the lighting of a fire on a cold hearth. The girl was more than the bright serviceable creature he had thought her. She had an eye to see and an ear to hear: he could show her things and tell her things, and taste the bliss of feeling that all he imparted left long reverberations and echoes he could wake at will.

It was during their night walks back to the farm that he felt most intensely the sweetness of this communion. He had always been more sensitive than the people about him to the appeal of natural beauty. His unfinished studies had given form to this sensibility and even in his unhappiest moments field and sky spoke to him with a deep and powerful persuasion. But hitherto the emotion had remained in him as a silent ache, veiling with sadness the beauty that evoked it. He did not even know whether any one else in the world felt as he did, or whether he was the sole victim of this mournful privilege. Then he learned that one other spirit had trembled with the same touch of wonder: that at his side, living under his roof and eating his bread, was a creature to whom he could say: "That's Orion down yonder; the big fellow to the right is Aldebaran, and the bunch of little ones—like bees swarming—they're the Pleiades . . ." or whom he could hold entranced before a ledge of granite thrusting up through the fern while he unrolled the huge panorama of the ice age, and the long dim stretches of succeeding time. The fact that admiration for his learning mingled with Mattie's wonder at what he taught was not the least part of his pleasure. And there were other sensations, less definable but more exquisite, which drew them together with a shock of silent joy: the cold red of sunset behind winter hills, the flight of cloud-flocks over slopes of golden stubble, or the intensely blue shadows of hemlocks on sunlit snow. When she said to him once: "It looks just as if it was painted!" it seemed to Ethan that the art of definition could go no farther, and that words had at last been found to utter his secret soul. . . .

As he stood in the darkness outside the church these memories came back with the poignancy of vanished things. Watching Mattie whirl down the floor from hand to hand he wondered how he could ever have thought that his dull talk interested her. To him, who was never gay but in her presence, her gaiety seemed plain proof of indifference. The face she lifted to her dancers was the same which, when she saw him, always looked like a window that has caught the sunset. He even noticed two or three gestures which, in his fatuity, he had thought she kept for him: a way of throwing her head back when she was amused, as if to taste her laugh before she let it out, and a trick of sinking her lids slowly when anything charmed or moved her.

The sight made him unhappy, and his unhappiness roused his latent fears. His wife had never shown any jealousy of Mattie, but of late she had grumbled increasingly over the house-work and found oblique ways of attracting attention to the girl's inefficiency. Zeena had always been what Starkfield called "sickly," and Frome had to admit that, if she were as ailing as she believed, she needed the help of a stronger arm than the one which lay so lightly in his during the night walks to the farm. Mattie had no natural turn for housekeeping, and her training had done nothing to remedy the defect. She was quick to learn, but forgetful and dreamy, and not disposed to take the matter seriously. Ethan had an idea that if she were to marry a man she was fond of the dormant instinct would wake, and her pies and biscuits become the pride of the county; but domesticity in the abstract did not interest her. At first she was so awkward that he could not help laughing at her; but she laughed with him and that made them better friends. He did his best to supplement her unskilled efforts, getting up earlier than usual to light the kitchen fire, carrying in the wood overnight, and neglecting the mill for the farm that he might help her about the house during the day. He even crept down on Saturday nights to scrub the kitchen floor after the women had gone to bed; and Zeena, one day, had surprised him at the churn and had turned away silently, with one of her queer looks.

Of late there had been other signs of her disfavour, as intangible but more disquieting. One cold winter morning, as he dressed in the dark, his candle flickering in the draught of the ill-fitting window, he had heard her speak from the bed behind him.

"The doctor don't want I should be left without anybody to do for me," she said in her flat whine.

He had supposed her to be asleep, and the sound of her voice had startled him, though she was given to abrupt explosions of speech after long intervals of secretive silence.

He turned and looked at her where she lay indistinctly outlined under the dark calico quilt, her high-boned face taking a grayish tinge from the whiteness of the pillow.

"Nobody to do for you?" he repeated.

"If you say you can't afford a hired girl when Mattie goes."

Frome turned away again, and taking up his razor stooped to catch the reflection of his stretched cheek in the blotched looking-glass above the wash-stand.

"Why on earth should Mattie go?"

"Well, when she gets married, I mean," his wife's drawl came from behind him.

"Oh, she'd never leave us as long as you needed her," he returned, scraping hard at his chin.

"I wouldn't ever have it said that I stood in the way of a poor girl like Mattie marrying a smart fellow like Denis Eady," Zeena answered in a tone of plaintive self-effacement.

Ethan, glaring at his face in the glass, threw his head back to draw the razor from ear to chin. His hand was steady, but the attitude was an excuse for not making an immediate reply.

"And the doctor don't want I should be left without anybody," Zeena continued. "He wanted I should speak to you about a girl he's heard about, that might come——"

Ethan laid down the razor and straightened himself with a laugh.

"Denis Eady! If that's all, I guess there's no such hurry to look round for a girl."

"Well, I'd like to talk to you about it," said Zeena obstinately.

He was getting into his clothes in fumbling haste. "All right. But I haven't got the time now; I'm late as it is," he returned, holding his old silver turnip-watch to the candle.

Zeena, apparently accepting this as final, lay watching him in silence while he pulled his suspenders over his shoulders and jerked his arms into his coat; but as he went toward the door she said, suddenly and incisively: "I guess you're always late, now you shave every morning."

That thrust had frightened him more than any vague insinuations about Denis Eady. It was a fact that since Mattie Silver's coming he had taken to shaving every day;

but his wife always seemed to be asleep when he left her side in the winter darkness, and he had stupidly assumed that she would not notice any change in his appearance. Once or twice in the past he had been faintly disquieted by Zenobia's way of letting things happen without seeming to remark them, and then, weeks afterward, in a casual phrase, revealing that she had all along taken her notes and drawn her inferences. Of late, however, there had been no room in his thoughts for such vague apprehensions. Zeena herself, from an oppressive reality, had faded into an insubstantial shade. All his life was lived in the sight and sound of Mattie Silver, and he could no longer conceive of its being otherwise. But now, as he stood outside the church, and saw Mattie spinning down the floor with Denis Eady, a throng of disregarded hints and menaces wove their cloud about his brain. . . .

CHAPTER II

As the dancers poured out of the hall Frome, drawing back behind the projecting storm-door, watched the segregation of the grotesquely muffled groups, in which a moving lantern ray now and then lit up a face flushed with food and dancing. The villagers, being afoot, were the first to climb the slope to the main street, while the country neighbours packed themselves more slowly into the sleighs under the shed.

"Ain't you riding, Mattie?" a woman's voice called back from the throng about the shed, and Ethan's heart gave a jump. From where he stood he could not see the persons coming out of the hall till they had advanced a few steps beyond the wooden sides of the storm-door; but through its cracks he heard a clear voice answer: "Mercy no! Not on such a night."

She was there, then, close to him, only a thin board between. In another moment she would step forth into the night, and his eyes, accustomed to the obscurity, would discern her as clearly as though she stood in daylight. A wave of shyness pulled him back into the dark angle of the wall, and he stood there in silence instead of making his presence known to her. It had been one of the wonders of their intercourse that from the first, she, the quicker, finer, more expressive, instead of crushing him by the contrast, had given him something of her own ease and freedom; but now he felt as heavy and loutish as in his student days, when he had tried to "jolly" the Worcester girls at a picnic.

He hung back, and she came out alone and paused within a few yards of him. She was almost the last to leave the hall, and she stood looking uncertainly about her as if wondering why he did not show himself. Then a man's figure approached, coming so close to her that under their formless wrappings they seemed merged in one dim outline.

"Gentleman friend gone back on you? Say, Matt, that's tough! No, I wouldn't be mean enough to tell the other girls. I ain't as low-down as that." (How Frome hated his cheap banter!) "But look a here, ain't it lucky I got the old man's cutter down there waiting for us?"

Frome heard the girl's voice, gaily incredulous: "What on earth's your father's cutter doin' down there?"

"Why, waiting for me to take a ride. I got the roan colt too. I kinder knew I'd want to take a ride to-night," Eady, in his triumph, tried to put a sentimental note into his bragging voice.

The girl seemed to waver, and Frome saw her twirl the end of her scarf irresolutely about her fingers. Not for the world would he have made a sign to her, though it seemed to him that his life hung on her next gesture.

"Hold on a minute while I unhitch the colt," Denis called to her, springing toward the shed.

She stood perfectly still, looking after him, in an attitude of tranquil expectancy torturing to the hidden watcher. Frome noticed that she no longer turned her head from side to side, as though peering through the night for another figure. She let Denis Eady lead out the horse, climb into the cutter and fling back the bearskin to make room for her at his side; then, with a swift motion of flight, she turned about and darted up the slope toward the front of the church.

"Good-bye! Hope you'll have a lovely ride!" she called back to him over her shoulder.

Denis laughed, and gave the horse a cut that brought him quickly abreast of her retreating figure.

"Come along! Get in quick! It's as slippery as thunder on this turn," he cried, leaning over to reach out a hand to her.

She laughed back at him: "Good-night! I'm not getting in."

By this time they had passed beyond Frome's earshot and he could only follow the shadowy pantomime of their silhouettes as they continued to move along the crest of the slope above him. He saw Eady, after a moment, jump from the cutter and go toward the girl with the reins over one arm. The other he tried to slip through hers; but she eluded him nimbly, and Frome's heart, which had swung out over a black void, trembled back to safety. A moment later he heard the jingle of departing sleigh bells and discerned a figure advancing along toward the empty expanse of snow before the church.

In the black shade of the Varnum spruces he caught up with her and she turned with a quick "Oh!"

"Think I'd forgotten you, Matt?" he asked with sheepish glee.

She answered seriously: "I thought maybe you couldn't come back for me."

"Couldn't? What on earth could stop me?"

"I knew Zeena wasn't feeling any too good to-day."

"Oh, she's in bed long ago." He paused, a question struggling in him. "Then you meant to walk home all alone?"

"Oh, I ain't afraid!" she laughed.

They stood together in the gloom of the spruces, an empty world glimmering about them wide and grey under the stars. He brought his question out.

"If you thought I hadn't come, why didn't you ride back with Denis Eady?"

"Why, where *were* you? How did you know? I never saw you!"

Her wonder and his laughter ran together like spring rills in a thaw. Ethan had the sense of having done something arch and ingenious. To prolong the effect he groped for a dazzling phrase, and brought out, in a growl of rapture: "Come along."

He slipped an arm through hers, as Eady had done, and fancied it was faintly pressed against her side; but neither of them moved. It was so dark under the spruces that he could barely see the shape of her head beside his shoulder. He longed to stoop his cheek and rub it against her scarf. He would have liked to stand there with her all night in the blackness. She moved forward a step or two and then paused again above the dip of the Corbury road. Its icy slope, scored by innumerable runners, looked like a mirror scratched by travellers at an inn.

"There was a whole lot of them coasting before the moon set," she said.

"Would you like to come in and coast with them some night?" he asked.

"Oh, *would* you, Ethan? It would be lovely!"

"We'll come to-morrow if there's a moon."

She lingered, pressing closer to his side. "Ned Hale and Ruth Varnum came just as *near* running into the big elm at the bottom. We were all sure they were killed." Her shiver ran down his arm. "Wouldn't it have been too awful? They're so happy!"

"Oh, Ned ain't much at steering. I guess I can take you down all right!" he said disdainfully.

He was aware that he was "talking big," like Denis Eady; but his reaction of joy had unsteadied him, and the inflection with which she had said of the engaged couple "They're so happy!" made the words sound as if she had been thinking of herself and him.

"The elm *is* dangerous, though. It ought to be cut down," she insisted.

"Would you be afraid of it, with me?"

"I told you I ain't the kind to be afraid," she tossed back, almost indifferently; and suddenly she began to walk on with a rapid step.

These alterations of mood were the despair and joy of Ethan Frome. The motions of her mind were as incalculable as the flit of a bird in the branches. The fact that he had no right to show his feelings, and thus provoke the expression of hers, made him attach a fantastic importance to every change in her look and tone. Now he thought she understood him, and feared; now he was sure she did not, and despaired. To-night the pressure of accumulated misgivings sent the scale drooping toward despair, and her indifference was the more chilling after the flush of joy into which she had plunged him by dismissing Denis Eady. He mounted School House Hill at her side and walked on in silence till they reached the lane leading to the saw-mill; then the need of some definite assurance grew too strong for him.

"You'd have found me right off if you hadn't gone back to have that last reel with Denis," he brought out awkwardly. He could not pronounce the name without a stiffening of the muscles of his throat.

"Why, Ethan, how could I tell you were there?"

"I suppose what folks say is true," he jerked out at her, instead of answering.

She stopped short, and he felt, in the darkness, that her face was lifted quickly to his. "Why, what do folks say?"

"It's natural enough you should be leaving us," he floundered on, following his thought.

"Is that what they say?" she mocked back at him; then, with a sudden drop of her sweet treble: "You mean that Zeena—ain't suited with me any more?" she faltered.

Their arms had slipped apart and they stood motionless, each seeking to distinguish the other's face.

"I know I ain't anything like as smart as I ought to be," she went on, while he vainly struggled for expression. "There's lots of things a hired girl could do that come awkward to me still—and I haven't got much strength in my arms. But if she'd only tell me I'd try. You know she hardly ever says anything, and sometimes I can see she ain't suited, and yet I don't know why." She turned on him with a sudden flash of indignation. "You'd ought to tell me, Ethan Frome—you'd ought to! Unless *you* want me to go too——"

Unless he wanted her to go too! The cry was balm to his raw wound. The iron heavens seemed to melt and rain down sweetness. Again he struggled for the all-expressive word, and again, his arm in hers, found only a deep "Come along."

They walked on in silence through the blackness of the hemlock-shaded lane, where Ethan's saw-mill gloomed through the night, and out again into the comparative clearness of the fields. On the farther side of the hemlock belt the open country rolled away before them grey and lonely under the stars. Sometimes their way led them under the shade of an overhanging bank or through the thin obscurity of a clump of leafless trees. Here and there a farmhouse stood far back among the fields, mute and cold as a grave-stone. The night was so still that they heard the frozen snow crackle under their feet. The crash of a loaded branch falling far off in the woods reverberated like a musket-shot, and once a fox barked, and Mattie shrank closer to Ethan, and quickened her steps.

At length they sighted the group of larches at Ethan's gate, and as they drew near it the sense that the walk was over brought back his words.

"Then you don't want to leave us, Matt?"

He had to stoop his head to catch her stifled whisper: "Where'd I go, if I did?"

The answer sent a pang through him but the tone suffused him with joy. He forgot what else he had meant to say and pressed her against him so closely that he seemed to feel her warmth in his veins.

"You ain't crying are you, Matt?"

"No, of course I'm not," she quavered.

They turned in at the gate and passed under the shaded knoll where, enclosed in a low fence, the Frome grave-stones slanted at crazy angles through the snow. Ethan looked at them curiously. For years that quiet company had mocked his restlessness, his desire for change and freedom. "We never got away—how should you?" seemed to be written on every headstone; and whenever he went in or out of his gate he thought with a shiver: "I shall just go on living here till I join them." But now all desire for change had vanished, and the sight of the little enclosure gave him a warm sense of continuance and stability.

"I guess we'll never let you go, Matt," he whispered, as though even the dead, lovers once, must conspire with him to keep her; and brushing by the graves, he thought: "We'll always go on living here together, and some day she'll lie there beside me."

He let the vision possess him as they climbed the hill to the house. He was never so happy with her as when he abandoned himself to these dreams. Half-way up the slope Mattie stumbled against some unseen obstruction and clutched his sleeve to steady herself. The wave of warmth that went through him was like the prolongation of his vision. For the first time he stole his arm about her, and she did not resist. They walked on as if they were floating on a summer stream.

Zeena always went to bed as soon as she had had her supper, and the shutterless windows of the house were dark. A dead cucumber-vine dangled from the porch like the crape streamer tied to the door for a death, and the thought flashed through Ethan's brain: "If it was there for Zeena—" Then he had a distinct sight of his wife lying in their bedroom asleep, her mouth slightly open, her false teeth in a tumbler by the bed . . .

They walked around to the back of the house, between the rigid gooseberry bushes. It was Zeena's habit, when they came back late from the village, to leave the key of the kitchen door under the mat. Ethan stood before the door, his head heavy with dreams, his arm still about Mattie. "Matt—" he began, not knowing what he meant to say.

She slipped out of his hold without speaking, and he stooped down and felt for the key.

"It's not there!" he said, straightening himself with a start.

They strained their eyes at each other through the icy darkness. Such a thing had never happened before.

"Maybe she's forgotten it," Mattie said in a tremulous whisper; but both of them knew that it was not like Zeena to forget.

"It might have fallen off into the snow," Mattie continued, after a pause during which they had stood intently listening.

"It must have been pushed off, then," he rejoined in the same tone. Another wild thought tore through him. What if tramps had been there—what if . . .

Again he listened, fancying he heard a distant sound in the house; then he felt in his pocket for a match, and kneeling down, passed its light slowly over the rough edges of snow about the doorstep.

He was still kneeling when his eyes, on a level with the lower panel of the door, caught a faint ray beneath it. Who could be stirring in that silent house? He heard a step on the stairs, and again for an instant the thought of tramps tore through him. Then the door opened and he saw his wife.

Against the dark background of the kitchen she stood up tall and angular, one hand drawing a quilted counterpane to her flat breast, while the other held a lamp. The light, on a level with her chin, drew out of the darkness her puckered throat and the projecting wrist of the hand that clutched the quilt, and deepened fantastically the hollows and prominences of her high-boned face under its ring of crimping-pins. To Ethan, still in the rosy haze of his hour with Mattie, the sight came with the intense precision of the last dream before waking. He felt as if he had never before known what his wife looked like.

She drew aside without speaking, and Mattie and Ethan passed into the kitchen, which had the deadly chill of a vault after the dry cold of the night.

"Guess you forgot about us, Zeena," Ethan joked, stamping the snow from his boots.

"No. I just felt so mean I couldn't sleep."

Mattie came forward, unwinding her wraps, the colour of the cherry scarf in her fresh lips and cheeks. "I'm so sorry, Zeena! Isn't there anything I can do?"

"No; there's nothing." Zeena turned away from her. "You might 'a' shook off that snow outside," she said to her husband.

She walked out of the kitchen ahead of them and pausing in the hall raised the lamp at arm's-length, as if to light them up the stairs.

Ethan paused also, affecting to fumble for the peg on which he hung his coat and cap. The doors of the two bedrooms faced each other across the narrow upper landing, and to-night it was peculiarly repugnant to him that Mattie should see him follow Zeena.

"I guess I won't come up yet awhile," he said, turning as if to go back to the kitchen.

Zeena stopped short and looked at him. "For the land's sake—what you going to do down here?"

"I've got the mill accounts to go over."

She continued to stare at him, the flame of the unshaded lamp bringing out with microscopic cruelty the fretful lines of her face.

"At this time o' night? You'll ketch your death. The fire's out long ago."

Without answering he moved away toward the kitchen. As he did so his glance crossed Mattie's and he fancied that a fugitive warning gleamed through her lashes. The next moment they sank to her flushed cheeks and she began to mount the stairs ahead of Zeena.

"That's so. It *is* powerful cold down here," Ethan assented; and with lowered head he went up in his wife's wake, and followed her across the threshold of their room.

CHAPTER III

There was some hauling to be done at the lower end of the wood-lot, and Ethan was out early the next day.

The winter morning was as clear as crystal. The sunrise burned red in a pure sky, the shadows on the rim of the wood-lot were darkly blue, and beyond the white and scintillating fields patches of far-off forest hung like smoke.

It was in the early morning stillness, when his muscles were swinging to their familiar task and his lungs expanding with long draughts of mountain air, that Ethan did his clearest thinking. He and Zeena had not exchanged a word after the door of their room had closed on them. She had measured out some drops from a medicine-bottle on a chair by the bed and, after swallowing them, and wrapping her head in a piece of yellow flannel, had lain down with her face turned away. Ethan undressed hurriedly and blew out the light so that he should not see her when he took his place at her side. As he lay there he could hear

Mattie moving about in her room, and her candle, sending its small ray across the landing, drew a scarcely perceptible line of light under his door. He kept his eyes fixed on the light till it vanished. Then the room grew perfectly black, and not a sound was audible but Zeena's asthmatic breathing. Ethan felt confusedly that there were many things he ought to think about, but through his tingling veins and tired brain only one sensation throbbed: the warmth of Mattie's shoulder against his. Why had he not kissed her when he held her there? A few hours earlier he would not have asked himself the question. Even a few minutes earlier, when they had stood alone outside the house, he would not have dared to think of kissing her. But since he had seen her lips in the lamplight he felt that they were his.

Now, in the bright morning air, her face was still before him. It was part of the sun's red and of the pure glitter on the snow. How the girl had changed since she had come to Starkfield! He remembered what a colourless slip of a thing she had looked the day he had met her at the station. And all the first winter, how she had shivered with cold when the northerly gales shook the thin clapboards and the snow beat like hail against the loose-hung windows!

He had been afraid that she would hate the hard life, the cold and loneliness; but not a sign of discontent escaped her. Zeena took the view that Mattie was bound to make the best of Starkfield since she hadn't any other place to go to; but this did not strike Ethan as conclusive. Zeena, at any rate, did not apply the principle in her own case.

He felt all the more sorry for the girl because misfortune had, in a sense, indentured her to them. Mattie Silver was the daughter of a cousin of Zenobia Frome's, who had inflamed his clan with mingled sentiments of envy and admiration by descending from the hills to Connecticut, where he had married a Stamford girl and succeeded to her father's thriving "drug" business. Unhappily Orin Silver, a man of far-reaching aims, had died too soon to prove that the end justifies the means. His accounts revealed merely what the means had been; and these were such that it was fortunate for his wife and daughter that his books were examined only after his impressive funeral. His wife died of the disclosure, and Mattie, at twenty, was left alone to make her way on the fifty dollars obtained from the sale of her piano. For this purpose her equipment, though varied, was inadequate. She could trim a hat, make molasses candy, recite "Curfew shall not ring to-night," and play "The Lost Chord" and a pot-pourri from "Carmen." When she tried to extend the field of her activities in the direction of stenography and book-keeping her health broke down, and six months on her feet behind the counter of a department store did not tend to restore it. Her nearest relations had been induced to place their savings in her father's hands, and though, after his death, they ungrudgingly acquitted themselves of the Christian duty of returning good for evil by giving his daughter all the advice at their disposal, they could hardly be expected to supplement it by material aid. But when Zenobia's doctor recommended her looking about for some one to help her with the house-work the clan instantly saw the chance of exacting a compensation from Mattie. Zenobia, though doubtful of the girl's efficiency, was tempted by the freedom to find fault without much risk of losing her; and so Mattie came to Starkfield.

Zenobia's fault-finding was of the silent kind, but not the less penetrating for that. During the first months Ethan alternately burned with the desire to see Mattie defy her and trembled with fear of the result. Then the situation grew less strained. The pure air, and the long summer hours in the open, gave back life and elasticity to Mattie, and Zeena, with more leisure to devote to her complex ailments, grew less watchful of the girl's omissions; so that Ethan, struggling on under the burden of his barren farm and failing saw-mill, could at least imagine that peace reigned in his house.

There was really, even now, no tangible evidence to the contrary; but since the previous night a vague dread had hung on his sky-line. It was formed of Zeena's obstinate silence, of Mattie's sudden look of warning, of the memory of just such fleeting imperceptible signs as those which told him, on certain stainless mornings, that before night there would be rain.

His dread was so strong that, man-like, he sought to postpone certainty. The hauling was not over till mid-day, and as the lumber was to be delivered to Andrew Hale, the Starkfield builder, it was really easier for Ethan to send Jotham Powell, the hired man, back to the farm on foot, and drive the load down to the village himself. He had scrambled up on the logs, and was sitting astride of them, close over his shaggy greys, when, coming between him and their streaming necks, he had a vision of the warning look that Mattie had given him the night before.

"If there's going to be any trouble I want to be there," was his vague reflection, as he threw to Jotham the unexpected order to unhitch the team and lead them back to the barn.

It was a slow trudge home through the heavy fields, and when the two men entered the kitchen Mattie was lifting the coffee from the stove and Zeena was already at the table. Her husband stopped short at sight of her. Instead of her usual calico wrapper and knitted shawl she wore her best dress of brown merino, and above her thin strands of hair, which still preserved the tight undulations of the crimping-pins, rose a hard perpendicular bonnet, as to which Ethan's clearest notion was that he had to pay five dollars for it at the Bettsbridge Emporium. On the floor beside her stood his old valise and a bandbox wrapped in newspapers.

"Why, where are you going, Zeena?" he exclaimed.

"I've got my shooting pains so bad that I'm going over to Bettsbridge to spend the night with Aunt Martha Pierce and see that new doctor," she answered in a matter-of-fact tone, as if she had said she was going into the store-room to take a look at the preserves, or up to the attic to go over the blankets.

In spite of her sedentary habits such abrupt decisions were not without precedent in Zeena's history. Twice or thrice before she had suddenly packed Ethan's valise and started off to Bettsbridge, or even Springfield, to seek the advice of some new doctor, and her husband had grown to dread these expeditions because of their cost. Zeena always came back laden with expensive remedies, and her last visit to Springfield had been commemorated by her paying twenty dollars for an electric battery of which she had never been able to learn the use. But for the moment his sense of relief was so great as to preclude all other feelings. He had now no doubt that Zeena had spoken the truth in saying, the night before, that she had sat up because she felt "too mean" to sleep: her abrupt resolve to seek medical advice showed that, as usual, she was wholly absorbed in her health.

As if expecting a protest, she continued plaintively; "If you're too busy with the hauling I presume you can let Jotham Powell drive me over with the sorrel in time to ketch the train at the Flats."

Her husband hardly heard what she was saying. During the winter months there was no stage between Starkfield and Bettsbridge, and the trains which stopped at Corbury Flats were slow and infrequent. A rapid calculation showed Ethan that Zeena could not be back at the farm before the following evening. . . .

"If I'd supposed you'd 'a' made any objection to Jotham Powell's driving me over—" she began again, as though his silence had implied refusal. On the brink of departure she was always seized with a flux of words. "All I know is," she continued, "I can't go on the way I am much longer. The pains are clear away down to my ankles now, or I'd 'a' walked in to Starkfield on my own feet, sooner'n put you out, and asked Michael Eady to let me ride over on his wagon to the Flats, when he sends to meet the train that brings his groceries. I'd 'a' had two hours to wait in the station, but I'd sooner 'a' done it, even with this cold, than to have you say——"

"Of course Jotham'll drive you over," Ethan roused himself to answer. He became suddenly conscious that he was looking at Mattie while Zeena talked to him, and with an effort he turned his eyes to his wife. She sat opposite the window, and the pale light reflected from the banks of snow made her face look more than usually drawn and bloodless, sharpened the three parallel creases between ear and cheek, and drew querulous lines from her thin nose to the corners of her mouth. Though she was but seven years her husband's senior, and he was only twenty-eight, she was already an old woman.

Ethan tried to say something befitting the occasion, but there was only one thought in his mind: the fact that, for the first time since Mattie had come to live with them, Zeena was to be away for a night. He wondered if the girl were thinking of it too. . . .

He knew that Zeena must be wondering why he did not offer to drive her to the Flats and let Jotham Powell take the lumber to Starkfield, and at first he could not think of a pretext for not doing so; then he said: "I'd take you over myself, only I've got to collect the cash for the lumber."

As soon as the words were spoken he regretted them, not only because they were untrue—there being no prospect of his receiving cash payment from Hale—but also because he knew from experience the imprudence of letting Zeena think he was in funds on the eve of one of her therapeutic excursions. At the moment, however, his one desire was to avoid the long drive with her behind the ancient sorrel who never went out of a walk.

Zeena made no reply: she did not seem to hear what he had said. She had already pushed her plate aside, and was measuring out a draught from a large bottle at her elbow.

"It ain't done me a speck of good, but I guess I might as well use it up," she remarked; adding, as she pushed the empty bottle toward Mattie: "If you can get the taste out it'll do for pickles."

CHAPTER IV

As soon as his wife had driven off Ethan took his coat and cap from the peg. Mattie was washing up the dishes, humming one of the dance tunes of the night before. He said "So long, Matt," and she answered gaily "So long, Ethan"; and that was all.

It was warm and bright in the kitchen. The sun slanted

through the south window on the girl's moving figure, on the cat dozing in a chair, and on the geraniums brought in from the door-way, where Ethan had planted them in the summer to "make a garden" for Mattie. He would have liked to linger on, watching her tidy up and then settle down to her sewing; but he wanted still more to get the hauling done and be back at the farm before night.

All the way down to the village he continued to think of his return to Mattie. The kitchen was a poor place, not "spruce" and shining as his mother had kept it in his boyhood; but it was surprising what a homelike look the mere fact of Zeena's absence gave it. And he pictured what it would be like that evening, when he and Mattie were there after supper. For the first time they would be alone together indoors, and they would sit there, one on each side of the stove, like a married couple, he in his stocking feet and smoking his pipe, she laughing and talking in that funny way she had, which was always as new to him as if he had never heard her before.

The sweetness of the picture, and the relief of knowing that his fears of "trouble" with Zeena were unfounded, sent up his spirits with a rush, and he, who was usually so silent, whistled and sang aloud as he drove through the snowy fields. There was in him a slumbering spark of sociability which the long Starkfield winters had not yet extinguished. By nature grave and inarticulate, he admired recklessness and gaiety in others and was warmed to the marrow by friendly human intercourse. At Worcester, though he had the name of keeping to himself and not being much of a hand at a good time, he had secretly gloried in being clapped on the back and hailed as "Old Ethe" or "Old Stiff"; and the cessation of such familiarities had increased the chill of his return to Starkfield.

There the silence had deepened about him year by year. Left alone, after his father's accident, to carry the burden of farm and mill, he had had no time for convivial loiterings in the village; and when his mother fell ill the loneliness of the house grew more oppressive than that of the fields. His mother had been a talker in her day, but after her "trouble" the sound of her voice was seldom heard, though she had not lost the power of speech.

Sometimes, in the long winter evenings, when in desperation her son asked her why she didn't "say something," she would lift a finger and answer: "Because I'm listening"; and on stormy nights, when the loud wind was about the house, she would complain, if he spoke to her: "They're talking so out there that I can't hear you."

It was only when she drew toward her last illness, and his cousin Zenobia Pierce came over from the next valley to help him nurse her, that human speech was heard again in the house. After the mortal silence of his long imprisonment Zeena's volubility was music in his ears. He felt that he might have "gone like his mother" if the sound of a new voice had not come to steady him. Zeena seemed to understand his case at a glance. She laughed at him for not knowing the simplest sick-bed duties and told him to "go right along out" and leave her to see to things. The mere fact of obeying her orders, of feeling free to go about his business again and talk with other men, restored his shaken balance and magnified his sense of what he owed her. Her efficiency shamed and dazzled him. She seemed to possess by instinct all the household wisdom that his long apprenticeship had not instilled in him. When the end came it was she who had to tell him to hitch up and go for the undertaker, and she thought it "funny" that he had not settled beforehand who was to have his mother's clothes and the sewing-machine. After the funeral, when he saw her preparing to go away, he was seized with an unreasoning dread of being left alone on the farm; and before he knew what he was doing he had asked her to stay there with him. He had often thought since that it would not have happened if his mother had died in spring instead of winter . . .

When they married it was agreed that, as soon as he could straighten out the difficulties resulting from Mrs. Frome's long illness, they would sell the farm and saw-mill and try their luck in a large town. Ethan's love of nature did not take the form of a taste for agriculture. He had always wanted to be an engineer, and to live in towns, where there were lectures and big libraries and "fellows doing things." A slight engineering job in Florida, put in his way during his period of study at Worcester, increased his faith in his ability as well as his eagerness to see the world; and he felt sure that, with a "smart" wife like Zeena, it would not be long before he had made himself a place in it.

Zeena's native village was slightly larger and nearer to the railway than Starkfield, and she had let her husband see from the first that life on an isolated farm was not what she had expected when she married. But purchasers were slow in coming, and while he waited for them Ethan learned the impossibility of transplanting her. She chose to look down on Starkfield, but she could not have lived in a place which looked down on her. Even Bettsbridge or Shadd's Falls would not have been sufficiently aware of her, and in the greater cities which attracted Ethan she would have suffered a complete loss of identity. And within a year of their marriage she developed the "sickliness" which had since made her notable even in a community rich in pathological instances. When she came to take care of his mother she had seemed to Ethan like the very genius of health, but he soon saw that her skill as a nurse had been acquired by the absorbed observation of her own symptoms.

Then she too fell silent. Perhaps it was the inevitable effect of life on the farm, or perhaps, as she sometimes said, it was because Ethan "never listened." The charge was not wholly unfounded. When she spoke it was only to complain, and to complain of things not in his power to remedy; and to check a tendency to impatient retort he had first formed the habit of not answering her, and finally of thinking of other things while she talked. Of late, however, since he had had reasons for observing her more closely, her silence had begun to trouble him. He recalled his mother's growing taciturnity, and wondered if Zeena were also turning "queer." Women did, he knew. Zeena, who had at her fingers' ends the pathological chart of the whole region, had cited many cases of the kind while she was nursing his mother; and he himself knew of certain lonely farm-houses in the neighbourhood where stricken creatures pined, and of others where sudden tragedy had come of their presence. At times, looking at Zeena's shut face, he felt the chill of such forebodings. At other times her silence seemed deliberately assumed to conceal far-reaching intentions, mysterious conclusions drawn from suspicions and resentments impossible to guess. That supposition was even more disturbing than the other; and it was the one which had come to him the night before, when he had seen her standing in the kitchen door.

Now her departure for Bettsbridge had once more eased his mind, and all his thoughts were on the prospect of his evening with Mattie. Only one thing weighed on him, and that was his having told Zeena that he was to receive cash for the lumber. He foresaw so clearly the consequences of this imprudence that with considerable reluctance he decided to ask Andrew Hale for a small advance on his load.

When Ethan drove into Hale's yard the builder was just getting out of his sleigh.

"Hello, Ethe!" he said. "This comes handy."

Andrew Hale was a ruddy man with a big grey moustache and a stubbly double-chin unconstrained by a collar; but his scrupulously clean shirt was always fastened by a small diamond stud. This display of opulence was misleading, for though he did a fairly good business it was known that his easygoing habits and the demands of his large family frequently kept him what Starkfield called "behind." He was an old friend of Ethan's family, and his house one of the few to which Zeena occasionally went, drawn there by the fact that Mrs. Hale, in her youth, had done more "doctoring" than any other woman in Starkfield, and was still a recognised authority on symptoms and treatment.

Hale went up to the greys and patted their sweating flanks.

"Well, sir," he said, "you keep them two as if they was pets."

Ethan set about unloading the logs and when he had finished his job he pushed open the glazed door of the shed which the builder used as his office. Hale sat with his feet up on the stove, his back propped against a battered desk strewn with papers: the place, like the man, was warm, genial and untidy.

"Sit right down and thaw out," he greeted Ethan.

The latter did not know how to begin, but at length he managed to bring out his request for an advance of fifty dollars. The blood rushed to his thin skin under the sting of Hale's astonishment. It was the builder's custom to pay at the end of three months, and there was no precedent between the two men for a cash settlement.

Ethan felt that if he had pleaded an urgent need Hale might have made shift to pay him; but pride, and an instinctive prudence, kept him from resorting to this argument. After his father's death it had taken time to get his head above water, and he did not want Andrew Hale, or any one else in Starkfield, to think he was going under again. Besides, he hated lying; if he wanted the money he wanted it, and it was nobody's business to ask why. He therefore made his demand with the awkwardness of a proud man who will not admit to himself that he is stooping; and he was not much surprised at Hale's refusal.

The builder refused genially, as he did everything else: he treated the matter as something in the nature of a practical joke, and wanted to know if Ethan meditated buying a grand piano or adding a "cupolo" to his house; offering, in the latter case, to give his services free of cost.

Ethan's arts were soon exhausted, and after an embarrassed pause he wished Hale good day and opened the door of the office. As he passed out the builder suddenly called after him: "See here—you ain't in a tight place, are you?"

"Not a bit," Ethan's pride retorted before his reason had time to intervene.

"Well, that's good! Because I *am*, a shade. Fact is, I was going to ask you to give me a little extra time on that payment. Business is pretty slack, to begin with, and then I'm fixing up a little house for Ned and Ruth when they're married. I'm glad to do it for 'em, but it costs." His look appealed to Ethan for sympathy. "The young people like things nice. You know how it is yourself: it's not so long ago since you fixed up your own place for Zeena."

Ethan left the greys in Hale's stable and went about some other business in the village. As he walked away the builder's last phrase lingered in his ears, and he reflected grimly that his seven years with Zeena seemed to Starkfield "not so long."

The afternoon was drawing to an end, and here and there a lighted pane spangled the cold grey dusk and made the snow look whiter. The bitter weather had driven every one indoors and Ethan had the long rural street to himself. Suddenly he heard the brisk play of sleigh-bells and a cutter passed him, drawn by a free-going horse. Ethan recognised Michael Eady's roan colt, and young Denis Eady, in a handsome new fur cap, leaned forward and waved a greeting. "Hello, Ethe!" he shouted and spun on.

The cutter was going in the direction of the Frome farm, and Ethan's heart contracted as he listened to the dwindling bells. What more likely than that Denis Eady had heard of Zeena's departure for Bettsbridge, and was profiting by the opportunity to spend an hour with Mattie? Ethan was ashamed of the storm of jealousy in his breast. It seemed unworthy of the girl that his thoughts of her should be so violent.

He walked on to the church corner and entered the shade of the Varnum spruces, where he had stood with her the night before. As he passed into their gloom he saw an indistinct outline just ahead of him. At his approach it melted for an instant into two separate shapes and then conjoined again, and he heard a kiss, and a half-laughing "Oh!" provoked by the discovery of his presence. Again the outline hastily disunited and the Varnum gate slammed on one half while the other hurried on ahead of him. Ethan smiled at the discomfiture he had caused. What did it matter to Ned Hale and Ruth Varnum if they were caught kissing each other? Everybody in Starkfield knew they were engaged. It pleased Ethan to have surprised a pair of lovers on the spot where he and Mattie had stood with such a thirst for each other in their hearts; but he felt a pang at the thought that these two need not hide their happiness.

He fetched the greys from Hale's stable and started on his long climb back to the farm. The cold was less sharp than earlier in the day and a thick fleecy sky threatened snow for the morrow. Here and there a star pricked through, showing behind it a deep well of blue. In an hour or two the moon would push over the ridge behind the farm, burn a gold-edged rent in the clouds, and then be swallowed by them. A mournful peace hung on the fields, as though they felt the relaxing grasp of the cold and stretched themselves in their long winter sleep.

Ethan's ears were alert for the jingle of sleighbells, but not a sound broke the silence of the lonely road. As he drew near the farm he saw, through the thin screen of larches at the gate, a light twinkling in the house above him. "She's up in her room," he said to himself, "fixing herself up for supper"; and he remembered Zeena's sarcastic stare when Mattie, on the evening of her arrival, had come down to supper with smoothed hair and a ribbon at her neck.

He passed by the graves on the knoll and turned his head to glance at one of the older headstones, which had interested him deeply as a boy because it bore his name.

SACRED TO THE MEMORY OF
ETHAN FROME AND ENDURANCE HIS WIFE,
WHO DWELLED TOGETHER IN PEACE
FOR FIFTY YEARS.

He used to think that fifty years sounded like a long time to live together, but now it seemed to him that they might pass in a flash. Then, with a sudden dart of irony, he wondered if, when their turn came, the same epitaph would be written over him and Zeena.

He opened the barn-door and craned his head into the obscurity, half-fearing to discover Denis Eady's roan colt in the stall beside the sorrel. But the old horse was there alone, mumbling his crib with toothless jaws, and Ethan whistled cheerfully while he bedded down the greys and shook an extra measure of oats into their mangers. His was not a tuneful throat, but harsh melodies burst from it as he locked the barn and sprang up the hill to the house. He reached the kitchen-porch and turned the door-handle; but the door did not yield to his touch.

Startled at finding it locked he rattled the handle violently; then he reflected that Mattie was alone and that it was natural she should barricade herself at nightfall. He stood in the darkness expecting to hear her step. It did not come, and after vainly straining his ears he called out in a voice that shook with joy: "Hello, Matt!"

Silence answered; but in a minute or two he caught a sound on the stairs and saw a line of light about the door-frame, as he had seen it the night before. So strange was the precision with which the incidents of the previous evening were repeating themselves that he half expected, when he heard the key turn, to see his wife before him on the threshold; but the door opened, and Mattie faced him.

She stood just as Zeena had stood, a lifted lamp in her hand, against the black background of the kitchen. She held the light at the same level, and it drew out with the same distinctness her slim young throat and the brown wrist no bigger than a child's. Then, striking upward, it threw a lustrous fleck on her lips, edged her eyes with velvet shade, and laid a milky whiteness above the black curve of her brows.

She wore her usual dress of darkish stuff, and there was no bow at her neck; but through her hair she had run a streak of crimson ribbon. This tribute to the unusual transformed and glorified her. She seemed to Ethan taller, fuller, more womanly in shape and motion. She stood aside, smiling silently, while he entered, and then moved away from him with something soft and flowing in her gait. She set the lamp on the table, and he saw that it was carefully laid for supper, with fresh doughnuts, stewed blueberries and his favourite pickles in a dish of gay red glass. A bright fire glowed in the stove and the cat lay stretched before it, watching the table with a drowsy eye.

Ethan was suffocated with the sense of well-being. He went out into the passage to hang up his coat and pull off his wet boots. When he came back Mattie had set the teapot on the table and the cat was rubbing itself persuasively against her ankles.

"Why, Puss! I nearly tripped over you," she cried, the laughter sparkling through her lashes.

Again Ethan felt a sudden twinge of jealousy. Could it be his coming that gave her such a kindled face?

"Well, Matt, any visitors?" he threw off, stooping down carelessly to examine the fastening of the stove.

She nodded and laughed "Yes, one," and he felt a blackness settling on his brows.

"Who was that?" he questioned, raising himself up to slant a glance at her beneath his scowl.

Her eyes danced with malice. "Why, Jotham Powell. He came in after he got back, and asked for a drop of coffee before he went down home."

The blackness lifted and light flooded Ethan's brain. "That all? Well, I hope you made out to let him have it." And after a pause he felt it right to add: "I suppose he got Zeena over to the Flats all right?"

"Oh, yes; in plenty of time."

The name threw a chill between them, and they stood a moment looking sideways at each other before Mattie said with a shy laugh, "I guess it's about time for supper."

They drew their seats up to the table, and the cat, unbidden, jumped between them into Zeena's empty chair. "Oh, Puss!" said Mattie, and they laughed again.

Ethan, a moment earlier, had felt himself on the brink of eloquence; but the mention of Zeena had paralysed him. Mattie seemed to feel the contagion of his embarrassment, and sat with downcast lids, sipping her tea, while he feigned an insatiable appetite for doughnuts and sweet pickles. At last, after casting about for an effective opening, he took a long gulp of tea, cleared his throat, and said: "Looks as if there'd be more snow."

She feigned great interest. "Is that so? Do you suppose it'll interfere with Zeena's getting back?" She flushed red as the question escaped her, and hastily set down the cup she was lifting.

Ethan reached over for another helping of pickles. "You never can tell, this time of year, it drifts so bad on the Flats." The name had benumbed him again, and once more he felt as if Zeena were in the room between them.

"Oh, Puss, you're too greedy!" Mattie cried.

The cat, unnoticed, had crept up on muffled paws from Zeena's seat to the table, and was stealthily elongating its body in the direction of the milk-jug, which stood between Ethan and Mattie. The two leaned forward at the same moment and their hands met on the handle of the jug. Mattie's hand was underneath, and Ethan kept his clasped on it a moment longer than was necessary. The cat, profiting by this unusual demonstration, tried to effect an unnoticed retreat, and in doing so backed into the pickle-dish, which fell to the floor with a crash.

Mattie, in an instant, had sprung from her chair and was down on her knees by the fragments.

"Oh, Ethan, Ethan—it's all to pieces! What will Zeena say?"

But this time his courage was up. "Well, she'll have to say it to the cat, any way!" he rejoined with a laugh, kneeling down at Mattie's side to scrape up the swimming pickles.

She lifted stricken eyes to him. "Yes, but, you see, she never meant it should be used, not even when there was company; and I had to get up on the step-ladder to reach it down from the top shelf of the china-closet, where she keeps it with all her best things, and of course she'll want to know why I did it——"

The case was so serious that it called forth all of Ethan's latent resolution.

"She needn't know anything about it if you keep quiet. I'll get another just like it to-morrow. Where did it come from? I'll go to Shadd's Falls for it if I have to!"

"Oh, you'll never get another even there! It was a wedding present—don't you remember? It came all the way from Philadelphia, from Zeena's aunt that married the minister. That's why she wouldn't ever use it. Oh, Ethan, Ethan, what in the world shall I do?"

She began to cry, and he felt as if every one of her tears were pouring over him like burning lead. "Don't, Matt, don't—oh, *don't*!" he implored her.

She struggled to her feet, and he rose and followed her helplessly while she spread out the pieces of glass on the kitchen dresser. It seemed to him as if the shattered fragments of their evening lay there.

"Here, give them to me," he said in a voice of sudden authority.

She drew aside, instinctively obeying his tone. "Oh, Ethan, what are you going to do?"

Without replying he gathered the pieces of glass into his broad palm and walked out of the kitchen to the passage. There he lit a candle-end, opened the china-closet, and, reaching his long arm up to the highest shelf, laid the pieces together with such accuracy of touch that a close inspection convinced him of the impossibility of detecting from below that the dish was broken. If he glued it together the next morning months might elapse before his wife noticed what had happened, and meanwhile he might after all be able to match the dish at Shadd's Falls or Bettsbridge. Having satisfied himself that there was no risk of immediate discovery he went back to the kitchen with a lighter step, and found Mattie disconsolately removing the last scraps of pickle from the floor.

"It's all right, Matt. Come back and finish supper," he commanded her.

Completely reassured, she shone on him through tear-hung lashes, and his soul swelled with pride as he saw how his tone subdued her. She did not even ask what he had done. Except when he was steering a big log down the mountain to his mill he had never known such a thrilling sense of mastery.

CHAPTER V

They finished supper, and while Mattie cleared the table Ethan went to look at the cows and then took a last turn about the house. The earth lay dark under a muffled sky and the air was so still that now and then he heard a lump of snow come thumping down from a tree far off on the edge of the wood-lot.

When he returned to the kitchen Mattie had pushed up his chair to the stove and seated herself near the lamp with a bit of sewing. The scene was just as he had dreamed of it that morning. He sat down, drew his pipe from his pocket and stretched his feet to the glow. His hard day's work in the keen air made him feel at once lazy and light of mood, and he had a confused sense of being in another world, where all was warmth and harmony and time could bring no change. The only drawback to his complete well-being was the fact that he could not see Mattie from where he sat; but he was too indolent to move and after a moment he said: "Come over here and sit by the stove."

Zeena's empty rocking-chair stood facing him. Mattie rose obediently, and seated herself in it. As her young brown head detached itself against the patch-work cushion that habitually framed his wife's gaunt countenance, Ethan had a momentary shock. It was almost as if the other face, the face of the superseded woman, had obliterated that of the intruder. After a moment Mattie seemed to be affected by the same sense of constraint. She changed her position, leaning forward to bend her head above her work, so that he saw only the foreshortened tip of her nose and the streak of red in her hair; then she slipped to her feet, saying "I can't see to sew," and went back to her chair by the lamp.

Ethan made a pretext of getting up to replenish the stove, and when he returned to his seat he pushed it sideways that he might get a view of her profile and of the lamplight falling on her hands. The cat, who had been a puzzled observer of these unusual movements, jumped up into Zeena's chair, rolled itself into a ball, and lay watching them with narrowed eyes.

Deep quiet sank on the room. The clock ticked above the dresser, a piece of charred wood fell now and then in the stove, and the faint sharp scent of the geraniums mingled with the odour of Ethan's smoke, which began to throw a blue haze about the lamp and to hang its greyish cobwebs in the shadowy corners of the room.

All constraint had vanished between the two, and they began to talk easily and simply. They spoke of every-day things, of the prospect of snow, of the next church sociable, of the loves and quarrels of Starkfield. The commonplace nature of what they said produced in Ethan an illusion of long-established intimacy which no outburst of emotion could have given, and he set his imagination adrift on the fiction that they had always spent their evenings thus and would always go on doing so . . .

"This is the night we were to have gone coasting,

Matt," he said at length, with the rich sense, as he spoke, that they could go on any other night they chose, since they had all time before them.

She smiled back at him. "I guess you forgot!"

"No, I didn't forget; but it's as dark as Egypt outdoors. We might go to-morrow if there's a moon."

She laughed with pleasure, her head tilted back, the lamplight sparkling on her lips and teeth. "That would be lovely, Ethan!"

He kept his eyes fixed on her, marvelling at the way her face changed with each turn of their talk, like a wheat-field under a summer breeze. It was intoxicating to find such magic in his clumsy words, and he longed to try new ways of using it.

"Would you be scared to go down the Corbury road with me on a night like this?" he asked.

Her cheeks burned redder. "I ain't any more scared than you are!"

"Well, *I'd* be scared, then; I wouldn't do it. That's an ugly corner down by the big elm. If a fellow didn't keep his eyes open he'd go plumb into it." He luxuriated in the sense of protection and authority which his words conveyed. To prolong and intensify the feeling he added: "I guess we're well enough here."

She let her lids sink slowly, in the way he loved. "Yes, we're well enough here," she sighed.

Her tone was so sweet that he took the pipe from his mouth and drew his chair up to the table. Leaning forward, he touched the farther end of the strip of brown stuff that she was hemming. "Say, Matt," he began with a smile, "what do you think I saw under the Varnum spruces, coming along home just now? I saw a friend of yours getting kissed."

The words had been on his tongue all the evening, but now that he had spoken them they struck him as inexpressibly vulgar and out of place.

Mattie blushed to the roots of her hair and pulled her needle rapidly twice or thrice through her work, insensibly drawing the end of it away from him. "I suppose it was Ruth and Ned," she said in a low voice, as though he had suddenly touched on something grave.

Ethan had imagined that his allusion might open the way to the accepted pleasantries, and these perhaps in turn to a harmless caress, if only a mere touch on her hand. But now he felt as if her blush had set a flaming guard about her. He supposed it was his natural awkwardness that made him feel so. He knew that most young men made nothing at all of giving a pretty girl a kiss, and he remembered that the night before, when he had put his arm about Mattie, she had not resisted. But that had been out-of-doors, under the open irresponsible night. Now, in the warm lamplit room, with all its ancient implications of conformity and order, she seemed infinitely farther away from him and more unapproachable.

To ease his constraint he said: "I suppose they'll be setting a date before long."

"Yes. I shouldn't wonder if they got married some time along in the summer." She pronounced the word *married* as if her voice caressed it. It seemed a rustling covert leading to enchanted glades. A pang shot through Ethan, and he said, twisting away from her in his chair: "It'll be your turn next, I wouldn't wonder."

She laughed a little uncertainly. "Why do you keep on saying that?"

He echoed her laugh. "I guess I do it to get used to the idea."

He drew up to the table again and she sewed on in silence, with dropped lashes, while he sat in fascinated contemplation of the way in which her hands went up and down above the strip of stuff, just as he had seen a pair of birds make short perpendicular flights over a nest they were building. At length, without turning her head or lifting her lids, she said in a low tone: "It's not because you think Zeena's got anything against me, is it?"

His former dread started up full-armed at the suggestion. "Why, what do you mean?" he stammered.

She raised distressed eyes to his, her work dropping on the table between them. "I don't know. I thought last night she seemed to have."

"I'd like to know what," he growled.

"Nobody can tell with Zeena." It was the first time they had ever spoken so openly of her attitude toward

Mattie, and the repetition of the name seemed to carry it to the farther corners of the room and send it back to them in long repercussions of sound. Mattie waited, as if to give the echo time to drop, and then went on: "She hasn't said anything to *you*?"

He shook his head. "No, not a word."

She tossed the hair back from her forehead with a laugh. "I guess I'm just nervous, then. I'm not going to think about it any more."

"Oh, no—don't let's think about it, Matt!"

The sudden heat of his tone made her colour mount again, not with a rush, but gradually, delicately, like the reflection of a thought stealing slowly across her heart. She sat silent, her hands clasped on her work, and it seemed to him that a warm current flowed toward him along the strip of stuff that still lay unrolled between them. Cautiously he slid his hand palm-downward along the table till his finger-tips touched the end of the stuff. A faint vibration of her lashes seemed to show that she was aware of his gesture, and that it had sent a counter-current back to her; and she let her hands lie motionless on the other end of the strip.

As they sat thus he heard a sound behind him and turned his head. The cat had jumped from Zeena's chair to dart at a mouse in the wainscot, and as a result of the sudden movement the empty chair had set up a spectral rocking.

"She'll be rocking in it herself this time to-morrow," Ethan thought. "I've been in a dream, and this is the only evening we'll ever have together." The return to reality was as painful as the return to consciousness after taking an anaesthetic. His body and brain ached with indescribable weariness, and he could think of nothing to say or to do that should arrest the mad flight of the moments.

His alteration of mood seemed to have communicated itself to Mattie. She looked up at him languidly, as though her lids were weighted with sleep and it cost her an effort to raise them. Her glance fell on his hand, which now completely covered the end of her work and grasped it as if it were a part of herself. He saw a scarcely perceptible tremor cross her face, and without knowing what he did he stooped his head and kissed the bit of stuff in his hold. As his lips rested on it he felt it glide slowly from beneath them, and saw that Mattie had risen and was silently rolling up her work. She fastened it with a pin, and then, finding her thimble and scissors, put them with the roll of stuff into the box covered with fancy paper which he had once brought to her from Bettsbridge.

He stood up also, looking vaguely about the room. The clock above the dresser struck eleven.

"Is the fire all right?" she asked in a low voice.

He opened the door of the stove and poked aimlessly at the embers. When he raised himself again he saw that she was dragging toward the stove the old soap-box lined with carpet in which the cat made its bed. Then she recrossed the floor and lifted two of the geranium pots in her arms, moving them away from the cold window. He followed her and brought the other geraniums, the hyacinth bulbs in a cracked custard bowl and the German ivy trained over an old croquet hoop.

When these nightly duties were performed there was nothing left to do but to bring in the tin candlestick from the passage, light the candle and blow out the lamp. Ethan put the candlestick in Mattie's hand and she went out of the kitchen ahead of him, the light that she carried before her making her dark hair look like a drift of mist on the moon.

"Good night, Matt," he said as she put her foot on the first step of the stairs.

She turned and looked at him a moment. "Good night, Ethan," she answered, and went up.

When the door of her room had closed on her he remembered that he had not even touched her hand.

CHAPTER VI

The next morning at breakfast Jotham Powell was between them, and Ethan tried to hide his joy under an air of exaggerated indifference, lounging back in his chair to throw scraps to the cat, growling at the weather, and not so much as offering to help Mattie when she rose to clear away the dishes.

He did not know why he was so irrationally happy, for nothing was changed in his life or hers. He had not even touched the tip of her fingers or looked her full in the eyes. But their evening together had given him a vision of what life at her side might be, and he was glad now that he had done nothing to trouble the sweetness of the picture. He had a fancy that she knew what had restrained him . . .

There was a last load of lumber to be hauled to the village, and Jotham Powell—who did not work regularly for Ethan in winter—had "come round" to help with the job. But a wet snow, melting to sleet, had fallen in the night and turned the roads to glass. There was more wet in the air and it seemed likely to both men that the weather would "milden" toward afternoon and make the going safer. Ethan therefore proposed to his assistant that they should load the sledge at the wood-lot, as they had done on the previous morning, and put off the "teaming" to Starkfield till later in the day. This plan had the advantage of enabling him to send Jotham to the Flats after dinner to meet Zenobia, while he himself took the lumber down to the village.

He told Jotham to go out and harness up the greys, and for a moment he and Mattie had the kitchen to themselves. She had plunged the breakfast dishes into a tin dish-pan and was bending above it with her slim arms bared to the elbow, the steam from the hot water beading her forehead and tightening her rough hair into little brown rings like the tendrils on the traveller's joy.

Ethan stood looking at her, his heart in his throat. He wanted to say: "We shall never be alone again like this." Instead, he reached down his tobacco-pouch from a shelf of the dresser, put it into his pocket and said: "I guess I can make out to be home for dinner."

She answered "All right, Ethan," and he heard her singing over the dishes as he went.

As soon as the sledge was loaded he meant to send Jotham back to the farm and hurry on foot into the village to buy the glue for the pickle-dish. With ordinary luck he should have had time to carry out this plan; but everything went wrong from the start. On the way over to the wood-lot one of the greys slipped on a glare of ice and cut his knee; and when they got him up again Jotham had to go back to the barn for a strip of rag to bind the cut. Then, when the loading finally began, a sleety rain was coming down once more, and the tree trunks were so slippery that it took twice as long as usual to lift them and get them in place on the sledge. It was what Jotham called a sour morning for work, and the horses, shivering and stamping under their wet blankets, seemed to like it as little as the men. It was long past the dinner-hour when the job was done, and Ethan had to give up going to the village because he wanted to lead the injured horse home and wash the cut himself.

He thought that by starting out again with the lumber as soon as he had finished his dinner he might get back to the farm with the glue before Jotham and the old sorrel had had time to fetch Zenobia from the Flats; but he knew the chance was a slight one. It turned on the state of the roads and on the possible lateness of the Bettsbridge train. He remembered afterward, with a grim flash of self-derision, what importance he had attached to the weighing of these probabilities . . .

As soon as dinner was over he set out again for the wood-lot, not daring to linger till Jotham Powell left. The hired man was still drying his wet feet at the stove, and Ethan could only give Mattie a quick look as he said beneath his breath: "I'll be back early."

He fancied that she nodded her comprehension; and

with that scant solace he had to trudge off through the rain.

He had driven his load half-way to the village when Jotham Powell overtook him, urging the reluctant sorrel toward the Flats. "I'll have to hurry up to do it," Ethan mused, as the sleigh dropped down ahead of him over the dip of the school-house hill. He worked like ten at the unloading, and when it was over hastened on to Michael Eady's for the glue. Eady and his assistant were both "down street," and young Denis, who seldom deigned to take their place, was lounging by the stove with a knot of the golden youth of Starkfield. They hailed Ethan with ironic compliment and offers of conviviality; but no one knew where to find the glue. Ethan, consumed with the longing for a last moment alone with Mattie, hung about impatiently while Denis made an ineffectual search in the obscurer corners of the store.

"Looks as if we were all sold out. But if you'll wait around till the old man comes along maybe he can put his hand on it."

"I'm obliged to you, but I'll try if I can get it down at Mrs. Homan's," Ethan answered, burning to be gone.

Denis's commercial instinct compelled him to aver on oath that what Eady's store could not produce would never be found at the widow Homan's; but Ethan, heedless of this boast, had already climbed to the sledge and was driving on to the rival establishment. Here, after considerable search, and sympathetic questions as to what he wanted it for, and whether ordinary flour paste wouldn't do as well if she couldn't find it, the widow Homan finally hunted down her solitary bottle of glue to its hiding-place in a medley of cough-lozenges and corset-laces.

"I hope Zeena ain't broken anything she sets store by," she called after him as he turned the greys toward home.

The fitful bursts of sleet had changed into a steady rain and the horses had heavy work even without a load behind them. Once or twice, hearing sleigh-bells, Ethan turned his head, fancying that Zeena and Jotham might overtake him; but the old sorrel was not in sight, and he set his face against the rain and urged on his ponderous pair.

The barn was empty when the horses turned into it

and, after giving them the most perfunctory ministrations they had ever received from him, he strode up to the house and pushed open the kitchen door.

Mattie was there alone, as he had pictured her. She was bending over a pan on the stove; but at the sound of his step she turned with a start and sprang to him.

"See, here, Matt, I've got some stuff to mend the dish with! Let me get at it quick," he cried, waving the bottle in one hand while he put her lightly aside; but she did not seem to hear him.

"Oh, Ethan—Zeena's come," she said in a whisper, clutching his sleeve.

They stood and stared at each other, pale as culprits.

"But the sorrel's not in the barn!" Ethan stammered.

"Jotham Powell brought some goods over from the Flats for his wife, and he drove right on home with them," she explained.

He gazed blankly about the kitchen, which looked cold and squalid in the rainy winter twilight.

"How is she?" he asked, dropping his voice to Mattie's whisper.

She looked away from him uncertainly. "I don't know. She went right up to her room."

"She didn't say anything?"

"No."

Ethan let out his doubts in a low whistle and thrust the bottle back into his pocket. "Don't fret; I'll come down and mend it in the night," he said. He pulled on his wet coat again and went back to the barn to feed the greys.

While he was there Jotham Powell drove up with the sleigh, and when the horses had been attended to Ethan said to him: "You might as well come back up for a bite." He was not sorry to assure himself of Jotham's neutralising presence at the supper table, for Zeena was always "nervous" after a journey. But the hired man, though seldom loth to accept a meal not included in his wages, opened his stiff jaws to answer slowly: "I'm obliged to you, but I guess I'll go along back."

Ethan looked at him in surprise. "Better come up and dry off. Looks as if there'd be something hot for supper."

Jotham's facial muscles were unmoved by this appeal

and, his vocabulary being limited, he merely repeated: "I guess I'll go along back."

To Ethan there was something vaguely ominous in this stolid rejection of free food and warmth, and he wondered what had happened on the drive to nerve Jotham to such stoicism. Perhaps Zeena had failed to see the new doctor or had not liked his counsels: Ethan knew that in such cases the first person she met was likely to be held responsible for her grievance.

When he re-entered the kitchen the lamp lit up the same scene of shining comfort as on the previous evening. The table had been as carefully laid, a clear fire glowed in the stove, the cat dozed in its warmth, and Mattie came forward carrying a plate of doughnuts.

She and Ethan looked at each other in silence; then she said, as she had said the night before: "I guess it's about time for supper."

CHAPTER VII

Ethan went out into the passage to hang up his wet garments. He listened for Zeena's step and, not hearing it, called her name up the stairs. She did not answer, and after a moment's hesitation he went up and opened her door. The room was almost dark, but in the obscurity he saw her sitting by the window, bolt upright, and knew by the rigidity of the outline projected against the pane that she had not taken off her travelling dress.

"Well, Zeena," he ventured from the threshold.

She did not move, and he continued: "Supper's about ready. Ain't you coming?"

She replied: "I don't feel as if I could touch a morsel."

It was the consecrated formula, and he expected it to be followed, as usual, by her rising and going down to supper. But she remained seated, and he could think of nothing more felicitous than: "I presume you're tired after the long ride."

Turning her head at this, she answered solemnly: "I'm a great deal sicker than you think."

Her words fell on his ear with a strange shock of wonder. He had often heard her pronounce them before—what if at last they were true?

He advanced a step or two into the dim room. "I hope that's not so, Zeena," he said.

She continued to gaze at him through the twilight with a mien of wan authority, as of one consciously singled out for a great fate. "I've got complications," she said.

Ethan knew the word for one of exceptional import. Almost everybody in the neighbourhood had "troubles," frankly localized and specified; but only the chosen had "complications." To have them was in itself a distinction, though it was also, in most cases, a death-warrant. People struggled on for years with "troubles," but they almost always succumbed to "complications."

Ethan's heart was jerking to and fro between two extremities of feeling, but for the moment compassion prevailed. His wife looked so hard and lonely, sitting there in the darkness with such thoughts.

"Is that what the new doctor told you?" he asked, instinctively lowering his voice.

"Yes. He says any regular doctor would want me to have an operation."

Ethan was aware that, in regard to the important question of surgical intervention, the female opinion of the neighbourhood was divided, some glorying in the prestige conferred by operations while others shunned them as indelicate. Ethan, from motives of economy, had always been glad that Zeena was of the latter faction.

In the agitation caused by the gravity of her announcement he sought a consolatory short cut. "What do you know about this doctor anyway? Nobody ever told you that before."

He saw his blunder before she could take it up: she wanted sympathy, not consolation.

"I didn't need to have anybody tell me I was losing ground every day. Everybody but you could see it. And everybody in Bettsbridge knows about Dr. Buck. He has his office in Worcester, and comes over once a fortnight to

Shadd's Falls and Bettsbridge for consultations. Eliza Spears was wasting away with kidney trouble before she went to him, and now she's up and around, and singing in the choir."

"Well, I'm glad of that. You must do just what he tells you," Ethan answered sympathetically.

She was still looking at him. "I mean to," she said. He was struck by a new note in her voice. It was neither whining nor reproachful, but drily resolute.

"What does he want you should do?" he asked, with a mounting vision of fresh expenses.

"He wants I should have a hired girl. He says I oughtn't to have to do a single thing around the house."

"A hired girl?" Ethan stood transfixed.

"Yes. And Aunt Martha found me one right off. Everybody said I was lucky to get a girl to come away out here, and I agreed to give her a dollar extry to make sure. She'll be over to-morrow afternoon."

Wrath and dismay contended in Ethan. He had foreseen an immediate demand for money, but not a permanent drain on his scant resources. He no longer believed what Zeena had told him of the supposed seriousness of her state: he saw in her expedition to Bettsbridge only a plot hatched between herself and her Pierce relations to foist on him the cost of a servant; and for the moment wrath predominated.

"If you meant to engage a girl you ought to have told me before you started," he said.

"How could I tell you before I started? How did I know what Dr. Buck would say?"

"Oh, Dr. Buck—" Ethan's incredulity escaped in a short laugh. "Did Dr. Buck tell you how I was to pay her wages?"

Her voice rose furiously with his. "No, he didn't. For I'd 'a' been ashamed to tell *him* that you grudged me the money to get back my health, when I lost it nursing your own mother!"

"*You* lost your health nursing mother?"

"Yes; and my folks all told me at the time you couldn't do no less than marry me after——"

"Zeena!"

Through the obscurity which hid their faces their thoughts seemed to dart at each other like serpents shooting venom. Ethan was seized with horror of the scene and shame at his own share in it. It was as senseless and savage as a physical fight between two enemies in the darkness.

He turned to the shelf above the chimney, groped for matches and lit the one candle in the room. At first its weak flame made no impression on the shadows; then Zeena's face stood grimly out against the uncurtained pane, which had turned from grey to black.

It was the first scene of open anger between the couple in their sad seven years together, and Ethan felt as if he had lost an irretrievable advantage in descending to the level of recrimination. But the practical problem was there and had to be dealt with.

"You know I haven't got the money to pay for a girl, Zeena. You'll have to send her back: I can't do it."

"The doctor says it'll be my death if I go on slaving the way I've had to. He doesn't understand how I've stood it as long as I have."

"Slaving!—" He checked himself again, "You sha'n't lift a hand, if he says so. I'll do everything round the house myself——"

She broke in: "You're neglecting the farm enough already," and this being true, he found no answer, and left her time to add ironically: "Better send me over to the almshouse and done with it . . . I guess there's been Fromes there afore now."

The taunt burned into him, but he let it pass. "I haven't got the money. That settles it."

There was a moment's pause in the struggle, as though the combatants were testing their weapons. Then Zeena said in a level voice: "I thought you were to get fifty dollars from Andrew Hale for that lumber."

"Andrew Hale never pays under three months." He had hardly spoken when he remembered the excuse he had made for not accompanying his wife to the station the day before; and the blood rose to his frowning brows.

"Why, you told me yesterday you'd fixed it up with

him to pay cash down. You said that was why you couldn't drive me over to the Flats."

Ethan had no suppleness in deceiving. He had never before been convicted of a lie, and all the resources of evasion failed him. "I guess that was a misunderstanding," he stammered.

"You ain't got the money?"

"No."

"And you ain't going to get it?"

"No."

"Well, I couldn't know that when I engaged the girl, could I?"

"No." He paused to control his voice. "But you know it now. I'm sorry, but it can't be helped. You're a poor man's wife, Zeena; but I'll do the best I can for you."

For a while she sat motionless, as if reflecting, her arms stretched along the arms of her chair, her eyes fixed on vacancy. "Oh, I guess we'll make out," she said mildly.

The change in her tone reassured him. "Of course we will! There's a whole lot more I can do for you, and Mattie——"

Zeena, while he spoke, seemed to be following out some elaborate mental calculation. She emerged from it to say: "There'll be Mattie's board less, anyhow——"

Ethan, supposing the discussion to be over, had turned to go down to supper. He stopped short, not grasping what he heard. "Mattie's board less—?" he began.

Zeena laughed. It was an odd unfamiliar sound—he did not remember ever having heard her laugh before. "You didn't suppose I was going to keep two girls, did you? No wonder you were scared at the expense!"

He still had but a confused sense of what she was saying. From the beginning of the discussion he had instinctively avoided the mention of Mattie's name, fearing he hardly knew what: criticism, complaints, or vague allusions to the imminent probability of her marrying. But the thought of a definite rupture had never come to him, and even now could not lodge itself in his mind.

"I don't know what you mean," he said. "Mattie Silver's not a hired girl. She's your relation."

"She's a pauper that's hung onto us all after her father'd

done his best to ruin us. I've kep' her here a whole year: it's somebody else's turn now."

As the shrill words shot out Ethan heard a tap on the door, which he had drawn shut when he turned back from the threshold.

"Ethan—Zeena!" Mattie's voice sounded gaily from the landing, "do you know what time it is? Supper's been ready half an hour."

Inside the room there was a moment's silence; then Zeena called out from her seat: "I'm not coming down to supper."

"Oh, I'm sorry! Aren't you well? Sha'n't I bring you up a bite of something?"

Ethan roused himself with an effort and opened the door. "Go along down, Matt. Zeena's just a little tired. I'm coming."

He heard her "All right!" and her quick step on the stairs; then he shut the door and turned back into the room. His wife's attitude was unchanged, her face inexorable, and he was seized with the despairing sense of his helplessness.

"You ain't going to do it, Zeena?"

"Do what?" she emitted between flattened lips.

"Send Mattie away—like this?"

"I never bargained to take her for life!"

He continued with rising vehemence: "You can't put her out of the house like a thief—a poor girl without friends or money. She's done her best for you and she's got no place to go to. You may forget she's your kin but everybody else'll remember it. If you do a thing like that what do you suppose folks'll say of you?"

Zeena waited a moment, as if giving him time to feel the full force of the contrast between his own excitement and her composure. Then she replied in the same smooth voice: "I know well enough what they say of my having kep' her here as long as I have."

Ethan's hand dropped from the door-knob, which he had held clenched since he had drawn the door shut on Mattie. His wife's retort was like a knife-cut across the sinews and he felt suddenly weak and powerless. He had meant to humble himself, to argue that Mattie's keep didn't cost much, after all, that he could make out to buy a stove and fix up a place in the attic for the hired girl—but Zeena's words revealed the peril of such pleadings.

"You mean to tell her she's got to go—at once?" he faltered out, in terror of letting his wife complete her sentence.

As if trying to make him see reason she replied impartially: "The girl will be over from Bettsbridge to-morrow, and I presume she's got to have somewheres to sleep."

Ethan looked at her with loathing. She was no longer the listless creature who had lived at his side in a state of sullen self-absorption, but a mysterious alien presence, an evil energy secreted from the long years of silent brooding. It was the sense of his helplessness that sharpened his antipathy. There had never been anything in her that one could appeal to; but as long as he could ignore and command he had remained indifferent. Now she had mastered him and he abhorred her. Mattie was her relation, not his: there were no means by which he could compel her to keep the girl under her roof. All the long misery of his baffled past, of his youth of failure, hardship and vain effort, rose up in his soul in bitterness and seemed to take shape before him in the woman who at every turn had barred his way. She had taken everything else from him; and now she meant to take the one thing that made up for all the others. For a moment such a flame of hate rose in him that it ran down his arm and clenched his fist against her. He took a wild step forward and then stopped.

"You're—you're not coming down?" he said in a bewildered voice.

"No. I guess I'll lay down on the bed a little while," she answered mildly; and he turned and walked out of the room.

In the kitchen Mattie was sitting by the stove, the cat curled up on her knees. She sprang to her feet as Ethan entered and carried the covered dish of meat-pie to the table.

"I hope Zeena isn't sick?" she asked.

"No."

She shone at him across the table. "Well, sit right down then. You must be starving." She uncovered the pie and pushed it over to him. So they were to have one more evening together, her happy eyes seemed to say!

He helped himself mechanically and began to eat; then disgust took him by the throat and he laid down his fork.

Mattie's tender gaze was on him and she marked the gesture.

"Why, Ethan, what's the matter? Don't it taste right?"

"Yes—it's first-rate. Only I—" He pushed his plate away, rose from his chair, and walked around the table to her side. She started up with frightened eyes.

"Ethan, there's something wrong! I *knew* there was!"

She seemed to melt against him in her terror, and he caught her in his arms, held her fast there, felt her lashes beat his cheek like netted butterflies.

"What is it—what is it?" she stammered; but he had found her lips at last and was drinking unconscious of everything but the joy they gave him.

She lingered a moment, caught in the same strong current; then she slipped from him and drew back a step or two, pale and troubled. Her look smote him with compunction, and he cried out, as if he saw her drowning in a dream: "You can't go, Matt! I'll never let you!"

"Go—go?" she stammered. "Must I go?"

The words went on sounding between them as though a torch of warning flew from hand to hand through a black landscape.

Ethan was overcome with shame at his lack of self-control in flinging the news at her so brutally. His head reeled and he had to support himself against the table. All the while he felt as if he were still kissing her, and yet dying of thirst for her lips.

"Ethan, what has happened? Is Zeena mad with me?"

Her cry steadied him, though it deepened his wrath and pity. "No, no," he assured her, "it's not that. But this new doctor has scared her about herself. You know she believes all they say the first time she sees them. And this one's told her she won't get well unless she lays up and don't do a thing about the house—not for months——"

He paused, his eyes wandering from her miserably. She stood silent a moment, drooping before him like a broken branch. She was so small and weak-looking that it wrung his heart; but suddenly she lifted her head and looked straight at him. "And she wants somebody handier in my place? Is that it?"

"That's what she says to-night."

"If she says it to-night she'll say it to-morrow."

Both bowed to the inexorable truth: they knew that Zeena never changed her mind, and that in her case a resolve once taken was equivalent to an act performed.

There was a long silence between them; then Mattie said in a low voice: "Don't be too sorry, Ethan."

"Oh, God—oh, God," he groaned. The glow of passion he had felt for her had melted to an aching tenderness. He saw her quick lids beating back the tears, and longed to take her in his arms and soothe her.

"You're letting your supper get cold," she admonished him with a pale gleam of gaiety.

"Oh, Matt—Matt—where'll you go to?"

Her lids sank and a tremor crossed her face. He saw that for the first time the thought of the future came to her distinctly. "I might get something to do over at Stamford," she faltered, as if knowing that he knew she had no hope.

He dropped back into his seat and hid his face in his hands. Despair seized him at the thought of her setting out alone to renew the weary quest for work. In the only place where she was known she was surrounded by indifference or animosity; and what chance had she, inexperienced and untrained, among the million bread-seekers of the cities? There came back to him miserable tales he had heard at Worcester, and the faces of girls whose lives had begun as hopefully as Mattie's. . . . It was not possible to think of such things without a revolt of his whole being. He sprang up suddenly.

"You can't go, Matt! I won't let you! She's always had her way, but I mean to have mine now——"

Mattie lifted her hand with a quick gesture, and he heard his wife's step behind him.

Zeena came into the room with her dragging down-at-the-heel step, and quietly took her accustomed seat between them.

"I felt a little mite better, and Dr. Buck says I ought to eat all I can to keep my strength up, even if I ain't got any appetite," she said in her flat whine, reaching across Mattie for the teapot. Her "good" dress had been replaced by the black calico and brown knitted shawl which formed her daily wear, and with them she had put on her usual face and manner. She poured out her tea, added a great deal of milk to it, helped herself largely to pie and pickles, and made the familiar gesture of adjusting her false teeth before she began to eat. The cat rubbed itself ingratiatingly against her, and she said "Good Pussy," stooped to stroke it and gave it a scrap of meat from her plate.

Ethan sat speechless, not pretending to eat, but Mattie nibbled valiantly at her food and asked Zeena one or two questions about her visit to Bettsbridge. Zeena answered in her every-day tone and, warming to the theme, regaled them with several vivid descriptions of intestinal disturbances among her friends and relatives. She looked straight at Mattie as she spoke, a faint smile deepening the vertical lines between her nose and chin.

When supper was over she rose from her seat and pressed her hand to the flat surface over the region of her heart. "That pie of yours always sets a mite heavy, Matt," she said, not ill-naturedly. She seldom abbreviated the girl's name, and when she did so it was always a sign of affability.

"I've a good mind to go and hunt up those stomach powders I got last year over in Springfield," she continued. "I ain't tried them for quite a while, and maybe they'll help the heartburn."

Mattie lifted her eyes. "Can't I get them for you, Zeena?" she ventured.

"No. They're in a place you don't know about," Zeena answered darkly, with one of her secret looks.

She went out of the kitchen and Mattie, rising, began to clear the dishes from the table. As she passed Ethan's chair their eyes met and clung together desolately. The warm still kitchen looked as peaceful as the night before. The cat had sprung to Zeena's rocking-chair, and the heat of the fire was beginning to draw out the faint sharp scent of the geraniums. Ethan dragged himself wearily to his feet.

"I'll go out and take a look around," he said, going toward the passage to get his lantern.

As he reached the door he met Zeena coming back into the room, her lips twitching with anger, a flush of excitement on her sallow face. The shawl had slipped from her shoulders and was dragging at her down-trodden heels, and in her hands she carried the fragments of the red glass pickle-dish.

"I'd like to know who done this," she said, looking sternly from Ethan to Mattie.

There was no answer, and she continued in a trembling voice: "I went to get those powders I'd put away in father's old spectacle-case, top of the china-closet, where I keep the things I set store by, so's folks sha'n't meddle with them—" Her voice broke, and two small tears hung on her lashless lids and ran slowly down her cheeks. "It takes the step-ladder to get at the top shelf, and I put Aunt Philura Maple's pickle-dish up there o' purpose when we was married, and it's never been down since, 'cept for the spring cleaning, and then I always lifted it with my own hands, so's 't shouldn't get broke." She laid the fragments reverently on the table. "I want to know who done this," she quavered.

At the challenge Ethan turned back into the room and faced her. "I can tell you, then. The cat done it."

"The *cat*?"

"That's what I said."

She looked at him hard, and then turned her eyes to Mattie, who was carrying the dish-pan to the table.

"I'd like to know how the cat got into my china-closet," she said.

"Chasin' mice, I guess," Ethan rejoiced. "There was a mouse round the kitchen all last evening."

Zeena continued to look from one to the other; then she emitted her small strange laugh. "I knew the cat was a smart cat," she said in a high voice, "but I didn't know he was smart enough to pick up the pieces of my pickle-dish and lay 'em edge to edge on the very shelf he knocked 'em off of."

Mattie suddenly drew her arms out of the steaming water. "It wasn't Ethan's fault, Zeena! The cat *did* break the dish; but I got it down from the china-closet, and I'm the one to blame for its getting broken."

Zeena stood beside the ruin of her treasure, stiffening into a stony image of resentment. "*You* got down my pickle-dish—what for?"

A bright flush flew to Mattie's cheeks. "I wanted to make the supper-table pretty," she said.

"You wanted to make the supper-table pretty; and you waited till my back was turned, and took the thing I set most store by of everything I've got, and wouldn't never use it, not even when the minister come to dinner, or Aunt Martha Pierce come over from Bettsbridge—" Zeena paused with a gasp, as if terrified by her own evocation of the sacrilege. "You're a bad girl, Mattie Silver, and I always known it. It's the way your father begun, and I was warned of it when I took you, and I tried to keep my things where you couldn't get at 'em—and now you've took from me the one I cared for most of all—" She broke off in a short spasm of sobs that passed and left her more than ever like a shape of stone.

"If I'd 'a' listened to folks, you'd 'a' gone before now, and this wouldn't 'a' happened," she said; and gathering up the bits of broken glass she went out of the room as if she carried a dead body . . .

CHAPTER VIII

When Ethan was called back to the farm by his father's illness his mother gave him, for his own use, a small room behind the untenanted "best parlour." Here he had nailed up shelves for his books, built himself a box-sofa out of boards and a mattress, laid out his papers on a kitchen-table, hung on the rough plaster wall an engraving of Abraham Lincoln and a calendar with "Thoughts from the Poets," and tried, with these meagre properties, to produce some likeness to the study of a "minister" who had been kind to him and lent him books when he was at Worcester. He still took refuge there in summer, but when Mattie came to live at the farm he had had to give her his stove, and consequently the room was uninhabitable for several months of the year.

To this retreat he descended as soon as the house was quiet, and Zeena's steady breathing from the bed had assured him that there was to be no sequel to the scene in the kitchen. After Zeena's departure he and Mattie had stood speechless, neither seeking to approach the other. Then the girl had returned to her task of clearing up the kitchen for the night and he had taken his lantern and gone on his usual round outside the house. The kitchen was empty when he came back to it; but his tobacco-pouch and pipe had been laid on the table, and under them was a scrap of paper torn from the back of a seedsman's catalogue, on which three words were written: "Don't trouble, Ethan."

Going into his cold dark "study" he placed the lantern on the table and, stooping to its light, read the message again and again. It was the first time that Mattie had ever written to him, and the possession of the paper gave him a strange new sense of her nearness; yet it deepened his anguish by reminding him that henceforth they would have no other way of communicating with each other. For the life of her smile, the warmth of her voice, only cold paper and dead words!

Confused motions of rebellion stormed in him. He was too young, too strong, too full of the sap of living, to submit so easily to the destruction of his hopes. Must he wear out all his years at the side of a bitter querulous woman? Other possibilities had been in him, possibilities sacrificed, one by one, to Zeena's narrow-mindedness and ignorance. And what good had come of it? She was a hundred times bitterer and more discontented than when he had married her: the one pleasure left her was to inflict pain on him. All the healthy instincts of self-defence rose up in him against such waste . . .

He bundled himself into his old coon-skin coat and lay down on the box-sofa to think. Under his cheek he felt a hard object with strange protuberances. It was a cushion which Zeena had made for him when they were engaged—the only piece of needlework he had ever seen her do. He flung it across the floor and propped his head against the wall . . .

He knew a case of a man over the mountain—a young fellow of about his own age—who had escaped from just such a life of misery by going West with the girl he cared for. His wife had divorced him, and he had married the girl and prospered. Ethan had seen the couple the summer before at Shadd's Falls, where they had come to visit relatives. They had a little girl with fair curls, who wore a gold locket and was dressed like a princess. The deserted wife had not done badly either. Her husband had given her the farm and she had managed to sell it, and with that and the alimony she had started a lunch-room at Bettsbridge and bloomed into activity and importance. Ethan was fired by the thought. Why should he not leave with Mattie the next day, instead of letting her go alone? He would hide his valise under the seat of the sleigh, and Zeena would suspect nothing till she went upstairs for her afternoon nap and found a letter on the bed . . .

His impulses were still near the surface, and he sprang up, re-lit the lantern, and sat down at the table. He rummaged in the drawer for a sheet of paper, found one, and began to write.

"Zeena, I've done all I could for you, and I don't see as it's been any use. I don't blame you, nor I don't blame myself. Maybe both of us will do better separate. I'm going to try my luck West, and you can sell the farm and mill, and keep the money——"

His pen paused on the word, which brought home to him the relentless conditions of his lot. If he gave the farm and mill to Zeena what would be left him to start his own life with? Once in the West he was sure of picking up work—he would not have feared to try his chance alone. But with Mattie depending on him the case was different. And what of Zeena's fate? Farm and mill were mortgaged to the limit of their value, and even if she found a purchaser—in itself an unlikely chance—it was doubtful if she could clear a thousand dollars on the sale. Meanwhile, how could she keep the farm going? It was only by incessant labour and personal supervision that Ethan drew a meagre living from his land, and his wife, even if she were in better health than she imagined, could never carry such a burden alone.

Well, she could go back to her people, then, and see what they would do for her. It was the fate she was forcing on Mattie—why not let her try it herself? By the time she had discovered his whereabouts, and brought suit for divorce, he would probably—wherever he was—be earning enough to pay her a sufficient alimony. And the alternative was to let Mattie go forth alone, with far less hope of ultimate provision . . .

He had scattered the contents of the table-drawer in his search for a sheet of paper, and as he took up his pen his eye fell on an old copy of the *Bettsbridge Eagle*. The advertising sheet was folded uppermost, and he read the seductive words: "Trips to the West: Reduced Rates."

He drew the lantern nearer and eagerly scanned the fares; then the paper fell from his hand and he pushed aside his unfinished letter. A moment ago he had wondered what he and Mattie were to live on when they reached the West; now he saw that he had not even the money to take her there. Borrowing was out of the question: six months before he had given his only security to raise funds for necessary repairs to the mill, and he knew that without security no one at Starkfield would lend him ten dollars. The inexorable facts closed in on him like prison-warders handcuffing a convict. There was no way out—none. He was a prisoner for life, and now his one ray of light was to be extinguished.

He crept back heavily to the sofa, stretching himself out with limbs so leaden that he felt as if they would never move again. Tears rose in his throat and slowly burned their way to his lids.

As he lay there, the window-pane that faced him, growing gradually lighter, inlaid upon the darkness a square of moon-suffused sky. A crooked tree-branch crossed it, a branch of the apple-tree under which, on summer evenings, he had sometimes found Mattie sitting when he came up from the mill. Slowly the rim of the rainy vapours caught fire and burnt away, and a pure moon swung into the blue. Ethan, rising on his elbow, watched the landscape whiten and shape itself under the sculpture of the moon. This was the night on which he was to have taken Mattie coasting, and there hung the lamp to light them! He looked out at the slopes bathed in lustre, the silver-edged darkness of the woods, the spectral purple of the hills against the sky, and it seemed as though all the beauty of the night had been poured out to mock his wretchedness . . .

He fell asleep, and when he woke the chill of the winter dawn was in the room. He felt cold and stiff and hungry, and ashamed of being hungry. He rubbed his eyes and went to the window. A red sun stood over the grey rim of the fields, behind trees that looked black and brittle. He said to himself: "This is Matt's last day," and tried to think what the place would be without her.

As he stood there he heard a step behind him and she entered.

"Oh, Ethan—were you here all night?"

She looked so small and pinched, in her poor dress, with the red scarf wound about her, and the cold light turning her paleness sallow, that Ethan stood before her without speaking.

"You must be frozen," she went on, fixing lustreless eyes on him.

He drew a step nearer. "How did you know I was here?"

"Because I heard you go down stairs again after I went to bed, and I listened all night, and you didn't come up."

All his tenderness rushed to his lips. He looked at her and said: "I'll come right along and make up the kitchen fire."

They went back to the kitchen, and he fetched the coal and kindlings and cleared out the stove for her, while she brought in the milk and the cold remains of the meat-pie. When warmth began to radiate from the stove, and the first ray of sunlight lay on the kitchen floor, Ethan's dark thoughts melted in the mellower air. The sight of Mattie going about her work as he had seen her on so many mornings made it seem impossible that she should ever cease to be a part of the scene. He said to himself that he had doubtless exaggerated the significance of Zeena's threats, and that she too, with the return of daylight, would come to a saner mood.

He went up to Mattie as she bent above the stove, and laid his hand on her arm. "I don't want you should trouble either," he said, looking down into her eyes with a smile.

She flushed up warmly and whispered back: "No, Ethan, I ain't going to trouble."

"I guess things'll straighten out," he added.

There was no answer but a quick throb of her lids, and he went on: "She ain't said anything this morning?"

"No. I haven't seen her yet."

"Don't you take any notice when you do."

With this injunction he left her and went out to the cow-barn. He saw Jotham Powell walking up the hill through the morning mist, and the familiar sight added to his growing conviction of security.

As the two men were clearing out the stalls Jotham rested on his pitch-fork to say: "Dan'l Byrne's goin' over to the Flats to-day noon, an' he c'd take Mattie's trunk along, and make it easier ridin' when I take her over in the sleigh."

Ethan looked at him blankly, and he continued: "Mis' Frome said the new girl'd be at the Flats at five, and I was to take Mattie then, so's 't she could ketch the six o'clock train for Stamford."

Ethan felt the blood drumming in his temples. He had to wait a moment before he could find voice to say: "Oh, it ain't so sure about Mattie's going——"

"That so?" said Jotham indifferently; and they went on with their work.

When they returned to the kitchen the two women were already at breakfast. Zeena had an air of unusual alertness and activity. She drank two cups of coffee and fed the cat with the scraps left in the pie-dish; then she rose from her seat and, walking over to the window, snipped two or three yellow leaves from the geraniums. "Aunt Martha's ain't got a faded leaf on 'em; but they pine away when they ain't cared for," she said reflectively. Then she turned to Jotham and asked: "What time'd you say Dan'l Byrne'd be along?"

The hired man threw a hesitating glance at Ethan. "Round about noon," he said.

Zeena turned to Mattie. "That trunk of yours is too heavy for the sleigh, and Dan'l Byrne'll be round to take it over to the Flats," she said.

"I'm much obliged to you, Zeena," said Mattie.

"I'd like to go over things with you first," Zeena continued in an unperturbed voice. "I know there's a huckabuck towel missing; and I can't take out what you done with that match-safe 't used to stand behind the stuffed owl in the parlour."

She went out, followed by Mattie, and when the men were alone Jotham said to his employer: "I guess I better let Dan'l come round, then."

Ethan finished his usual morning tasks about the house and barn; then he said to Jotham: "I'm going down to Starkfield. Tell them not to wait dinner."

The passion of rebellion had broken out in him again. That which had seemed incredible in the sober light of day had really come to pass, and he was to assist as a helpless spectator at Mattie's banishment. His manhood was humbled by the part he was compelled to play and by the thought of what Mattie must think of him. Confused impulses struggled in him as he strode along to the village. He had made up his mind to do something, but he did not know what it would be.

The early mist had vanished and the fields lay like a silver shield under the sun. It was one of the days when the glitter of winter shines through a pale haze of spring. Every yard of the road was alive with Mattie's presence, and there was hardly a branch against the sky or a tangle of brambles on the bank in which some bright shred of memory was not caught. Once, in the stillness, the call of a bird in a mountain ash was so like her laughter that his heart tightened and then grew large; and all these things made him see that something must be done at once.

Suddenly it occurred to him that Andrew Hale, who was a kind-hearted man, might be induced to reconsider his refusal and advance a small sum on the lumber if he were told that Zeena's ill-health made it necessary to hire a servant. Hale, after all, knew enough of Ethan's situation to make it possible for the latter to renew his appeal without too much loss of pride; and, moreover, how much did pride count in the ebullition of passions in his breast?

The more he considered his plan the more hopeful it seemed. If he could get Mrs. Hale's ear he felt certain of success, and with fifty dollars in his pocket nothing could keep him from Mattie . . .

His first object was to reach Starkfield before Hale had started for his work; he knew the carpenter had a job down the Corbury road and was likely to leave his house early. Ethan's long strides grew more rapid with the accelerated beat of his thoughts, and as he reached the foot of School House Hill he caught sight of Hale's sleigh in the distance. He hurried forward to meet it, but as it drew nearer he saw that it was driven by the carpenter's youngest boy and that the figure at his side, looking like a large upright cocoon in spectacles, was that of Mrs. Hale. Ethan signed to them to stop, and Mrs. Hale leaned forward, her pink wrinkles twinkling with benevolence.

"Mr. Hale? Why, yes, you'll find him down home now. He ain't going to his work this forenoon. He woke up with a touch o' lumbago, and I just made him put on one of old Dr. Kidder's plasters and set right up into the fire."

Beaming maternally on Ethan, she bent over to add: "I on'y just heard from Mr. Hale 'bout Zeena's going over to Bettsbridge to see that new doctor. I'm real sorry she's feeling so bad again! I hope he thinks he can do something for her. I don't know anybody round here's had more sickness than Zeena. I always tell Mr. Hale I don't know what she'd 'a' done if she hadn't 'a' had you to look after her; and I used to say the same thing 'bout your mother. You've had an awful mean time, Ethan Frome."

She gave him a last nod of sympathy while her son chirped to the horse; and Ethan, as she drove off, stood in the middle of the road and stared after the retreating sleigh.

It was a long time since any one had spoken to him as kindly as Mrs. Hale. Most people were either indifferent to his troubles, or disposed to think it natural that a young fellow of his age should have carried without repining the burden of three crippled lives. But Mrs. Hale had said, "You've had an awful mean time, Ethan Frome," and he felt less alone with his misery. If the Hales were sorry for him they would surely respond to his appeal . . .

He started down the road toward their house, but at the end of a few yards he pulled up sharply, the blood in his face. For the first time, in the light of the words he had just heard, he saw what he was about to do. He was planning to take advantage of the Hales' sympathy to obtain money from them on false pretences. That was a plain statement of the cloudy purpose which had driven him in headlong to Starkfield.

With the sudden perception of the point to which his madness had carried him, the madness fell and he saw his life before him as it was. He was a poor man, the husband of a sickly woman, whom his desertion would leave alone and destitute; and even if he had had the heart to desert her he could have done so only by deceiving two kindly people who had pitied him.

He turned and walked slowly back to the farm.

CHAPTER IX

At the kitchen door Daniel Byrne sat in his sleigh behind a big-boned grey who pawed the snow and swung his long head restlessly from side to side.

Ethan went into the kitchen and found his wife by the stove. Her head was wrapped in her shawl, and she was reading a book called "Kidney Troubles and Their Cure" on which he had had to pay extra postage only a few days before.

Zeena did not move or look up when he entered, and after a moment he asked: "Where's Mattie?"

Without lifting her eyes from the page she replied: "I presume she's getting down her trunk."

The blood rushed to his face. "Getting down her trunk—alone?"

"Jotham Powell's down in the wood-lot, and Dan'l Byrne says he darsn't leave that horse," she returned.

Her husband, without stopping to hear the end of the phrase, had left the kitchen and sprung up the stairs. The door of Mattie's room was shut, and he wavered a moment on the landing. "Matt," he said in a low voice; but there was no answer, and he put his hand on the door-knob.

He had never been in her room except once, in the early summer, when he had gone there to plaster up a leak in the eaves, but he remembered exactly how everything had looked: the red-and-white quilt on her narrow bed, the pretty pin-cushion on the chest of drawers, and over it the enlarged photograph of her mother, in an oxydized frame, with a bunch of dyed grasses at the back. Now these and all other tokens of her presence had vanished and the room looked as bare and comfortless as when Zeena had shown her into it on the day of her arrival. In the middle of the floor stood her trunk, and on the trunk she sat in her Sunday dress, her back turned to the door and her face in her hands. She had not heard Ethan's call because she was sobbing and she did not hear his step till he stood close behind her and laid his hands on her shoulders.

"Matt—oh, don't—oh, *Matt*!"

She started up, lifting her wet face to his. "Ethan—I thought I wasn't ever going to see you again!"

He took her in his arms, pressing her close, and with a trembling hand smoothed away the hair from her forehead.

"Not see me again? What do you mean?"

She sobbed out: "Jotham said you told him we wasn't to wait dinner for you, and I thought——"

"You thought I meant to cut it?" he finished for her grimly.

She clung to him without answering, and he laid his lips on her hair, which was soft yet springy, like certain mosses on warm slopes, and had the faint woody fragrance of fresh sawdust in the sun.

Through the door they heard Zeena's voice calling out from below: "Dan'l Byrne says you better hurry up if you want him to take that trunk."

They drew apart with stricken faces. Words of resistance rushed to Ethan's lips and died there. Mattie found her handkerchief and dried her eyes; then, bending down, she took hold of a handle of the trunk.

Ethan put her aside. "You let go, Matt," he ordered her.

She answered: "It takes two to coax it round the corner"; and submitting to this argument he grasped the other handle, and together they manœuvred the heavy trunk out to the landing.

"Now let go," he repeated; then he shouldered the trunk and carried it down the stairs and across the passage to the kitchen. Zeena, who had gone back to her seat by the stove, did not lift her head from her book as he passed. Mattie followed him out of the door and helped him to lift the trunk into the back of the sleigh. When it was in place they stood side by side on the door-step, watching Daniel Byrne plunge off behind his fidgety horse.

It seemed to Ethan that his heart was bound with cords which an unseen hand was tightening with every tick of the clock. Twice he opened his lips to speak to Mattie and found no breath. At length, as she turned to re-enter the house, he laid a detaining hand on her.

"I'm going to drive you over, Matt," he whispered.

She murmured back: "I think Zeena wants I should go with Jotham."

"I'm going to drive you over," he repeated; and she went into the kitchen without answering.

At dinner Ethan could not eat. If he lifted his eyes they rested on Zeena's pinched face, and the corners of her straight lips seemed to quiver away into a smile. She ate well, declaring that the mild weather made her feel better, and pressed a second helping of beans on Jotham Powell, whose wants she generally ignored.

Mattie, when the meal was over, went about her usual task of clearing the table and washing up the dishes. Zeena, after feeding the cat, had returned to her rocking-chair by the stove, and Jotham Powell, who always lingered last, reluctantly pushed back his chair and moved toward the door.

On the threshold he turned back to say to Ethan: "What time'll I come round for Mattie?"

Ethan was standing near the window, mechanically filling his pipe while he watched Mattie move to and fro. He answered: "You needn't come round; I'm going to drive her over myself."

He saw the rise of the colour in Mattie's averted cheek, and the quick lifting of Zeena's head.

"I want you should stay here this afternoon, Ethan," his wife said. "Jotham can drive Mattie over."

Mattie flung an imploring glance at him, but he repeated curtly: "I'm going to drive her over myself."

Zeena continued in the same even tone: "I wanted you should stay and fix up that stove in Mattie's room afore the girl gets here. It ain't been drawing right for nigh on a month now."

Ethan's voice rose indignantly. "If it was good enough for Mattie I guess it's good enough for a hired girl."

"That girl that's coming told me she was used to a house where they had a furnace," Zeena persisted with the same monotonous mildness.

"She'd better ha' stayed there then," he flung back at her; and turning to Mattie he added in a hard voice: "You be ready by three, Matt; I've got business at Corbury."

Jotham Powell had started for the barn, and Ethan strode down after him aflame with anger. The pulses in his temples throbbed and a fog was in his eyes. He went about his task without knowing what force directed him, or whose hands and feet were fulfilling its orders. It was not till he led out the sorrel and backed him between the shafts of the sleigh that he once more became conscious of what he was doing. As he passed the bridle over the horse's head, and wound the traces around the shafts, he remembered the day when he had made the same preparations in order to drive over and meet his wife's cousin at the Flats. It was little more than a year ago, on just such a soft afternoon, with a "feel" of spring in the air. The sorrel, turning the same big ringed eye on him, nuzzled the palm of his hand in the same way; and one by one all the days between rose up and stood before him . . .

He flung the bearskin into the sleigh, climbed to the seat, and drove up to the house. When he entered the kitchen it was empty, but Mattie's bag and shawl lay ready by the door. He went to the foot of the stairs and listened. No sound reached him from above, but presently he thought he heard some one moving about in his deserted study, and pushing open the door he saw Mattie, in her hat and jacket, standing with her back to him near the table.

She started at his approach and turning quickly, said: "Is it time?"

"What are you doing here, Matt?" he asked her.

She looked at him timidly. "I was just taking a look round—that's all," she answered, with a wavering smile.

They went back into the kitchen without speaking, and Ethan picked up her bag and shawl.

"Where's Zeena?" he asked.

"She went upstairs right after dinner. She said she had those shooting pains again, and didn't want to be disturbed."

"Didn't she say good-bye to you?"

"No. That was all she said."

Ethan, looking slowly about the kitchen, said to himself with a shudder that in a few hours he would be returning to it alone. Then the sense of unreality overcame him once more, and he could not bring himself to believe that Mattie stood there for the last time before him.

"Come on," he said almost gaily, opening the door and putting her bag into the sleigh. He sprang to his seat and bent over to tuck the rug about her as she slipped into the place at his side. "Now then, go 'long," he said, with a shake of the reins that sent the sorrel placidly jogging down the hill.

"We got lots of time for a good ride, Matt!" he cried, seeking her hand beneath the fur and pressing it in his. His face tingled and he felt dizzy, as if he had stopped in at the Starkfield saloon on a zero day for a drink.

At the gate, instead of making for Starkfield, he turned the sorrel to the right, up the Bettsbridge road. Mattie sat silent, giving no sign of surprise; but after a moment she said: "Are you going round by Shadow Pond?"

He laughed and answered: "I knew you'd know!"

She drew closer under the bearskin, so that, looking sideways around his coat-sleeve, he could just catch the tip of her nose and a blown brown wave of hair. They drove slowly up the road between fields glistening under the pale sun, and then bent to the right down a lane edged with spruce and larch. Ahead of them, a long way off, a range of hills stained by mottlings of black forest flowed away in round white curves against the sky. The lane passed into a pine-wood with boles reddening in the afternoon sun and delicate blue shadows on the snow. As they entered it the breeze fell and a warm stillness seemed to drop from the branches with the dropping needles. Here the snow was so pure that the tiny tracks of wood-animals had left on it intricate lace-like patterns, and the bluish cones caught in its surface stood out like ornaments of bronze.

Ethan drove on in silence till they reached a part of the wood where the pines were more widely spaced, then he drew up and helped Mattie to get out of the sleigh. They passed between the aromatic trunks, the snow breaking crisply under their feet, till they came to a small sheet of water with steep wooded sides. Across its frozen surface, from the farther bank, a single hill rising against the western sun threw the long conical shadow which gave the lake its name. It was a shy secret spot, full of the same dumb melancholy that Ethan felt in his heart.

He looked up and down the little pebbly beach till his eye lit on a fallen tree-trunk half submerged in snow.

"There's where we sat at the picnic," he reminded her.

The entertainment of which he spoke was one of the few that they had taken part in together: a "church picnic" which, on a long afternoon of the preceding summer, had filled the retired place with merry-making. Mattie had begged him to go with her but he had refused. Then, toward sunset, coming down from the mountain where he had been felling timber, he had been caught by some strayed revellers and drawn into the group by the lake, where Mattie, encircled by facetious youths, and bright as a blackberry under her spreading hat, was brewing coffee over a gipsy fire. He remembered the shyness he had felt at approaching her in his uncouth clothes, and then the lighting up of her face, and the way she had broken through the group to come to him with a cup in her hand. They had sat for a few minutes on the fallen log by the pond, and she had missed her gold locket, and set the young men searching for it; and it was Ethan who had spied it in the moss. . . . That was all; but all their intercourse had been made up of just such inarticulate flashes, when they seemed to come suddenly upon happiness as if they had surprised a butterfly in the winter woods . . .

"It was right there I found your locket," he said, pushing his foot into a dense tuft of blueberry bushes.

"I never saw anybody with such sharp eyes!" she answered.

She sat down on the tree-trunk in the sun and he sat down beside her.

"You were as pretty as a picture in that pink hat," he said.

She laughed with pleasure. "Oh, I guess it was the hat!" she rejoined."

They had never before avowed their inclination so openly, and Ethan, for a moment, had the illusion that he was a free man, wooing the girl he meant to marry. He looked at her hair and longed to touch it again, and to tell her that it smelt of the woods; but he had never learned to say such things.

Suddenly she rose to her feet and said: "We mustn't stay here any longer."

He continued to gaze at her vaguely, only half-roused from his dream. "There's plenty of time," he answered.

They stood looking at each other as if the eyes of each were straining to absorb and hold fast the other's image. There were things he had to say to her before they parted, but he could not say them in that place of summer memories, and he turned and followed her in silence to the sleigh. As they drove away the sun sank behind the hill and the pine-boles turned from red to grey.

By a devious track between the fields they wound back to the Starkfield road. Under the open sky the light was still clear, with a reflection of cold red on the eastern hills. The clumps of trees in the snow seemed to draw together in ruffled lumps, like birds with their heads under their wings; and the sky, as it paled, rose higher, leaving the earth more alone.

As they turned into the Starkfield road Ethan said: "Matt, what do you mean to do?"

She did not answer at once, but at length she said: "I'll try to get a place in a store."

"You know you can't do it. The bad air and the standing all day nearly killed you before."

"I'm a lot stronger than I was before I came to Starkfield."

"And now you're going to throw away all the good it's done you!"

There seemed to be no answer to this, and again they drove on for a while without speaking. With every yard of the way some spot where they had stood, and laughed together or been silent, clutched at Ethan and dragged him back.

"Isn't there any of your father's folks could help you?"

"There isn't any of 'em I'd ask."

He lowered his voice to say: "You know there's nothing I wouldn't do for you if I could."

"I know there isn't."

"But I can't——"

She was silent, but he felt a slight tremor in the shoulder against his.

"Oh, Matt," he broke out, "if I could ha' gone with you now I'd ha' done it——"

She turned to him, pulling a scrap of paper from her breast. "Ethan—I found this," she stammered. Even in the failing light he saw it was the letter to his wife that he had begun the night before and forgotten to destroy. Through his astonishment there ran a fierce thrill of joy. "Matt—" he cried; "if I could ha' done it, would you?"

"Oh, Ethan, Ethan—what's the use?" With a sudden movement she tore the letter in shreds and sent them fluttering off into the snow.

"Tell me, Matt! Tell me!" he adjured her.

She was silent for a moment; then she said, in such a low tone that he had to stoop his head to hear her: "I used to think of it sometimes, summer nights, when the moon was so bright I couldn't sleep."

His heart reeled with the sweetness of it. "As long ago as that?"

She answered, as if the date had long been fixed for her: "The first time was at Shadow Pond."

"Was that why you gave me my coffee before the others?"

"I don't know. Did I? I was dreadfully put out when you wouldn't go to the picnic with me; and then, when I saw you coming down the road, I thought maybe you'd gone home that way o' purpose; and that made me glad."

They were silent again. They had reached the point where the road dipped to the hollow by Ethan's mill and as they descended the darkness descended with them, dropping down like a black veil from the heavy hemlock boughs.

"I'm tied hand and foot, Matt. There isn't a thing I can do," he began again.

"You must write to me sometimes, Ethan."

"Oh, what good'll writing do? I want to put my hand out and touch you. I want to do for you and care for you. I want to be there when you're sick and when you're lonesome."

"You mustn't think but what I'll do all right."

"You won't need me, you mean? I suppose you'll marry!"

"Oh, Ethan!" she cried.

"I don't know how it is you make me feel, Matt. I'd a'most rather have you dead than that!"

"Oh, I wish I was, I wish I was!" she sobbed.

The sound of her weeping shook him out of his dark anger, and he felt ashamed.

"Don't let's talk that way," he whispered.

"Why shouldn't we, when it's true? I've been wishing it every minute of the day."

"Matt! You be quiet! Don't you say it."

"There's never anybody been good to me but you."

"Don't say that either, when I can't lift a hand for you!"

"Yes; but it's true just the same."

They had reached the top of School House Hill and Starkfield lay below them in the twilight. A cutter, mounting the road from the village, passed them by in a joyous flutter of bells, and they straightened themselves and looked ahead with rigid faces. Along the main street lights had begun to shine from the house-fronts and stray figures were turning in here and there at the gates. Ethan, with a touch of his whip, roused the sorrel to a languid trot.

As they drew near the end of the village the cries of children reached them, and they saw a knot of boys, with sleds behind them, scattering across the open space before the church.

"I guess this'll be their last coast for a day or two," Ethan said, looking up at the mild sky.

Mattie was silent, and he added: "We were to have gone down last night."

Still she did not speak and, prompted by an obscure desire to help himself and her through their miserable last hour, he went on discursively: "Ain't it funny we haven't been down together but just that once last winter?"

She answered: "It wasn't often I got down to the village."

"That's so," he said.

They had reached the crest of the Corbury road, and between the indistinct white glimmer of the church and the black curtain of the Varnum spruces the slope stretched away below them without a sled on its length. Some erratic impulse prompted Ethan to say: "How'd you like me to take you down now?"

She forced a laugh. "Why, there isn't time!"

"There's all the time we want. Come along!" His one desire now was to postpone the moment of turning the sorrel toward the Flats.

"But the girl," she faltered. "The girl'll be waiting at the station."

"Well, let her wait. You'd have to if she didn't. Come!"

The note of authority in his voice seemed to subdue her, and when he had jumped from the sleigh she let him help her out, saying only, with a vague feint of reluctance: "But there isn't a sled round anywheres."

"Yes, there is! Right over there under the spruces."

He threw the bearskin over the sorrel, who stood passively by the roadside, hanging a meditative head. Then he caught Mattie's hand and drew her after him toward the sled.

She seated herself obediently and he took his place behind her, so close that her hair brushed his face. "All right, Matt?" he called out, as if the width of the road had been between them.

She turned her head to say: "It's dreadfully dark. Are you sure you can see?"

He laughed contemptuously: "I could go down this coast with my eyes tied!" and she laughed with him, as if she liked his audacity. Nevertheless he sat still a moment, straining his eyes down the long hill, for it was the most confusing hour of the evening, the hour when the last clearness from the upper sky is merged with the rising night in a blur that disguises landmarks and falsifies distances.

"Now!" he cried.

The sled started with a bound, and they flew on through the dusk, gathering smoothness and speed as they went, with the hollow night opening out below them and the air singing by like an organ. Mattie sat perfectly still, but as they reached the bend at the foot of the hill, where the big elm thrust out a deadly elbow, he fancied that she shrank a little closer.

"Don't be scared, Matt!" he cried exultantly, as they spun safely past it and flew down the second slope; and when they reached the level ground beyond, and the speed of the sled began to slacken, he heard her give a little laugh of glee.

They sprang off and started to walk back up the hill. Ethan dragged the sled with one hand and passed the other through Mattie's arm.

"Were you scared I'd run you into the elm?" he asked with a boyish laugh.

"I told you I was never scared with you," she answered.

The strange exaltation of his mood had brought on one of his rare fits of boastfulness. "It *is* a tricky place, though. The least swerve, and we'd never ha' come up again. But I can measure distances to a hair's-breadth—always could."

She murmured: "I always say you've got the surest eye . . ."

Deep silence had fallen with the starless dusk, and they leaned on each other without speaking; but at every step of their climb Ethan said to himself: "It's the last time we'll ever walk together."

They mounted slowly to the top of the hill. When they were abreast of the church he stooped his head to her to ask: "Are you tired?" and she answered, breathing quickly: "It was splendid!"

With a pressure of his arm he guided her toward the Norway spruces. "I guess this sled must be Ned Hale's.

Anyhow I'll leave it where I found it." He drew the sled up to the Varnum gate and rested it against the fence. As he raised himself he suddenly felt Mattie close to him among the shadows.

"Is this where Ned and Ruth kissed each other?" she whispered breathlessly, and flung her arms about him. Her lips, groping for his, swept over his face, and he held her fast in a rapture of surprise.

"Good-bye—good-bye," she stammered, and kissed him again.

"Oh, Matt, I can't let you go!" broke from him in the same old cry.

She freed herself from his hold and he heard her sobbing. "Oh, I can't go either!" she wailed.

"Matt! What'll we do? What'll we do?"

They clung to each other's hands like children, and her body shook with desperate sobs.

Through the stillness they heard the church clock striking five.

"Oh, Ethan, it's time!" she cried.

He drew her back to him. "Time for what? You don't suppose I'm going to leave you now?"

"If I missed my train where'd I go?"

"Where are you going if you catch it?"

She stood silent, her hands lying cold and relaxed in his.

"What's the good of either of us going anywheres without the other one now?" he said.

She remained motionless, as if she had not heard him. Then she snatched her hands from his, threw her arms about his neck, and pressed a sudden drenched cheek against his face. "Ethan! Ethan! I want you to take me down again!"

"Down where?"

"The coast. Right off," she panted. "So 't we'll never come up any more."

"Matt! What on earth do you mean?"

She put her lips close against his ear to say: "Right into the big elm. You said you could. So 't we'd never have to leave each other any more."

"Why, what are you talking of? You're crazy!"

"I'm not crazy; but I will be if I leave you."

"Oh, Matt, Matt—" he groaned.

She tightened her fierce hold about his neck. Her face lay close to his face.

"Ethan, where'll I go if I leave you? I don't know how to get along alone. You said so yourself just now. Nobody but you was ever good to me. And there'll be that strange girl in the house . . . and she'll sleep in my bed, where I used to lay nights and listen to hear you come up the stairs . . ."

The words were like fragments torn from his heart. With them came the hated vision of the house he was going back to—of the stairs he would have to go up every night, of the woman who would wait for him there. And the sweetness of Mattie's avowal, the wild wonder of knowing at last that all that had happened to him had happened to her too, made the other vision more abhorrent, the other life more intolerable to return to . . .

Her pleadings still came to him between short sobs, but he no longer heard what she was saying. Her hat had slipped back and he was stroking her hair. He wanted to get the feeling of it into his hand, so that it would sleep there like a seed in winter. Once he found her mouth again, and they seemed to be by the pond together in the burning August sun. But his cheek touched hers, and it was cold and full of weeping, and he saw the road to the Flats under the night and heard the whistle of the train up the line.

The spruces swathed them in blackness and silence. They might have been in their coffins underground. He said to himself: "Perhaps it'll feel like this . . ." and then again: "After this I sha'n't feel anything . . ."

Suddenly he heard the old sorrel whinny across the road, and thought: "He's wondering why he doesn't get his supper . . ."

"Come," Mattie whispered, tugging at his hand.

Her sombre violence constrained him: she seemed the embodied instrument of fate. He pulled the sled out, blinking like a night-bird as he passed from the shade of the spruces into the transparent dusk of the open. The slope below them was deserted. All Starkfield was at supper, and not a figure crossed the open space before the church. The sky, swollen with the clouds that announce a thaw, hung as low as before a summer storm. He strained his eyes through the dimness, and they seemed less keen, less capable than usual.

He took his seat on the sled and Mattie instantly placed herself in front of him. Her hat had fallen into the snow and his lips were in her hair. He stretched out his legs, drove his heels into the road to keep the sled from slipping forward, and bent her head back between his hands. Then suddenly he sprang up again.

"Get up," he ordered her.

It was the tone she always heeded, but she cowered down in her seat, repeating vehemently: "No, no, no!"

"Get up!"

"Why?"

"I want to sit in front."

"No, no! How can you steer in front?"

"I don't have to. We'll follow the track."

They spoke in smothered whispers, as though the night were listening.

"Get up! Get up!" he urged her; but she kept on repeating: "Why do you want to sit in front?"

"Because I—because I want to feel you holding me," he stammered, and dragged her to her feet.

The answer seemed to satisfy her, or else she yielded to the power of his voice. He bent down, feeling in the obscurity for the glassy slide worn by preceding coasters, and placed the runners carefully between its edges. She waited while he seated himself with crossed legs in the front of the sled; then she crouched quickly down at his back and clasped her arms about him. Her breath in his neck set him shuddering again, and he almost sprang from his seat. But in a flash he remembered the alternative. She was right: this was better than parting. He leaned back and drew her mouth to his . . .

Just as they started he heard the sorrel's whinny again, and the familiar wistful call, and all the confused images it brought with it, went with him down the first reach of the road. Half-way down there was a sudden drop, then a rise, and after that another long delirious descent. As they took wing for this it seemed to him that they were flying indeed, flying far up into the cloudy night, with Starkfield immeasurably below them, falling away like a speck in space . . . Then the big elm shot up ahead, lying in wait for them at the bend of the road, and he said between his teeth: "We can fetch it; I know we can fetch it——"

As they flew toward the tree Mattie pressed her arms tighter, and her blood seemed to be in his veins. Once or twice the sled swerved a little under them. He slanted his body to keep it headed for the elm, repeating to himself again and again: "I know we can fetch it"; and little phrases she had spoken ran through his head and danced before him on the air. The big tree loomed bigger and closer, and as they bore down on it he thought: "It's waiting for us: it seems to know." But suddenly his wife's face, with twisted monstrous lineaments, thrust itself between him and his goal, and he made an instinctive movement to brush it aside. The sled swerved in response, but he righted it again, kept it straight, and drove down on the black projecting mass. There was a last instant when the air shot past him like millions of fiery wires; and then the elm . . .

The sky was still thick, but looking straight up he saw a single star, and tried vaguely to reckon whether it were Sirius, or—or— The effort tired him too much, and he closed his heavy lids and thought that he would sleep . . . The stillness was so profound that he heard a little animal twittering somewhere near by under the snow. It made a small frightened *cheep* like a field mouse, and he wondered languidly if it were hurt. Then he understood that it must be in pain: pain so excruciating that he seemed, mysteriously, to feel it shooting through his own body. He tried in vain to roll over in the direction of the sound, and stretched his left arm out across the snow. And now it was as though he felt rather than heard the twittering; it seemed to be under his palm, which rested on something soft and springy. The thought of the animal's suffering was intolerable to him and he struggled to raise himself, and could not because a rock, or some huge mass, seemed to be lying on him. But he continued to finger about cautiously with his left hand, thinking he might get hold of the little creature and help it; and all at once he knew that the soft thing he had touched was Mattie's hair and that his hand was on her face.

He dragged himself to his knees, the monstrous load on him moving with him as he moved, and his hand went over and over her face, and he felt that the twittering came from her lips . . .

He got his face down close to hers, with his ear to her mouth, and in the darkness he saw her eyes open and heard her say his name.

"Oh, Matt, I thought we'd fetched it," he moaned; and far off, up the hill, he heard the sorrel whinny, and thought: "I ought to be getting him his feed . . ."

The querulous drone ceased as I entered Frome's kitchen, and of the two women sitting there I could not tell which had been the speaker.

One of them, on my appearing, raised her tall bony figure from her seat, not as if to welcome me—for she threw me no more than a brief glance of surprise—but simply to set about preparing the meal which Frome's absence had delayed. A slatternly calico wrapper hung from her shoulders and the wisps of her thin grey hair were drawn away from a high forehead and fastened at the back by a broken comb. She had pale opaque eyes which revealed nothing and reflected nothing, and her narrow lips were of the same sallow colour as her face.

The other woman was much smaller and slighter. She sat huddled in an arm-chair near the stove, and when I came in she turned her head quickly toward me, without the least corresponding movement of her body. Her hair was as grey as her companion's, her face as bloodless and shrivelled, but amber-tinted, with swarthy shadows sharpening the nose and hollowing the temples. Under her shapeless dress her body kept its limp immobility, and her dark eyes had the bright witch-like stare that disease of the spine sometimes gives.

Even for that part of the country the kitchen was a poor-looking place. With the exception of the dark-eyed woman's chair, which looked like a soiled relic of luxury bought at a country auction, the furniture was of the roughest kind. Three coarse china plates and a broken-nosed milk-jug had been set on a greasy table scored with knife-cuts, and a couple of straw-bottomed chairs and a kitchen dresser of unpainted pine stood meagrely against the plaster walls.

"My, it's cold here! The fire must be 'most out," Frome said, glancing about him apologetically as he followed me in.

The tall woman, who had moved away from us toward the dresser, took no notice; but the other, from her cushioned niche, answered complainingly, in a high thin voice. "It's on'y just been made up this very minute. Zeena fell asleep and slep' ever so long, and I thought I'd be frozen stiff before I could wake her up and get her to 'tend to it."

I knew then that it was she who had been speaking when we entered.

Her companion, who was just coming back to the table with the remains of a cold mince-pie in a battered pie-dish, set down her unappetising burden without appearing to hear the accusation brought against her.

Frome stood hesitatingly before her as she advanced; then he looked at me and said: "This is my wife, Mis' Frome." After another interval he added, turning toward the figure in the arm-chair: "And this is Miss Mattie Silver . . ."

Mrs. Hale, tender soul, had pictured me as lost in the Flats and buried under a snow-drift; and so lively was her satisfaction on seeing me safely restored to her the next morning that I felt my peril had caused me to advance several degrees in her favour.

Great was her amazement, and that of old Mrs. Varnum,

on learning that Ethan Frome's old horse had carried me to and from Corbury Junction through the worst blizzard of the winter; greater still their surprise when they heard that his master had taken me in for the night.

Beneath their wondering exclamations I felt a secret curiosity to know what impressions I had received from my night in the Frome household, and divined that the best way of breaking down their reserve was to let them try to penetrate mine. I therefore confined myself to saying, in a matter-of-fact tone, that I had been received with great kindness, and that Frome had made a bed for me in a room on the ground-floor which seemed in happier days to have been fitted up as a kind of writing-room or study.

"Well," Mrs. Hale mused, "in such a storm I suppose he felt he couldn't do less than take you in—but I guess it went hard with Ethan. I don't believe but what you're the only stranger has set foot in that house for over twenty years. He's that proud he don't even like his oldest friends to go there; and I don't know as any do, any more, except myself and the doctor . . ."

"You still go there, Mrs. Hale?" I ventured.

"I used to go a good deal after the accident, when I was first married; but after awhile I got to think it made 'em feel worse to see us. And then one thing and another came, and my own troubles . . . But I generally make out to drive over there round about New Year's, and once in the summer. Only I always try to pick a day when Ethan's off somewheres. It's bad enough to see the two women sitting there—but *his* face, when he looks round that bare place, just kills me . . . You see, I can look back and call it up in his mother's day, before their troubles."

Old Mrs. Varnum, by this time, had gone up to bed, and her daughter and I were sitting alone, after supper, in the austere seclusion of the horse-hair parlour. Mrs. Hale glanced at me tentatively, as though trying to see how much footing my conjectures gave her; and I guessed that if she had kept silence till now it was because she had been waiting, through all the years, for some one who should see what she alone had seen.

I waited to let her trust in me gather strength before I

said: "Yes, it's pretty bad, seeing all three of them there together."

She drew her mild brows into a frown of pain. "It was just awful from the beginning. I was here in the house when they were carried up—they laid Mattie Silver in the room you're in. She and I were great friends, and she was to have been my bridesmaid in the spring . . . When she came to I went up to her and stayed all night. They gave her things to quiet her, and she didn't know much till to'rd morning, and then all of a sudden she woke up just like herself, and looked straight at me out of her big eyes, and said . . . Oh, I don't know why I'm telling you all this," Mrs. Hale broke off, crying.

She took off her spectacles, wiped the moisture from them, and put them on again with an unsteady hand. "It got about the next day," she went on, "that Zeena Frome had sent Mattie off in a hurry because she had a hired girl coming, and the folks here could never rightly tell what she and Ethan were doing that night coasting, when they'd ought to have been on their way to the Flats to ketch the train . . . I never knew myself what Zeena thought—I don't to this day. Nobody knows Zeena's thoughts. Anyhow, when she heard o' the accident she came right in and stayed with Ethan over to the minister's, where they'd carried him. And as soon as the doctors said that Mattie could be moved, Zeena sent for her and took her back to the farm."

"And there she's been ever since?"

Mrs. Hale answered simply: "There was nowhere else for her to go;" and my heart tightened at the thought of the hard compulsions of the poor.

"Yes, there she's been," Mrs. Hale continued, "and Zeena's done for her, and done for Ethan, as good as she could. It was a miracle, considering how sick she was—but she seemed to be raised right up just when the call came to her. Not as she's ever given up doctoring, and she's had sick spells right along; but she's had the strength given her to care for those two for over twenty years, and before the accident came she thought she couldn't even care for herself."

Mrs. Hale paused a moment, and I remained silent,

plunged in the vision of what her words evoked. "It's horrible for them all," I murmured.

"Yes: it's pretty bad. And they ain't any of 'em easy people either. Mattie *was,* before the accident; I never knew a sweeter nature. But she's suffered too much—that's what I always say when folks tell me how she's soured. And Zeena, she was always cranky. Not but what she bears with Mattie wonderful—I've seen that myself. But sometimes the two of them get going at each other, and then Ethan's face'd break your heart . . . When I see that, I think it's *him* that suffers most . . . anyhow it ain't Zeena, because she ain't got the time . . . It's a pity, though," Mrs. Hale ended, sighing, "that they're all shut up there'n that one kitchen. In the summertime, on pleasant days, they move Mattie into the parlour, or out in the door-yard, and that makes it easier . . . but winters there's the fires to be thought of; and there ain't a dime to spare up at the Fromes'."

Mrs. Hale drew a deep breath, as though her memory were eased of its long burden, and she had no more to say; but suddenly an impulse of complete avowal seized her.

She took off her spectacles again, leaned toward me across the bead-work table-cover, and went on with lowered voice: "There was one day, about a week after the accident, when they all thought Mattie couldn't live. Well, I say it's a pity she *did.* I said it right out to our minister once, and he was shocked at me. Only he wasn't with me that morning when she first came to . . . And I say, if she'd ha' died, Ethan might ha' lived; and the way they are now, I don't see's there's much difference between the Fromes up at the farm and the Fromes down in the graveyard; 'cept that down there they're all quiet, and the women have got to hold their tongues."

O PIONEERS!

by Willa Cather

To the memory of
SARAH ORNE JEWETT
in whose beautiful and delicate work
there is the perfection
that endures

"Those fields, colored by various grain!"

MICKIEWICZ

PRAIRIE SPRING

Evening and the flat land,
Rich and sombre and always silent;
The miles of fresh-plowed soil,
Heavy and black, full of strength and harshness;
The growing wheat, the growing weeds,
The toiling horses, the tired men;
The long empty roads,
Sullen fires of sunset, fading,
The eternal, unresponsive sky.
Against all this, Youth.
Flaming like the wild roses,
Singing like the larks over the plowed fields,
Flashing like a star out of the twilight;
Youth with its insupportable sweetness,
Its fierce necessity,
Its sharp desire,
Singing and singing,
Out of the lips of silence,
Out of the earthy dusk.

PART I

•

The Wild Land

CHAPTER I

One January day, thirty years ago, the little town of Hanover, anchored on a windy Nebraska tableland, was trying not to be blown away. A mist of fine snowflakes was curling and eddying about the cluster of low drab buildings huddled on the gray prairie, under a gray sky. The dwelling-houses were set about haphazard on the tough prairie sod; some of them looked as if they had been moved in overnight, and others as if they were straying off by themselves, headed straight for the open plain. None of them had any appearance of permanence, and the howling wind blew under them as well as over them. The main street was a deeply rutted road, now frozen hard, which ran from the squat red railway station and the grain "elevator" at the north end of the town to the lumber yard and the horse pond at the south end. On either side of this road straggled two uneven rows of wooden buildings; the general merchandise stores, the two banks, the drug store, the feed store, the saloon, the post-office. The board sidewalks were gray with trampled snow, but at two o'clock in the afternoon the shopkeepers, having come back from dinner, were keeping well behind their frosty windows. The children were all in school, and there was nobody abroad in the streets but a few rough-looking countrymen in coarse overcoats, with their long caps pulled down to their noses. Some of them had brought their wives to town, and now and then a red or a plaid shawl flashed out of one store into the shelter of another. At the hitch-bars along the street a few heavy work-horses, harnessed to farm wagons, shivered under their blankets. About the station everything was quiet, for there would not be another train in until night.

On the sidewalk in front of one of the stores sat a little Swede boy, crying bitterly. He was about five years old. His black cloth coat was much too big for him and made him look like a little old man. His shrunken brown flannel dress had been washed many times and left a long stretch of stocking between the hem of his skirt and the tops of his clumsy, copper-toed shoes. His cap was pulled down over his ears; his nose and his chubby cheeks were chapped and red with cold. He cried quietly, and the few people who hurried by did not notice him. He was afraid to stop any one, afraid to go into the store and ask for help, so he sat wringing his long sleeves and looking up a telegraph pole beside him, whimpering, "My kitten, oh, my kitten! Her will fweeze!" At the top of the pole crouched a shivering gray kitten, mewing faintly and clinging desperately to the wood with her claws. The boy had been left at the store while his sister went to the doctor's office, and in her absence a dog had chased his kitten up the pole. The little creature had never been so high before, and she was too frightened to move. Her master was sunk in despair. He was a little country boy, and this village was to him a very strange and perplexing place, where people wore fine clothes and had hard hearts. He always felt shy and awkward here, and wanted to hide behind things for fear some one might laugh at him. Just now, he was too unhappy to care who laughed. At last he seemed to see a ray of hope: his sister was coming, and he got up and ran toward her in his heavy shoes.

His sister was a tall, strong girl, and she walked rapidly and resolutely, as if she knew exactly where she was going and what she was going to do next. She wore a man's long ulster (not as if it were an affliction, but as if it were very comfortable and belonged to her; carried it like a young soldier), and a round plush cap, tied down with a thick veil. She had a serious, thoughtful face, and her clear, deep blue eyes were fixed intently on the distance, without seeming to see anything, as if she were in trouble. She did not notice the little boy until he pulled her by the coat. Then she stopped short and stooped down to wipe his wet face.

"Why, Emil! I told you to stay in the store and not to come out. What is the matter with you?"

"My kitten, sister, my kitten! A man put her out, and a dog chased her up there." His forefinger, projecting from the sleeve of his coat, pointed up to the wretched little creature on the pole.

"Oh, Emil! Didn't I tell you she'd get us into trouble of some kind, if you brought her? What made you tease me so? But there, I ought to have known better myself." She went to the foot of the pole and held out her arms, crying, "Kitty, kitty, kitty," but the kitten only mewed and faintly waved its tail. Alexandra turned away decidedly. "No, she won't come down. Somebody will have to go up after her. I saw the Linstrums' wagon in town. I'll go and see if I can find Carl. Maybe he can do something. Only you must stop crying, or I won't go a step. Where's your comforter? Did you leave it in the store? Never mind. Hold still, till I put this on you."

She unwound the brown veil from her head and tied it about his throat. A shabby little traveling man, who was just then coming out of the store on his way to the saloon, stopped and gazed stupidly at the shining mass of hair she bared when she took off her veil; two thick braids, pinned about her head in the German way, with a fringe of reddish-yellow curls blowing out from under her cap. He took his cigar out of his mouth and held the wet end between the fingers of his woolen glove. "My God, girl, what a head of hair!" he exclaimed, quite innocently and foolishly. She stabbed him with a glance of Amazonian fierceness and drew in her lower lip—most unnecessary severity. It gave the little clothing drummer such a start that he actually let his cigar fall to the sidewalk and went off weakly in the teeth of the wind to the saloon. His hand was still unsteady when he took his glass from the bartender. His feeble flirtatious instincts had been crushed before, but never so mercilessly. He felt cheap and ill-used, as if some one had taken advantage of him. When a drummer had been knocking about in little drab towns and crawling across the wintry country in dirty smoking-cars, was he to be blamed if, when he chanced upon a fine human creature, he suddenly wished himself more of a man?

While the little drummer was drinking to recover his nerve, Alexandra hurried to the drug store as the most likely place to find Carl Linstrum. There he was, turning over a portfolio of chromo "studies" which the druggist sold to the Hanover women who did china-painting. Alexandra explained her predicament, and the boy followed her to the corner, where Emil still sat by the pole.

"I'll have to go up after her, Alexandra. I think at the depot they have some spikes I can strap on my feet. Wait a minute." Carl thrust his hands into his pockets, lowered his head, and darted up the street against the north wind. He was a tall boy of fifteen, slight and narrow-chested. When he came back with the spikes, Alexandra asked him what he had done with his overcoat.

"I left it in the drug store. I couldn't climb in it, anyhow. Catch me if I fall, Emil," he called back as he began his ascent. Alexandra watched him anxiously; the cold was bitter enough on the ground. The kitten would not budge an inch. Carl had to go to the very top of the pole, and then had some difficulty in tearing her from her hold. When he reached the ground, he handed the cat to her tearful little master. "Now go into the store with her, Emil, and get warm." He opened the door for the child. "Wait a minute, Alexandra. Why can't I drive for you as far as our place? It's getting colder every minute. Have you seen the doctor?"

"Yes. He is coming over to-morrow. But he says father can't get better; can't get well." The girl's lip trembled. She looked fixedly up the bleak street as if she were gathering her strength to face something, as if she were trying with all her might to grasp a situation which, no matter how painful, must be met and dealt with somehow. The wind flapped the skirts of her heavy coat about her.

Carl did not say anything, but she felt his sympathy. He, too, was lonely. He was a thin, frail boy, with brooding dark eyes, very quiet in all his movements. There was a delicate pallor in his thin face, and his mouth was too sensitive for a boy's. The lips had already a little curl of bitterness and skepticism. The two friends stood for a few moments on the windy street corner, not speaking a word, as two travelers, who have lost their way, sometimes stand and admit their perplexity in silence. When Carl turned away he said, "I'll see to your team." Alexandra went into the store to have her purchases packed in the egg-boxes, and to get warm before she set out on her long cold drive.

When she looked for Emil, she found him sitting on a step of the staircase that led up to the clothing and carpet department. He was playing with a little Bohemian girl, Marie Tovesky, who was tying her handkerchief over the kitten's head for a bonnet. Marie was a stranger in the country, having come from Omaha with her mother to visit her uncle, Joe Tovesky. She was a dark child, with brown curly hair, like a brunette doll's, a coaxing little red mouth, and round, yellow-brown eyes. Every one noticed her eyes; the brown iris had golden glints that made them look like gold-stone, or, in softer lights, like that Colorado mineral called tiger-eye.

The country children thereabouts wore their dresses to their shoe-tops, but this city child was dressed in what was then called the "Kate Greenaway" manner, and her red cashmere frock, gathered full from the yoke, came almost to the floor. This, with her poke bonnet, gave her the look of a quaint little woman. She had a white fur tippet about her neck and made no fussy objections when Emil fingered it admiringly. Alexandra had not the heart to take him away from so pretty a playfellow, and she let them tease the kitten together until Joe Tovesky came in noisily and picked up his little niece, setting her on his shoulder for every one to see. His children were all boys, and he adored this little creature. His cronies formed a circle about him, admiring and teasing the little girl, who took their jokes with great good nature. They were all delighted with her, for they seldom saw so pretty and carefully nurtured a child. They told her that she must choose one of them for a sweetheart, and each began pressing his suit and offering her bribes: candy, and little pigs, and spotted calves. She looked archly into the big, brown, mustached faces, smelling of spirits and tobacco, then she ran her tiny forefinger delicately over Joe's bristly chin and said, "Here is my sweetheart."

The Bohemians roared with laughter, and Marie's uncle hugged her until she cried, "Please don't, Uncle Joe! You hurt me." Each of Joe's friends gave her a bag of candy, and she kissed them all around, though she did not like country candy very well. Perhaps that was why she bethought herself of Emil. "Let me down, Uncle Joe," she said, "I want to give some of my candy to that nice little boy I found." She walked graciously over to Emil, followed by her lusty admirers, who formed a new circle and teased the little boy until he hid his face in his sister's skirts, and she had to scold him for being such a baby.

The farm people were making preparations to start for home. The women were checking over their groceries and pinning their big red shawls about their heads. The men were buying tobacco and candy with what money they had left, were showing each other new boots and gloves and blue flannel shirts. Three big Bohemians were drinking raw alcohol, tinctured with oil of cinnamon. This was said to fortify one effectually against the cold, and they smacked their lips after each pull at the flask. Their volubility drowned every other noise in the place, and the overheated store sounded of their spirited language as it reeked of pipe smoke, damp woolens, and kerosene.

Carl came in, wearing his overcoat and carrying a wooden box with a brass handle. "Come," he said, "I've fed and watered your team, and the wagon is ready." He carried Emil out and tucked him down in the straw in the wagon-box. The heat had made the little boy sleepy, but he still clung to his kitten.

"You were awful good to climb so high and get my kitten, Carl. When I get big I'll climb and get little boys' kittens for them," he murmured drowsily. Before the horses were over the first hill, Emil and his cat were both fast asleep.

Although it was only four o'clock, the winter day was fading. The road led southwest, toward the streak of pale, watery light that glimmered in the leaden sky. The light fell upon the two sad young faces that were turned mutely toward it: upon the eyes of the girl, who seemed to be looking with such anguished perplexity into the future; upon the sombre eyes of the boy, who seemed already to be looking into the past. The little town behind them had vanished as if it had never been, had fallen behind the swell of the prairie, and the stern frozen country received them into its bosom. The homesteads were few and far apart; here and there a windmill gaunt against the sky, a sod house crouching in a hollow. But the great fact was the land itself, which seemed to overwhelm the little beginnings of human society that struggled in its sombre wastes. It was from facing this vast hardness that the boy's mouth had become so bitter; because he felt that men were too weak to make any mark here, that the land wanted to be let alone, to preserve its own fierce strength, its peculiar, savage kind of beauty, its uninterrupted mournfulness.

The wagon jolted along over the frozen road. The two friends had less to say to each other than usual, as if the cold had somehow penetrated to their hearts.

"Did Lou and Oscar go to the Blue to cut wood today?" Carl asked.

"Yes. I'm almost sorry I let them go, it's turned so cold. But mother frets if the wood gets low." She stopped and put her hand to her forehead, brushing back her hair. "I don't know what is to become of us, Carl, if father has to die. I don't dare to think about it. I wish we could all go with him and let the grass grow back over everything."

Carl made no reply. Just ahead of them was the Norwegian graveyard, where the grass had, indeed, grown back over everything, shaggy and red, hiding even the wire fence. Carl realized that he was not a very helpful companion, but there was nothing he could say.

"Of course," Alexandra went on, steadying her voice a little, "the boys are strong and work hard, but we've always depended so on father that I don't see how we can go ahead. I almost feel as if there were nothing to go ahead for."

"Does your father know?"

"Yes, I think he does. He lies and counts on his fingers all day. I think he is trying to count up what he is leaving for us. It's a comfort to him that my chickens are laying right on through the cold weather and bringing in a little money. I wish we could keep his mind off such things, but I don't have much time to be with him now."

"I wonder if he'd like to have me bring my magic lantern over some evening?"

Alexandra turned her face toward him. "Oh, Carl! Have you got it?"

"Yes. It's back there in the straw. Didn't you notice the box I was carrying? I tried it all morning in the drug-store cellar, and it worked ever so well, makes fine big pictures."

"What are they about?"

"Oh, hunting pictures in Germany, and Robinson Crusoe and funny pictures about cannibals. I'm going to paint some slides for it on glass, out of the Hans Andersen book."

Alexandra seemed actually cheered. There is often a good deal of the child left in people who have had to grow up too soon. "Do bring it over, Carl. I can hardly wait to see it, and I'm sure it will please father. Are the pictures colored? Then I know he'll like them. He likes the calendars I get him in town. I wish I could get more. You must leave me here, mustn't you? It's been nice to have company."

Carl stopped the horses and looked dubiously up at the black sky. "It's pretty dark. Of course the horses will take you home, but I think I'd better light your lantern, in case you should need it."

He gave her the reins and climbed back into the wagon-box, where he crouched down and made a tent of his overcoat. After a dozen trials he succeeded in lighting the lantern, which he placed in front of Alexandra, half covering it with a blanket so that the light would not shine in her eyes. "Now, wait until I find my box. Yes, here it is. Good-night, Alexandra. Try not to worry." Carl sprang to the ground and ran off across the fields toward the Linstrum homestead. "Hoo, hoo-o-o-o!" he called back as he disappeared over a ridge and dropped into a sand gully. The wind answered him like an echo, "Hoo, hoo-o-o-o-o-o!" Alexandra drove off alone. The rattle of her wagon was lost in the howling of the wind, but her lantern, held firmly between her feet, made a moving point of light along the highway, going deeper and deeper into the dark country.

CHAPTER II

On one of the ridges of that wintry waste stood the low log house in which John Bergson was dying. The Bergson homestead was easier to find than many another, because it overlooked Norway Creek, a shallow, muddy stream that sometimes flowed, and sometimes stood still, at the bottom of a winding ravine with steep, shelving sides overgrown with brush and cottonwoods and dwarf ash. This creek gave a sort of identity to the farms that bordered upon it. Of all the bewildering things about a new country, the absence of human landmarks is one of the most depressing and disheartening. The houses on the Divide were small and were usually tucked away in low places; you did not see them until you came directly upon them. Most of them were built of the sod itself, and were only the unescapable ground in another form. The roads were but faint tracks in the grass, and the fields were scarcely noticeable. The record of the plow was insignificant, like the feeble scratches on stone left by prehistoric races, so indeterminate that they may, after all, be only the markings of glaciers, and not a record of human strivings.

In eleven long years John Bergson had made but little impression upon the wild land he had come to tame. It was still a wild thing that had its ugly moods; and no one knew when they were likely to come, or why. Mischance hung over it. Its Genius was unfriendly to man. The sick man was feeling this as he lay looking out of the window, after the doctor had left him, on the day following Alexandra's trip to town. There it lay outside his door, the same land, the same lead-colored miles. He knew every ridge and draw and gully between him and the horizon. To the south, his plowed fields; to the east, the sod stables, the cattle corral, the pond,—and then the grass.

Bergson went over in his mind the things that had held him back. One winter his cattle had perished in a blizzard. The next summer one of his plow horses broke its leg in a prairie-dog hole and had to be shot. Another summer he lost his hogs from cholera, and a valuable stallion died from a rattlesnake bite. Time and again his crops had failed. He had lost two children, boys, that came between Lou and Emil, and there had been the cost of sickness and death. Now, when he had at last struggled out of debt, he was going to die himself. He was only forty-six, and had, of course, counted upon more time.

Bergson had spent his first five years on the Divide getting into debt, and the last six getting out. He had paid off his mortgages and had ended pretty much where he began, with the land. He owned exactly six hundred and forty acres of what stretched outside his door; his own original homestead and timber claim, making three hundred and twenty acres, and the half-section adjoining, the homestead of a younger brother who had given up the fight, gone back to Chicago to work in a fancy bakery and distinguish himself in a Swedish athletic club. So far John had not attempted to cultivate the second half-section, but used it for pasture land, and one of his sons rode herd there in open weather.

John Bergson had the Old-World belief that land, in itself, is desirable. But this land was an enigma. It was like a horse that no one knows how to break to harness, that runs wild and kicks things to pieces. He had an idea that no one understood how to farm it properly, and this he often discussed with Alexandra. Their neighbors, certainly, knew even less about farming than he did. Many of them had never worked on a farm until they took up their homesteads. They had been *handwerkers* at home; tailors, locksmiths, joiners, cigar-makers, etc. Bergson himself had worked in a shipyard.

For weeks, John Bergson had been thinking about these things. His bed stood in the sitting-room, next to the kitchen. Through the day, while the baking and washing and ironing were going on, the father lay and looked up at the roof beams that he himself had hewn, or out at the cattle in the corral. He counted the cattle over and over. It diverted him to speculate as to how much weight each of the steers would probably put on by spring. He often called his daughter in to talk to her about this.

Before Alexandra was twelve years old she had begun to be a help to him, and as she grew older he had come to depend more and more upon her resourcefulness and good judgment. His boys were willing enough to work, but when he talked with them they usually irritated him. It was Alexandra who read the papers and followed the markets, and who learned by the mistakes of their neighbors. It was Alexandra who could always tell about what it had cost to fatten each steer, and who could guess the weight of a hog before it went on the scales closer than John Bergson himself. Lou and Oscar were industrious, but he could never teach them to use their heads about their work.

Alexandra, her father often said to himself, was like her grandfather; which was his way of saying that she was intelligent. John Bergson's father had been a shipbuilder, a man of considerable force and of some fortune. Late in life he married a second time, a Stockholm woman of questionable character, much younger than he, who goaded him into every sort of extravagance. On the shipbuilder's part, this marriage was an infatuation, the despairing folly of a powerful man who cannot bear to grow old. In a few years his unprincipled wife warped the probity of a lifetime. He speculated, lost his own fortune and funds entrusted to him by poor seafaring men, and died disgraced, leaving his children nothing. But when all was said, he had come up from the sea himself, had built up a proud little business with no capital but his own skill and foresight, and had proved himself a man. In his daughter, John Bergson recognized the strength of will, and the simple direct way of thinking things out, that had characterized his father in his better days. He would much rather, of course, have seen this likeness in one of his sons, but it was not a question of choice. As he lay there day after day he had to accept the situation as it was, and to be thankful that there was one among his children to whom he could entrust the future of his family and the possibilities of his hard-won land.

The winter twilight was fading. The sick man heard his wife strike a match in the kitchen, and the light of a lamp glimmered through the cracks of the door. It seemed like a light shining far away. He turned painfully in his bed and looked at his white hands, with all the work gone out of them. He was ready to give up, he felt. He did not know how it had come about, but he was quite willing to go deep under his fields and rest, where the plow could not find him. He was tired of making mistakes. He was content to leave the tangle to other hands; he thought of his Alexandra's strong ones.

"*Dotter*," he called feebly, "*dotter!*" He heard her quick step and saw her tall figure appear in the doorway, with the light of the lamp behind her. He felt her youth and strength, how easily she moved and stooped and lifted. But he would not have had it again if he could, not he! He knew the end too well to wish to begin again. He knew where it all went to, what it all became.

His daughter came and lifted him up on his pillows. She called him by an old Swedish name that she used to call him when she was little and took his dinner to him in the shipyard.

"Tell the boys to come here, daughter. I want to speak to them."

"They are feeding the horses, father. They have just come back from the Blue. Shall I call them?"

He sighed. "No, no. Wait until they come in. Alexandra, you will have to do the best you can for your brothers. Everything will come on you."

"I will do all I can, father."

"Don't let them get discouraged and go off like Uncle Otto. I want them to keep the land."

"We will, father. We will never lose the land."

There was a sound of heavy feet in the kitchen. Alexandra went to the door and beckoned to her brothers, two strapping boys of seventeen and nineteen. They came in and stood at the foot of the bed. Their father looked at them searchingly, though it was too dark to see their faces; they were just the same boys, he told himself, he had not been mistaken in them. The square head and heavy shoulders belonged to Oscar, the elder. The younger boy was quicker, but vacillating.

"Boys," said the father wearily, "I want you to keep the land together and to be guided by your sister. I have talked to her since I have been sick, and she knows all my wishes. I want no quarrels among my children, and so long as there is one house there must be one head. Alexandra is the oldest, and she knows my wishes. She will do the best she can. If she makes mistakes, she will not make so many as I have made. When you marry, and want a house of your own, the land will be divided fairly, according to the courts. But for the next few years you will have it hard, and you must all keep together. Alexandra will manage the best she can."

Oscar, who was usually the last to speak, replied because he was the older, "Yes, father. It would be so anyway, without your speaking. We will all work the place together."

"And you will be guided by your sister, boys, and be good brothers to her, and good sons to your mother? That is good. And Alexandra must not work in the fields any more. There is no necessity now. Hire a man when you need help. She can make much more with her eggs and butter than the wages of a man. It was one of my mistakes that I did not find that out sooner. Try to break a little more land every year; sod corn is good for fodder. Keep turning the land, and always put up more hay than you need. Don't grudge your mother a little time for plowing her garden and setting out fruit trees, even if it comes in a busy season. She has been a good mother to you, and she has always missed the old country."

When they went back to the kitchen the boys sat down silently at the table. Throughout the meal they looked down at their plates and did not lift their red eyes. They did not eat much, although they had been working in the cold all day, and there was a rabbit stewed in gravy for supper, and prune pies.

John Bergson had married beneath him, but he had married a good housewife. Mrs. Bergson was a fair-skinned, corpulent woman, heavy and placid like her son, Oscar, but there was something comfortable about her; perhaps it was her own love of comfort. For eleven years she had worthily striven to maintain some semblance of household order amid conditions that made order very difficult. Habit was very strong with Mrs. Bergson, and her unremitting efforts to repeat the routine of her old life among new surroundings had done a great deal to keep the family from disintegrating morally and getting careless in their ways. The Bergsons had a log house, for instance, only because Mrs. Bergson would not live in a sod house. She missed the fish diet of her own country, and twice every summer she sent the boys to the river, twenty miles to the southward, to fish for channel cat. When the children were little she used to load them all into the wagon, the baby in its crib, and go fishing herself.

Alexandra often said that if her mother were cast upon a desert island, she would thank God for her deliverance, make a garden, and find something to preserve. Preserving was almost a mania with Mrs. Bergson. Stout as she was, she roamed the scrubby banks of Norway Creek looking for fox grapes and goose plums, like a wild creature in search of prey. She made a yellow jam of the insipid ground-cherries that grew on the prairie, flavoring it with lemon peel; and she made a sticky dark conserve of garden tomatoes. She had experimented even with the rank buffalo-pea, and she could not see a fine bronze cluster of them without shaking her head and murmuring, "What a pity!" When there was nothing more to preserve, she began to pickle. The amount of sugar she used in these processes was sometimes a serious drain upon the family resources. She was a good mother, but she was glad when her children were old enough not to be in her way in the kitchen. She had never quite forgiven John Bergson for bringing her to the end of the earth; but, now that she was there, she wanted to be let alone to reconstruct her old life insofar as that was possible. She could still take some comfort in the world if she had bacon in the cave, glass jars on the shelves, and sheets in the press. She disapproved of all her neighbors because of their slovenly housekeeping, and the women thought her very proud. Once when Mrs. Bergson, on her way to Norway Creek, stopped to see old Mrs. Lee, the old woman hid in the haymow "for fear Mis' Bergson would catch her barefoot."

CHAPTER III

One Sunday afternoon in July, six months after John Bergson's death, Carl was sitting in the doorway of the Linstrum kitchen, dreaming over an illustrated paper, when he heard the rattle of a wagon along the hill road. Looking up he recognized the Bergsons' team, with two seats in the wagon, which meant they were off for a pleasure excursion. Oscar and Lou, on the front seat, wore their cloth hats and coats, never worn except on Sundays, and Emil, on the second seat with Alexandra, sat proudly in his new trousers, made from a pair of his father's, and a pink-striped shirt, with a wide ruffled collar. Oscar stopped the horses and waved to Carl, who caught up his hat and ran through the melon patch to join them.

"Want to go with us?" Lou called. "We're going to Crazy Ivar's to buy a hammock."

"Sure." Carl ran up panting, and clambering over the wheel sat down beside Emil. "I've always wanted to see Ivar's pond. They say it's the biggest in all the country. Aren't you afraid to go to Ivar's in that new shirt, Emil? He might want it and take it right off your back."

Emil grinned. "I'd be awful scared to go," he admitted, "if you big boys weren't along to take care of me. Did you ever hear him howl, Carl? People say sometimes he runs about the country howling at night because he is afraid the Lord will destroy him. Mother thinks he must have done something awful wicked."

Lou looked back and winked at Carl. "What would you do, Emil, if you was out on the prairie by yourself and seen him coming?"

Emil stared. "Maybe I could hide in a badger-hole," he suggested doubtfully.

"But suppose there wasn't any badger-hole," Lou persisted. "Would you run?"

"No, I'd be too scared to run," Emil admitted mournfully, twisting his fingers. "I guess I'd sit right down on the ground and say my prayers."

The big boys laughed, and Oscar brandished his whip over the broad backs of the horses.

"He wouldn't hurt you, Emil," said Carl persuasively. "He came to doctor our mare when she ate green corn and swelled up most as big as the water-tank. He petted her just like you do your cats. I couldn't understand much he said, for he don't talk any English, but he kept patting her and groaning as if he had the pain himself, and saying, 'There now, sister, that's easier, that's better!' "

Lou and Oscar laughed, and Emil giggled delightedly and looked up at his sister.

"I don't think he knows anything at all about doctoring," said Oscar scornfully. "They say when horses have distemper he takes the medicine himself, and then prays over the horses."

Alexandra spoke up. "That's what the Crows said, but he cured their horses, all the same. Some days his mind is cloudy, like. But if you can get him on a clear day, you can learn a great deal from him. He understands animals. Didn't I see him take the horn off the Berquist's cow when she had torn it loose and went crazy? She was tearing all over the place, knocking herself against things. And at last she ran out on the roof of the old dugout and her legs went through and there she stuck, bellowing. Ivar came running with his white bag, and the moment he got to her she was quiet and let him saw her horn off and daub the place with tar."

Emil had been watching his sister, his face reflecting the sufferings of the cow. "And then didn't it hurt her any more?" he asked.

Alexandra patted him. "No, not any more. And in two days they could use her milk again."

The road to Ivar's homestead was a very poor one. He had settled in the rough country across the county line, where no one lived but some Russians,—half a dozen families who dwelt together in one long house, divided off like barracks. Ivar had explained his choice by saying that the fewer neighbors he had, the fewer temptations. Nevertheless, when one considered that his chief business was horse-doctoring, it seemed rather short-sighted of him to live in the most inaccessible place he could find. The Bergson wagon lurched along over the rough hummocks and grass banks, followed the bottom of winding draws, or skirted the margin of wide lagoons, where the golden coreopsis grew up out of the clear water and the wild ducks rose with a whirr of wings.

Lou looked after them helplessly. "I wish I'd brought my gun, anyway, Alexandra," he said fretfully. "I could have hidden it under the straw in the bottom of the wagon."

"Then we'd have had to lie to Ivar. Besides, they say he can smell dead birds. And if he knew, we wouldn't get anything out of him, not even a hammock. I want to talk to him, and he won't talk sense if he's angry. It makes him foolish."

Lou sniffed. "Whoever heard of him talking sense, anyhow! I'd rather have ducks for supper than Crazy Ivar's tongue."

Emil was alarmed. "Oh, but, Lou, you don't want to make him mad! He might howl!"

They all laughed again, and Oscar urged the horses up the crumbling side of a clay bank. They had left the lagoons and the red grass behind them. In Crazy Ivar's country the grass was short and gray, the draws deeper than they were in the Bergsons' neighborhood, and the land was all broken up into hillocks and clay ridges. The wild flowers disappeared, and only in the bottom of the draws and gullies grew a few of the very toughest and hardiest: shoestring, and ironweed, and snow-on-the-mountain.

"Look, look, Emil, there's Ivar's big pond!" Alexandra pointed to a shining sheet of water that lay at the bottom of a shallow draw. At one end of the pond was an earthen dam, planted with green willow bushes, and above it a door and a single window were set into the hillside. You would not have seen them at all but for the reflection of the sunlight upon the four panes of window-glass. And that was all you saw. Not a shed, not a corral, not a well, not even a path broken in the curly grass. But for the piece of rusty stovepipe sticking up through the sod, you could have walked over the roof of Ivar's dwelling without dreaming that you were near a human habitation. Ivar had lived for three years in the clay bank, without defiling the face of nature any more than the coyote that had lived there before him had done.

When the Bergsons drove over the hill, Ivar was sitting in the doorway of his house, reading the Norwegian Bible. He was a queerly shaped old man, with a thick, powerful body set on short bow-legs. His shaggy white hair, falling in a thick mane about his ruddy cheeks, made him look older than he was. He was barefoot, but he wore a clean shirt of unbleached cotton, open at the neck. He always put on a clean shirt when Sunday morning came round, though he never went to church. He had a peculiar religion of his own and could not get on with any of the denominations. Often he did not see anybody from one week's end to another. He kept a calendar, and every morning he checked off a day, so that he was never in any doubt as to which day of the week it was. Ivar hired himself out in threshing and corn-husking time, and he doctored sick animals when he was sent for. When he was at home, he made hammocks out of twine and committed chapters of the Bible to memory.

Ivar found contentment in the solitude he had sought out for himself. He disliked the litter of human dwellings: the broken food, the bits of broken china, the old wash-boilers and tea-kettles thrown into the sunflower patch. He preferred the cleanness and tidiness of the wild sod. He always said that the badgers had cleaner houses than people, and that when he took a housekeeper her name would be Mrs. Badger. He best expressed his preference for his wild homestead by saying that his Bible seemed truer to him there. If one stood in the doorway of his cave, and looked off at the rough land, the smiling sky, the curly grass white in the hot sunlight; if one listened to the rapturous song of the lark, the drumming of the quail, the burr of the locust against that vast silence, one understood what Ivar meant.

On this Sunday afternoon his face shone with happiness. He closed the book on his knee, keeping the place with his horny finger, and repeated softly:—

He sendeth the springs into the valleys, which run
among the hills;
They give drink to every beast of the field; the wild
asses quench their thirst.
The trees of the Lord are full of sap; the cedars of
Lebanon which he hath planted;
Where the birds make their nests: as for the stork,
the fir trees are her house.
The high hills are a refuge for the wild goats; and the
rocks for the conies.

Before he opened his Bible again, Ivar heard the Bergsons' wagon approaching, and he sprang up and ran toward it.

"No guns, no guns!" he shouted, waving his arms distractedly.

"No, Ivar, no guns," Alexandra called reassuringly.

He dropped his arms and went up to the wagon, smiling amiably and looking at them out of his pale blue eyes.

"We want to buy a hammock, if you have one," Alexandra explained, "and my little brother, here, wants to see your big pond, where so many birds come."

Ivar smiled foolishly, and began rubbing the horses' noses and feeling about their mouths behind the bits. "Not many birds just now. A few ducks this morning; and some snipe come to drink. But there was a crane last week. She spent one night and came back the next evening. I don't know why. It is not her season, of course. Many of them go over in the fall. Then the pond is full of strange voices every night."

Alexandra translated for Carl, who looked thoughtful. "Ask him, Alexandra, if it is true that a sea gull came here once. I have heard so."

She had some difficulty in making the old man understand. He looked puzzled at first, then smote his hands together as he remembered. "Oh, yes, yes! A big white bird with long wings and pink feet. My! what a voice she had! She came in the afternoon and kept flying about the pond and screaming until dark. She was in trouble of some sort, but I could not understand her. She was going over to the other ocean, maybe, and did not know how far it was. She was afraid of never getting there. She was more mournful than our birds here; she cried in the night. She saw the light from my window and darted up to it. Maybe she thought my house was a boat, she was such a wild thing. Next morning, when the sun rose, I went out to take her food, but she flew up into the sky and went on her way." Ivar ran his fingers through his thick hair. "I have many strange birds stop with me here. They come from very far away and are great company. I hope you boys never shoot wild birds?"

Lou and Oscar grinned, and Ivar shook his bushy head. "Yes, I know boys are thoughtless. But these wild things are God's birds. He watches over them and counts them, as we do our cattle; Christ says so in the New Testament."

"Now, Ivar," Lou asked, "may we water our horses at your pond and give them some feed? It's a bad road to your place."

"Yes, yes, it is." The old man scrambled about and began to loose the tugs. "A bad road, eh, girls? And the bay with a colt at home!"

Oscar brushed the old man aside. "We'll take care of the horses, Ivar. You'll be finding some disease on them. Alexandra wants to see your hammocks."

Ivar led Alexandra and Emil to his little cave house. He had but one room, neatly plastered and whitewashed, and there was a wooden floor. There was a kitchen stove, a table covered with oilcloth, two chairs, a clock, a calendar, a few books on the window-shelf; nothing more. But the place was as clean as a cupboard.

"But where do you sleep, Ivar?" Emil asked, looking about.

Ivar unslung a hammock from a hook on the wall; in it was rolled a buffalo robe. "There, my son. A hammock is a good bed, and in winter I wrap up in this skin. Where I go to work, the beds are not half so easy as this."

By this time Emil had lost all his timidity. He thought a cave a very superior kind of house. There was something pleasantly unusual about it and about Ivar. "Do the birds know you will be kind to them, Ivar? Is that why so many come?" he asked.

Ivar sat down on the floor and tucked his feet under him. "See, little brother, they have come from a long way, and they are very tired. From up there where they are flying, our country looks dark and flat. They must have water to drink and to bathe in before they can go on with their journey. They look this way and that, and far below them they see something shining, like a piece of glass set in the dark earth. That is my pond. They come to it and are not disturbed. Maybe I sprinkle a little corn. They tell the other birds, and next year more come this way. They have their roads up there, as we have down here."

Emil rubbed his knees thoughtfully. "And is that true, Ivar, about the head ducks falling back when they are tired, and the hind ones taking their place?"

"Yes. The point of the wedge gets the worst of it; they cut the wind. They can only stand it there a little while—half an hour, maybe. Then they fall back and the wedge splits a little, while the rear ones come up the middle to the front. Then it closes up and they fly on, with a new edge. They are always changing like that, up in the air. Never any confusion; just like soldiers who have been drilled."

Alexandra had selected her hammock by the time the boys came up from the pond. They would not come in, but sat in the shade of the bank outside while Alexandra and Ivar talked about the birds and about his housekeeping, and why he never ate meat, fresh or salt.

Alexandra was sitting on one of the wooden chairs, her arms resting on the table. Ivar was sitting on the floor at her feet. "Ivar," she said suddenly, beginning to trace the pattern on the oilcloth with her forefinger, "I came to-day more because I wanted to talk to you than because I wanted to buy a hammock."

"Yes?" The old man scraped his bare feet on the plank floor.

"We have a big bunch of hogs, Ivar. I wouldn't sell in the spring, when everybody advised me to, and now so many people are losing their hogs that I am frightened. What can be done?"

Ivar's little eyes began to shine. They lost their vagueness.

"You feed them swill and such stuff? Of course! And sour milk? Oh, yes! And keep them in a stinking pen? I tell you, sister, the hogs of this country are put upon! They become unclean, like the hogs in the Bible. If you kept your chickens like that, what would happen? You have a little sorghum patch, maybe? Put a fence around it, and turn the hogs in. Build a shed to give them shade, a thatch on poles. Let the boys haul water to them in barrels, clean water, and plenty. Get them off the old stinking ground, and do not let them go back there until winter. Give them only grain and clean feed, such as you would give horses or cattle. Hogs do not like to be filthy."

The boys outside the door had been listening. Lou nudged his brother. "Come, the horses are done eating. Let's hitch up and get out of here. He'll fill her full of notions. She'll be for having the pigs sleep with us, next."

Oscar grunted and got up. Carl, who could not understand what Ivar said, saw that the two boys were displeased. They did not mind hard work, but they hated experiments and could never see the use of taking pains. Even Lou, who was more elastic than his older brother, disliked to do anything different from their neighbors. He felt that it made them conspicuous and gave people a chance to talk about them.

Once they were on the homeward road, the boys forgot their ill-humor and joked about Ivar and his birds. Alexandra did not propose any reforms in the care of the pigs, and they hoped she had forgotten Ivar's talk. They agreed that he was crazier than ever, and would never be able to prove up on his land because he worked it so little. Alexandra privately resolved that she would have a talk with Ivar about this and stir him up. The boys persuaded Carl to stay for supper and go swimming in the pasture pond after dark.

That evening, after she had washed the supper dishes, Alexandra sat down on the kitchen doorstep, while her mother was mixing the bread. It was a still, deep-breathing summer night, full of the smell of the hay fields. Sounds of laughter and splashing came up from the pasture, and when the moon rose rapidly above the bare rim of the prairie, the pond glittered like polished metal, and she could see the flash of white bodies as the boys ran about the edge, or jumped into the water. Alexandra watched the shimmering pool dreamily, but eventually her eyes went back to the sorghum patch south of the barn, where she was planning to make her new pig corral.

CHAPTER IV

For the first three years after John Bergson's death, the affairs of his family prospered. Then came the hard times that brought every one on the Divide to the brink of despair; three years of drouth and failure, the last struggle of a wild soil against the encroaching plowshare. The first of these fruitless summers the Bergson boys bore courageously. The failure of the corn crop made labor cheap. Lou and Oscar hired two men and put in bigger crops than ever before. They lost everything they spent. The whole country was discouraged. Farmers who were already in debt had to give up their land. A few foreclosures demoralized the country. The settlers sat about on the wooden sidewalks in the little town and told each other that the country was never meant for men to live in; the thing to do was to get back to Iowa, to Illinois, to any place that had been proved habitable. The Bergson boys, certainly, would have been happier with their uncle Otto, in the bakery shop in Chicago. Like most of their neighbors, they were meant to follow in paths already marked out for them, not to break trails in a new country. A steady job, a few holidays, nothing to think about, and they would have been very happy. It was no fault of theirs that they had been dragged into the wilderness when they were little boys. A pioneer should have imagination, should be able to enjoy the idea of things more than the things themselves.

The second of these barren summers was passing. One September afternoon Alexandra had gone over to the garden across the draw to dig sweet potatoes—they had been thriving upon the weather that was fatal to everything else. But when Carl Linstrum came up the garden rows to find her, she was not working. She was standing lost in thought, leaning upon her pitchfork, her sunbonnet lying beside her on the ground. The dry garden patch smelled of drying vines and was strewn with yellow seed-cucumbers and pumpkins and citrons. At one end, next to the rhubarb, grew feathery asparagus, with red berries. Down the middle of the garden was a row of gooseberry and currant bushes. A few tough zenias and marigolds and a row of scarlet sage bore witness to the buckets of water that Mrs. Bergson had carried there after sundown, against the prohibition of her sons. Carl came quietly and slowly up the garden path, looking intently at Alexandra. She did not hear him. She was standing perfectly still, with that serious ease so characteristic of her. Her thick, reddish braids, twisted about her head, fairly burned in the sunlight. The air was cool enough to make the warm sun pleasant on one's back and shoulders, and so clear that the eye could follow a hawk up and up, into the blazing blue depths of the sky. Even Carl, never a very cheerful boy, and considerably darkened by these last two bitter years, loved the country on days like this, felt something strong and young and wild come out of it, that laughed at care.

"Alexandra," he said as he approached her, "I want to talk to you. Let's sit down by the gooseberry bushes." He picked up her sack of potatoes and they crossed the garden. "Boys gone to town?" he asked as he sank down on the warm, sun-baked earth. "Well, we have made up our minds at last, Alexandra. We are really going away."

She looked at him as if she were a little frightened. "Really, Carl? Is it settled?"

"Yes, father has heard from St. Louis, and they will give him back his old job in the cigar factory. He must be there by the first of November. They are taking on new men then. We will sell the place for whatever we can get, and auction the stock. We haven't enough to ship. I am going to learn engraving with a German engraver there, and then try to get work in Chicago."

Alexandra's hands dropped in her lap. Her eyes became dreamy and filled with tears.

Carl's sensitive lower lip trembled. He scratched in the soft earth beside him with a stick. "That's all I hate about it, Alexandra," he said slowly. "You've stood by us through so much and helped father out so many times, and now it seems as if we were running off and leaving you to face the worst of it. But it isn't as if we could really ever be of any help to you. We are only one more drag, one more thing you look out for and feel responsible for. Father was never meant for a farmer, you know that. And I hate it. We'd only get in deeper and deeper."

"Yes, yes, Carl, I know. You are wasting your life here. You are able to do much better things. You are nearly nineteen now, and I wouldn't have you stay. I've always hoped you would get away. But I can't help feeling scared when I think how I will miss you—more than you will ever know." She brushed the tears from her cheeks, not trying to hide them.

"But, Alexandra," he said sadly and wistfully, "I've never been any real help to you, beyond sometimes trying to keep the boys in a good humor."

Alexandra smiled and shook her head. "Oh, it's not that. Nothing like that. It's by understanding me, and the boys, and mother, that you've helped me. I expect that is the only way one person ever really can help another. I think you are about the only one that ever helped me. Somehow it will take more courage to bear your going than everything that has happened before."

Carl looked at the ground. "You see, we've all depended so on you," he said, "even father. He makes me laugh. When anything comes up he always says, 'I wonder what the Bergsons are going to do about that? I guess I'll go and ask her.' I'll never forget that time, when we first came here, and our horse had the colic, and I ran over to your place—your father was away, and you came home with me and showed father how to let the wind out of the horse. You were only a little girl then, but you knew ever so much more about farm work than poor father. You remember how homesick I used to get, and what long talks we used to have coming from school? We've someway always felt alike about things."

"Yes, that's it; we've liked the same things and we've liked them together, without anybody else knowing. And we've had good times, hunting for Christmas trees and going for ducks and making our plum wine together every year. We've never either of us had any other close friend. And now"— Alexandra wiped her eyes with the corner of her apron— "and now I must remember that you are going where you will have many friends, and will find the work you were meant to do. But you'll write to me, Carl? That will mean a great deal to me here."

"I'll write as long as I live," cried the boy impetuously. "And I'll be working for you as much as for myself, Alexandra. I want to do something you'll like and be proud of. I'm a fool here, but I know I can do something!" He sat up and frowned at the red grass.

Alexandra sighed. "How discouraged the boys will be when they hear. They always come home from town discouraged, anyway. So many people are trying to leave the country, and they talk to our boys and make them low-spirited. I'm afraid they are beginning to feel hard toward me because I won't listen to any talk about going. Sometimes I feel like I'm getting tired of standing up for this country."

"I won't tell the boys yet, if you'd rather not."

"Oh, I'll tell them myself, to-night, when they come home. They'll be talking wild, anyway, and no good comes of keeping bad news. It's all harder on them than it is on me. Lou wants to get married, poor boy, and he can't until times are better. See, there goes the sun, Carl. I must be getting back. Mother will want her potatoes. It's chilly already, the moment the light goes."

Alexandra rose and looked about. A golden afterglow throbbed in the west, but the country already looked empty and mournful. A dark moving mass came over the western hill, the Lee boy was bringing in the herd from the other half-section. Emil ran from the windmill to open the corral gate. From the log house, on the little rise across the draw, the smoke was curling. The cattle lowed and bellowed. In the sky the pale half-moon was slowly silvering. Alexandra and Carl walked together down the potato rows. "I have to keep telling myself what is going to happen," she said softly. "Since you have been here, ten years now, I have never really been lonely. But I can remember what it was like before. Now I shall have nobody but Emil. But he is my boy, and he is tender-hearted."

That night, when the boys were called to supper, they sat down moodily. They had worn their coats to town, but they ate in their striped shirts and suspenders. They were grown men now, and, as Alexandra said, for the last few years they had been growing more and more like themselves. Lou was still the slighter of the two, the quicker and more intelligent, but apt to go off at half-cock. He had a lively blue eye, a thin, fair skin (always burned red to the neckband of his shirt in summer), stiff, yellow hair that would not lie down on his head, and a bristly little yellow mustache, of which he was very proud. Oscar could not grow a mustache; his pale face was as bare as an egg, and his white eyebrows gave it an empty look. He was a man of powerful body and unusual endurance; the sort of man you could attach to a corn-sheller as you would an engine. He would turn it all day, without hurrying, without slowing down. But he was as indolent of mind as he was unsparing of his body. His love of routine amounted to a vice. He worked like an insect, always doing the same thing over in the same way, regardless of whether it was best or not. He felt that there was a sovereign virtue in mere bodily toil, and he rather liked to do things in the hardest way. If a field had once been in corn, he couldn't bear to put it into wheat. He liked to begin his corn-planting at the same time every year, whether the season were backward or forward. He seemed to feel that by his own irreproachable regularity he would clear himself of blame and reprove the weather. When the wheat crop failed, he threshed the straw at a dead loss to demonstrate how little grain there was, and thus prove his case against Providence.

Lou, on the other hand, was fussy and flighty; always planned to get through two days' work in one, and often got only the least important things done. He liked to keep the place up, but he never got round to doing odd jobs until he had to neglect more pressing work to attend to them. In the middle of the wheat harvest, when the grain was over-ripe and every hand was needed, he would stop to mend fences or to patch the harness; then dash down to the field and overwork and be laid up in bed for a week. The two boys balanced each other, and they pulled well together. They had been good friends since they were children. One seldom went anywhere, even to town, without the other.

To-night, after they sat down to supper, Oscar kept looking at Lou as if he expected him to say something, and Lou blinked his eyes and frowned at his plate. It was Alexandra herself who at last opened the discussion.

"The Linstrums," she said calmly, as she put another plate of hot biscuit on the table, "are going back to St. Louis. The old man is going to work in the cigar factory again."

At this Lou plunged in. "You see, Alexandra, everybody who can crawl out is going away. There's no use of us trying to stick it out, just to be stubborn. There's something in knowing when to quit."

"Where do you want to go, Lou?"

"Any place where things will grow," said Oscar grimly.

Lou reached for a potato. "Chris Arnson has traded his half-section for a place down on the river."

"Who did he trade with?"

"Charley Fuller, in town."

"Fuller the real estate man? You see, Lou, that Fuller has a head on him. He's buying and trading for every bit of land he can get up here. It'll make him a rich man, some day."

"He's rich now, that's why he can take a chance."

"Why can't we? We'll live longer than he will. Some day the land itself will be worth more than all we can ever raise on it."

Lou laughed. "It could be worth that, and still not be worth much. Why, Alexandra, you don't know what you're talking about. Our place wouldn't bring now what it would six years ago. The fellows that settled up here just made a mistake. Now they're beginning to see this high land wasn't never meant to grow nothing on, and everybody who ain't fixed to graze cattle is trying to crawl out. It's too high to farm up here. All the Americans are skinning out. That man Percy Adams, north of town, told me that he was going to let Fuller take his land and stuff for four hundred dollars and a ticket to Chicago."

"There's Fuller again!" Alexandra exclaimed. "I wish that man would take me for a partner. He's feathering his nest! If only poor people could learn a little from rich people! But all these fellows who are running off are bad farmers, like poor Mr. Linstrum. They couldn't get ahead even in good years, and they all got into debt while father was getting out. I think we ought to hold on as long as we can on father's account. He was so set on keeping this land. He must have seen harder times than this, here. How was it in the early days, mother?"

Mrs. Bergson was weeping quietly. These family discussions always depressed her, and made her remember all that she had been torn away from. "I don't see why the boys are always taking on about going away," she said, wiping her eyes. "I don't want to move again; out to some raw place, maybe, where we'd be worse off than we are here, and all to do over again. I won't move! If the rest of you go, I will ask some of the neighbors to take me in, and stay and be buried by father. I'm not going to leave him by himself on the prairie, for cattle to run over." She began to cry more bitterly.

The boys looked angry. Alexandra put a soothing hand on her mother's shoulder. "There's no question of that, mother. You don't have to go if you don't want to. A third of the place belongs to you by American law, and we can't sell without your consent. We only want you to advise us. How did it use to be when you and father first came? Was it really as bad as this, or not?"

"Oh, worse! Much worse," moaned Mrs. Bergson. "Drouth, chince-bugs, hail, everything! My garden all cut to pieces like sauerkraut. No grapes on the creek, no nothing. The people all lived just like coyotes."

Oscar got up and tramped out of the kitchen. Lou followed him. They felt that Alexandra had taken an unfair advantage in turning their mother loose on them. The next morning they were silent and reserved. They did not offer to take the women to church, but went down to the barn immediately after breakfast and stayed there all day. When Carl Linstrum came over in the afternoon, Alexandra winked to him and pointed toward the barn. He understood her and went down to play cards with the boys. They believed that a very wicked thing to do on Sunday, and it relieved their feelings.

Alexandra stayed in the house. On Sunday afternoon Mrs. Bergson always took a nap, and Alexandra read. During the week she read only the newspaper, but on Sunday, and in the long evenings of winter, she read a good deal; read a few things over a great many times. She knew long portions of the *Frithjof Saga* by heart, and, like most Swedes who read at all, she was fond of Longfellow's verse,—the ballads and the "Golden Legend" and "The Spanish Student." To-day she sat in the wooden rocking-chair with the Swedish Bible open on her knees, but she was not reading. She was looking thoughtfully away at the point where the upland road disappeared over the rim of the prairie. Her body was in an attitude of perfect repose, such as it was apt to take when she was thinking earnestly. Her mind was slow, truthful, steadfast. She had not the least spark of cleverness.

All afternoon the sitting-room was full of quiet and sunlight. Emil was making rabbit traps in the kitchen shed. The hens were clucking and scratching brown holes in the flower beds, and the wind was teasing the prince's feather by the door.

That evening Carl came in with the boys to supper.

"Emil," said Alexandra, when they were all seated at the table, "how would you like to go traveling? Because I am going to take a trip, and you can go with me if you want to."

The boys looked up in amazement; they were always afraid of Alexandra's schemes. Carl was interested.

"I've been thinking, boys," she went on, "that maybe I am too set against making a change. I'm going to take Brigham and the buckboard to-morrow and drive down to the river country and spend a few days looking over what they've got down there. If I find anything good, you boys can go down and make a trade."

"Nobody down there will trade for anything up here," said Oscar gloomily.

"That's just what I want to find out. Maybe they are just as discontented down there as we are up here. Things away from home often look better than they are. You know what your Hans Andersen book says, Carl, about the Swedes liking to buy Danish bread and the Danes liking to buy Swedish bread, because people always think the bread of another country is better than their own. Anyway, I've heard so much about the river farms, I won't be satisfied till I've seen for myself."

Lou fidgeted. "Look out! Don't agree to anything. Don't let them fool you."

Lou was apt to be fooled himself. He had not yet learned to keep away from the shell-game wagons that followed the circus.

After supper Lou put on a necktie and went across the fields to court Annie Lee, and Carl and Oscar sat down to a game of checkers, while Alexandra read *The Swiss Family Robinson* aloud to her mother and Emil. It was not long before the two boys at the table neglected their game to listen. They were all big children together, and they found the adventures of the family in the tree house so absorbing that they gave them their undivided attention.

CHAPTER V

Alexandra and Emil spent five days down among the river farms, driving up and down the valley. Alexandra talked to the men about their crops and to the women about their poultry. She spent a whole day with one young farmer who had been away at school, and who was experimenting with a new kind of clover hay. She learned a great deal. As they drove along, she and Emil talked and planned. At last, on the sixth day, Alexandra turned Brigham's head northward and left the river behind.

"There's nothing in it for us down there, Emil. There are a few fine farms, but they are owned by the rich men in town, and couldn't be bought. Most of the land is rough and hilly. They can always scrape along down there, but they can never do anything big. Down there they have a little certainty, but up with us there is a big chance. We must have faith in the high land, Emil. I want to hold on harder than ever, and when you're a man you'll thank me." She urged Brigham forward.

When the road began to climb the first long swells of the Divide, Alexandra hummed an old Swedish hymn, and Emil wondered why his sister looked so happy. Her face was so radiant that he felt shy about asking her. For the first time, perhaps, since that land emerged from the waters of geologic ages, a human face was set toward it with love and yearning. It seemed beautiful to her, rich and strong and glorious. Her eyes drank in the breadth of it, until her tears blinded her. Then the Genius of the Divide, the great, free spirit which breathes across it, must have bent lower than it ever bent to a human will before. The history of every country begins in the heart of a man or a woman.

Alexandra reached home in the afternoon. That evening she held a family council and told her brothers all that she had seen and heard.

"I want you boys to go down yourselves and look it over. Nothing will convince you like seeing with your own eyes. The river land was settled before this, and so they are a few years ahead of us, and have learned more about farming. The land sells for three times as much as this, but in five years we will double it. The rich men down there own all the best land, and they are buying all they can get. The thing to do is to sell our cattle and what little old corn we have, and buy the Linstrum place. Then the next thing to do is to take out two loans on our half-sections, and buy Peter Crow's place; raise every dollar we can, and buy every acre we can."

"Mortgage the homestead again?" Lou cried. He sprang up and began to wind the clock furiously. "I won't slave to pay off another mortgage. I'll never do it. You'd just as soon kill us all, Alexandra, to carry out some scheme!"

Oscar rubbed his high, pale forehead. "How do you propose to pay off your mortgages?"

Alexandra looked from one to the other and bit her lip. They had never seen her so nervous. "See here," she brought out at last. "We borrow the money for six years. Well, with the money we buy a half-section from Linstrum and a half from Crow, and a quarter from Struble, maybe. That will give us upwards of fourteen hundred acres, won't it? You won't have to pay off your mortgages for six years. By that time, any of this land will be worth thirty dollars an acre—it will be worth fifty, but we'll say thirty; then you can sell a garden patch anywhere, and pay off a debt of sixteen hundred dollars. It's not the principal I'm worried about, it's the interest and taxes. We'll have to strain to meet the payments. But as sure as we are sitting here to-night, we can sit down here ten years from now independent landowners, not struggling farmers any longer. The chance that father was always looking for has come."

Lou was pacing the floor. "But how do you *know* that land is going to go up enough to pay the mortgages and—"

"And make us rich besides?" Alexandra put in firmly. "I can't explain that, Lou. You'll have to take my word for it. I *know,* that's all. When you drive about over the country you can feel it coming."

Oscar had been sitting with his head lowered, his hands hanging between his knees. "But we can't work so much land," he said dully, as if he were talking to himself. "We can't even try. It would just lie there and we'd work ourselves to death." He sighed, and laid his calloused fist on the table.

Alexandra's eyes filled with tears. She put her hand on his shoulder. "You poor boy, you won't have to work it. The men in town who are buying up other people's land don't try to farm it. They are the men to watch, in a new country. Let's try to do like the shrewd ones and not like these stupid fellows. I don't want you boys always to have to work like this. I want you to be independent, and Emil to go to school."

Lou held his head as if it were splitting. "Everybody will say we are crazy. It must be crazy, or everybody would be doing it."

"If they were, we wouldn't have much chance. No, Lou, I was talking about that with the smart young man who is raising the new kind of clover. He says the right thing is usually just what everybody don't do. Why are we better fixed than any of our neighbors? Because father had more brains. Our people were better people than these in the old country. We *ought* to do more than they do, and see further ahead. Yes, mother, I'm going to clear the table now."

Alexandra rose. The boys went to the stable to see to the stock, and they were gone a long while. When they came back Lou played on his *dragharmonika* and Oscar sat figuring at his father's secretary all evening. They said nothing more about Alexandra's project, but she felt sure now that they would consent to it. Just before bedtime Oscar went out for a pail of water. When he did not come back, Alexandra threw a shawl over her head and ran down the path to the windmill. She found him sitting there with his head in his hands, and she sat down beside him.

"Don't do anything you don't want to do, Oscar," she whispered. She waited a moment, but he did not stir. "I won't say any more about it, if you'd rather not. What makes you so discouraged?"

"I dread signing my name to them pieces of paper," he said slowly. "All the time I was a boy we had a mortgage hanging over us."

"Then don't sign one. I don't want you to, if you feel that way."

Oscar shook his head. "No, I can see there's a chance that way. I've thought a good while there might be. We're in so deep now, we might as well go deeper. But it's hard work pulling out of debt. Like pulling a threshing-machine out of the mud; breaks your back. Me and Lou's worked hard, and I can't see it's got us ahead much."

"Nobody knows about that as well as I do, Oscar. That's why I want to try an easier way. I don't want you to have to grub for every dollar."

"Yes, I know what you mean. Maybe it'll come out right. But signing papers is signing papers. There ain't no maybe about that." He took his pail and trudged up the path to the house.

Alexandra drew her shawl closer about her and stood

leaning against the frame of the mill, looking at the stars which glittered so keenly through the frosty autumn air. She always loved to watch them, to think of their vastness and distance, and of their ordered march. It fortified her to reflect upon the great operations of nature, and when she thought of the law that lay behind them, she felt a sense of personal security. That night she had a new consciousness of the country, felt almost a new relation to it. Even her talk with the boys had not taken away the feeling that had overwhelmed her when she drove back to the Divide that afternoon. She had never known before how much the country meant to her. The chirping of the insects down in the long grass had been like the sweetest music. She had felt as if her heart were hiding down there, somewhere, with the quail and the plover and all the little wild things that crooned or buzzed in the sun. Under the long shaggy ridges, she felt the future stirring.

PART II

•

Neighboring Fields

CHAPTER I

It is sixteen years since John Bergson died. His wife now lies beside him, and the white shaft that marks their graves gleams across the wheatfields. Could he rise from beneath it, he would not know the country under which he has been asleep. The shaggy coat of the prairie, which they lifted to make him a bed, has vanished forever. From the Norwegian graveyard one looks out over a vast checker-board, marked off in squares of wheat and corn; light and dark, dark and light. Telephone wires hum along the white roads, which always run at right angles. From the graveyard gate one can count a dozen gayly painted farm-houses; the gilded weather-vanes on the big red barns wink at each other across the green and brown and yellow fields. The light steel windmills tremble throughout their frames and tug at their moorings, as they vibrate in the wind that often blows from one week's end to another across that high, active, resolute stretch of country.

The Divide is now thickly populated. The rich soil yields heavy harvests; the dry, bracing climate and the smoothness of the land make labor easy for men and beasts. There are few scenes more gratifying than a spring plowing in that country, where the furrows of a single field often lie a mile in length, and the brown earth, with such a strong, clean smell, and such a power of growth and fertility in it, yields itself eagerly to the plow; rolls away from the shear, not even dimming the brightness of the metal, with a soft, deep sigh of happiness. The wheat-cutting sometimes goes on all night as well as all day, and in good seasons there are scarcely men and horses enough to do the harvesting. The grain is so heavy that it bends toward the blade and cuts like velvet.

There is something frank and joyous and young in the open face of the country. It gives itself ungrudgingly to the moods of the season, holding nothing back. Like the plains of Lombardy, it seems to rise a little to meet the sun. The air and the earth are curiously mated and intermingled, as if the one were the breath of the other. You feel in the atmosphere the same tonic, puissant quality that is in the tilth, the same strength and resoluteness.

One June morning a young man stood at the gate of the Norwegian graveyard, sharpening his scythe in strokes unconsciously timed to the tune he was whistling. He wore a flannel cap and duck trousers, and the sleeves of his white flannel shirt were rolled back to the elbow. When he was satisfied with the edge of his blade, he slipped the whetstone into his hip pocket and began to swing his scythe, still whistling, but softly, out of respect to the quiet folk about him. Unconscious respect, probably, for he seemed intent upon his own thoughts, and, like the Gladiator's, they were far away. He was a splendid figure of a boy, tall and straight as a young pine tree, with a handsome head, and stormy gray eyes, deeply set under a serious brow. The space between his two front teeth, which were unusually far apart, gave him the proficiency in whistling for which he was distinguished at college. (He also played the cornet in the University band.)

When the grass required his close attention, or when he had to stoop to cut about a headstone, he paused in his lively air,—the "Jewel" song,—taking it up where he had left it when his scythe swung free again. He was not thinking about the tired pioneers over whom his blade glittered. The old wild country, the struggle in which his sister was destined to succeed while so many men broke their hearts and died, he can scarcely remember. That is all among the dim things of childhood and has been forgotten in the brighter pattern life weaves to-day, in the bright facts of being captain of the track team, and holding the interstate record for the high jump, in the all-suffusing brightness of being twenty-one. Yet sometimes, in the pauses of his work, the young man frowned and looked at the ground with an intentness which suggested that even twenty-one might have its problems.

When he had been mowing the better part of an hour, he heard the rattle of a light cart on the road behind him. Supposing that it was his sister coming back from one of her farms, he kept on with his work. The cart stopped at the gate and a merry contralto voice called, "Almost through, Emil?" He dropped his scythe and went toward the fence, wiping his face and neck with his handkerchief. In the cart sat a young woman who wore driving gauntlets and a wide shade hat, trimmed with red poppies. Her face, too, was rather like a poppy, round and brown, with rich color in her cheeks and lips, and her dancing yellow-brown eyes bubbled with gayety. The wind was flapping her big hat and teasing a curl of her chestnut-colored hair. She shook her head at the tall youth.

"What time did you get over here? That's not much of a job for an athlete. Here I've been to town and back. Alexandra lets you sleep late. Oh, I know! Lou's wife was telling me about the way she spoils you. I was going to give you a lift, if you were done." She gathered up her reins.

"But I will be, in a minute. Please wait for me, Marie," Emil coaxed. "Alexandra sent me to mow our lot, but I've done half a dozen others, you see. Just wait till I finish off the Kourdnas'. By the way, they were Bohemians. Why aren't they up in the Catholic graveyard?"

"Free-thinkers," replied the young woman laconically.

"Lots of the Bohemian boys at the University are," said Emil, taking up his scythe again. "What did you ever burn John Huss for, anyway? It's made an awful row. They still jaw about it in history classes."

"We'd do it right over again, most of us," said the young woman hotly. "Don't they ever teach you in your history classes that you'd all be heathen Turks if it hadn't been for the Bohemians?"

Emil had fallen to mowing. "Oh, there's no denying you're a spunky little bunch, you Czechs," he called back over his shoulder.

Marie Shabata settled herself in her seat and watched the rhythmical movement of the young man's long arms, swinging her foot as if in time to some air that was going through her mind. The minutes passed. Emil mowed vigorously and Marie sat sunning herself and watching the long grass fall. She sat with the ease that belongs to persons of an essentially happy nature, who can find a comfortable spot almost anywhere; who are supple, and quick in adapting themselves to circumstances. After a final swish, Emil snapped the gate and sprang into the cart, holding his scythe well out over the wheel. "There," he sighed. "I gave old man Lee a cut or so, too. Lou's wife needn't talk. I never see Lou's scythe over here."

Marie clucked to her horse. "Oh, you know Annie!" She looked at the young man's bare arms. "How brown you've got since you came home. I wish I had an athlete to mow my orchard. I get wet to my knees when I go down to pick cherries."

"You can have one, any time you want him. Better wait until after it rains." Emil squinted off at the horizon as if he were looking for clouds.

"Will you? Oh, there's a good boy!" She turned her head to him with a quick, bright smile. He felt it rather than saw it. Indeed, he had looked away with the purpose of not seeing it. "I've been up looking at Angélique's wedding clothes," Marie went on, "and I'm so excited I can hardly wait until Sunday. Amédée will be a handsome bridegroom. Is anybody but you going to stand up with him? Well, then it will be a handsome wedding party." She made a droll face at Emil, who flushed. "Frank," Marie continued, flicking her horse, "is cranky at me because I loaned his saddle to Jan Smirka, and I'm terribly afraid he won't take me to the dance in the evening. Maybe the supper will tempt him. All Angélique's folks are baking for it, and all Amédée's twenty cousins. There will be barrels of beer. If once I get Frank to the supper, I'll see that I stay for the dance. And by the way, Emil, you mustn't dance with me but once or twice. You must dance with all the French girls. It hurts their feelings if you don't. They think you're proud because you've been away to school or something."

Emil sniffed. "How do you know they think that?"

"Well, you didn't dance with them much at Raoul Marcel's party, and I could tell how they took it by the way they looked at you—and at me."

"All right," said Emil shortly, studying the glittering blade of his scythe.

They drove westward toward Norway Creek, and toward a big white house that stood on a hill, several miles across the fields. There were so many sheds and outbuildings grouped about it that the place looked not unlike a tiny village. A stranger, approaching it, could not help noticing the beauty and fruitfulness of the outlying fields. There was something individual about the great farm, a most unusual trimness and care for detail. On either side of the road, for a mile before you reached the foot of the hill, stood tall osage orange hedges, their glossy green marking off the yellow fields. South of the hill, in a low, sheltered swale, surrounded by a mulberry hedge, was the orchard, its fruit trees knee-deep in timothy grass. Any one thereabouts would have told you that this was one of the richest farms on the Divide, and that the farmer was a woman, Alexandra Bergson.

If you go up the hill and enter Alexandra's big house, you will find that it is curiously unfinished and uneven in comfort. One room is papered, carpeted, over-furnished; the next is almost bare. The pleasantest rooms in the house are the kitchen—where Alexandra's three young Swedish girls chatter and cook and pickle and preserve all summer long—and the sitting-room, in which Alexandra has brought together the old homely furniture that the Bergsons used in their first log house, the family portraits, and the few things her mother brought from Sweden.

When you go out of the house into the flower garden, there you feel again the order and fine arrangement manifest all over the great farm; in the fencing and hedging, in the windbreaks and sheds, in the symmetrical pasture ponds, planted with scrub willows to give shade to the cattle in fly-time. There is even a white row of beehives in the orchard, under the walnut trees. You feel that, properly, Alexandra's house is the big out-of-doors, and that it is in the soil that she expresses herself best.

CHAPTER II

Emil reached home a little past noon, and when he went into the kitchen Alexandra was already seated at the head of the long table, having dinner with her men, as she always did unless there were visitors. He slipped into his empty place at his sister's right. The three pretty young Swedish girls who did Alexandra's housework were cutting pies, refilling coffee-cups, placing platters of bread and meat and potatoes upon the red tablecloth, and continually getting in each other's way between the table and the stove. To be sure they always wasted a good deal of time getting in each other's way and giggling at each other's mistakes. But, as Alexandra had pointedly told her sisters-in-law, it was to hear them giggle that she kept three young things in her kitchen; the work she could do herself, if it were necessary. These girls, with their long letters from home, their finery, and their love-affairs, afforded her a great deal of entertainment, and they were company for her when Emil was away at school.

Of the youngest girl, Signa, who has a pretty figure, mottled pink cheeks, and yellow hair, Alexandra is very fond, though she keeps a sharp eye upon her. Signa is apt to be skittish at mealtime, when the men are about, and to spill the coffee or upset the cream. It is supposed that Nelse Jensen, one of the six men at the dinner-table, is courting Signa, though he has been so careful not to commit himself that no one in the house, least of all Signa, can tell just how far the matter has progressed. Nelse watches her glumly as she waits upon the table, and in the evening he sits on a bench behind the stove with his *dragharmonika*, playing mournful airs and watching her as she goes about her work. When Alexandra asked Signa whether she thought Nelse was in earnest, the poor child hid her hands under her apron and murmured, "I don't know, ma'm. But he scolds me about everything, like as if he wanted to have me!"

At Alexandra's left sat a very old man, barefoot and wearing a long blue blouse, open at the neck. His shaggy head is scarcely whiter than it was sixteen years ago, but his little blue eyes have become pale and watery, and his ruddy face is withered, like an apple that has clung all winter to the tree. When Ivar lost his land through mismanagement a dozen years ago, Alexandra took him in, and he has been a member of her household ever since. He is too old to work in the fields, but he hitches and unhitches the work-teams and looks after the health of the stock. Sometimes of a winter evening Alexandra calls him into the sitting-room to read the Bible aloud to her, for he still reads very well. He dislikes human habitations, so Alexandra has fitted him up a room in the barn, where he is very comfortable, being near the horses and, as he says, further from temptations. No one has ever found out what his temptations are. In cold weather he sits by the kitchen fire and makes hammocks or mends harness until it is time to go to bed. Then he says his prayers at great length behind the stove, puts on his buffalo-skin coat and goes out to his room in the barn.

Alexandra herself has changed very little. Her figure is fuller, and she has more color. She seems sunnier and more vigorous than she did as a young girl. But she still has the same calmness and deliberation of manner, the same clear eyes, and she still wears her hair in two braids wound round her head. It is so curly that fiery ends escape from the braids and make her head look like one of the big double sunflowers that fringe her vegetable garden. Her face is always tanned in summer, for her sunbonnet is oftener on her arm than on her head. But where her collar falls away from her neck, or where her sleeves are pushed back from her wrist, the skin is of such smoothness and whiteness as none but Swedish women ever possess; skin with the freshness of the snow itself.

Alexandra did not talk much at the table, but she encouraged her men to talk, and she always listened attentively, even when they seemed to be talking foolishly.

To-day Barney Flinn, the big red-headed Irishman who had been with Alexandra for five years and who was actually her foreman, though he had no such title, was grumbling about the new silo she had put up that spring. It happened to be the first silo on the Divide, and Alexandra's neighbors and her men were skeptical about it. "To be sure, if the thing don't work, we'll have plenty of feed without it, indeed," Barney conceded.

Nelse Jensen, Signa's gloomy suitor, had his word. "Lou, he says he wouldn't have no silo on his place if you'd give it to him. He says the feed outen it gives the stock the bloat. He heard of somebody lost four head of horses, feedin' 'em that stuff."

Alexandra looked down the table from one to another. "Well, the only way we can find out is to try. Lou and I have different notions about feeding stock, and that's a good thing. It's bad if all the members of a family think alike. They never get anywhere. Lou can learn by my mistakes and I can learn by his. Isn't that fair, Barney?"

The Irishman laughed. He had no love for Lou, who was always uppish with him and who said that Alexandra paid her hands too much. "I've not thought but to give the thing an honest try, mum. 'T would be only right, after puttin' so much expense into it. Maybe Emil will come out an' have a look at it wid me." He pushed back his chair, took his hat from the nail, and marched out with Emil, who, with his university ideas, was supposed to have instigated the silo. The other hands followed them, all except old Ivar. He had been depressed throughout the meal and had paid no heed to the talk of the men, even when they mentioned cornstalk bloat, upon which he was sure to have opinions.

"Did you want to speak to me, Ivar?" Alexandra asked as she rose from the table. "Come into the sitting-room."

The old man followed Alexandra, but when she motioned him to a chair he shook his head. She took up her workbasket and waited for him to speak. He stood looking at the carpet, his bushy head bowed, his hands clasped in front of him. Ivar's bandy legs seemed to have grown shorter with years, and they were completely misfitted to his broad, thick body and heavy shoulders.

"Well, Ivar, what is it?" Alexandra asked after she had waited longer than usual.

Ivar had never learned to speak English and his Norwegian was quaint and grave, like the speech of the more old-fashioned people. He always addressed Alexandra in terms of the deepest respect, hoping to set a good example to the kitchen girls, whom he thought too familiar in their manners.

"Mistress," he began faintly, without raising his eyes, "the folk have been looking coldly at me of late. You know there has been talk."

"Talk about what, Ivar?"

"About sending me away; to the asylum."

Alexandra put down her sewing-basket. "Nobody has come to me with such talk," she said decidedly. "Why need you listen? You know I would never consent to such a thing."

Ivar lifted his shaggy head and looked at her out of his little eyes. "They say that you cannot prevent it if the folk complain of me, if your brothers complain to the authorities. They say that your brothers are afraid—God forbid! —that I may do you some injury when my spells are on me. Mistress, how can any one think that?—that I could bite the hand that fed me!" The tears trickled down on the old man's beard.

Alexandra frowned. "Ivar, I wonder at you, that you should come bothering me with such nonsense. I am still running my own house, and other people have nothing to do with either you or me. So long as I am suited with you, there is nothing to be said."

Ivar pulled a red handkerchief out of the breast of his blouse and wiped his eyes and beard. "But I should not wish you to keep me if, as they say, it is against your interests, and if it is hard for you to get hands because I am here."

Alexandra made an impatient gesture, but the old man put out his hand and went on earnestly:—

"Listen, mistress, it is right that you should take these things into account. You know that my spells come from God, and that I would not harm any living creature. You believe that every one should worship God in the way revealed to him. But that is not the way of this country. The way here is for all to do alike. I am despised because I do not wear shoes, because I do not cut my hair, and because I have visions. At home, in the old country, there were many like me, who had been touched by God, or who had seen things in the graveyard at night and were different afterward. We thought nothing of it, and let them alone. But here, if a man is different in his feet or in his head, they put him in the asylum. Look at Peter Kralik; when he was a boy, drinking out of a creek, he swallowed a snake, and always after that he could eat only such food as the creature liked, for when he ate anything else, it became enraged and gnawed him. When he felt it whipping about in him, he drank alcohol to stupefy it and get some ease for himself. He could work as good as any man, and his head was clear, but they locked him up for being different in his stomach. That is the way; they have built the asylum for people who are different, and they will not even let us live in the holes with the badgers. Only your great prosperity has protected me so far. If you had had ill-fortune, they would have taken me to Hastings long ago."

As Ivar talked, his gloom lifted. Alexandra had found that she could often break his fasts and long penances by talking to him and letting him pour out the thoughts that troubled him. Sympathy always cleared his mind, and ridicule was poison to him.

"There is a great deal in what you say, Ivar. Like as not they will be wanting to take me to Hastings because I have built a silo; and then I may take you with me. But at present I need you here. Only don't come to me again telling me what people say. Let people go on talking as they like, and we will go on living as we think best. You have been with me now for twelve years, and I have gone to you for advice oftener than I have ever gone to any one. That ought to satisfy you."

Ivar bowed humbly. "Yes, mistress, I shall not trouble you with their talk again. And as for my feet, I have observed your wishes all these years, though you have never questioned me; washing them every night, even in winter."

Alexandra laughed. "Oh, never mind about your feet, Ivar. We can remember when half our neighbors went barefoot in summer. I expect old Mrs. Lee would love to slip her shoes off now sometimes, if she dared. I'm glad I'm not Lou's mother-in-law."

Ivar looked about mysteriously and lowered his voice almost to a whisper. "You know what they have over at Lou's house? A great white tub, like the stone water-troughs in the old country, to wash themselves in. When you sent me over with the strawberries, they were all in town but the old woman Lee and the baby. She took me in and showed me the thing, and she told me it was impossible to wash yourself clean in it, because, in so much water, you could not make a strong suds. So when they fill it up and send her in there, she pretends, and makes a splashing noise. Then, when they are all asleep, she washes herself in a little wooden tub she keeps under her bed."

Alexandra shook with laughter. "Poor old Mrs. Lee! They won't let her wear nightcaps, either. Never mind; when she comes to visit me, she can do all the old things in the old way, and have as much beer as she wants. We'll start an asylum for old-time people, Ivar."

Ivar folded his big handkerchief carefully and thrust it back into his blouse. "This is always the way, mistress. I come to you sorrowing, and you send me away with a light heart. And will you be so good as to tell the Irishman that he is not to work the brown gelding until the sore on its shoulder is healed?"

"That I will. Now go and put Emil's mare to the cart. I am going to drive up to the north quarter to meet the man from town who is to buy my alfalfa hay."

CHAPTER III

Alexandra was to hear more of Ivar's case, however. On Sunday her married brothers came to dinner. She had asked them for that day because Emil, who hated family parties, would be absent, dancing at Amédée Chevalier's wedding, up in the French country. The table was set for company in the dining-room, where highly varnished wood and colored glass and useless pieces of china were conspicuous enough to satisfy the standards of the new prosperity. Alexandra had put herself into the hands of the Hanover furniture dealer, and he had conscientiously done his best to make her dining-room look like his display window. She said frankly that she knew nothing about such things, and she was willing to be governed by the general conviction that the more useless and utterly unusable objects were, the greater their virtue as ornament. That seemed reasonable enough. Since she liked plain things herself, it was all the more necessary to have jars and punchbowls and candlesticks in the company rooms for people who did appreciate them. Her guests liked to see about them these reassuring emblems of prosperity.

The family party was complete except for Emil, and Oscar's wife who, in the country phrase, "was not going anywhere just now." Oscar sat at the foot of the table and his four tow-headed little boys, aged from twelve to five, were ranged at one side. Neither Oscar nor Lou has changed much; they have simply, as Alexandra said of them long ago, grown to be more and more like themselves. Lou now looks the older of the two; his face is thin and shrewd and wrinkled about the eyes, while Oscar's is thick and dull. For all his dullness, however, Oscar makes more money than his brother, which adds to Lou's sharpness and uneasiness and tempts him to make a show. The trouble with Lou is that he is tricky, and his neighbors have found out that, as Ivar says, he has not a fox's face for nothing. Politics being the natural field for such talents, he neglects his farm to attend conventions and to run for county offices.

Lou's wife, formerly Annie Lee, has grown to look curiously like her husband. Her face has become longer, sharper, more aggressive. She wears her yellow hair in a high pompadour, and is bedecked with rings and chains and "beauty pins." Her tight, high-heeled shoes give her an awkward walk, and she is always more or less preoccupied with her clothes. As she sat at the table, she kept telling her youngest daughter to "be careful now, and not drop anything on mother."

The conversation at the table was all in English. Oscar's wife, from the malaria district of Missouri, was ashamed of marrying a foreigner, and his boys do not understand a word of Swedish. Annie and Lou sometimes speak Swedish at home, but Annie is almost as much afraid of being "caught" at it as ever her mother was of being caught barefoot. Oscar still has a thick accent, but Lou speaks like anybody from Iowa.

"When I was in Hastings to attend the convention," he was saying, "I saw the superintendent of the asylum, and I was telling him about Ivar's symptoms. He says Ivar's case is one of the most dangerous kind, and it's a wonder he hasn't done something violent before this."

Alexandra laughed good-humoredly. "Oh, nonsense, Lou! The doctors would have us all crazy if they could. Ivar's queer, certainly, but he has more sense than half the hands I hire."

Lou flew at his fried chicken. "Oh, I guess the doctor knows his business, Alexandra. He was very much surprised when I told him how you'd put up with Ivar. He says he's likely to set fire to the barn any night, or to take after you and the girls with an axe."

Little Signa, who was waiting on the table, giggled and fled to the kitchen. Alexandra's eyes twinkled. "That was too much for Signa, Lou. We all know that Ivar's perfectly harmless. The girls would as soon expect me to chase them with an axe."

Lou flushed and signaled to his wife. "All the same, the neighbors will be having a say about it before long. He may burn anybody's barn. It's only necessary for one property-owner in the township to make complaint, and he'll be taken up by force. You'd better send him yourself and not have any hard feelings."

Alexandra helped one of her little nephews to gravy. "Well, Lou, if any of the neighbors try that, I'll have myself appointed Ivar's guardian and take the case to court, that's all. I am perfectly satisfied with him."

"Pass the preserves, Lou," said Annie in a warning tone. She had reasons for not wishing her husband to cross Alexandra too openly. "But don't you sort of hate to have people see him around here, Alexandra?" she went on with persuasive smoothness. "He *is* a disgraceful object, and you're fixed up so nice now. It sort of makes people distant with you, when they never know when they'll hear him scratching about. My girls are afraid as death of him, aren't you, Milly, dear?"

Milly was fifteen, fat and jolly and pompadoured, with a creamy complexion, square white teeth, and a short upper lip. She looked like her grandmother Bergson, and had her comfortable and comfort-loving nature. She grinned at her aunt, with whom she was a great deal more at ease than she was with her mother. Alexandra winked a reply.

"Milly needn't be afraid of Ivar. She's an especial favorite of his. In my opinion Ivar has just as much right to his own way of dressing and thinking as we have. But I'll see that he doesn't bother other people. I'll keep him at home, so don't trouble any more about him, Lou. I've been wanting to ask you about your new bathtub. How does it work?"

Annie came to the fore to give Lou time to recover himself. "Oh, it works something grand! I can't keep him out of it. He washes himself all over three times a week now, and uses all the hot water. I think it's weakening to stay in as long as he does. You ought to have one, Alexandra."

"I'm thinking of it. I might have one put in the barn for Ivar, if it will ease people's minds. But before I get a bathtub, I'm going to get a piano for Milly."

Oscar, at the end of the table, looked up from his plate. "What does Milly want of a pianny? What's the matter with her organ? She can make some use of that, and play in church."

Annie looked flustered. She had begged Alexandra not to say anything about this plan before Oscar, who was apt to be jealous of what his sister did for Lou's children. Alexandra did not get on with Oscar's wife at all. "Milly can play in church just the same, and she'll still play on the organ. But practising on it so much spoils her touch. Her teacher says so," Annie brought out with spirit.

Oscar rolled his eyes. "Well, Milly must have got on pretty good if she's got past the organ. I know plenty of grown folks that ain't," he said bluntly.

Annie threw up her chin. "She has got on good, and

she's going to play for her commencement when she graduates in town next year."

"Yes," said Alexandra firmly, "I think Milly deserves a piano. All the girls around here have been taking lessons for years, but Milly is the only one of them who can ever play anything when you ask her. I'll tell you when I first thought I would like to give you a piano, Milly, and that was when you learned that book of old Swedish songs that your grandfather used to sing. He had a sweet tenor voice, and when he was a young man he loved to sing. I can remember hearing him singing with the sailors down in the shipyard, when I was no bigger than Stella here," pointing to Annie's younger daughter.

Milly and Stella both looked through the door into the sitting-room, where a crayon portrait of John Bergson hung on the wall. Alexandra had had it made from a little photograph, taken for his friends just before he left Sweden; a slender man of thirty-five, with soft hair curling about his high forehead, a drooping mustache, and wondering, sad eyes that looked forward into the distance, as if they already beheld the New World.

After dinner Lou and Oscar went to the orchard to pick cherries—they had neither of them had the patience to grow an orchard of their own—and Annie went down to gossip with Alexandra's kitchen girls while they washed the dishes. She could always find out more about Alexandra's domestic economy from the prattling maids than from Alexandra herself, and what she discovered she used to her own advantage with Lou. On the Divide, farmers' daughters no longer went out into service, so Alexandra got her girls from Sweden, by paying their fare over. They stayed with her until they married, and were replaced by sisters or cousins from the old country.

Alexandra took her three nieces into the flower garden. She was fond of the little girls, especially of Milly, who came to spend a week with her aunt now and then, and read aloud to her from the old books about the house, or listened to stories about the early days on the Divide. While they were walking among the flower beds, a buggy drove up the hill and stopped in front of the gate. A man got out and stood talking to the driver. The little girls were delighted at the advent of a stranger, some one from very far away, they knew by his clothes, his gloves, and the sharp, pointed cut of his dark beard. The girls fell behind their aunt and peeped out at him from among the castor beans. The stranger came up to the gate and stood holding his hat in his hand, smiling, while Alexandra advanced slowly to meet him. As she approached he spoke in a low, pleasant voice.

"Don't you know me, Alexandra? I would have known you, anywhere."

Alexandra shaded her eyes with her hand. Suddenly she took a quick step forward. "Can it be!" she exclaimed with feeling; "can it be that it is Carl Linstrum? Why, Carl, it is!" She threw out both her hands and caught his across the gate. "Sadie, Milly, run tell your father and Uncle Oscar that our old friend Carl Linstrum is here. Be quick! Why, Carl, how did it happen? I can't believe this!" Alexandra shook the tears from her eyes and laughed.

The stranger nodded to his driver, dropped his suitcase inside the fence, and opened the gate. "Then you are glad to see me, and you can put me up overnight? I couldn't go through this country without stopping off to have a look at you. How little you have changed! Do you know, I was sure it would be like that. You simply couldn't be different. How fine you are!" He stepped back and looked at her admiringly.

Alexandra blushed and laughed again. "But you yourself, Carl—with that beard—how could I have known you? You went away a little boy." She reached for his suitcase and when he intercepted her she threw up her hands. "You see, I give myself away. I have only women come to visit me, and I do not know how to behave. Where is your trunk?"

"It's in Hanover. I can stay only a few days. I am on my way to the coast."

They started up the path. "A few days? After all these years!" Alexandra shook her finger at him. "See this, you have walked into a trap. You do not get away so easy." She put her hand affectionately on his shoulder. "You owe me a visit for the sake of old times. Why must you go to the coast at all?"

"Oh, I must! I am a fortune hunter. From Seattle I go on to Alaska."

"Alaska?" She looked at him in astonishment. "Are you going to paint the Indians?"

"Paint?" the young man frowned. "Oh! I'm not a painter, Alexandra. I'm an engraver. I have nothing to do with painting."

"But on my parlor wall I have the paintings—"

He interrupted nervously. "Oh, water-color sketches—done for amusement. I sent them to remind you of me, not because they were good. What a wonderful place you have made of this, Alexandra." He turned and looked back at the wide, map-like prospect of field and hedge and pasture. "I would never have believed it could be done. I'm disappointed in my own eye, in my imagination."

At this moment Lou and Oscar came up the hill from the orchard. They did not quicken their pace when they saw Carl; indeed, they did not openly look in his direction. They advanced distrustfully, and as if they wished the distance were longer.

Alexandra beckoned to them. "They think I am trying to fool them. Come, boys, it's Carl Linstrum, our old Carl!"

Lou gave the visitor a quick, sidelong glance and thrust out his hand. "Glad to see you." Oscar followed with "How d' do." Carl could not tell whether their offishness came from unfriendliness or from embarrassment. He and Alexandra led the way to the porch.

"Carl," Alexandra explained, "is on his way to Seattle. He is going to Alaska."

Oscar studied the visitor's yellow shoes. "Got business there?" he asked.

Carl laughed. "Yes, very pressing business. I'm going there to get rich. Engraving's a very interesting profession, but a man never makes any money at it. So I'm going to try the goldfields."

Alexandra felt that this was a tactful speech, and Lou looked up with some interest. "Ever done anything in that line before?"

"No, but I'm going to join a friend of mine who went out from New York and has done well. He has offered to break me in."

"Turrible cold winters, there, I hear," remarked Oscar. "I thought people went up there in the spring."

"They do. But my friend is going to spend the winter in Seattle and I am to stay with him there and learn something about prospecting before we start north next year."

Lou looked skeptical. "Let's see, how long have you been away from here?"

"Sixteen years. You ought to remember that, Lou, for you were married just after we went away."

"Going to stay with us some time?" Oscar asked.

"A few days, if Alexandra can keep me."

"I expect you'll be wanting to see your old place," Lou observed more cordially. "You won't hardly know it. But there's a few chunks of your old sod house left. Alexandra wouldn't never let Frank Shabata plough over it."

Annie Lee, who, ever since the visitor was announced, had been touching up her hair and settling her lace and wishing she had worn another dress, now emerged with her three daughters and introduced them. She was greatly impressed by Carl's urban appearance, and in her excitement talked very loud and threw her head about. "And you ain't married yet? At your age, now! Think of that! You'll have to wait for Milly. Yes, we've got a boy, too. The youngest. He's at home with his grandma. You must come over to see mother and hear Milly play. She's the musician of the family. She does pyrography, too. That's burnt wood, you know. You wouldn't believe what she can do with her poker. Yes, she goes to school in town, and she is the youngest in her class by two years."

Milly looked uncomfortable and Carl took her hand again. He liked her creamy skin and happy, innocent eyes, and he could see that her mother's way of talking distressed her. "I'm sure she's a clever little girl," he murmured, looking at her thoughtfully. "Let me see—Ah, it's your mother that she looks like, Alexandra. Mrs. Bergson must have looked just like this when she was a little girl. Does Milly run about over the country as you and Alexandra used to, Annie?"

Milly's mother protested. "Oh, my, no! Things has changed since we was girls. Milly has it very different. We are going to rent the place and move into town as soon as the girls are old enough to go out into company. A good many are doing that here now. Lou is going into business."

Lou grinned. "That's what she says. You better go get your things on. Ivar's hitching up," he added, turning to Annie.

Young farmers seldom address their wives by name. It is always "you," or "she."

Having got his wife out of the way, Lou sat down on the step and began to whittle. "Well, what do folks in New York think of William Jennings Bryan?" Lou began to bluster, as he always did when he talked politics. "We gave Wall Street a scare in ninety-six, all right, and we're fixing another to hand them. Silver wasn't the only issue," he nodded mysteriously. "There's a good many things got to be changed. The West is going to make itself heard."

Carl laughed. "But, surely, it did do that, if nothing else."

Lou's thin face reddened up to the roots of his bristly hair. "Oh, we've only begun. We're waking up to a sense of our responsibilities, out here, and we ain't afraid, neither. You fellows back there must be a tame lot. If you had any nerve you'd get together and march down to Wall Street and blow it up. Dynamite it, I mean," with a threatening nod.

He was so much in earnest that Carl scarcely knew how to answer him. "That would be a waste of powder. The same business would go on in another street. The street doesn't matter. But what have you fellows out here got to kick about? You have the only safe place there is. Morgan himself couldn't touch you. One only has to drive through this country to see that you're all as rich as barons."

"We have a good deal more to say than we had when we were poor," said Lou threateningly. "We're getting on to a whole lot of things."

As Ivar drove a double carriage up to the gate, Annie came out in a hat that looked like the model of a battleship. Carl rose and took her down to the carriage, while Lou lingered for a word with his sister.

"What do you suppose he's come for?" he asked, jerking his head toward the gate.

"Why, to pay us a visit. I've been begging him to for years."

Oscar looked at Alexandra. "He didn't let you know he was coming?"

"No. Why should he? I told him to come at any time."

Lou shrugged his shoulders. "He doesn't seem to have done much for himself. Wandering around this way!"

Oscar spoke solemnly, as from the depths of a cavern. "He never was much account."

Alexandra left them and hurried down to the gate where Annie was rattling on to Carl about her new dining-room furniture. "You must bring Mr. Linstrum over real soon, only be sure to telephone me first," she called back, as Carl helped her into the carriage. Old Ivar, his white head bare, stood holding the horses. Lou came down the path and climbed into the front seat, took up the reins, and drove off without saying anything further to any one. Oscar picked up his youngest boy and trudged off down the road, the other three trotting after him. Carl, holding the gate open for Alexandra, began to laugh. "Up and coming on the Divide, eh, Alexandra?" he cried gayly.

CHAPTER IV

Carl had changed, Alexandra felt, much less than one might have expected. He had not become a trim, self-satisfied city man. There was still something homely and wayward and definitely personal about him. Even his clothes, his Norfolk coat and his very high collars, were a little unconventional. He seemed to shrink into himself as he used to do; to hold himself away from things, as if he were afraid of being hurt. In short, he was more self-conscious than a man of thirty-five is expected to be. He looked older than his years and not very strong. His black hair, which still hung in a triangle over his pale forehead, was thin at the crown, and there were fine, relentless lines about his eyes. His back, with its high, sharp shoulders, looked like the back of an overworked German professor off on his holiday. His face was intelligent, sensitive, unhappy.

That evening after supper, Carl and Alexandra were sitting by the clump of castor beans in the middle of the flower garden. The gravel paths glittered in the moonlight, and below them the fields lay white and still.

"Do you know, Alexandra," he was saying, "I've been thinking how strangely things work out. I've been away engraving other men's pictures, and you've stayed at home and made your own." He pointed with his cigar toward the sleeping landscape. "How in the world have you done it? How have your neighbors done it?"

"We hadn't any of us much to do with it, Carl. The land did it. It had its little joke. It pretended to be poor because nobody knew how to work it right; and then, all at once, it worked itself. It woke up out of its sleep and stretched itself, and it was so big, so rich, that we suddenly found we were rich, just from sitting still. As for me, you remember when I began to buy land. For years after that I was always squeezing and borrowing until I was ashamed to show my face in the banks. And then, all at once, men began to come to me offering to lend me money—and I didn't need it! Then I went ahead and built this house. I really built it for Emil. I want you to see Emil, Carl. He is so different from the rest of us!"

"How different?"

"Oh, you'll see! I'm sure it was to have sons like Emil, and to give them a chance, that father left the old country. It's curious, too; on the outside Emil is just like an American boy,—he graduated from the State University in June, you know,—but underneath he is more Swedish than any of us. Sometimes he is so like father that he frightens me; he is so violent in his feelings like that."

"Is he going to farm here with you?"

"He shall do whatever he wants to," Alexandra declared warmly. "He is going to have a chance, a whole chance; that's what I've worked for. Sometimes he talks about studying law, and sometimes, just lately, he's been talking about going out into the sand hills and taking up more land. He has his sad times, like father. But I hope he won't do that. We have land enough, at last!" Alexandra laughed.

"How about Lou and Oscar? They've done well, haven't they?"

"Yes, very well; but they are different, and now that they have farms of their own I do not see so much of them. We divided the land equally when Lou married. They have their own way of doing things, and they do not altogether like my way, I am afraid. Perhaps they think me too independent. But I have had to think for myself a good many years and am not likely to change. On the whole, though, we take as much comfort in each other as most brothers and sisters do. And I am very fond of Lou's oldest daughter."

"I think I liked the old Lou and Oscar better, and they probably feel the same about me. I even, if you can keep a secret,"—Carl leaned forward and touched her arm, smiling,—"I even think I liked the old country better. This is all very splendid in its way, but there was something about this country when it was a wild old beast that has haunted me all these years. Now, when I come back to all this milk and honey, I feel like the old German song, 'Wo bist du, wo bist du, mein geliebtest Land?'—Do you ever feel like that, I wonder?"

"Yes, sometimes, when I think about father and mother and those who are gone; so many of our old neighbors." Alexandra paused and looked up thoughtfully at the stars. "We can remember the graveyard when it was wild prairie, Carl, and now—"

"And now the old story has begun to write itself over there," said Carl softly. "Isn't it queer: there are only two or three human stories, and they go on repeating themselves as fiercely as if they had never happened before; like the larks in this country, that have been singing the same five notes over for thousands of years."

"Oh, yes! The young people, they live so hard. And yet I sometimes envy them. There is my little neighbor, now; the people who bought your old place. I wouldn't have sold it to any one else, but I was always fond of that girl. You must remember her, little Marie Tovesky, from Omaha, who used to visit here? When she was eighteen she ran away from the convent school and got married, crazy child! She came out here a bride, with her father and husband. He had nothing, and the old man was willing to buy them a place and set them up. Your farm took her fancy, and I was glad to have her so near me. I've never been sorry, either. I even try to get along with Frank on her account."

"Is Frank her husband?"

"Yes. He's one of these wild fellows. Most Bohemians are good-natured, but Frank thinks we don't appreciate him here, I guess. He's jealous about everything, his farm and his horses and his pretty wife. Everybody likes her, just the same as when she was little. Sometimes I go up to the Catholic church with Emil, and it's funny to see Marie standing there laughing and shaking hands with people, looking so excited and gay, with Frank sulking behind her as if he could eat everybody alive. Frank's not a bad neighbor, but to get on with him you've got to make a fuss over him and act as if you thought he was a very important person all the time, and different from other people. I find it hard to keep that up from one year's end to another."

"I shouldn't think you'd be very successful at that kind of thing, Alexandra." Carl seemed to find the idea amusing.

"Well," said Alexandra firmly, "I do the best I can, on Marie's account. She has it hard enough, anyway. She's too young and pretty for this sort of life. We're all ever so much older and slower. But she's the kind that won't be downed easily. She'll work all day and go to a Bohemian wedding and dance all night, and drive the hay wagon for a cross man next morning. I could stay by a job, but I never had the go in me that she has, when I was going my best. I'll have to take you over to see her to-morrow."

Carl dropped the end of his cigar softly among the castor beans and sighed. "Yes, I suppose I must see the old place. I'm cowardly about things that remind me of myself. It took courage to come at all, Alexandra. I wouldn't have, if I hadn't wanted to see you very, very much."

Alexandra looked at him with her calm, deliberate eyes. "Why do you dread things like that, Carl?" she asked earnestly. "Why are you dissatisfied with yourself?"

Her visitor winced. "How direct you are, Alexandra!

Just like you used to be. Do I give myself away so quickly? Well, you see, for one thing, there's nothing to look forward to in my profession. Wood-engraving is the only thing I care about, and that had gone out before I began. Everything's cheap metal work nowadays, touching up miserable photographs, forcing up poor drawings, and spoiling good ones. I'm absolutely sick of it all." Carl frowned. "Alexandra, all the way out from New York I've been planning how I could deceive you and make you think me a very enviable fellow, and here I am telling you the truth the first night. I waste a lot of time pretending to people, and the joke of it is, I don't think I ever deceive any one. There are too many of my kind; people know us on sight."

Carl paused. Alexandra pushed her hair back from her brow with a puzzled, thoughtful gesture. "You see," he went on calmly, "measured by your standards here, I'm a failure. I couldn't buy even one of your cornfields. I've enjoyed a great many things, but I've got nothing to show for it all."

"But you show for it yourself, Carl. I'd rather have had your freedom than my land."

Carl shook his head mournfully. "Freedom so often means that one isn't needed anywhere. Here you are an individual, you have a background of your own, you would be missed. But off there in the cities there are thousands of rolling stones like me. We are all alike; we have no ties, we know nobody, we own nothing. When one of us dies, they scarcely know where to bury him. Our landlady and the delicatessen man are our mourners, and we leave nothing behind us but a frock-coat and a fiddle, or an easel, or a typewriter, or whatever tool we got our living by. All we have ever managed to do is to pay our rent, the exorbitant rent that one has to pay for a few square feet of space near the heart of things. We have no house, no place, no people of our own. We live in the streets, in the parks, in the theatres. We sit in restaurants and concert halls and look about at the hundreds of our own kind and shudder."

Alexandra was silent. She sat looking at the silver spot the moon made on the surface of the pond down in the pasture. He knew that she understood what he meant. At last she said slowly, "And yet I would rather have Emil grow up like that than like his two brothers. We pay a high rent, too, though we pay differently. We grow hard and heavy here. We don't move lightly and easily as you do, and our minds get stiff. If the world were no wider than my cornfields, if there were not something beside this, I wouldn't feel that it was much worthwhile to work. No, I would rather have Emil like you than like them. I felt that as soon as you came."

"I wonder why you feel like that?" Carl mused.

"I don't know. Perhaps I am like Carrie Jensen, the sister of one of my hired men. She had never been out of the cornfields, and a few years ago she got despondent and said life was just the same thing over and over, and she didn't see the use of it. After she had tried to kill herself once or twice, her folks got worried and sent her over to Iowa to visit some relations. Ever since she's come back she's been perfectly cheerful, and she says she's contented to live and work in a world that's so big and interesting. She said that anything as big as the bridges over the Platte and the Missouri reconciled her. And it's what goes on in the world that reconciles me."

CHAPTER V

Alexandra did not find time to go to her neighbor's the next day, nor the next. It was a busy season on the farm, with the corn-plowing going on, and even Emil was in the field with a team and cultivator. Carl went about over the farms with Alexandra in the morning, and in the afternoon and evening they found a great deal to talk about. Emil, for all his track practice, did not stand up under farmwork very well, and by night he was too tired to talk or even to practice on his cornet.

On Wednesday morning Carl got up before it was light, and stole downstairs and out of the kitchen door just as old Ivar was making his morning ablutions at the pump. Carl nodded to him and hurried up the draw, past the garden, and into the pasture where the milking cows used to be kept.

The dawn in the east looked like the light from some great fire that was burning under the edge of the world. The color was reflected in the globules of dew that sheathed the short gray pasture grass. Carl walked rapidly until he came to the crest of the second hill, where the Bergson pasture joined the one that had belonged to his father. There he sat down and waited for the sun to rise. It was just there that he and Alexandra used to do their milking together, he on his side of the fence, she on hers. He could remember exactly how she looked when she came over the close-cropped grass, her skirts pinned up, her head bare, a bright tin pail in either hand, and the milky light of the early morning all about her. Even as a boy he used to feel, when he saw her coming with her free step, her upright head and calm shoulders, that she looked as if she had walked straight out of the morning itself. Since then, when he had happened to see the sun come up in the country or on the water, he had often remembered the young Swedish girl and her milking pails.

Carl sat musing until the sun leaped above the prairie, and in the grass about him all the small creatures of day began to tune their tiny instruments. Birds and insects without number began to chirp, to twitter, to snap and whistle, to make all manner of fresh shrill noises. The pasture was flooded with light; every clump of ironweed and snow-on-the-mountain threw a long shadow, and the golden light seemed to be rippling through the curly grass like the tide racing in.

He crossed the fence into the pasture that was now the Shabatas' and continued his walk toward the pond. He had not gone far, however, when he discovered that he was not the only person abroad. In the draw below, his gun in his hands, was Emil, advancing cautiously, with a young woman beside him. They were moving softly, keeping close together, and Carl knew that they expected to find ducks on the pond. At the moment when they came in sight of the bright spot of water, he heard a whirr of wings and the ducks shot up into the air. There was a sharp crack from the gun, and five of the birds fell to the ground. Emil and his companion laughed delightedly, and Emil ran to pick them up. When he came back, dangling the ducks by their feet, Marie held her apron and he dropped them into it. As she stood looking down at them, her face changed. She took up one of the birds, a rumpled ball of feathers with the blood dripping slowly from its mouth, and looked at the live color that still burned on its plumage.

As she let it fall, she cried in distress, "Oh, Emil, why did you?"

"I like that!" the boy exclaimed indignantly. "Why, Marie, you asked me to come yourself."

"Yes, yes, I know," she said tearfully, "but I didn't think. I hate to see them when they are first shot. They were having such a good time, and we've spoiled it all for them."

Emil gave a rather sore laugh. "I should say we had! I'm not going hunting with you any more. You're as bad as Ivar. Here, let me take them." He snatched the ducks out of her apron.

"Don't be cross, Emil. Only—Ivar's right about wild things. They're too happy to kill. You can tell just how they felt when they flew up. They were scared, but they didn't really think anything could hurt them. No, we won't do that any more."

"All right," Emil assented. "I'm sorry I made you feel bad." As he looked down into her tearful eyes, there was a curious, sharp young bitterness in his own.

Carl watched them as they moved slowly down the draw. They had not seen him at all. He had not overheard much of their dialogue, but he felt the import of it. It made him, somehow, unreasonably mournful to find two young things abroad in the pasture in the early morning. He decided that he needed his breakfast.

CHAPTER VI

At dinner that day Alexandra said she thought they must really manage to go over to the Shabatas' that afternoon. "It's not often I let three days go by without seeing Marie. She will think I have forsaken her, now that my old friend has come back."

After the men had gone back to work, Alexandra put on a white dress and her sun-hat, and she and Carl set forth across the fields. "You see we have kept up the old path, Carl. It has been so nice for me to feel that there was a friend at the other end of it again."

Carl smiled a little ruefully. "All the same, I hope it hasn't been *quite* the same."

Alexandra looked at him with surprise. "Why, no, of course not. Not the same. She could not very well take your place, if that's what you mean. I'm friendly with all my neighbors, I hope. But Marie is really a companion, some one I can talk to quite frankly. You wouldn't want me to be more lonely than I have been, would you?"

Carl laughed and pushed back the triangular lock of hair with the edge of his hat. "Of course I don't. I ought to be thankful that this path hasn't been worn by—well, by friends with more pressing errands than your little Bohemian is likely to have." He paused to give Alexandra his hand as she stepped over the stile. "Are you the least bit disappointed in our coming together again?" he asked abruptly. "Is it the way you hoped it would be?"

Alexandra smiled at this. "Only better. When I've thought about your coming, I've sometimes been a little afraid of it. You have lived where things move so fast, and everything is slow here; the people slowest of all. Our lives are like the years, all made up of weather and crops and cows. How you hated cows!" She shook her head and laughed to herself.

"I didn't when we milked together. I walked up to the pasture corners this morning. I wonder whether I shall ever be able to tell you all that I was thinking about up there. It's a strange thing, Alexandra; I find it easy to be frank with you about everything under the sun except—yourself!"

"You are afraid of hurting my feelings, perhaps." Alexandra looked at him thoughtfully.

"No, I'm afraid of giving you a shock. You've seen yourself for so long in the dull minds of the people about you, that if I were to tell you how you seem to me, it would startle you. But you must see that you astonish me. You must feel when people admire you."

Alexandra blushed and laughed with some confusion. "I felt that you were pleased with me, if you mean that."

"And you've felt when other people were pleased with you?" he insisted.

"Well, sometimes. The men in town, at the banks and the county offices, seem glad to see me. I think, myself, it is more pleasant to do business with people who are clean and healthy-looking," she admitted blandly.

Carl gave a little chuckle as he opened the Shabatas' gate for her. "Oh, do you?" he asked dryly.

There was no sign of life about the Shabatas' house except a big yellow cat, sunning itself on the kitchen doorstep.

Alexandra took the path that led to the orchard. "She often sits there and sews. I didn't telephone her we were coming, because I didn't want her to go to work and bake cake and freeze ice-cream. She'll always make a party if you give her the least excuse. Do you recognize the apple trees, Carl?"

Linstrum looked about him. "I wish I had a dollar for every bucket of water I've carried for those trees. Poor father, he was an easy man, but he was perfectly merciless when it came to watering the orchard."

"That's one thing I like about Germans; they make an orchard grow if they can't make anything else. I'm so glad these trees belong to some one who takes comfort in them. When I rented this place, the tenants never kept the orchard up, and Emil and I used to come over and take care of it ourselves. It needs mowing now. There she is, down in the corner. Maria-a-a!" she called.

A recumbent figure started up from the grass and came running toward them through the flickering screen of light and shade.

"Look at her! Isn't she like a little brown rabbit?" Alexandra laughed.

Marie ran up panting and threw her arms about Alexandra. "Oh, I had begun to think you were not coming at all, maybe. I knew you were so busy. Yes, Emil told me about Mr. Linstrum being here. Won't you come up to the house?"

"Why not sit down there in your corner? Carl wants to see the orchard. He kept all these trees alive for years, watering them with his own back."

Marie turned to Carl. "Then I'm thankful to you, Mr. Linstrum. We'd never have bought the place if it hadn't been for this orchard, and then I wouldn't have had Alexandra, either." She gave Alexandra's arm a little squeeze as she walked beside her. "How nice your dress smells, Alexandra; you put rosemary leaves in your chest, like I told you."

She led them to the northwest corner of the orchard, sheltered on one side by a thick mulberry hedge and bordered on the other by a wheatfield, just beginning to yellow. In this corner the ground dipped a little, and the bluegrass, which the weeds had driven out in the upper part of the orchard, grew thick and luxuriant. Wild roses were flaming in the tufts of bunchgrass along the fence. Under a white mulberry tree there was an old wagon-seat. Beside it lay a book and a workbasket.

"You must have the seat, Alexandra. The grass would stain your dress," the hostess insisted. She dropped down on the ground at Alexandra's side and tucked her feet under her. Carl sat at a little distance from the two women, his back to the wheatfield, and watched them. Alexandra took off her shade-hat and threw it on the ground. Marie picked it up and played with the white ribbons, twisting them about her brown fingers as she talked. They made a pretty picture in the strong sunlight, the leafy pattern surrounding them like a net; the Swedish woman so white and gold, kindly and amused, but armored in calm, and the alert brown one, her full lips parted, points of yellow light dancing in her eyes as she laughed and chattered. Carl had never forgotten little Marie Tovesky's eyes, and he was glad to have an opportunity to study them. The brown iris, he found, was curiously slashed with yellow, the color of sunflower honey, or of old amber. In each eye one of these streaks must have been larger than the others, for the effect was that of two dancing points of light, two little yellow bubbles, such as rise in a glass of champagne. Sometimes they seemed like the sparks from a forge. She seemed so easily excited, to kindle with a fierce little flame if one but breathed upon her. "What a waste," Carl reflected. "She ought to be doing all that for a sweetheart. How awkwardly things come about!"

It was not very long before Marie sprang up out of the grass again. "Wait a moment. I want to show you something." She ran away and disappeared behind the low-growing apple trees.

"What a charming creature," Carl murmured. "I don't wonder that her husband is jealous. But can't she walk? Does she always run?"

Alexandra nodded. "Always. I don't see many people, but I don't believe there are many like her, anywhere."

Marie came back with a branch she had broken from an apricot tree, laden with pale-yellow, pink-cheeked fruit. She dropped it beside Carl. "Did you plant those, too? They are such beautiful little trees."

Carl fingered the blue-green leaves, porous like blotting-paper and shaped like birch leaves, hung on waxen red stems. "Yes, I think I did. Are these the circus trees, Alexandra?"

"Shall I tell her about them?" Alexandra asked. "Sit down like a good girl, Marie, and don't ruin my poor hat, and I'll tell you a story. A long time ago, when Carl and I were, say, sixteen and twelve, a circus came to Hanover and we went to town in our wagon, with Lou and Oscar, to see the parade. We hadn't money enough to go to the circus. We followed the parade out to the circus grounds and hung around until the show began and the crowd went inside the tent. Then Lou was afraid we looked foolish standing outside in the pasture, so we went back to

Hanover feeling very sad. There was a man in the streets selling apricots, and we had never seen any before. He had driven down from somewhere up in the French country, and he was selling them twenty-five cents a peck. We had a little money our fathers had given us for candy, and I bought two pecks and Carl bought one. They cheered us a good deal, and we saved all the seeds and planted them. Up to the time Carl went away, they hadn't borne at all."

"And now he's come back to eat them," cried Marie, nodding at Carl. "That *is* a good story. I can remember you a little, Mr. Linstrum. I used to see you in Hanover sometimes, when Uncle Joe took me to town. I remember you because you were always buying pencils and tubes of paint at the drug store. Once, when my uncle left me at the store, you drew a lot of little birds and flowers for me on a piece of wrapping-paper. I kept them for a long while. I thought you were very romantic because you could draw and had such black eyes."

Carl smiled. "Yes, I remember that time. Your uncle bought you some kind of a mechanical toy, a Turkish lady sitting on an ottoman and smoking a hookah, wasn't it? And she turned her head backwards and forwards."

"Oh, yes! Wasn't she splendid! I knew well enough I ought not to tell Uncle Joe I wanted it, for he had just come back from the saloon and was feeling good. You remember how he laughed? She tickled him, too. But when we got home, my aunt scolded him for buying toys when she needed so many things. We wound our lady up every night, and when she began to move her head my aunt used to laugh as hard as any of us. It was a music-box, you know, and the Turkish lady played a tune while she smoked. That was how she made you feel so jolly. As I remember her, she was lovely, and had a gold crescent on her turban."

Half an hour later, as they were leaving the house, Carl and Alexandra were met in the path by a strapping fellow in overalls and a blue shirt. He was breathing hard, as if he had been running, and was muttering to himself.

Marie ran forward, and, taking him by the arm, gave him a little push toward her guests. "Frank, this is Mr. Linstrum."

Frank took off his broad straw hat and nodded to Alexandra. When he spoke to Carl, he showed a fine set of white teeth. He was burned a dull red down to his neckband, and there was a heavy three-days' stubble on his face. Even in his agitation he was handsome, but he looked a rash and violent man.

Barely saluting the callers, he turned at once to his wife and began, in an outraged tone, "I have to leave my team to drive the old woman Hiller's hogs out-a my wheat. I go to take dat old woman to de court if she ain't careful, I tell you!"

His wife spoke soothingly. "But, Frank, she has only her lame boy to help her. She does the best she can."

Alexandra looked at the excited man and offered a suggestion. "Why don't you go over there some afternoon and hog-tight her fences? You'd save time for yourself in the end."

Frank's neck stiffened. "Not-a-much, I won't. I keep my hogs home. Other peoples can do like me. See? If that Louis can mend shoes, he can mend fence."

"Maybe," said Alexandra placidly; "but I've found it sometimes pays to mend other people's fences. Good-bye, Marie. Come to see me soon."

Alexandra walked firmly down the path and Carl followed her.

Frank went into the house and threw himself on the sofa, his face to the wall, his clenched fist on his hip. Marie, having seen her guests off, came in and put her hand coaxingly on his shoulder.

"Poor Frank! You've run until you've made your head ache, now haven't you? Let me make you some coffee."

"What else am I to do?" he cried hotly in Bohemian. "Am I to let any old woman's hogs root up my wheat? Is that what I work myself to death for?"

"Don't worry about it, Frank. I'll speak to Mrs. Hiller again. But, really, she almost cried last time they got out, she was so sorry."

Frank bounced over on his other side. "That's it; you always side with them against me. They all know it. Anybody here feels free to borrow the mower and break it, or turn their hogs in on me. They know you won't care!"

Marie hurried away to make his coffee. When she came back, he was fast asleep. She sat down and looked at him for a long while, very thoughtfully. When the kitchen clock struck six she went out to get supper, closing the door gently behind her. She was always sorry for Frank when he worked himself into one of these rages, and she was sorry to have him rough and quarrelsome with his neighbors. She was perfectly aware that the neighbors had a good deal to put up with, and that they bore with Frank for her sake.

CHAPTER VII

Marie's father, Albert Tovesky, was one of the more intelligent Bohemians who came West in the early seventies. He settled in Omaha and became a leader and adviser among his people there. Marie was his youngest child, by a second wife, and was the apple of his eye. She was barely sixteen, and was in the graduating class of the Omaha High School, when Frank Shabata arrived from the old country and set all the Bohemian girls in a flutter. He was easily the buck of the beer-gardens, and on Sunday he was a sight to see, with his silk hat and tucked shirt and blue frock-coat, wearing gloves and carrying a little wisp of a yellow cane. He was tall and fair, with splendid teeth and close-cropped yellow curls, and he wore a slightly disdainful expression, proper for a young man with high connections, whose mother had a big farm in the Elbe valley. There was often an interesting discontent in his blue eyes, and every Bohemian girl he met imagined herself the cause of that unsatisfied expression. He had a way of drawing out his cambric handkerchief slowly, by one corner, from his breast-pocket, that was melancholy and romantic in the extreme. He took a little flight with each of the more eligible Bohemian girls, but it was when he was with little Marie Tovesky that he drew his handkerchief out most slowly, and, after he had lit a fresh cigar, dropped the match most despairingly. Any one could see, with half an eye, that his proud heart was bleeding for somebody.

One Sunday, late in the summer after Marie's graduation, she met Frank at a Bohemian picnic down the river and went rowing with him all the afternoon. When she got home that evening she went straight to her father's room and told him that she was engaged to Shabata. Old Tovesky was having a comfortable pipe before he went to bed. When he heard his daughter's announcement, he first prudently corked his beer bottle and then leaped to his feet and had a turn of temper. He characterized Frank Shabata by a Bohemian expression which is the equivalent of stuffed shirt.

"Why don't he go to work like the rest of us did? His farm in the Elbe valley, indeed! Ain't he got plenty brothers and sisters? It's his mother's farm, and why don't he stay at home and help her? Haven't I seen his mother out in the morning at five o'clock with her ladle and her big bucket on wheels, putting liquid manure on the cabbages? Don't I know the look of old Eva Shabata's hands? Like an old horse's hoofs they are—and this fellow wearing gloves and rings! Engaged, indeed! You aren't fit to be out of school, and that's what's the matter with you. I will send you off to the Sisters of the Sacred Heart in St. Louis, and they will teach you some sense, *I* guess!"

Accordingly, the very next week, Albert Tovesky took his daughter, pale and tearful, down the river to the convent. But the way to make Frank want anything was to tell him he couldn't have it. He managed to have an interview with Marie before she went away, and whereas he had been only half in love with her before, he now persuaded himself that he would not stop at anything. Marie took with her to the convent, under the canvas lining of her trunk, the results of a laborious and satisfying morning on Frank's part; no less than a dozen photographs of himself, taken in a dozen different love-lorn attitudes. There was a little round photograph for her watch-case, photographs for her wall and dresser, and even long narrow ones to be used as bookmarks. More than once the handsome gentleman was torn to pieces before the French class by an indignant nun.

Marie pined in the convent for a year, until her eighteenth birthday was passed. Then she met Frank Shabata in the Union Station in St. Louis and ran away with him. Old Tovesky forgave his daughter because there was nothing else to do, and bought her a farm in the country that she had loved so well as a child. Since then her story had been a part of the history of the Divide. She and Frank had been living there for five years when Carl Linstrum came back to pay his long deferred visit to Alexandra. Frank had, on the whole, done better than one might have expected. He had flung himself at the soil with savage energy. Once a year he went to Hastings or to Omaha, on a spree. He stayed away for a week or two, and then came home and worked like a demon. He did work; if he felt sorry for himself, that was his own affair.

CHAPTER VIII

On the evening of the day of Alexandra's call at the Shabatas', a heavy rain set in. Frank sat up until a late hour reading the Sunday newspapers. One of the Goulds was getting a divorce, and Frank took it as a personal affront. In printing the story of the young man's marital troubles, the knowing editor gave a sufficiently colored account of his career, stating the amount of his income and the manner in which he was supposed to spend it. Frank read English slowly, and the more he read about this divorce case, the angrier he grew. At last he threw down the page with a snort. He turned to his farm-hand who was reading the other half of the paper.

"By God! If I have that young feller in de hayfield once, I show him somet'ing. Listen here what he do wit his money." And Frank began the catalogue of the young man's reputed extravagances.

Marie sighed. She thought it hard that the Goulds, for whom she had nothing but good will, should make her so much trouble. She hated to see the Sunday newspapers come into the house. Frank was always reading about the doings of rich people and feeling outraged. He had an inexhaustible stock of stories about their crimes and follies, how they bribed the courts and shot down their butlers with impunity whenever they chose. Frank and Lou Bergson had very similar ideas, and they were two of the political agitators of the county.

The next morning broke clear and brilliant, but Frank said the ground was too wet to plough, so he took the cart and drove over to Sainte-Agnes to spend the day at Moses Marcel's saloon. After he was gone, Marie went out to the back porch to begin her butter-making. A brisk wind had come up and was driving puffy white clouds across the sky. The orchard was sparkling and rippling in the sun. Marie stood looking toward it wistfully, her hand on the lid of the churn, when she heard a sharp ring in the air, the merry sound of the whetstone on the scythe. That invitation decided her. She ran into the house, put on a short skirt and a pair of her husband's boots, caught up a tin pail and started for the orchard. Emil had already begun work and was mowing vigorously. When he saw her coming, he stopped and wiped his brow. His yellow canvas leggings and khaki trousers were splashed to the knees.

"Don't let me disturb you, Emil. I'm going to pick cherries. Isn't everything beautiful after the rain? Oh, but I'm glad to get this place mowed! When I heard it raining in the night, I thought maybe you would come and do it for me to-day. The wind wakened me. Didn't it blow dreadfully? Just smell the wild roses! They are always so spicy after a rain. We never had so many of them in here before. I suppose it's the wet season. Will you have to cut them, too?"

"If I cut the grass, I will," Emil said teasingly. "What's the matter with you? What makes you so flighty?"

"Am I flighty? I suppose that's the wet season, too, then. It's exciting to see everything growing so fast,—and to get the grass cut! Please leave the roses till last, if you must cut them. Oh, I don't mean all of them, I mean that low place down by my tree, where there are so many. Aren't you splashed! Look at the spider-webs all over the grass. Good-bye. I'll call you if I see a snake."

She tripped away and Emil stood looking after her. In a few moments he heard the cherries dropping smartly into the pail, and he began to swing his scythe with that long, even stroke that few American boys ever learn. Marie picked cherries and sang softly to herself, stripping one glittering branch after another, shivering when she caught a shower of raindrops on her neck and hair. And Emil mowed his way slowly down toward the cherry trees.

That summer the rains had been so many and opportune that it was almost more than Shabata and his man could do to keep up with the corn; the orchard was a neglected wilderness. All sorts of weeds and herbs and flowers had grown up there; splotches of wild larkspur, pale green-and-white spikes of hoarhound, plantations of wild cotton, tangles of foxtail and wild wheat. South of the apricot trees, cornering on the wheatfield, was Frank's alfalfa, where myriads of white and yellow butterflies were always fluttering above the purple blossoms. When Emil reached the lower corner by the hedge, Marie was sitting under her white mulberry tree, the pailful of cherries beside her, looking off at the gentle, tireless swelling of the wheat.

"Emil," she said suddenly—he was mowing quietly about under the tree so as not to disturb her—"what religion did the Swedes have away back, before they were Christians?"

Emil paused and straightened his back. "I don't know. About like the Germans', wasn't it?"

Marie went on as if she had not heard him. "The Bohemians, you know, were tree worshipers before the missionaries came. Father says the people in the mountains still do queer things, sometimes,—they believe that trees bring good or bad luck."

Emil looked superior. "Do they? Well, which are the lucky trees? I'd like to know."

"I don't know all of them, but I know lindens are. The old people in the mountains plant lindens to purify the forest, and to do away with the spells that come from the old trees they say have lasted from heathen times. I'm a good Catholic, but I think I could get along with caring for trees, if I hadn't anything else."

"That's a poor saying," said Emil, stooping over to wipe his hands in the wet grass.

"Why is it? If I feel that way, I feel that way. I like trees because they seem more resigned to the way they have to live than other things do. I feel as if this tree knows everything I ever think of when I sit here. When I come back to it, I never have to remind it of anything; I begin just where I left off."

Emil had nothing to say to this. He reached up among the branches and began to pick the sweet, insipid fruit, —long ivory-colored berries, tipped with faint pink, like white coral, that fall to the ground unheeded all summer through. He dropped a handful into her lap.

"Do you like Mr. Linstrum?" Marie asked suddenly.

"Yes. Don't you?"

"Oh, ever so much; only he seems kind of staid and school-teachery. But, of course, he is older than Frank, even. I'm sure I don't want to live to be more than thirty, do you? Do you think Alexandra likes him very much?"

"I suppose so. They were old friends."

"Oh, Emil, you know what I mean!" Marie tossed her head impatiently. "Does she really care about him? When she used to tell me about him, I always wondered whether she wasn't a little in love with him."

"Who, Alexandra?" Emil laughed and thrust his hands into his trousers pockets. "Alexandra's never been in love, you crazy!" He laughed again. "She wouldn't know how to go about it. The idea!"

Marie shrugged her shoulders. "Oh, you don't know Alexandra as well as you think you do! If you had any eyes, you would see that she is very fond of him. It would serve you all right if she walked off with Carl. I like him because he appreciates her more than you do."

Emil frowned. "What are you talking about, Marie? Alexandra's all right. She and I have always been good friends. What more do you want? I like to talk to Carl about New York and what a fellow can do there."

"Oh, Emil! Surely you are not thinking of going off there?"

"Why not? I must go somewhere, mustn't I?" The

young man took up his scythe and leaned on it. "Would you rather I went off in the sand hills and lived like Ivar?"

Marie's face fell under his brooding gaze. She looked down at his wet leggings. "I'm sure Alexandra hopes you will stay on here," she murmured.

"Then Alexandra will be disappointed," the young man said roughly. "What do I want to hang around here for? Alexandra can run the farm all right, without me. I don't want to stand around and look on. I want to be doing something on my own account."

"That's so," Marie sighed. "There are so many, many things you can do. Almost anything you choose."

"And there are so many, many things I can't do." Emil echoed her tone sarcastically. "Sometimes I don't want to do anything at all, and sometimes I want to pull the four corners of the Divide together"—he threw out his arm and brought it back with a jerk—"so, like a table-cloth. I get tired of seeing men and horses going up and down, up and down."

Marie looked up at his defiant figure and her face clouded. "I wish you weren't so restless, and didn't get so worked up over things," she said sadly.

"Thank you," he returned shortly.

She sighed despondently. "Everything I say makes you cross, don't it? And you never used to be cross to me."

Emil took a step nearer and stood frowning down at her bent head. He stood in an attitude of self-defense, his feet well apart, his hands clenched and drawn up at his sides, so that the cords stood out on his bare arms. "I can't play with you like a little boy any more," he said slowly. "That's what you miss, Marie. You'll have to get some other little boy to play with." He stopped and took a deep breath. Then he went on in a low tone, so intense that it was almost threatening: "Sometimes you seem to understand perfectly, and then sometimes you pretend you don't. You don't help things any by pretending. It's then that I want to pull the corners of the Divide together. If you *won't* understand, you know, I could make you!"

Marie clasped her hands and started up from her seat. She had grown very pale and her eyes were shining with excitement and distress. "But, Emil, if I understand, then all our good times are over, we can never do nice things together any more. We shall have to behave like Mr. Linstrum. And, anyhow, there's nothing to understand!" She struck the ground with her little foot fiercely. "That won't last. It will go away, and things will be just as they used to. I wish you were a Catholic. The Church helps people, indeed it does. I pray for you, but that's not the same as if you prayed yourself."

She spoke rapidly and pleadingly, looked entreatingly into his face. Emil stood defiant, gazing down at her.

"I can't pray to have the things I want," he said slowly, "and I won't pray not to have them, not if I'm damned for it."

Marie turned away, wringing her hands. "Oh, Emil, you won't try! Then all our good times are over."

"Yes, over. I never expect to have any more."

Emil gripped the hand-holds of his scythe and began to mow. Marie took up her cherries and went slowly toward the house, crying bitterly.

CHAPTER IX

On Sunday afternoon, a month after Carl Linstrum's arrival, he rode with Emil up into the French country to attend a Catholic fair. He sat for most of the afternoon in the basement of the church, where the fair was held, talking to Marie Shabata, or strolled about the gravel terrace, thrown up on the hillside in front of the basement doors, where the French boys were jumping and wrestling and throwing the discus. Some of the boys were in their white baseball suits; they had just come up from a Sunday practice game down in the ballgrounds. Amédée, the newly married, Emil's best friend, was their pitcher, renowned among the country towns for his dash and skill. Amédée was a little fellow, a year younger than Emil and much more boyish in appearance; very lithe and active and neatly made, with a clear brown and white skin, and flashing white teeth. The Sainte-Agnes boys were to play the Hastings nine in a fortnight, and Amédée's lightning balls were the hope of his team. The little Frenchman seemed to get every ounce there was in him behind the ball as it left his hand.

"You'd have made the battery at the University for sure, 'Médée," Emil said as they were walking from the ballgrounds back to the church on the hill. "You're pitching better than you did in the spring."

Amédée grinned. "Sure! A married man don't lose his head no more." He slapped Emil on the back as he caught step with him. "Oh, Emil, you wanna get married right off quick! It's the greatest thing ever!"

Emil laughed. "How am I going to get married without any girl?"

Amédée took his arm. "Pooh! There are plenty girls will have you. You wanna get some nice French girl, now. She treat you well; always be jolly. See"—he began checking off on his fingers—"there is Sévérine, and Alphosen, and Joséphine, and Hectorine, and Louise, and Malvina—why, I could love any of them girls! Why don't you get after them? Are you stuck up, Emil, or is anything the matter with you? I never did know a boy twenty-two years old before that didn't have no girl. You wanna be a priest, maybe? Not-a for me!" Amédée swaggered. "I bring many good Catholics into this world, I hope, and that's a way I help the Church."

Emil looked down and patted him on the shoulder. "Now you're windy, 'Médée. You Frenchies like to brag."

But Amédée had the zeal of the newly married, and he was not to be lightly shaken off. "Honest and true, Emil, don't you want *any* girl? Maybe there's some young lady in Lincoln, now, very grand"—Amédée waved his hand languidly before his face to denote the fan of heartless beauty—"and you lost your heart up there. Is that it?"

"Maybe," said Emil.

But Amédée saw no appropriate glow in his friend's face. "Bah!" he exclaimed in disgust. "I tell all the French girls to keep 'way from you. You gotta rock in there," thumping Emil on the ribs.

When they reached the terrace at the side of the church, Amédée, who was excited by his success on the ballgrounds, challenged Emil to a jumping-match, though he knew he would be beaten. They belted themselves up, and Raoul Marcel, the choir tenor and Father Duchesne's pet, and Jean Bordelau held the string over which they vaulted. All the French boys stood round, cheering and humping themselves up when Emil or Amédée went over the wire, as if they were helping in the lift. Emil stopped at five-feet-five, declaring that he would spoil his appetite for supper if he jumped any more.

Angélique, Amédée's pretty bride, as blonde and fair as her name, who had come out to watch the match, tossed her head at Emil and said:—

" 'Médée could jump much higher than you if he were as tall. And anyhow, he is much more graceful. He goes over like a bird, and you have to hump yourself all up."

"Oh, I do, do I?" Emil caught her and kissed her saucy mouth squarely, while she laughed and struggled and called, " 'Médée! 'Médée!"

"There, you see your 'Médée isn't even big enough to get you away from me. I could run away with you right now and he could only sit down and cry about it. I'll show you whether I have to hump myself!" Laughing and panting, he picked Angélique up in his arms and began running about the rectangle with her. Not until he saw Marie Shabata's tiger eyes flashing from the gloom of the basement doorway did he hand the disheveled bride over to her husband. "There, go to your graceful; I haven't the heart to take you away from him."

Angélique clung to her husband and made faces at Emil over the white shoulder of Amédée's ball-shirt. Emil was greatly amused at her air of proprietorship and at Amédée's shameless submission to it. He was delighted with his friend's good fortune. He liked to see and to think about Amédée's sunny, natural, happy love.

He and Amédée had ridden and wrestled and larked together since they were lads of twelve. On Sundays and holidays they were always arm in arm. It seemed strange that now he should have to hide the thing that Amédée was so proud of, that the feeling which gave one of them such happiness should bring the other such despair. It was like that when Alexandra tested her seed-corn in the spring, he mused. From two ears that had grown side by side, the grains of one shot up joyfully into the light, projecting themselves into the future, and the grains from the other lay still in the earth and rotted; and nobody knew why.

CHAPTER X

While Emil and Carl were amusing themselves at the fair, Alexandra was at home, busy with her account-books, which had been neglected of late. She was almost through with her figures when she heard a cart drive up to the gate, and looking out of the window she saw her two older brothers. They had seemed to avoid her ever since Carl Linstrum's arrival, four weeks ago that day, and she hurried to the door to welcome them. She saw at once that they had come with some very definite purpose. They followed her stiffly into the sitting-room. Oscar sat down, but Lou walked over to the window and remained standing, his hands behind him.

"You are by yourself?" he asked, looking toward the doorway into the parlor.

"Yes. Carl and Emil went up to the Catholic fair."

For a few moments neither of the men spoke.

Then Lou came out sharply. "How soon does he intend to go away from here?"

"I don't know, Lou. Not for some time, I hope." Alexandra spoke in an even, quiet tone that often exasperated her brothers. They felt that she was trying to be superior with them.

Oscar spoke up grimly. "We thought we ought to tell you that people have begun to talk," he said meaningly.

Alexandra looked at him. "What about?"

Oscar met her eyes blankly. "About you, keeping him here so long. It looks bad for him to be hanging on to a woman this way. People think you're getting taken in."

Alexandra shut her account-book firmly. "Boys," she said seriously, "don't let's go on with this. We won't come out anywhere. I can't take advice on such a matter. I know you mean well, but you must not feel responsible for me in things of this sort. If we go on with this talk it will only make hard feeling."

Lou whipped about from the window. "You ought to think a little about your family. You're making us all ridiculous."

"How am I?"

"People are beginning to say you want to marry the fellow."

"Well, and what is ridiculous about that?"

Lou and Oscar exchanged outraged looks. "Alexandra! Can't you see he's just a tramp and he's after your money? He wants to be taken care of, he does!"

"Well, suppose I want to take care of him? Whose business is it but my own?"

"Don't you know he'd get hold of your property?"

"He'd get hold of what I wished to give him, certainly."

Oscar sat up suddenly and Lou clutched at his bristly hair.

"Give him?" Lou shouted. "Our property, our homestead?"

"I don't know about the homestead," said Alexandra quietly. "I know you and Oscar have always expected that it would be left to your children, and I'm not sure but that you're right. But I'll do exactly as I please with the rest of my land, boys."

"The rest of your land!" cried Lou, growing more excited every minute. "Didn't all the land come out of the homestead? It was bought with money borrowed on the homestead, and Oscar and me worked ourselves to the bone paying interest on it."

"Yes, you paid the interest. But when you married we made a division of the land, and you were satisfied. I've made more on my farms since I've been alone than when we all worked together."

"Everything you've made has come out of the original land that us boys worked for, hasn't it? The farms and all that comes out of them belongs to us as a family."

Alexandra waved her hand impatiently. "Come now, Lou. Stick to the facts. You are talking nonsense. Go to the county clerk and ask him who owns my land, and whether my titles are good."

Lou turned to his brother. "This is what comes of letting a woman meddle in business," he said bitterly. "We ought to have taken things in our own hands years ago. But she liked to run things, and we humored her. We thought you had good sense, Alexandra. We never thought you'd do anything foolish."

Alexandra rapped impatiently on her desk with her knuckles. "Listen, Lou. Don't talk wild. You say you ought to have taken things into your own hands years ago. I suppose you mean before you left home. But how could you take hold of what wasn't there? I've got most of what I have now since we divided the property; I've built it up myself, and it has nothing to do with you."

Oscar spoke up solemnly. "The property of a family really belongs to the men of the family, no matter about the title. If anything goes wrong, it's the men that are held responsible."

"Yes, of course," Lou broke in. "Everybody knows that. Oscar and me have always been easy-going and we've never made any fuss. We were willing you should hold the land and have the good of it, but you got no right to part with any of it. We worked in the fields to pay for the first land you bought, and whatever's come out of it has got to be kept in the family."

Oscar reinforced his brother, his mind fixed on the one point he could see. "The property of a family belongs to the men of the family, because they are held responsible, and because they do the work."

Alexandra looked from one to the other, her eyes full of indignation. She had been impatient before, but now she was beginning to feel angry. "And what about my work?" she asked in an unsteady voice.

Lou looked at the carpet. "Oh, now, Alexandra, you always took it pretty easy! Of course we wanted you to. You liked to manage round, and we always humored you. We realize you were a great deal of help to us. There's no woman anywhere around that knows as much about business as you do, and we've always been proud of that, and thought you were pretty smart. But, of course, the real work always fell on us. Good advice is all right, but it don't get the weeds out of the corn."

"Maybe not, but it sometimes puts in the crop, and it sometimes keeps the fields for corn to grow in," said Alexandra dryly. "Why, Lou, I can remember when you and Oscar wanted to sell this homestead and all the improvements to old preacher Ericson for two thousand dollars. If I'd consented, you'd have gone down to the river and scraped along on poor farms for the rest of your lives. When I put in our first field of alfalfa you both opposed me, just because I first heard about it from a young man who had been to the University. You said I was being taken in then, and all the neighbors said so. You know as well as I do that alfalfa has been the salvation of this country. You all laughed at me when I said our land here was about ready for wheat, and I had to raise three big wheat crops before the neighbors quit putting all their land in corn. Why, I remember you cried, Lou, when we put in the first big wheat-planting, and said everybody was laughing at us."

Lou turned to Oscar. "That's the woman of it; if she tells you to put in a crop, she thinks she's put it in. It makes women conceited to meddle in business. I shouldn't think you'd want to remind us how hard you were on us, Alexandra, after the way you baby Emil."

"Hard on you? I never meant to be hard. Conditions were hard. Maybe I would never have been very soft, anyhow; but I certainly didn't choose to be the kind of girl I was. If you take even a vine and cut it back again and again, it grows hard, like a tree."

Lou felt that they were wandering from the point, and that in digression Alexandra might unnerve him. He wiped his forehead with a jerk of his handkerchief. "We never doubted you, Alexandra. We never questioned anything you did. You've always had your own way. But you can't expect us to sit like stumps and see you done out of the property by any loafer who happens along, and making yourself ridiculous into the bargain."

Oscar rose. "Yes," he broke in, "everybody's laughing to see you get took in; at your age, too. Everybody knows he's nearly five years younger than you, and is after your money. Why, Alexandra, you are forty years old!"

"All that doesn't concern anybody but Carl and me. Go to town and ask your lawyers what you can do to restrain me from disposing of my own property. And I advise you to do what they tell you; for the authority you can exert by law is the only influence you will ever have over me again." Alexandra rose. "I think I would rather not have lived to find out what I have to-day," she said quietly, closing her desk.

Lou and Oscar looked at each other questioningly. There seemed to be nothing to do but to go, and they walked out.

"You can't do business with women," Oscar said heavily as he clambered into the cart. "But anyhow, we've had our say, at last."

Lou scratched his head. "Talk of that kind might come too high, you know; but she's apt to be sensible. You hadn't ought to have said that about her age, though, Oscar. I'm afraid that hurt her feelings; and the worst thing we can do is to make her sore at us. She'd marry him out of contrariness."

"I only meant," said Oscar, "that she is old enough to know better, and she is. If she was going to marry, she ought to done it long ago, and not go making a fool of herself now."

Lou looked anxious, nevertheless. "Of course," he reflected hopefully and inconsistently, "Alexandra ain't much like other women-folks. Maybe it won't make her sore. Maybe she'd as soon be forty as not!"

CHAPTER XI

Emil came home at about half-past seven o'clock that evening. Old Ivar met him at the windmill and took his horse, and the young man went directly into the house. He called to his sister and she answered from her bedroom, behind the sitting-room, saying that she was lying down.

Emil went to her door.

"Can I see you for a minute?" he asked. "I want to talk to you about something before Carl comes."

Alexandra rose quickly and came to the door. "Where is Carl?"

"Lou and Oscar met us and said they wanted to talk to him, so he rode over to Oscar's with them. Are you coming out?" Emil asked impatiently.

"Yes, sit down. I'll be dressed in a moment."

Alexandra closed her door, and Emil sank down on the old slat lounge and sat with his head in his hands. When his sister came out, he looked up, not knowing whether the interval had been short or long, and he was surprised to see that the room had grown quite dark. That was just as well; it would be easier to talk if he were not under the gaze of those clear, deliberate eyes, that saw so far in some directions and were so blind in others. Alexandra, too, was glad of the dusk. Her face was swollen from crying.

Emil started up and then sat down again. "Alexandra," he said slowly, in his deep young baritone, "I don't want to go away to law school this fall. Let me put it off another year. I want to take a year off and look around. It's awfully easy to rush into a profession you don't really like, and awfully hard to get out of it. Linstrum and I have been talking about that."

"Very well, Emil. Only don't go off looking for land." She came up and put her hand on his shoulder. "I've been wishing you could stay with me this winter."

"That's just what I don't want to do, Alexandra. I'm restless. I want to go to a new place. I want to go down to the City of Mexico to join one of the University fellows who's at the head of an electrical plant. He wrote me he could give me a little job, enough to pay my way, and I could look around and see what I want to do. I want to go as soon as harvest is over. I guess Lou and Oscar will be sore about it."

"I suppose they will." Alexandra sat down on the lounge beside him. "They are very angry with me, Emil. We have had a quarrel. They will not come here again."

Emil scarcely heard what she was saying; he did not

notice the sadness of her tone. He was thinking about the reckless life he meant to live in Mexico.

"What about?" he asked absently.

"About Carl Linstrum. They are afraid I am going to marry him, and that some of my property will get away from them."

Emil shrugged his shoulders. "What nonsense!" he murmured. "Just like them."

Alexandra drew back. "Why nonsense, Emil?"

"Why, you've never thought of such a thing, have you? They always have to have something to fuss about."

"Emil," said his sister slowly, "you ought not to take things for granted. Do you agree with them that I have no right to change my way of living?"

Emil looked at the outline of his sister's head in the dim light. They were sitting close together and he somehow felt that she could hear his thoughts. He was silent for a moment, and then said in an embarrassed tone, "Why, no, certainly not. You ought to do whatever you want to. I'll always back you."

"But it would seem a little bit ridiculous to you if I married Carl?"

Emil fidgeted. The issue seemed to him too far-fetched to warrant discussion. "Why, no. I should be surprised if you wanted to. I can't see exactly why. But that's none of my business. You ought to do as you please. Certainly you ought not to pay any attention to what the boys say."

Alexandra sighed. "I had hoped you might understand, a little, why I do want to. But I suppose that's too much to expect. I've had a pretty lonely life, Emil. Besides Marie, Carl is the only friend I have ever had."

Emil was awake now; a name in her last sentence roused him. He put out his hand and took his sister's awkwardly. "You ought to do just as you wish, and I think Carl's a fine fellow. He and I would always get on. I don't believe any of the things the boys say about him, honest I don't. They are suspicious of him because he's intelligent. You know their way. They've been sore at me ever since you let me go away to college. They're always trying to catch me up. If I were you, I wouldn't pay any attention to them. There's nothing to get upset about. Carl's a sensible fellow. He won't mind them."

"I don't know. If they talk to him the way they did to me, I think he'll go away."

Emil grew more and more uneasy. "Think so? Well, Marie said it would serve us all right if you walked off with him."

"Did she? Bless her little heart! *She* would." Alexandra's voice broke.

Emil began unlacing his leggings. "Why don't you talk to her about it? There's Carl, I hear his horse. I guess I'll go upstairs and get my boots off. No, I don't want any supper. We had supper at five o'clock, at the fair."

Emil was glad to escape and get to his own room. He was a little ashamed for his sister, though he had tried not to show it. He felt that there was something indecorous in her proposal, and she did seem to him somewhat ridiculous. There was trouble enough in the world, he reflected, as he threw himself upon his bed, without people who were forty years old imagining they wanted to get married. In the darkness and silence Emil was not likely to think long about Alexandra. Every image slipped away but one. He had seen Marie in the crowd that afternoon. She sold candy at the fair. *Why* had she ever run away with Frank Shabata, and how could she go on laughing and working and taking an interest in things? Why did she like so many people, and why had she seemed pleased when all the French and Bohemian boys, and the priest himself, crowded round her candy stand? Why did she care about any one but him? Why could he never, never find the thing he looked for in her playful, affectionate eyes?

Then he fell to imagining that he looked once more and found it there, and what it would be like if she loved him,—she who, as Alexandra said, could give her whole heart. In that dream he could lie for hours, as if in a trance. His spirit went out of his body and crossed the fields to Marie Shabata.

At the University dances the girls had often looked wonderingly at the tall young Swede with the fine head, leaning against the wall and frowning, his arms folded, his eyes fixed on the ceiling or the floor. All the girls were a little afraid of him. He was distinguished-looking, and not the jollying kind. They felt that he was too intense and preoccupied. There was something queer about him. Emil's fraternity rather prided itself upon its dances, and sometimes he did his duty and danced every dance. But whether he was on the floor or brooding in a corner, he was always thinking about Marie Shabata. For two years the storm had been gathering in him.

CHAPTER XII

Carl came into the sitting-room while Alexandra was lighting the lamp. She looked up at him as she adjusted the shade. His sharp shoulders stooped as if he were very tired, his face was pale, and there were bluish shadows under his dark eyes. His anger had burned itself out and left him sick and disgusted.

"You have seen Lou and Oscar?" Alexandra asked.

"Yes." His eyes avoided hers.

Alexandra took a deep breath. "And now you are going away. I thought so."

Carl threw himself into a chair and pushed the dark lock back from his forehead with his white, nervous hand. "What a hopeless position you are in, Alexandra!" he exclaimed feverishly. "It is your fate to be always surrounded by little men. And I am no better than the rest. I am too little to face the criticism of even such men as Lou and Oscar. Yes, I am going away; to-morrow. I cannot even ask you to give me a promise until I have something to offer you. I thought, perhaps, I could do that; but I find I can't."

"What good comes of offering people things they don't need?" Alexandra asked sadly. "I don't need money. But I have needed you for a great many years. I wonder why I have been permitted to prosper, if it is only to take my friends away from me."

"I don't deceive myself," Carl said frankly. "I know that I am going away on my own account. I must make the usual effort. I must have something to show for myself. To take what you would give me, I should have to be either a very large man or a very small one, and I am only in the middle class."

Alexandra sighed. "I have a feeling that if you go away, you will not come back. Something will happen to one of us, or to both. People have to snatch at happiness when they can, in this world. It is always easier to lose than to find. What I have is yours, if you care enough about me to take it."

Carl rose and looked up at the picture of John Bergson. "But I can't, my dear, I can't! I will go North at once. Instead of idling about in California all winter, I shall be getting my bearings up there. I won't waste another week. Be patient with me, Alexandra. Give me a year!"

"As you will," said Alexandra wearily. "All at once, in a single day, I lose everything; and I do not know why. Emil, too, is going away." Carl was still studying John Bergson's face and Alexandra's eyes followed his. "Yes," she said, "if he could have seen all that would come of the task he gave me, he would have been sorry. I hope he does not see me now. I hope that he is among the old people of his blood and country, and that tidings do not reach him from the New World."

PART III

•

Winter Memories

CHAPTER I

Winter has settled down over the Divide again; the season in which Nature recuperates, in which she sinks to sleep between the fruitfulness of autumn and the passion of spring. The birds have gone. The teeming life that goes on down in the long grass is exterminated. The prairie-dog keeps his hole. The rabbits run shivering from one frozen garden patch to another and are hard put to it to find frost-bitten cabbage-stalks. At night the coyotes roam the wintry waste, howling for food. The variegated fields are all one color now; the pastures, the stubble, the roads, the sky are the same leaden gray. The hedgerows and trees are scarcely perceptible against the bare earth, whose slaty hue they have taken on. The ground is frozen so hard that it bruises the foot to walk in the roads or in the ploughed fields. It is like an iron country, and the spirit is oppressed by its rigor and melancholy. One could easily believe that in that dead landscape the germs of life and fruitfulness were extinct forever.

Alexandra has settled back into her old routine. There are weekly letters from Emil. Lou and Oscar she has not seen since Carl went away. To avoid awkward encounters in the presence of curious spectators, she has stopped going to the Norwegian Church and drives up to the Reform Church at Hanover, or goes with Marie Shabata to the Catholic Church, locally known as "the French Church." She has not told Marie about Carl, or her differences with her brothers. She was never very communicative about her own affairs, and when she came to the point, an instinct told her that about such things she and Marie would not understand one another.

Old Mrs. Lee had been afraid that family misunderstandings might deprive her of her yearly visit to Alexandra. But on the first day of December Alexandra telephoned Annie that to-morrow she would send Ivar over for her mother, and the next day the old lady arrived with her bundles. For twelve years Mrs. Lee had always entered Alexandra's sitting-room with the same exclamation, "Now we be yust-a like old times!" She enjoyed the liberty Alexandra gave her, and hearing her own language about her all day long. Here she could wear her nightcap and sleep with all her windows shut, listen to Ivar reading the Bible, and here she could run about among the stables in a pair of Emil's old boots. Though she was bent almost double, she was as spry as a gopher. Her face was as brown as if it had been varnished, and as full of wrinkles as a washerwoman's hands. She had three jolly old teeth left in the front of her mouth, and when she grinned she looked very knowing, as if when you found out how to take it, life wasn't half bad. While she and Alexandra patched and pieced and quilted, she talked incessantly about stories she read in a Swedish family paper, telling the plots in great detail; or about her life on a dairy farm in Gottland when she was a girl. Sometimes she forgot which were the printed stories and which were the real stories, it all seemed so far away. She loved to take a little brandy, with hot water and sugar, before she went to bed, and Alexandra always had it ready for her. "It sends good dreams," she would say with a twinkle in her eye.

When Mrs. Lee had been with Alexandra for a week, Marie Shabata telephoned one morning to say that Frank had gone to town for the day, and she would like them to come over for coffee in the afternoon. Mrs. Lee hurried to wash out and iron her new cross-stitched apron, which she had finished only the night before; a checked gingham apron worked with a design ten inches broad across the bottom; a hunting scene, with fir trees and a stag and dogs and huntsmen. Mrs. Lee was firm with herself at dinner, and refused a second helping of apple dumplings. "I ta-ank I save up," she said with a giggle.

At two o'clock in the afternoon Alexandra's cart drove up to the Shabatas' gate, and Marie saw Mrs. Lee's red shawl come bobbing up the path. She ran to the door and pulled the old woman into the house with a hug, helping her to take off her wraps while Alexandra blanketed the horse outside. Mrs. Lee had put on her best black satine dress—she abominated woolen stuffs, even in winter—and a crocheted collar, fastened with a big pale gold pin, containing faded daguerreotypes of her father and mother. She had not worn her apron for fear of rumpling it, and now she shook it out and tied it round her waist with a conscious air. Marie drew back and threw up her hands, exclaiming, "Oh, what a beauty! I've never seen this one before, have I, Mrs. Lee?"

The old woman giggled and ducked her head. "No, yust las' night I ma-ake. See dis tread; verra strong, no wa-ash out, no fade. My sister send from Sveden. I yust-a ta-ank you like dis."

Marie ran to the door again. "Come in, Alexandra. I have been looking at Mrs. Lee's apron. Do stop on your way home and show it to Mrs. Hiller. She's crazy about cross-stitch."

While Alexandra removed her hat and veil, Mrs. Lee went out to the kitchen and settled herself in a wooden rocking-chair by the stove, looking with great interest at the table, set for three, with a white cloth, and a pot of pink geraniums in the middle. "My, a-an't you gotta fine plants; such-a much flower. How you keep from freeze?"

She pointed to the window-shelves, full of blooming fuchsias and geraniums.

"I keep the fire all night, Mrs. Lee, and when it's very cold I put them all on the table, in the middle of the room. Other nights I only put newspapers behind them. Frank laughs at me for fussing, but when they don't bloom he says, 'What's the matter with the darned things?'— What do you hear from Carl, Alexandra?"

"He got to Dawson before the river froze, and now I suppose I won't hear any more until spring. Before he left California he sent me a box of orange flowers, but they didn't keep very well. I have brought a bunch of Emil's letters for you." Alexandra came out from the sitting-room and pinched Marie's cheek playfully. "You don't look as if the weather ever froze you up. Never have colds, do you? That's a good girl. She had dark red cheeks like this when she was a little girl, Mrs. Lee. She looked like some queer foreign kind of a doll. I've never forgot the first time I saw you in Mieklejohn's store, Marie, the time father was lying sick. Carl and I were talking about that before he went away."

"I remember, and Emil had his kitten along. When are you going to send Emil's Christmas box?"

"It ought to have gone before this. I'll have to send it by mail now, to get it there in time."

Marie pulled a dark purple silk necktie from her work-basket. "I knit this for him. It's a good color, don't you think? Will you please put it in with your things and tell him it's from me, to wear when he goes serenading."

Alexandra laughed. "I don't believe he goes serenading much. He says in one letter that the Mexican ladies are said to be very beautiful, but that don't seem to me very warm praise."

Marie tossed her head. "Emil can't fool me. If he's bought a guitar, he goes serenading. Who wouldn't, with all those Spanish girls dropping flowers down from their windows! I'd sing to them every night, wouldn't you, Mrs. Lee?"

The old lady chuckled. Her eyes lit up as Marie bent down and opened the oven door. A delicious hot fragrance blew out into the tidy kitchen. "My, somet'ing smell good!" She turned to Alexandra with a wink, her three yellow teeth making a brave show, "I ta-ank dat stop my yaw from ache no more!" she said contentedly.

Marie took out a pan of delicate little rolls, stuffed with stewed apricots, and began to dust them over with powdered sugar. "I hope you'll like these, Mrs. Lee; Alexandra does. The Bohemians always like them with their coffee. But if you don't, I have a coffee-cake with nuts and poppy seeds. Alexandra, will you get the cream jug? I put it in the window to keep cool."

"The Bohemians," said Alexandra, as they drew up to the table, "certainly know how to make more kinds of bread than any other people in the world. Old Mrs. Hiller told me once at the church supper that she could make seven kinds of fancy bread, but Marie could make a dozen."

Mrs. Lee held up one of the apricot rolls between her brown thumb and forefinger and weighed it critically. "Yust like-a fedders," she pronounced with satisfaction.

"My, a-an't dis nice!" she exclaimed as she stirred her coffee. "I yust ta-ake a liddle yelly now, too, I ta-ank."

Alexandra and Marie laughed at her forehandedness, and fell to talking of their own affairs. "I was afraid you had a cold when I talked to you over the telephone the other night, Marie. What was the matter, had you been crying?"

"Maybe I had," Marie smiled guiltily. "Frank was out late that night. Don't you get lonely sometimes in the winter, when everybody has gone away?"

"I thought it was something like that. If I hadn't had company, I'd have run over to see for myself. If you get down-hearted, what will become of the rest of us?" Alexandra asked.

"I don't, very often. There's Mrs. Lee without any coffee!"

Later, when Mrs. Lee declared that her powers were spent, Marie and Alexandra went upstairs to look for some crochet patterns the old lady wanted to borrow. "Better put on your coat, Alexandra. It's cold up there, and I have no idea where those patterns are. I may have to look through my old trunks." Marie caught up a shawl and opened the stair door, running up the steps ahead of her guest. "While I go through the bureau drawers, you might look in those hat-boxes on the closet-shelf, over where Frank's clothes hang. There are a lot of odds and ends in them."

She began tossing over the contents of the drawers, and Alexandra went into the clothes-closet. Presently she came back, holding a slender elastic yellow stick in her hand.

"What in the world is this, Marie? You don't mean to tell me Frank ever carried such a thing?"

Marie blinked at it with astonishment and sat down on the floor. "Where did you find it? I didn't know he had kept it. I haven't seen it for years."

"It really is a cane, then?"

"Yes. One he brought from the old country. He used to carry it when I first knew him. Isn't it foolish? Poor Frank!"

Alexandra twirled the stick in her fingers and laughed. "He must have looked funny!"

Marie was thoughtful. "No, he didn't, really. It didn't seem out of place. He used to be awfully gay like that when he was a young man. I guess people always get what's hardest for them, Alexandra." Marie gathered the shawl closer about her and still looked hard at the cane. "Frank would be all right in the right place," she said reflectively. "He ought to have a different kind of wife, for one thing. Do you know, Alexandra, I could pick out exactly the right sort of woman for Frank—now. The trouble is you almost have to marry a man before you can find out the sort of wife he needs; and usually it's exactly the sort you are not. Then what are you going to do about it?" she asked candidly.

Alexandra confessed she didn't know. "However," she added, "it seems to me that you get along with Frank about as well as any woman I've ever seen or heard of could."

Marie shook her head, pursing her lips and blowing her warm breath softly out into the frosty air. "No; I was spoiled at home. I like my own way, and I have a quick tongue. When Frank brags, I say sharp things, and he never forgets. He goes over and over it in his mind; I can feel him. Then I'm too giddy. Frank's wife ought to be timid, and she ought not to care about another living thing in the world but just Frank! I didn't when I married him, but I suppose I was too young to stay like that." Marie sighed.

Alexandra had never heard Marie speak so frankly about her husband before, and she felt that it was wiser not to encourage her. No good, she reasoned, ever came from talking about such things, and while Marie was thinking aloud, Alexandra had been steadily searching the hat-boxes. "Aren't these the patterns, Marie?"

Marie sprang up from the floor. "Sure enough, we were looking for patterns, weren't we? I'd forgot about everything but Frank's other wife. I'll put that away."

She poked the cane behind Frank's Sunday clothes, and though she laughed, Alexandra saw there were tears in her eyes.

When they went back to the kitchen, the snow had begun to fall, and Marie's visitors thought they must be getting home. She went out to the cart with them, and tucked the robes about old Mrs. Lee while Alexandra took the blanket off her horse. As they drove away, Marie turned and went slowly back to the house. She took up the package of letters Alexandra had brought, but she did not read them. She turned them over and looked at the foreign stamps, and then sat watching the flying snow while the dusk deepened in the kitchen and the stove sent out a red glow.

Marie knew perfectly well that Emil's letters were written more for her than for Alexandra. They were not the sort of letters that a young man writes to his sister. They were both more personal and more painstaking; full of descriptions of the gay life in the old Mexican capital in the days when the strong hand of Porfirio Diaz was still strong. He told about bull-fights and cock-fights, churches and *fiestas*, the flower-markets and the fountains, the music and dancing, the people of all nations he met in the Italian restaurants on San Francisco Street. In short, they were the kind of letters a young man writes to a woman when he wishes himself and his life to seem interesting to her, when he wishes to enlist her imagination in his behalf.

Marie, when she was alone or when she sat sewing in the evening, often thought about what it must be like down there where Emil was; where there were flowers and street bands everywhere, and carriages rattling up and down, and where there was a little blind boot-black in front of the cathedral who could play any tune you asked for by dropping the lids of blacking-boxes on the stone steps. When everything is done and over for one at twenty-three, it is pleasant to let the mind wander forth and follow a young adventurer who has life before him. "And if it had not been for me," she thought, "Frank might still be free like that, and having a good time making people admire him. Poor Frank, getting married wasn't very good for him either. I'm afraid I do set people against him, as he says. I seem, somehow, to give him away all the time. Perhaps he would try to be agreeable to people again, if I were not around. It seems as if I always make him just as bad as he can be."

Later in the winter, Alexandra looked back upon that

afternoon as the last satisfactory visit she had had with Marie. After that day the younger woman seemed to shrink more and more into herself. When she was with Alexandra she was not spontaneous and frank as she used to be. She seemed to be brooding over something, and holding something back. The weather had a good deal to do with their seeing less of each other than usual. There had not been such snowstorms in twenty years, and the path across the fields was drifted deep from Christmas until March. When the two neighbors went to see each other, they had to go round by the wagon-road, which was twice as far. They telephoned each other almost every night, though in January there was a stretch of three weeks when the wires were down, and when the postman did not come at all.

Marie often ran in to see her nearest neighbor, old Mrs. Hiller, who was crippled with rheumatism and had only her son, the lame shoemaker, to take care of her; and she went to the French Church, whatever the weather. She was a sincerely devout girl. She prayed for herself and for Frank, and for Emil, among the temptations of that gay, corrupt old city. She found more comfort in the Church that winter than ever before. It seemed to come closer to her, and to fill an emptiness that ached in her heart. She tried to be patient with her husband. He and his hired man usually played California Jack in the evening. Marie sat sewing or crocheting and tried to take a friendly interest in the game, but she was always thinking about the wide fields outside, where the snow was drifting over the fences; and about the orchard, where the snow was falling and packing, crust over crust. When she went out into the dark kitchen to fix her plants for the night, she used to stand by the window and look out at the white fields, or watch the currents of snow whirling over the orchard. She seemed to feel the weight of all the snow that lay down there. The branches had become so hard that they wounded your hand if you but tried to break a twig. And yet, down under the frozen crusts, at the roots of the trees, the secret of life was still safe, warm as the blood in one's heart; and the spring would come again! Oh, it would come again!

CHAPTER II

If Alexandra had had much imagination she might have guessed what was going on in Marie's mind, and she would have seen long before what was going on in Emil's. But that, as Emil himself had more than once reflected, was Alexandra's blind side, and her life had not been of the kind to sharpen her vision. Her training had all been toward the end of making her proficient in what she had undertaken to do. Her personal life, her own realization of herself, was almost a subconscious existence; like an underground river that came to the surface only here and there, at intervals months apart, and then sank again to flow on under her own fields. Nevertheless, the underground stream was there, and it was because she had so much personality to put into her enterprises and succeeded in putting it into them so completely, that her affairs prospered better than those of her neighbors.

There were certain days in her life, outwardly uneventful, which Alexandra remembered as peculiarly happy; days when she was close to the flat, fallow world about her, and felt, as it were, in her own body the joyous germination in the soil. There were days, too, which she and Emil had spent together, upon which she loved to look back. There had been such a day when they were down on the river in the dry year, looking over the land. They had made an early start one morning and had driven a long way before noon. When Emil said he was hungry, they drew back from the road, gave Brigham his oats among the bushes, and climbed up to the top of a grassy bluff to eat their lunch under the shade of some little elm trees. The river was clear there, and shallow, since there had been no rain, and it ran in ripples over the sparkling sand. Under the overhanging willows of the opposite bank there was an inlet where the water was deeper and flowed so slowly that it seemed to sleep in the sun. In this little bay a single wild duck was swimming and diving and preening her feathers, disporting herself very happily in the flickering light and shade. They sat for a long time, watching the solitary bird take its pleasure. No living thing had ever seemed to Alexandra as beautiful as that wild duck. Emil must have felt about it as she did, for afterward, when they were at home, he used sometimes to say, "Sister, you know our duck down there—" Alexandra remembered that day as one of the happiest in her life. Years afterward she thought of the duck as still there, swimming and diving all by herself in the sunlight, a kind of enchanted bird that did not know age or change.

Most of Alexandra's happy memories were as impersonal as this one; yet to her they were very personal. Her mind was a white book, with clear writing about weather and beasts and growing things. Not many people would have cared to read it; only a happy few. She had never been in love, she had never indulged in sentimental reveries. Even as a girl she had looked upon men as work-fellows. She had grown up in serious times.

There was one fancy indeed, which persisted through her girlhood. It most often came to her on Sunday mornings, the one day in the week when she lay late abed listening to the familiar morning sounds; the windmill singing in the brisk breeze, Emil whistling as he blacked his boots down by the kitchen door. Sometimes, as she lay thus luxuriously idle, her eyes closed, she used to have an illusion of being lifted up bodily and carried lightly by some one very strong. It was a man, certainly, who carried her, but he was like no man she knew; he was much larger and stronger and swifter, and he carried her as easily as if she were a sheaf of wheat. She never saw him, but, with eyes closed, she could feel that he was yellow like the sunlight, and there was the smell of ripe cornfields about him. She could feel him approach, bend over her and lift her, and then she could feel herself being carried swiftly off across the fields. After such a reverie she would rise hastily, angry with herself, and go down to the bath-house that was partitioned off the kitchen shed. There she would stand in a tin tub and prosecute her bath with vigor, finishing it by pouring buckets of cold well-water over her gleaming white body which no man on the Divide could have carried very far.

As she grew older, this fancy more often came to her when she was tired than when she was fresh and strong. Sometimes, after she had been in the open all day, overseeing the branding of the cattle or the loading of the pigs, she would come in chilled, take a concoction of spices and warm home-made wine, and go to bed with her body actually aching with fatigue. Then, just before she went to sleep, she had the old sensation of being lifted and carried by a strong being who took from her all her bodily weariness.

PART IV

•

The White Mulberry Tree

CHAPTER I

The French Church, properly the Church of Sainte-Agnes, stood upon a hill. The high, narrow, red-brick building, with its tall steeple and steep roof, could be seen for miles across the wheatfields, though the little town of Sainte-Agnes was completely hidden away at the foot of the hill. The church looked powerful and triumphant there on its eminence, so high above the rest of the landscape, with miles of warm color lying at its feet, and by its position and setting it reminded one of some of the churches built long ago in the wheat-lands of middle France.

Late one June afternoon Alexandra Bergson was driving along one of the many roads that led through the rich French farming country to the big church. The sunlight was shining directly in her face, and there was a blaze of light all about the red church on the hill. Beside Alexandra lounged a strikingly exotic figure in a tall Mexican hat, a silk sash, and a black velvet jacket sewn with silver buttons. Emil had returned only the night before, and his sister was so proud of him that she decided at once to take him up to the church supper, and to make him wear the Mexican costume he had brought home in his trunk. "All the girls who have stands are going to wear fancy costumes," she argued, "and some of the boys. Marie is going to tell fortunes, and she sent to Omaha for a Bohemian dress her father brought back from a visit to the old country. If you wear those clothes, they will all be pleased. And you must take your guitar. Everybody ought to do what they can to help along, and we have never done much. We are not a talented family."

The supper was to be at six o'clock, in the basement of the church, and afterward there would be a fair, with charades and an auction. Alexandra had set out from home early, leaving the house to Signa and Nelse Jensen, who were to be married next week. Signa had shyly asked to have the wedding put off until Emil came home.

Alexandra was well satisfied with her brother. As they drove through the rolling French country toward the westering sun and the stalwart church, she was thinking of that time long ago when she and Emil drove back from the river valley to the still unconquered Divide. Yes, she told herself, it had been worthwhile; both Emil and the country had become what she had hoped. Out of her father's children there was one who was fit to cope with the world, who had not been tied to the plow, and who had a personality apart from the soil. And that, she reflected, was what she had worked for. She felt well satisfied with her life.

When they reached the church, a score of teams were hitched in front of the basement doors that opened from the hillside upon the sanded terrace, where the boys wrestled and had jumping-matches. Amédée Chevalier, a proud father of one week, rushed out and embraced Emil. Amédée was an only son,—hence he was a very rich young man,—but he meant to have twenty children himself, like his uncle Xavier. "Oh, Emil," he cried, hugging his old friend rapturously, "why ain't you been up to see my boy? You come to-morrow, sure? Emil, you wanna get a boy right off! It's the greatest thing ever! No, no, no! Angel not sick at all. Everything just fine. That boy he come into this world laughin', and he been laughin' ever since. You come an' see!" He pounded Emil's ribs to emphasize each announcement.

Emil caught his arms. "Stop, Amédée. You're knocking the wind out of me. I brought him cups and spoons and blankets and moccasins enough for an orphan asylum. I'm awful glad it's a boy, sure enough!"

The young men crowded round Emil to admire his costume and to tell him in a breath everything that had happened since he went away. Emil had more friends up here in the French country than down on Norway Creek. The French and Bohemian boys were spirited and jolly, liked variety, and were as much predisposed to favor anything new as the Scandinavian boys were to reject it. The Norwegian and Swedish lads were much more self-centered, apt to be egotistical and jealous. They were cautious and reserved with Emil because he had been away to college, and were prepared to take him down if he should try to put on airs with them. The French boys liked a bit of swagger, and they were always delighted to hear about anything new: new clothes, new games, new songs, new dances. Now they carried Emil off to show him the club room they had just fitted up over the post-office, down in the village. They ran down the hill in a drove, all laughing and chattering at once, some in French, some in English.

Alexandra went into the cool, whitewashed basement where the women were setting the tables. Marie was standing on a chair, building a little tent of shawls where she was to tell fortunes. She sprang down and ran toward Alexandra, stopping short and looking at her in disappointment. Alexandra nodded to her encouragingly.

"Oh, he will be here, Marie. The boys have taken him off to show him something. You won't know him. He is a man now, sure enough. I have no boy left. He smokes terrible-smelling Mexican cigarettes and talks Spanish. How pretty you look, child. Where did you get those beautiful earrings?"

"They belonged to father's mother. He always promised them to me. He sent them with the dress and said I could keep them."

Marie wore a short red skirt of stoutly woven cloth, a white bodice and kirtle, a yellow silk turban wound low over her brown curls, and long coral pendants in her ears. Her ears had been pierced against a piece of cork by her great-aunt when she was seven years old. In those germless days she had worn bits of broomstraw, plucked from the common sweeping-broom, in the lobes until the holes were healed and ready for little gold rings.

When Emil came back from the village, he lingered outside on the terrace with the boys. Marie could hear him talking and strumming on his guitar while Raoul Marcel sang falsetto. She was vexed with him for staying out there. It made her very nervous to hear him and not to see him; for, certainly, she told herself, she was not going out to look for him. When the supper bell rang and the boys came trooping in to get seats at the first table, she forgot all about her annoyance and ran to greet the tallest of the crowd, in his conspicuous attire. She didn't mind showing her embarrassment at all. She blushed and laughed excitedly as she gave Emil her hand, and looked delightedly at the black velvet coat that brought out his fair skin and fine blond head. Marie was incapable of being lukewarm about anything that pleased her. She simply did not know how to give a half-hearted response. When she was delighted, she was as likely as not to stand on her tip-toes and clap her hands. If people laughed at her, she laughed with them.

"Do the men wear clothes like that every day, in the street?" She caught Emil by his sleeve and turned him about. "Oh, I wish I lived where people wore things like that! Are the buttons real silver? Put on the hat, please. What a heavy thing! How do you ever wear it? Why don't you tell us about the bull-fights?"

She wanted to wring all his experiences from him at once, without waiting a moment. Emil smiled tolerantly and stood looking down at her with his old, brooding gaze, while the French girls fluttered about him in their white dresses and ribbons, and Alexandra watched the scene with pride. Several of the French girls, Marie knew, were hoping that Emil would take them to supper, and she was relieved when he took only his sister. Marie caught Frank's arm and dragged him to the same table, managing to get seats opposite the Bergsons, so that she could hear what they were talking about. Alexandra made Emil tell Mrs. Xavier Chevalier, the mother of the twenty, about how he had seen a famous matador killed in the bull-ring. Marie listened to every word, only taking her eyes from Emil to watch Frank's plate and keep it filled. When Emil finished his account,—bloody enough to satisfy Mrs. Xavier and to make her feel thankful that she was not a matador,—Marie broke out with a volley of questions. How did the women dress when they went to bull-fights? Did they wear mantillas? Did they never wear hats?

After supper the young people played charades for the amusement of their elders, who sat gossiping between their guesses. All the shops in Sainte-Agnes were closed at eight o'clock that night, so that the merchants and their clerks could attend the fair. The auction was the liveliest part of the entertainment, for the French boys always lost their heads when they began to bid, satisfied that their extravagance was in a good cause. After all the pincushions and sofa pillows and embroidered slippers were sold, Emil precipitated a panic by taking out one of his turquoise shirt studs, which every one had been admiring, and handing it to the auctioneer. All the French girls clamored for it, and their sweethearts bid against each other recklessly. Marie wanted it, too, and she kept making signals to Frank, which he took a sour pleasure in disregarding. He didn't see the use of making a fuss over a fellow just because he was dressed like a clown. When the turquoise went to Malvina Sauvage, the French banker's daughter, Marie shrugged her shoulders and betook herself to her little tent of shawls, where she began to shuffle her cards by the light of a tallow candle, calling out, "Fortunes, fortunes!"

The young priest, Father Duchesne, went first to have his fortune read. Marie took his long white hand, looked at it, and then began to run off her cards. "I see a long journey across water for you, Father. You will go to a town all cut up by water; built on islands, it seems to be, with rivers and green fields all about. And you will visit an old lady with a white cap and gold hoops in her ears, and you will be very happy there."

"Mais, oui," said the priest, with a melancholy smile. "C'est L'Isle-Adam, chez ma mère. Vous êtes très savante, ma fille." He patted her yellow turban, calling, "Venez donc, mes garçons! Il y a ici une véritable clairvoyante!"

Marie was clever at fortune-telling, indulging in a light irony that amused the crowd. She told old Brunot, the miser, that he would lose all his money, marry a girl of sixteen, and live happily on a crust. Sholte, the fat Russian boy, who lived for his stomach, was to be disappointed in love, grow thin, and shoot himself from despondency. Amédée was to have twenty children, and nineteen of them were to be girls. Amédée slapped Frank on the back and asked him why he didn't see what the fortune-teller would promise him. But Frank shook off his friendly hand and grunted, "She tell my fortune long ago; bad enough!" Then he withdrew to a corner and sat glowering at his wife.

Frank's case was all the more painful because he had no one in particular to fix his jealousy upon. Sometimes he could have thanked the man who would bring him evidence against his wife. He had discharged a good farm-boy, Jan Smirka, because he thought Marie was fond of him; but she had not seemed to miss Jan when he was gone, and she had been just as kind to the next boy. The farm-hands would always do anything for Marie; Frank couldn't find one so surly that he would not make an effort to please her. At the bottom of his heart Frank knew well enough that if he could once give up his grudge, his wife would come back to him. But he could never in the world do that. The grudge was fundamental. Perhaps he could not have given it up if he had tried. Perhaps he got more satisfaction out of feeling himself abused than he would have got out of being loved. If he could once have made Marie thoroughly unhappy, he might have relented and raised her from the dust. But she had never humbled herself. In the first days of their love she had been his slave; she had admired him abandonedly. But the moment he began to bully her and to be unjust, she began to draw away; at first in tearful amazement, then in quiet, unspoken disgust. The distance between them had widened and hardened. It no longer contracted and brought them suddenly together. The spark of her life went somewhere else, and he was always watching to surprise it. He knew that somewhere she must get a feeling to live upon, for she was not a woman who could live without loving. He wanted to prove to himself the wrong he felt. What did she hide in her heart? Where did it go? Even Frank had his churlish delicacies; he never reminded her of how much she had once loved him. For that Marie was grateful to him.

While Marie was chattering to the French boys, Amédée called Emil to the back of the room and whispered to him that they were going to play a joke on the girls. At eleven o'clock, Amédée was to go up to the switchboard in the vestibule and turn off the electric lights, and every boy would have a chance to kiss his sweetheart before Father Duchesne could find his way up the stairs to turn the current on again. The only difficulty was the candle in

Marie's tent; perhaps, as Emil had no sweetheart, he would oblige the boys by blowing out the candle. Emil said he would undertake to do that.

At five minutes to eleven he sauntered up to Marie's booth, and the French boys dispersed to find their girls. He leaned over the card-table and gave himself up to looking at her. "Do you think you could tell my fortune?" he murmured. It was the first word he had had alone with her for almost a year. "My luck hasn't changed any. It's just the same."

Marie had often wondered whether there was anyone else who could look his thoughts to you as Emil could. To-night, when she met his steady, powerful eyes, it was impossible not to feel the sweetness of the dream he was dreaming; it reached her before she could shut it out, and hid itself in her heart. She began to shuffle her cards furiously. "I'm angry with you, Emil," she broke out with petulance. "Why did you give them that lovely blue stone to sell? You might have known Frank wouldn't buy it for me, and I wanted it awfully!"

Emil laughed shortly. "People who want such little things surely ought to have them," he said dryly. He thrust his hand into the pocket of his velvet trousers and brought out a handful of uncut turquoises, as big as marbles. Leaning over the table he dropped them into her lap. "There, will those do? Be careful, don't let any one see them. Now, I suppose you want me to go away and let you play with them?"

Marie was gazing in rapture at the soft blue color of the stones. "Oh, Emil! Is everything down there beautiful like these? How could you ever come away?"

At that instant Amédée laid hands on the switchboard. There was a shiver and a giggle, and every one looked toward the red blur that Marie's candle made in the dark. Immediately that, too, was gone. Little shrieks and currents of soft laughter ran up and down the dark hall. Marie started up,—directly into Emil's arms. In the same instant she felt his lips. The veil that had hung uncertainly between them for so long was dissolved. Before she knew what she was doing, she had committed herself to that kiss that was at once a boy's and a man's, as timid as it was tender; so like Emil and so unlike any one else in the world. Not until it was over did she realize what it meant. And Emil, who had so often imagined the shock of this first kiss, was surprised at its gentleness and naturalness. It was like a sigh which they had breathed together; almost sorrowful, as if each were afraid of wakening something in the other.

When the lights came on again, everybody was laughing and shouting, and all the French girls were rosy and shining with mirth. Only Marie, in her little tent of shawls, was pale and quiet. Under her yellow turban the red coral pendants swung against white cheeks. Frank was still staring at her, but he seemed to see nothing. Years ago, he himself had had the power to take the blood from her cheeks like that. Perhaps he did not remember—perhaps he had never noticed! Emil was already at the other end of the hall, walking about with the shoulder-motion he had acquired among the Mexicans, studying the floor with his intent, deep-set eyes. Marie began to take down and fold her shawls. She did not glance up again. The young people drifted to the other end of the hall where the guitar was sounding. In a moment she heard Emil and Raoul singing:

"Across the Rio Grand-e
There lies a sunny land-e,
My bright-eyed Mexico!"

Alexandra Bergson came up to the card booth. "Let me help you, Marie. You look tired."

She placed her hand on Marie's arm and felt her shiver. Marie stiffened under that kind, calm hand. Alexandra drew back, perplexed and hurt.

There was about Alexandra something of the impervious calm of the fatalist, always disconcerting to very young people, who cannot feel that the heart lives at all unless it is still at the mercy of storms; unless its strings can scream to the touch of pain.

CHAPTER II

Signa's wedding supper was over. The guests, and the tiresome little Norwegian preacher who had performed the marriage ceremony, were saying good-night. Old Ivar was hitching the horses to the wagon to take the wedding presents and the bride and groom up to their new home, on Alexandra's north quarter. When Ivar drove up to the gate, Emil and Marie Shabata began to carry out the presents, and Alexandra went into her bedroom to bid Signa good-bye and to give her a few words of good counsel. She was surprised to find that the bride had changed her slippers for heavy shoes and was pinning up her skirts. At that moment Nelse appeared at the gate with the two milk cows that Alexandra had given Signa for a wedding present.

Alexandra began to laugh. "Why, Signa, you and Nelse are to ride home. I'll send Ivar over with the cows in the morning."

Signa hesitated and looked perplexed. When her husband called her, she pinned her hat on resolutely. "I ta-ank I better do yust like he say," she murmured in confusion.

Alexandra and Marie accompanied Signa to the gate and saw the party set off, old Ivar driving ahead in the wagon and the bride and groom following on foot, each leading a cow. Emil burst into a laugh before they were out of hearing.

"Those two will get on," said Alexandra as they turned back to the house. "They are not going to take any chances. They will feel safer with those cows in their own stable. Marie, I am going to send for an old woman next. As soon as I get the girls broken in, I marry them off."

"I've no patience with Signa, marrying that grumpy fellow!" Marie declared. "I wanted her to marry that nice Smirka boy who worked for us last winter. I think she liked him, too."

"Yes, I think she did," Alexandra assented, "but I suppose she was too much afraid of Nelse to marry any one else. Now that I think of it, most of my girls have married men they were afraid of. I believe there is a good deal of the cow in most Swedish girls. You high-strung Bohemians can't understand us. We're a terribly practical people, and I guess we think a cross man makes a good manager."

Marie shrugged her shoulders and turned to pin up a lock of hair that had fallen on her neck. Somehow Alexandra had irritated her of late. Everybody irritated her. She was tired of everybody. "I'm going home alone, Emil, so you needn't get your hat," she said as she wound her scarf quickly about her head. "Good-night, Alexandra," she called back in a strained voice, running down the gravel walk.

Emil followed with long strides until he overtook her. Then she began to walk slowly. It was a night of warm wind and faint starlight, and the fireflies were glimmering over the wheat.

"Marie," said Emil after they had walked for a while, "I wonder if you know how unhappy I am?"

Marie did not answer him. Her head, in its white scarf, drooped forward a little.

Emil kicked a clod from the path and went on:—

"I wonder whether you are really shallow-hearted, like you seem? Sometimes I think one boy does just as well as another for you. It never seems to make much difference whether it is me or Raoul Marcel or Jan Smirka. Are you like that?"

"Perhaps I am. What do you want me to do? Sit around and cry all day? When I've cried until I can't cry any more, then—I must do something else."

"Are you sorry for me?" he persisted.

"No, I'm not. If I were big and free like you, I wouldn't let anything make me unhappy. As old Napoleon Brunot said at the fair, I wouldn't go lovering after no woman. I'd take the first train and go off and have all the fun there is."

"I tried that, but it didn't do any good. Everything reminded me. The nicer the place was, the more I wanted you." They had come to the stile and Emil pointed to it persuasively. "Sit down a moment, I want to ask you something." Marie sat down on the top step and Emil drew nearer. "Would you tell me something that's none of my business if you thought it would help me out? Well, then, tell me, *please* tell me, why you ran away with Frank Shabata!"

Marie drew back. "Because I was in love with him," she said firmly.

"Really?" he asked incredulously.

"Yes, indeed. Very much in love with him. I think I was the one who suggested our running away. From the first it was more my fault than his."

Emil turned away his face.

"And now," Marie went on, "I've got to remember that. Frank is just the same now as he was then, only then I would see him as I wanted him to be. I would have my own way. And now I pay for it."

"You don't do all the paying."

"That's it. When one makes a mistake, there's no telling where it will stop. But you can go away; you can leave all this behind you."

"Not everything. I can't leave you behind. Will you go away with me, Marie?"

Marie started up and stepped across the stile. "Emil! How wickedly you talk! I am not that kind of a girl, and you know it. But what am I going to do if you keep tormenting me like this!" she added plaintively.

"Marie, I won't bother you any more if you will tell me just one thing. Stop a minute and look at me. No, nobody can see us. Everybody's asleep. That was only a firefly. Marie, *stop* and tell me!"

Emil overtook her and catching her by the shoulders shook her gently, as if he were trying to awaken a sleepwalker.

Marie hid her face on his arm. "Don't ask me anything more. I don't know anything except how miserable I am. And I thought it would be all right when you came back. Oh, Emil," she clutched his sleeve and began to cry, "what am I to do if you don't go away? I can't go, and one of us must. Can't you see?"

Emil stood looking down at her, holding his shoulders stiff and stiffening the arm to which she clung. Her white dress looked gray in the darkness. She seemed like a troubled spirit, like some shadow out of the earth, clinging to him and entreating him to give her peace. Behind her the fireflies were weaving in and out over the wheat. He put his hand on her bent head. "On my honor, Marie, if you will say you love me, I will go away."

She lifted her face to his. "How could I help it? Didn't you know?"

Emil was the one who trembled, through all his frame. After he left Marie at her gate, he wandered about the fields all night, till morning put out the fireflies and the stars.

CHAPTER III

One evening, a week after Signa's wedding, Emil was kneeling before a box in the sitting-room, packing his books. From time to time he rose and wandered about the house, picking up stray volumes and bringing them listlessly back to his box. He was packing without enthusiasm. He was not very sanguine about his future. Alexandra sat sewing by the table. She had helped him pack his trunk in the afternoon. As Emil came and went by her chair with his books, he thought to himself that it had not been so hard to leave his sister since he first went away to school. He was going directly to Omaha, to read law in the office of a Swedish lawyer until October, when he would enter the law school at Ann Arbor. They had planned that Alexandra was to come to Michigan—a long journey for her—at Christmas time, and spend several weeks with him. Nevertheless, he felt that this leavetaking would be more final than his earlier ones had been; that it meant a definite break with his old home and the beginning of something new—he did not know what. His ideas about the future would not crystallize; the more he tried to think about it, the vaguer his conception of it became. But one thing was clear, he told himself; it was high time that he made good to Alexandra, and that ought to be incentive enough to begin with.

As he went about gathering up his books he felt as if he were uprooting things. At last he threw himself down on the old slat lounge where he had slept when he was little, and lay looking up at the familiar cracks in the ceiling.

"Tired, Emil?" his sister asked.

"Lazy," he murmured, turning on his side and looking at her. He studied Alexandra's face for a long time in the lamplight. It had never occurred to him that his sister was a handsome woman until Marie Shabata had told him so. Indeed, he had never thought of her as being a woman at all, only a sister. As he studied her bent head, he looked up at the picture of John Bergson above the lamp. "No," he thought to himself, "she didn't get it there. I suppose I am more like that."

"Alexandra," he said suddenly, "that old walnut secretary you use for a desk was father's, wasn't it?"

Alexandra went on stitching. "Yes. It was one of the first things he bought for the old log house. It was a great extravagance in those days. But he wrote a great many letters back to the old country. He had many friends there, and they wrote to him up to the time he died. No one ever blamed him for grandfather's disgrace. I can see him now, sitting there on Sundays, in his white shirt, writing pages and pages, so carefully. He wrote a fine, regular hand, almost like engraving. Yours is something like his, when you take pains."

"Grandfather was really crooked, was he?"

"He married an unscrupulous woman, and then—then I'm afraid he was really crooked. When we first came here father used to have dreams about making a great fortune and going back to Sweden to pay back to the poor sailors the money grandfather had lost."

Emil stirred on the lounge. "I say, that would have been worthwhile, wouldn't it? Father wasn't a bit like Lou or Oscar, was he? I can't remember much about him before he got sick."

"Oh, not at all!" Alexandra dropped her sewing on her knee. "He had better opportunities; not to make money, but to make something of himself. He was a quiet man, but he was very intelligent. You would have been proud of him, Emil."

Alexandra felt that he would like to know there had been a man of his kin whom he could admire. She knew that Emil was ashamed of Lou and Oscar, because they were bigoted and self-satisfied. He never said much about them, but she could feel his disgust. His brothers had shown their disapproval of him ever since he first went away to school. The only thing that would have satisfied them would have been his failure at the University. As it was, they resented every change in his speech, in his dress, in his point of view; though the latter they had to conjecture, for Emil avoided talking to them about any but family matters. All his interests they treated as affectations.

Alexandra took up her sewing again. "I can remember father when he was quite a young man. He belonged to some kind of a musical society, a male chorus, in Stockholm. I can remember going with mother to hear them sing. There must have been a hundred of them, and they all wore long black coats and white neckties. I was used to seeing father in a blue coat, a sort of jacket, and when I recognized him on the platform, I was very proud. Do you remember that Swedish song he taught you, about the ship boy?"

"Yes. I used to sing it to the Mexicans. They like anything different." Emil paused. "Father had a hard fight here, didn't he?" he added thoughtfully.

"Yes, and he died in a dark time. Still, he had hope. He believed in the land."

"And in you, I guess," Emil said to himself. There was another period of silence; that warm, friendly silence, full of perfect understanding, in which Emil and Alexandra had spent many of their happiest half-hours.

At last Emil said abruptly, "Lou and Oscar would be better off if they were poor, wouldn't they?"

Alexandra smiled. "Maybe. But their children wouldn't. I have great hopes of Milly."

Emil shivered. "I don't know. Seems to me it gets worse as it goes on. The worst of the Swedes is that they're never willing to find out how much they don't know. It was like that at the University. Always so pleased with themselves! There's no getting behind that conceited Swedish grin. The Bohemians and Germans were so different."

"Come, Emil, don't go back on your own people. Father wasn't conceited, Uncle Otto wasn't. Even Lou and Oscar weren't when they were boys."

Emil looked incredulous, but he did not dispute the point. He turned on his back and lay still for a long time, his hands locked under his head, looking up at the ceiling. Alexandra knew that he was thinking of many things. She felt no anxiety about Emil. She had always believed in him, as she had believed in the land. He had been more like himself since he got back from Mexico; seemed glad to be at home, and talked to her as he used to do. She had no doubt that his wandering fit was over, and that he would soon be settled in life.

"Alexandra," said Emil suddenly, "do you remember the wild duck we saw down on the river that time?"

His sister looked up. "I often think of her. It always seems to me she's there still, just like we saw her."

"I know. It's queer what things one remembers and what things one forgets." Emil yawned and sat up. "Well, it's time to turn in." He rose, and going over to Alexandra stooped down and kissed her lightly on the cheek. "Good-night, sister. I think you did pretty well by us."

Emil took up his lamp and went upstairs. Alexandra sat finishing his new nightshirt, that must go in the top tray of his trunk.

CHAPTER IV

The next morning Angélique, Amédée's wife, was in the kitchen baking pies, assisted by old Mrs. Chevalier. Between the mixing-board and the stove stood the old cradle that had been Amédée's, and in it was his black-eyed son. As Angélique, flushed and excited, with flour on her hands, stopped to smile at the baby, Emil Bergson rode up to the kitchen door on his mare and dismounted.

"'Médée is out in the field, Emil," Angélique called as she ran across the kitchen to the oven. "He begins to cut his wheat to-day; the first wheat ready to cut anywhere about here. He bought a new header, you know, because all the wheat's so short this year. I hope he can rent it to the neighbors, it cost so much. He and his cousins bought a steam thresher on shares. You ought to go out and see that header work. I watched it an hour this morning, busy as I am with all the men to feed. He has a lot of hands, but he's the only one that knows how to drive the header or how to run the engine, so he has to be everywhere at once. He's sick, too, and ought to be in his bed."

Emil bent over Hector Baptiste, trying to make him blink his round, bead-like black eyes. "Sick? What's the matter with your daddy, kid? Been making him walk the floor with you?"

Angélique sniffed. "Not much! We don't have that kind of babies. It was his father that kept Baptiste awake. All night I had to be getting up and making mustard plasters to put on his stomach. He had an awful colic. He said he felt better this morning, but I don't think he ought to be out in the field, overheating himself."

Angélique did not speak with much anxiety, not because she was indifferent, but because she felt so secure in their good fortune. Only good things could happen to a rich, energetic, handsome young man like Amédée, with a new baby in the cradle and a new header in the field.

Emil stroked the black fuzz on Baptiste's head. "I say, Angélique, one of 'Médée's grandmothers, 'way back, must have been a squaw. This kid looks exactly like the Indian babies."

Angélique made a face at him, but old Mrs. Chevalier had been touched on a sore point, and she let out such a stream of fiery *patois* that Emil fled from the kitchen and mounted his mare.

Opening the pasture gate from the saddle, Emil rode across the field to the clearing where the thresher stood, driven by a stationary engine and fed from the header boxes. As Amédée was not on the engine, Emil rode on to the wheatfield, where he recognized, on the header, the slight, wiry figure of his friend, coatless, his white shirt puffed out by the wind, his straw hat stuck jauntily on the side of his head. The six big work-horses that drew, or rather pushed, the header, went abreast at a rapid walk, and as they were still green at the work they required a good deal of management on Amédée's part; especially when they turned the corners, where they divided, three and three, and then swung round into line again with a movement that looked as complicated as a wheel of artillery. Emil felt a new thrill of admiration for his friend, and with it the old pang of envy at the way in which Amédée could do with his might what his hand found to do, and feel that, whatever it was, it was the most important thing in the world. "I'll have to bring Alexandra up to see this thing work," Emil thought; "it's splendid!"

When he saw Emil, Amédée waved to him and called to one of his twenty cousins to take the reins. Stepping off the header without stopping it, he ran up to Emil who had dismounted. "Come along," he called. "I have to go over to the engine for a minute. I gotta green man running it, and I gotta keep an eye on him."

Emil thought the lad was unnaturally flushed and more excited than even the cares of managing a big farm at a critical time warranted. As they passed behind a last year's stack, Amédée clutched at his right side and sank down for a moment on the straw.

"Ouch! I got an awful pain in me, Emil. Something's the matter with my insides, for sure."

Emil felt his fiery cheek. "You ought to go straight to bed, 'Médée, and telephone for the doctor; that's what you ought to do."

Amédée staggered up with a gesture of despair. "How can I? I got no time to be sick. Three thousand dollars' worth of new machinery to manage, and the wheat so ripe it will begin to shatter next week. My wheat's short but it's gotta grand full berries. What's he slowing down for? We haven't got header boxes enough to feed the thresher, I guess."

Amédée started hot-foot across the stubble, leaning a

little to the right as he ran, and waved to the engineer not to stop the engine.

Emil saw that this was no time to talk about his own affairs. He mounted his mare and rode on to Sainte-Agnes, to bid his friends there good-bye. He went first to see Raoul Marcel, and found him innocently practicing the "Gloria" for the big confirmation service on Sunday while he polished the mirrors of his father's saloon.

As Emil rode homewards at three o'clock in the afternoon, he saw Amédée staggering out of the wheatfield, supported by two of his cousins. Emil stopped and helped them put the boy to bed.

CHAPTER V

When Frank Shabata came in from work at five o'clock that evening, old Moses Marcel, Raoul's father, telephoned him that Amédée had had a seizure in the wheatfield, and that Doctor Paradis was going to operate on him as soon as the Hanover doctor got there to help. Frank dropped a word of this at the table, bolted his supper, and rode off to Sainte-Agnes, where there would be sympathetic discussion of Amédée's case at Marcel's saloon.

As soon as Frank was gone, Marie telephoned Alexandra. It was a comfort to hear her friend's voice. Yes, Alexandra knew what there was to be known about Amédée. Emil had been there when they carried him out of the field, and had stayed with him until the doctors operated for appendicitis at five o'clock. They were afraid it was too late to do much good; it should have been done three days ago. Amédée was in a very bad way. Emil had just come home, worn out and sick himself. She had given him some brandy and put him to bed.

Marie hung up the receiver. Poor Amédée's illness had taken on a new meaning to her, now that she knew Emil had been with him. And it might so easily have been the other way—Emil who was ill and Amédée who was sad! Marie looked about the dusky sitting-room. She had seldom felt so utterly lonely. If Emil was asleep, there was not even a chance of his coming; and she could not go to Alexandra for sympathy. She meant to tell Alexandra everything, as soon as Emil went away. Then whatever was left between them would be honest.

But she could not stay in the house this evening. Where should she go? She walked slowly down through the orchard, where the evening air was heavy with the smell of wild cotton. The fresh, salty scent of the wild roses had given way before this more powerful perfume of midsummer. Wherever those ashes-of-rose balls hung on their milky stalks, the air about them was saturated with their breath. The sky was still red in the west and the evening star hung directly over the Bergsons' windmill. Marie crossed the fence at the wheatfield corner, and walked slowly along the path that led to Alexandra's. She could not help feeling hurt that Emil had not come to tell her about Amédée. It seemed to her most unnatural that he should not have come. If she were in trouble, certainly he was the one person in the world she would want to see. Perhaps he wished her to understand that for her he was as good as gone already.

Marie stole slowly, flutteringly, along the path, like a white night-moth out of the fields. The years seemed to stretch before her like the land; spring, summer, autumn, winter, spring; always the same patient fields, the patient little trees, the patient lives; always the same yearning, the same pulling at the chain—until the instinct to live had torn itself and bled and weakened for the last time, until the chain secured a dead woman, who might cautiously be released. Marie walked on, her face lifted toward the remote, inaccessible evening star.

When she reached the stile she sat down and waited. How terrible it was to love people when you could not really share their lives!

Yes, insofar as she was concerned, Emil was already gone. They couldn't meet any more. There was nothing for them to say. They had spent the last penny of their small change; there was nothing left but gold. The day of love-tokens was past. They had now only their hearts to give each other. And Emil being gone, what was her life to be like? In some ways, it would be easier. She would not, at least, live in perpetual fear. If Emil were once away and settled at work, she would not have the feeling that she was spoiling his life. With the memory he left her, she could be as rash as she chose. Nobody could be the worse for it but herself; and that, surely, did not matter. Her own case was clear. When a girl had loved one man, and then loved another while that man was still alive, everybody knew what to think of her. What happened to her was of little consequence, so long as she did not drag other people down with her. Emil once away, she could let everything else go and live a new life of perfect love.

Marie left the stile reluctantly. She had, after all, thought he might come. And how glad she ought to be, she told herself, that he was asleep. She left the path and went across the pasture. The moon was almost full. An owl was hooting somewhere in the fields. She had scarcely thought about where she was going when the pond glittered before her, where Emil had shot the ducks. She stopped and looked at it. Yes, there would be a dirty way out of life, if one chose to take it. But she did not want to die. She wanted to live and dream—a hundred years, forever! As long as this sweetness welled up in her heart, as long as her breast could hold this treasure of pain! She felt as the pond must feel when it held the moon like that; when it encircled and swelled with that image of gold.

In the morning, when Emil came downstairs, Alexandra met him in the sitting-room and put her hands on his shoulders. "Emil, I went to your room as soon as it was light, but you were sleeping so sound I hated to wake you. There was nothing you could do, so I let you sleep. They telephoned from Sainte-Agnes that Amédée died at three o'clock this morning."

CHAPTER VI

The Church has always held that life is for the living. On Saturday, while half the village of Sainte-Agnes was mourning for Amédée and preparing the funeral black for his burial on Monday, the other half was busy with white dresses and white veils for the great confirmation service to-morrow, when the bishop was to confirm a class of one hundred boys and girls. Father Duchesne divided his time between the living and the dead. All day Saturday the church was a scene of bustling activity, a little hushed by the thought of Amédée. The choir were busy rehearsing a mass of Rossini, which they had studied and practiced for this occasion. The women were trimming the altar, the boys and girls were bringing flowers.

On Sunday morning the bishop was to drive overland to Sainte-Agnes from Hanover, and Emil Bergson had been asked to take the place of one of Amédée's cousins in the cavalcade of forty French boys who were to ride across country to meet the bishop's carriage. At six o'clock on Sunday morning the boys met at the church. As they stood holding their horses by the bridle, they talked in low tones of their dead comrade. They kept repeating that Amédée had always been a good boy, glancing toward the red brick church which had played so large a part in Amédée's life, had been the scene of his most serious moments and of his happiest hours. He had played and wrestled and sung and courted under its shadow. Only three weeks ago he had proudly carried his baby there to be christened. They could not doubt that that invisible arm was still about Amédée; that through the church on earth he had passed to the church triumphant, the goal of the hopes and faith of so many hundred years.

When the word was given to mount, the young men rode at a walk out of the village; but once out among the wheatfields in the morning sun, their horses and their own youth got the better of them. A wave of zeal and fiery enthusiasm swept over them. They longed for a Jerusalem to deliver. The thud of their galloping hoofs interrupted many a country breakfast and brought many a woman and child to the door of the farmhouses as they passed. Five miles east of Sainte-Agnes they met the bishop in his open carriage, attended by two priests. Like one man the boys swung off their hats in a broad salute, and bowed their heads as the handsome old man lifted his two fingers in the episcopal blessing. The horsemen closed about the carriage like a guard, and whenever a restless horse broke from control and shot down the road ahead of the body, the bishop laughed and rubbed his plump hands together. "What fine boys!" he said to his priests. "The Church still has her cavalry."

As the troop swept past the graveyard half a mile east of the town,—the first frame church of the parish had stood there,—old Pierre Séguin was already out with his pick and spade, digging Amédée's grave. He knelt and uncovered as the bishop passed. The boys with one accord looked away from old Pierre to the red church on the hill, with the gold cross flaming on its steeple.

Mass was at eleven. While the church was filling, Emil Bergson waited outside, watching the wagons and buggies drive up the hill. After the bell began to ring, he saw Frank Shabata ride up on horseback and tie his horse to the hitch-bar. Marie, then, was not coming. Emil turned and went into the church. Amédée's was the only empty pew, and he sat down in it. Some of Amédée's cousins were there, dressed in black and weeping. When all the pews were full, the old men and boys packed the open space at the back of the church, kneeling on the floor. There was scarcely a family in town that was not represented in the confirmation class, by a cousin, at least. The new communicants, with their clear, reverent faces, were beautiful to look upon as they entered in a body and took the front benches reserved for them. Even before the Mass began, the air was charged with feeling. The choir had never sung so well and Raoul Marcel, in the "Gloria," drew even the bishop's eyes to the organ loft. For the offertory he sang Gounod's "Ave Maria,"—always spoken of in Sainte-Agnes as "the Ave Maria."

Emil began to torture himself with questions about Marie. Was she ill? Had she quarreled with her husband? Was she too unhappy to find comfort even here? Had she, perhaps, thought that he would come to her? Was she waiting for him? Overtaxed by excitement and sorrow as he was, the rapture of the service took hold upon his body and mind. As he listened to Raoul, he seemed to emerge from the conflicting emotions which had been whirling him about and sucking him under. He felt as if a clear light broke upon his mind, and with it a conviction that good was, after all, stronger than evil, and that good was possible to men. He seemed to discover that there was a kind of rapture in which he could love forever without faltering and without sin. He looked across the heads of the people at Frank Shabata with calmness. That rapture was for those who could feel it; for people who could not, it was non-existent. He coveted nothing that was Frank Shabata's. The spirit he had met in music was his own. Frank Shabata had never found it; would never find it if he lived beside it a thousand years; would have destroyed it if he had found it, as Herod slew the innocents, as Rome slew the martyrs.

San—cta Mari-i-i-a,

wailed Raoul from the organ loft;

O—ra pro no-o-bis!

And it did not occur to Emil that any one had ever reasoned thus before, that music had ever before given a man this equivocal revelation.

The confirmation service followed the Mass. When it was over, the congregation thronged about the newly confirmed. The girls, and even the boys, were kissed and embraced and wept over. All the aunts and grandmothers wept with joy. The housewives had much ado to tear themselves away from the general rejoicing and hurry back to their kitchens. The country parishioners were staying in town for dinner, and nearly every house in Sainte-Agnes entertained visitors that day. Father Duchesne, the bishop, and the visiting priests dined with Fabien Sauvage, the banker. Emil and Frank Shabata were both guests of old Moïse Marcel. After dinner Frank and old Moïse retired to the rear room of the saloon to play California Jack and drink their cognac, and Emil went over to the banker's with Raoul, who had been asked to sing for the bishop.

At three o'clock, Emil felt that he could stand it no longer. He slipped out under cover of "The Holy City," followed by Malvina's wistful eye, and went to the stable for his mare. He was at that height of excitement from which everything is foreshortened, from which life seems short and simple, death very near, and the soul seems to soar like an eagle. As he rode past the graveyard he looked at the brown hole in the earth where Amédée was to lie, and felt no horror. That, too, was beautiful, that simple doorway into forgetfulness. The heart, when it is too much alive, aches for that brown earth, and ecstasy has no fear of death. It is the old and the poor and the maimed who shrink from that brown hole; its wooers are found among the young, the passionate, the gallant-hearted. It was not until he had passed the graveyard that Emil realized where he was going. It was the hour for saying good-bye. It might be the last time that he would see her alone, and today he could leave her without rancor, without bitterness.

Everywhere the grain stood ripe and the hot afternoon was full of the smell of the ripe wheat, like the smell of bread baking in an oven. The breath of the wheat and the sweet clover passed him like pleasant things in a dream. He could feel nothing but the sense of diminishing distance. It seemed to him that his mare was flying, or running on wheels, like a railway train. The sunlight, flashing on the window-glass of the big red barns, drove him wild with joy. He was like an arrow shot from the bow. His life poured itself out along the road before him as he rode to the Shabata farm.

When Emil alighted at the Shabatas' gate, his horse was in a lather. He tied her in the stable and hurried to the house. It was empty. She might be at Mrs. Hiller's or with Alexandra. But anything that reminded him of her would be enough, the orchard, the mulberry tree . . .

When he reached the orchard the sun was hanging low over the wheatfield. Long fingers of light reached through the apple branches as through a net; the orchard was riddled and shot with gold; light was the reality, the trees were merely interferences that reflected and refracted light. Emil went softly down between the cherry trees toward the wheatfield. When he came to the corner, he stopped short and put his hand over his mouth. Marie was lying on her side under the white mulberry tree, her face half hidden in the grass, her eyes closed, her hands lying limply where they had happened to fall. She had lived a day of her new life of perfect love, and it had left her like this. Her breast rose and fell faintly, as if she were asleep. Emil threw himself down beside her and took her in his arms. The blood came back to her cheeks, her amber eyes opened slowly, and in them Emil saw his own face and the orchard and the sun. "I was dreaming this," she whispered, hiding her face against him, "don't take my dream away!"

CHAPTER VII

When Frank Shabata got home that night, he found Emil's mare in his stable. Such an impertinence amazed him. Like everybody else, Frank had had an exciting day. Since noon he had been drinking too much, and he was in a bad temper. He talked bitterly to himself while he put his own horse away, and as he went up the path and saw that the house was dark he felt an added sense of injury. He approached quietly and listened on the doorstep. Hearing nothing, he opened the kitchen door and went softly from one room to another. Then he went through the house again, upstairs and down, with no better result. He sat down on the bottom step of the box stairway and tried to get his wits together. In that unnatural quiet there was no sound but his own heavy breathing. Suddenly an owl began to hoot out in the fields. Frank lifted his head. An idea flashed into his mind, and his sense of injury and outrage grew. He went into his bedroom and took his murderous 405 Winchester from the closet.

When Frank took up his gun and walked out of the house, he had not the faintest purpose of doing anything with it. He did not believe that he had any real grievance. But it gratified him to feel like a desperate man. He had got into the habit of seeing himself always in desperate straits. His unhappy temperament was like a cage; he could never get out of it; and he felt that other people, his wife in particular, must have put him there. It had never more than dimly occurred to Frank that he made his own unhappiness. Though he took up his gun with dark projects in his mind, he would have been paralyzed with fright had he known that there was the slightest probability of his ever carrying any of them out.

Frank went slowly down to the orchard gate, stopped and stood for a moment lost in thought. He retraced his steps and looked through the barn and the hayloft. Then he went out to the road, where he took the footpath along the outside of the orchard hedge. The hedge was twice as tall as Frank himself, and so dense that one could see through it only by peering closely between the leaves. He could see the empty path a long way in the moonlight. His mind traveled ahead to the stile, which he always thought of as haunted by Emil Bergson. But why had he left his horse?

At the wheatfield corner, where the orchard hedge ended and the path led across the pasture to the Bergsons', Frank stopped. In the warm, breathless night air he heard a murmuring sound, perfectly inarticulate, as low as the sound of water coming from a spring, where there is no fall, and where there are no stones to fret it. Frank strained his ears. It ceased. He held his breath and began to tremble. Resting the butt of his gun on the ground, he parted the mulberry leaves softly with his fingers and peered through the hedge at the dark figures on the grass, in the shadow of the mulberry tree. It seemed to him that they must feel his eyes, that they must hear him breathing. But they did not. Frank, who had always wanted to see things blacker than they were, for once wanted to believe less than he saw. The woman lying in the shadow might so easily be one of the Bergsons' farm-girls. . . . Again the murmur, like water welling out of the ground. This time he heard it more distinctly, and his blood was quicker than his brain. He began to act, just as a man who falls into the fire begins to act. The gun sprang to his shoulder, he sighted mechanically and fired three times without stopping, stopped without knowing why. Either he shut his eyes or he had vertigo. He did not see anything while he was firing. He thought he heard a cry simultaneous with the second report, but he was not sure. He peered again through the hedge, at the two dark figures under the tree. They had fallen a little apart from each other, and were perfectly still— No, not quite; in a white patch of light, where the moon shone through the branches, a man's hand was plucking spasmodically at the grass.

Suddenly the woman stirred and uttered a cry, then another, and another. She was living! She was dragging herself toward the hedge! Frank dropped his gun and ran back along the path, shaking, stumbling, gasping. He had never imagined such horror. The cries followed him. They grew fainter and thicker, as if she were choking. He dropped on his knees beside the hedge and crouched like a rabbit, listening; fainter, fainter; a sound like a whine; again—a moan—another—silence. Frank scrambled to his feet and ran on, groaning and praying. From habit he went toward the house, where he was used to being soothed when he had worked himself into a frenzy, but at the sight of the black, open door, he started back. He knew that he had murdered somebody, that a woman was bleeding and moaning in the orchard, but he had not realized before that it was his wife. The gate stared him in the face. He threw his hands over his head. Which way to turn? He lifted his tormented face and looked at the sky. "Holy Mother of God, not to suffer! She was a good girl—not to suffer!"

Frank had been wont to see himself in dramatic situations; but now, when he stood by the windmill, in the bright space between the barn and the house, facing his own black doorway, he did not see himself at all. He stood like the hare when the dogs are approaching from all sides. And he ran like a hare, back and forth about that moonlit space, before he could make up his mind to go into the dark stable for a horse. The thought of going into a doorway was terrible to him. He caught Emil's horse by the bit and led it out. He could not have buckled a bridle on his own. After two or three attempts, he lifted himself into the saddle and started for Hanover. If he could catch the one o'clock train, he had money enough to get as far as Omaha.

While he was thinking dully of this in some less sensitized part of his brain, his acuter faculties were going over and over the cries he had heard in the orchard. Terror was the only thing that kept him from going back to her, terror that she might still be she, that she might still be suffering. A woman, mutilated and bleeding in his orchard—it was because it was a woman that he was so afraid. It was inconceivable that he should have hurt a woman. He would rather be eaten by wild beasts than see her move on the ground as she had moved in the orchard. Why had she been so careless? She knew he was like a crazy man when he was angry. She had more than once taken that gun away from him and held it, when he was angry with other people. Once it had gone off while they were struggling over it! She was never afraid. But, when she knew him, why hadn't she been more careful? Didn't she have all summer before her to love Emil Bergson in, without taking such chances? Probably she had met the Smirka boy, too, down there in the orchard. He didn't care. She could have met all the men on the Divide there, and welcome, if only she hadn't brought this horror on him.

There was a wrench in Frank's mind. He did not honestly believe that of her. He knew that he was doing her wrong. He stopped his horse to admit this to himself the more directly, to think it out the more clearly. He knew that he was to blame. For three years he had been trying to break her spirit. She had a way of making the best of things that seemed to him a sentimental affectation. He wanted his wife to resent that he was wasting his best years among these stupid and unappreciative people; but she had seemed to find the people quite good enough. If he ever got rich he meant to buy her pretty clothes and take her to California in a Pullman car, and treat her like a lady; but in the meantime he wanted her to feel that life was as ugly and as unjust as he felt it. He had tried to make her life ugly. He had refused to share any of the little pleasures she was so plucky about making for herself. She could be gay about the least thing in the world; but she must be gay! When she first came to him, her faith in him, her adoration—Frank struck the mare with his fist. Why had Marie made him do this thing; why had she brought this upon him? He was overwhelmed by sickening misfortune. All at once he heard her cries again—he had forgotten for a moment. "Marie," he sobbed aloud, "Marie!"

When Frank was halfway to Hanover, the motion of his horse brought on a violent attack of nausea. After it had passed, he rode on again, but he could think of nothing except his physical weakness and his desire to be comforted by his wife. He wanted to get into his own bed! Had his wife been at home, he would have turned and gone back to her meekly enough.

CHAPTER VIII

When old Ivar climbed down from his loft at four o'clock the next morning, he came upon Emil's mare, jaded and lather-stained, her bridle broken, chewing the scattered tufts of hay outside the stable door. The old man was thrown into a fright at once. He put the mare in her stall, threw her a measure of oats, and then set out as fast as his bow-legs could carry him on the path to the nearest neighbor.

"Something is wrong with that boy. Some misfortune has come upon us. He would never have used her so, in his right senses. It is not his way to abuse his mare," the old man kept muttering, as he scuttled through the short, wet pasture grass on his bare feet.

While Ivar was hurrying across the fields, the first long rays of the sun were reaching down between the orchard boughs to those two dew-drenched figures. The story of what had happened was written plainly on the orchard grass, and on the white mulberries that had fallen in the night and were covered with dark stain. For Emil the chapter had been short. He was shot in the heart, and had rolled over on his back and died. His face was turned up to the sky and his brows were drawn in a frown, as if he had realized that something had befallen him. But for Marie Shabata it had not been so easy. One ball had torn through her right lung, another had shattered the carotid artery. She must have started up and gone toward the hedge, leaving a trail of blood. There she had fallen and bled. From that spot there was another trail, heavier than the first, where she must have dragged herself back to Emil's body. Once there, she seemed not to have struggled any more. She had lifted her head to her lover's breast, taken his hand in both her own, and bled quietly to death. She was lying on her right side in an easy and natural position, her cheek on Emil's shoulder. On her face there was a look of ineffable content. Her lips were parted a little; her eyes were lightly closed, as if in a day-dream or a light slumber. After she lay down there, she seemed not to have moved an eyelash. The hand she held was covered with dark stains, where she had kissed it.

But the stained, slippery grass, the darkened mulberries, told only half the story. Above Marie and Emil, two white butterflies from Frank's alfalfa-field were fluttering in and out among the interlacing shadows; diving and soaring, now close together, now far apart; and in the long grass by the fence the last wild roses of the year opened their pink hearts to die.

When Ivar reached the path by the hedge, he saw Shabata's rifle lying in the way. He turned and peered through the branches, falling upon his knees as if his legs had been mowed from under him. "Merciful God!" he groaned; "merciful, merciful God!"

Alexandra, too, had risen early that morning, because of her anxiety about Emil. She was in Emil's room upstairs when, from the window, she saw Ivar coming along the path that led from the Shabatas'. He was running like a spent man, tottering and lurching from side to side. Ivar never drank, and Alexandra thought at once that one of his spells had come upon him, and that he must be in a very bad way indeed. She ran downstairs and hurried out to meet him, to hide his infirmity from the eyes of her household. The old man fell in the road at her feet and caught her hand, over which he bowed his shaggy head. "Mistress, mistress," he sobbed, "it has fallen! Sin and death for the young ones! God have mercy upon us!"

PART V

•

Alexandra

CHAPTER I

Ivar was sitting at a cobbler's bench in the barn, mending harness by the light of a lantern and repeating to himself the 101st Psalm. It was only five o'clock of a mid-October day, but a storm had come up in the afternoon, bringing black clouds, a cold wind and torrents of rain. The old man wore his buffalo-skin coat, and occasionally stopped to warm his fingers at the lantern. Suddenly a woman burst into the shed, as if she had been blown in, accompanied by a shower of rain-drops. It was Signa, wrapped in a man's overcoat and wearing a pair of boots over her shoes. In time of trouble Signa had come back to stay with her mistress, for she was the only one of the maids from whom Alexandra would accept much personal service. It was three months now since the news of the terrible thing that had happened in Frank Shabata's orchard had first run like a fire over the Divide. Signa and Nelse were staying on with Alexandra until winter.

"Ivar," Signa exclaimed as she wiped the rain from her face, "do you know where she is?"

The old man put down his cobbler's knife. "Who, the mistress?"

"Yes. She went away about three o'clock. I happened to look out of the window and saw her going across the fields in her thin dress and sun-hat! And now this storm has come on. I thought she was going to Mrs. Hiller's and I telephoned as soon as the thunder stopped, but she had not been there. I'm afraid she is out somewhere and will get her death of cold."

Ivar put on his cap and took up the lantern. "*Ja, ja,* we will see. I will hitch the boy's mare to the cart and go."

Signa followed him across the wagon-shed to the horses' stable. She was shivering with cold and excitement. "Where do you suppose she can be, Ivar?"

The old man lifted a set of single harness carefully from its peg. "How should I know?"

"But you think she is at the graveyard, don't you?" Signa persisted. "So do I. Oh, I wish she would be more like herself! I can't believe it's Alexandra Bergson come to this, with no head about anything. I have to tell her when to eat and when to go to bed."

"Patience, patience, sister," muttered Ivar as he settled the bit in the horse's mouth. "When the eyes of the flesh are shut, the eyes of the spirit are open. She will have a message from those who are gone, and that will bring her peace. Until then we must bear with her. You and I are the only ones who have weight with her. She trusts us."

"How awful it's been these last three months." Signa held the lantern so that he could see to buckle the straps. "It don't seem right that we must all be so miserable. Why do we all have to be punished? Seems to me like good times would never come again."

Ivar expressed himself in a deep sigh, but said nothing. He stooped and took a sandburr from his toe.

"Ivar," Signa asked suddenly, "will you tell me why you go barefoot? All the time I lived here in the house I wanted to ask you. Is it for a penance, or what?"

"No, sister. It is for the indulgence of the body. From my youth up I have had a strong, rebellious body, and have been subject to every kind of temptation. Even in age my temptations are prolonged. It was necessary to make some allowances; and the feet, as I understand it, are free members. There is no divine prohibition for them in the Ten Commandments. The hands, the tongue, the eyes, the heart, all the bodily desires we are commanded to subdue; but the feet are free members. I indulge them without harm to any one, even to trampling in filth when my desires are low. They are quickly cleaned again."

Signa did not laugh. She looked thoughtful as she followed Ivar out to the wagon-shed and held the shafts up for him, while he backed in the mare and buckled the hold-backs. "You have been a good friend to the mistress, Ivar," she murmured.

"And you, God be with you," replied Ivar as he clambered into the cart and put the lantern under the oilcloth lap-cover. "Now for a ducking, my girl," he said to the mare, gathering up the reins.

As they emerged from the shed, a stream of water, running off the thatch, struck the mare on the neck. She tossed her head indignantly, then struck out bravely on the soft ground, slipping back again and again as she climbed the hill to the main road. Between the rain and the darkness Ivar could see very little, so he let Emil's mare have the rein, keeping her head in the right direction. When the ground was level, he turned her out of the dirt road upon the sod, where she was able to trot without slipping.

Before Ivar reached the graveyard, three miles from the house, the storm had spent itself, and the downpour had died into a soft, dripping rain. The sky and the land were a dark smoke color, and seemed to be coming together, like two waves. When Ivar stopped at the gate and swung out his lantern, a white figure rose from beside John Bergson's white stone.

The old man sprang to the ground and shuffled toward the gate calling, "Mistress, mistress!"

Alexandra hurried to meet him and put her hand on his shoulder. "*Tyst!* Ivar. There's nothing to be worried about. I'm sorry if I've scared you all. I didn't notice the storm till it was on me, and I couldn't walk against it. I'm glad you've come. I am so tired I didn't know how I'd ever get home!"

Ivar swung the lantern up so that it shone in her face. "*Gud!* You are enough to frighten us, mistress. You look like a drowned woman. How could you do such a thing!"

Groaning and mumbling he led her out of the gate and helped her into the cart, wrapping her in the dry blankets on which he had been sitting.

Alexandra smiled at his solicitude. "Not much use in that, Ivar. You will only shut the wet in. I don't feel so cold now; but I'm heavy and numb. I'm glad you came."

Ivar turned the mare and urged her into a sliding trot. Her feet sent back a continual spatter of mud.

Alexandra spoke to the old man as they jogged along through the sullen gray twilight of the storm. "Ivar, I think it has done me good to get cold clear through like this, once. I don't believe I shall suffer so much any more. When you get so near the dead, they seem more real than the living. Worldly thoughts leave one. Ever since Emil died, I've suffered so when it rained. Now that I've been out in it with him, I shan't dread it. After you once get cold clear through, the feeling of the rain on you is sweet. It seems to bring back feelings you had when you were a baby. It carries you back into the dark, before you were born; you can't see things, but they come to you, somehow, and you know them and aren't afraid of them. Maybe it's like that with the dead. If they feel anything at all, it's the old things, before they were born, that comfort people like the feeling of their own bed does when they are little."

"Mistress," said Ivar reproachfully, "those are bad thoughts. The dead are in Paradise."

Then he hung his head, for he did not believe that Emil was in Paradise.

When they got home, Signa had a fire burning in the sitting-room stove. She undressed Alexandra and gave her a hot footbath, while Ivar made ginger tea in the kitchen. When Alexandra was in bed, wrapped in hot blankets, Ivar came in with his tea and saw that she drank it. Signa asked permission to sleep on the slat lounge outside her door. Alexandra endured their attentions patiently, but she was glad when they put out the lamp and left her. As she lay alone in the dark, it occurred to her for the first time that perhaps she was actually tired of life. All the physical operations of life seemed difficult and painful. She longed to be free from her own body, which ached and was so heavy. And longing itself was heavy: she yearned to be free of that.

As she lay with her eyes closed, she had again, more vividly than for many years, the old illusion of her girlhood, of being lifted and carried lightly by some one very strong. He was with her a long while this time, and carried her very far, and in his arms she felt free from pain. When he laid her down on her bed again, she opened her eyes, and, for the first time in her life, she saw him, saw him clearly, though the room was dark, and his face was covered. He was standing in the doorway of her room. His white cloak was thrown over his face, and his head was bent a little forward. His shoulders seemed as strong as the foundations of the world. His right arm, bared from the elbow, was dark and gleaming, like bronze, and she knew at once that it was the arm of the mightiest of all lovers. She knew at last for whom it was she had waited, and where he would carry her. That, she told herself, was very well. Then she went to sleep.

Alexandra wakened in the morning with nothing worse than a hard cold and a stiff shoulder. She kept her bed for several days, and it was during that time that she formed a resolution to go to Lincoln to see Frank Shabata. Ever since she last saw him in the courtroom, Frank's haggard face and wild eyes had haunted her. The trial had lasted only three days. Frank had given himself up to the police in Omaha and pleaded guilty of killing without malice and without premeditation. The gun was, of course, against him, and the judge had given him the full sentence,—ten years. He had now been in the State Penitentiary for a month.

Frank was the only one, Alexandra told herself, for whom anything could be done. He had been less in the wrong than any of them, and he was paying the heaviest penalty. She often felt that she herself had been more to blame than poor Frank. From the time the Shabatas had first moved to the neighboring farm, she had omitted no opportunity of throwing Marie and Emil together. Because she knew Frank was surly about doing little things to help his wife, she was always sending Emil over to spade or plant or carpenter for Marie. She was glad to have Emil see as much as possible of an intelligent, city-bred girl like their neighbor; she noticed that it improved his manners. She knew that Emil was fond of Marie, but it had never occurred to her that Emil's feeling might be different from her own. She wondered at herself now, but she had never thought of danger in that direction. If Marie had been unmarried,—oh, yes! Then she would have kept her eyes open. But the mere fact that she was Shabata's wife, for Alexandra, settled everything. That she was beautiful, impulsive, barely two years older than Emil, these facts had had no weight with Alexandra. Emil was a good boy, and only bad boys ran after married women.

Now, Alexandra could in a measure realize that Marie was, after all, Marie; not merely a "married woman." Sometimes, when Alexandra thought of her, it was with an aching tenderness. The moment she had reached them in the orchard that morning, everything was clear to her. There was something about those two lying in the grass, something in the way Marie had settled her cheek on Emil's shoulder, that told her everything. She wondered then how they could have helped loving each other; how she could have helped knowing that they must. Emil's cold, frowning face, the girl's content—Alexandra had felt awe of them, even in the first shock of her grief.

The idleness of those days in bed, the relaxation of body which attended them, enabled Alexandra to think more calmly than she had done since Emil's death. She and Frank, she told herself, were left out of that group of friends who had been overwhelmed by disaster. She must certainly see Frank Shabata. Even in the courtroom her heart had grieved for him. He was in a strange country, he had no kinsmen or friends, and in a moment he had ruined his life. Being what he was, she felt, Frank could not have acted otherwise. She could understand his behavior more easily than she could understand Marie's. Yes, she must go to Lincoln to see Frank Shabata.

The day after Emil's funeral, Alexandra had written to Carl Linstrum; a single page of note-paper, a bare statement of what had happened. She was not a woman who could write much about such a thing, and about her own feelings she could never write very freely. She knew that Carl was away from post-offices, prospecting somewhere in the interior. Before he started he had written her where he expected to go, but her ideas about Alaska were vague. As the weeks went by and she heard nothing from him, it seemed to Alexandra that her heart grew hard against Carl. She began to wonder whether she would not do better to finish her life alone. What was left of life seemed unimportant.

CHAPTER II

Late in the afternoon of a brilliant October day, Alexandra Bergson, dressed in a black suit and traveling-hat, alighted at the Burlington depot in Lincoln. She drove to the Lindell Hotel, where she had stayed two years ago when she came up for Emil's Commencement. In spite of her usual air of sureness and self-possession, Alexandra felt ill at ease in hotels, and she was glad, when she went to the clerk's desk to register, that there were not many people in the lobby. She had her supper early, wearing her hat and black jacket down to the dining-room and carrying her handbag. After supper she went out for a walk.

It was growing dark when she reached the university campus. She did not go into the grounds, but walked slowly up and down the stone walk outside the long iron fence, looking through at the young men who were running from one building to another, at the lights shining from the armory and the library. A squad of cadets were going through their drill behind the armory, and the commands of their young officer rang out at regular intervals, so sharp and quick that Alexandra could not understand them. Two stalwart girls came down the library steps and out through one of the iron gates. As they passed her, Alexandra was pleased to hear them speaking Bohemian to each other. Every few moments a boy would come running down the flagged walk and dash out into the street as if he were rushing to announce some wonder to the world. Alexandra felt a great tenderness for them all. She wished one of them would stop and speak to her. She wished she could ask them whether they had known Emil.

As she lingered by the south gate she actually did encounter one of the boys. He had on his drill cap and was swinging his books at the end of a long strap. It was dark by this time; he did not see her and ran against her. He snatched off his cap and stood bareheaded and panting.

"I'm awfully sorry," he said in a bright, clear voice, with a rising inflection, as if he expected her to say something.

"Oh, it was my fault!" said Alexandra eagerly. "Are you an old student here, may I ask?"

"No, ma'am. I'm a Freshie, just off the farm. Cherry County. Were you hunting somebody?"

"No, thank you. That is—" Alexandra wanted to detain him. "That is, I would like to find some of my brother's friends. He graduated two years ago."

"Then you'd have to try the Seniors, wouldn't you? Let's see; I don't know any of them yet, but there'll be sure to be some of them around the library. That red building, right there," he pointed.

"Thank you, I'll try there," said Alexandra lingeringly.

"Oh, that's all right! Good-night." The lad clapped his cap on his head and ran straight down Eleventh Street. Alexandra looked after him wistfully.

She walked back to her hotel unreasonably comforted. "What a nice voice that boy had, and how polite he was. I know Emil was always like that to women." And again, after she had undressed and was standing in her nightgown, brushing her long, heavy hair by the electric light, she remembered him and said to herself: "I don't think I ever heard a nicer voice than that boy had. I hope he will get on well here. Cherry County; that's where the hay is so fine, and the coyotes can scratch down to water."

At nine o'clock the next morning Alexandra presented herself at the warden's office in the State Penitentiary. The warden was a German, a ruddy, cheerful-looking man who had formerly been a harness-maker. Alexandra had a letter to him from the German banker in Hanover. As he glanced at the letter, Mr. Schwartz put away his pipe.

"That big Bohemian, is it? Sure, he's gettin' along fine," said Mr. Schwartz cheerfully.

"I am glad to hear that. I was afraid he might be quarrelsome and get himself into more trouble. Mr. Schwartz, if you have time, I would like to tell you a little about Frank Shabata, and why I am interested in him."

The warden listened genially while she told him briefly something of Frank's history and character, but he did not seem to find anything unusual in her account.

"Sure, I'll keep an eye on him. We'll take care of him all right," he said, rising. "You can talk to him here, while I go to see to things in the kitchen. I'll have him sent in. He ought to be done washing out his cell by this time. We have to keep 'em clean, you know."

The warden paused at the door, speaking back over his shoulder to a pale young man in convicts' clothes who was seated at a desk in the corner, writing in a big ledger.

"Bertie, when 1037 is brought in, you just step out and give this lady a chance to talk."

The young man bowed his head and bent over his ledger again.

When Mr. Schwartz disappeared, Alexandra thrust her black-edged handkerchief nervously into her handbag. Coming out on the street-car she had not had the least dread of meeting Frank. But since she had been here the sounds and smells in the corridor, the look of the men in convicts' clothes who passed the glass door of the warden's office, affected her unpleasantly.

The warden's clock ticked, the young convict's pen scratched busily in the big book, and his sharp shoulders were shaken every few seconds by a loose cough which he tried to smother. It was easy to see that he was a sick man. Alexandra looked at him timidly, but he did not once raise his eyes. He wore a white shirt under his striped jacket, a high collar, and a necktie, very carefully tied. His hands were thin and white and well cared for, and he had a seal ring on his little finger. When he heard steps approaching in the corridor, he rose, blotted his book, put his pen in the rack, and left the room without raising his eyes. Through the door he opened a guard came in, bringing Frank Shabata.

"You the lady that wanted to talk to 1037? Here he is. Be on your good behavior, now. He can set down, lady," seeing that Alexandra remained standing. "Push that white button when you're through with him, and I'll come."

The guard went out and Alexandra and Frank were left alone.

Alexandra tried not to see his hideous clothes. She tried to look straight into his face, which she could scarcely believe was his. It was already bleached to a chalky gray.

His lips were colorless, his fine teeth looked yellowish. He glanced at Alexandra sullenly, blinked as if he had come from a dark place, and one eyebrow twitched continually. She felt at once that this interview was a terrible ordeal to him. His shaved head, showing the conformation of his skull, gave him a criminal look which he had not had during the trial.

Alexandra held out her hand. "Frank," she said, her eyes filling suddenly, "I hope you'll let me be friendly with you. I understand how you did it. I don't feel hard toward you. They were more to blame than you."

Frank jerked a dirty blue handkerchief from his trousers pocket. He had begun to cry. He turned away from Alexandra. "I never did mean to do not'ing to dat woman," he muttered. "I never mean to do not'ing to dat boy. I ain't had not'ing ag'in' dat boy. I always like dat boy fine. An' then I find him—" He stopped. The feeling went out of his face and eyes. He dropped into a chair and sat looking stolidly at the floor, his hands hanging loosely between his knees, the handkerchief lying across his striped leg. He seemed to have stirred up in his mind a disgust that had paralyzed his faculties.

"I haven't come up here to blame you, Frank. I think they were more to blame than you." Alexandra, too, felt benumbed.

Frank looked up suddenly and stared out of the office window. "I guess dat place all go to hell what I work so hard on," he said with a slow, bitter smile. "I not care a damn." He stopped and rubbed the palm of his hand over the light bristles on his head with annoyance. "I no can t'ink without my hair," he complained. "I forget English. We not talk here, except swear."

Alexandra was bewildered. Frank seemed to have undergone a change of personality. There was scarcely anything by which she could recognize her handsome Bohemian neighbor. He seemed, somehow, not altogether human. She did not know what to say to him.

"You do not feel hard to me, Frank?" she asked at last.

Frank clenched his fist and broke out in excitement. "I not feel hard at no woman. I tell you I not that kind-a man. I never hit my wife. No, never I hurt her when she devil me something awful!" He struck his fist down on the warden's desk so hard that he afterward stroked it absently. A pale pink crept over his neck and face. "Two, t'ree years I know dat woman don' care no more 'bout me, Alexandra Bergson. I know she after some other man. I know her, oo-oo! An' I ain't never hurt her. I never would-a done dat, if I ain't had dat gun along. I don' know what in hell make me take dat gun. She always say I ain't no man to carry gun. If she been in dat house, where she ought-a been— But das a foolish talk."

Frank rubbed his head and stopped suddenly, as he had stopped before. Alexandra felt that there was something strange in the way he chilled off, as if something came up in him that extinguished his power of feeling or thinking.

"Yes, Frank," she said kindly. "I know you never meant to hurt Marie."

Frank smiled at her queerly. His eyes filled slowly with tears. "You know, I most forgit dat woman's name. She ain't got no name for me no more. I never hate my wife, but dat woman what make me do dat— Honest to God, but I hate her! I no man to fight. I don' want to kill no boy and no woman. I not care how many men she take under dat tree. I no care for not'ing but dat fine boy I kill, Alexandra Bergson. I guess I go crazy sure 'nough."

Alexandra remembered the little yellow cane she had found in Frank's clothes-closet. She thought of how he had come to this country a gay young fellow, so attractive that the prettiest Bohemian girl in Omaha had run away with him. It seemed unreasonable that life should have landed him in such a place as this. She blamed Marie bitterly. And why, with her happy, affectionate nature, should she have brought destruction and sorrow to all who had loved her, even to poor old Joe Tovesky, the uncle who used to carry her about so proudly when she was a little girl? That was the strangest thing of all. Was there, then, something wrong in being warm-hearted and impulsive like that? Alexandra hated to think so. But there was Emil, in the Norwegian graveyard at home, and here was Frank Shabata. Alexandra rose and took him by the hand.

"Frank Shabata, I am never going to stop trying until I

get you pardoned. I'll never give the Governor any peace. I know I can get you out of this place."

Frank looked at her distrustfully, but he gathered confidence from her face. "Alexandra," he said earnestly, "if I git out-a here, I not trouble dis country no more. I go back where I come from; see my mother."

Alexandra tried to withdraw her hand, but Frank held on to it nervously. He put out his finger and absently touched a button on her black jacket. "Alexandra," he said in a low tone, looking steadily at the button, "you ain' t'ink I use dat girl awful bad before—"

"No, Frank. We won't talk about that," Alexandra said, pressing his hand. "I can't help Emil now, so I'm going to do what I can for you. You know I don't go away from home often, and I came up here on purpose to tell you this."

The warden at the glass door looked in inquiringly. Alexandra nodded, and he came in and touched the white button on his desk. The guard appeared, and with a sinking heart Alexandra saw Frank led away down the corridor. After a few words with Mr. Schwartz, she left the prison and made her way to the street-car. She had refused with horror the warden's cordial invitation to "go through the institution." As the car lurched over its uneven roadbed, back toward Lincoln, Alexandra thought of how she and Frank had been wrecked by the same storm and of how, although she could come out into the sunlight, she had not much more left in her life than he. She remembered some lines from a poem she had liked in her schooldays:

> Henceforth the world will only be
> A wider prison-house to me,—

and sighed. A disgust of life weighed upon her heart; some such feeling as had twice frozen Frank Shabata's features while they talked together. She wished she were back on the Divide.

When Alexandra entered her hotel, the clerk held up one finger and beckoned her. As she approached his desk, he handed her a telegram. Alexandra took the yellow envelope and looked at it in perplexity, then stepped into the elevator without opening it. As she walked down the corridor toward her room, she reflected that she was, in a manner, immune from evil tidings. On reaching her room she locked the door, and sitting down on a chair by the dresser, opened the telegram. It was from Hanover, and it read:

> Arrived Hanover last night. Shall wait here until you come. Please hurry.
>
> CARL LINSTRUM.

Alexandra put her head down on the dresser and burst into tears.

CHAPTER III

The next afternoon Carl and Alexandra were walking across the fields from Mrs. Hiller's. Alexandra had left Lincoln after midnight, and Carl had met her at the Hanover station early in the morning. After they reached home, Alexandra had gone over to Mrs. Hiller's to leave a little present she had bought for her in the city. They stayed at the old lady's door but a moment, and then came out to spend the rest of the afternoon in the sunny fields.

Alexandra had taken off her black traveling-suit and put on a white dress; partly because she saw that her black clothes made Carl uncomfortable and partly because she felt oppressed by them herself. They seemed a little like the prison where she had worn them yesterday, and to be out of place in the open fields. Carl had changed very little. His cheeks were browner and fuller. He looked less like a tired scholar than when he went away a year ago, but no one, even now, would have taken him for a man of business. His soft, lustrous black eyes, his whimsical smile, would be less against him in the Klondike than on the Divide. There are always dreamers on the frontier.

Carl and Alexandra had been talking since morning.

Her letter had never reached him. He had first learned of her misfortune from a San Francisco paper, four weeks old, which he had picked up in a saloon, and which contained a brief account of Frank Shabata's trial. When he put down the paper, he had already made up his mind that he could reach Alexandra as quickly as a letter could; and ever since he had been on the way; day and night, by the fastest boats and trains he could catch. His steamer had been held back two days by rough weather.

As they came out of Mrs. Hiller's garden they took up their talk again where they had left it.

"But could you come away like that, Carl, without arranging things? Could you just walk off and leave your business?" Alexandra asked.

Carl laughed. "Prudent Alexandra! You see, my dear, I happen to have an honest partner. I trust him with everything. In fact, it's been his enterprise from the beginning, you know. I'm in it only because he took me in. I'll have to go back in the spring. Perhaps you will want to go with me then. We haven't turned up millions yet, but we've got a start that's worth following. But this winter I'd like to spend with you. You won't feel that we ought to wait longer, on Emil's account, will you, Alexandra?"

Alexandra shook her head. "No, Carl; I don't feel that way about it. And surely you needn't mind anything Lou and Oscar say now. They are much angrier with me about Emil, now, than about you. They say it was all my fault. That I ruined him by sending him to college."

"No, I don't care a button for Lou or Oscar. The moment I knew you were in trouble, the moment I thought you might need me, it all looked different. You've always been a triumphant kind of person." Carl hesitated, looking sidewise at her strong, full figure. "But you do need me now, Alexandra?"

She put her hand on his arm. "I needed you terribly when it happened, Carl. I cried for you at night. Then everything seemed to get hard inside of me, and I thought perhaps I should never care for you again. But when I got your telegram yesterday, then—then it was just as it used to be. You are all I have in the world, you know."

Carl pressed her hand in silence. They were passing

the Shabatas' empty house now, but they avoided the orchard path and took one that led over by the pasture pond.

"Can you understand it, Carl?" Alexandra murmured. "I have had nobody but Ivar and Signa to talk to. Do talk to me. Can you understand it? Could you have believed that of Marie Tovesky? I would have been cut to pieces, little by little, before I would have betrayed her trust in me!"

Carl looked at the shining spot of water before them. "Maybe she was cut to pieces, too, Alexandra. I am sure she tried hard; they both did. That was why Emil went to Mexico, of course. And he was going away again, you tell me, though he had only been home three weeks. You remember that Sunday when I went with Emil up to the French Church fair? I thought that day there was some kind of feeling, something unusual, between them. I meant to talk to you about it. But on my way back I met Lou and Oscar and got so angry that I forgot everything else. You mustn't be hard on them, Alexandra. Sit down here by the pond a minute. I want to tell you something."

They sat down on the grass-tufted bank and Carl told her how he had seen Emil and Marie out by the pond that morning, more than a year ago, and how young and charming and full of grace they had seemed to him. "It happens like that in the world sometimes, Alexandra," he added earnestly. "I've seen it before. There are women who spread ruin around them through no fault of theirs, just by being too beautiful, too full of life and love. They can't help it. People come to them as people go to a warm fire in winter. I used to feel that in her when she was a little girl. Do you remember how all the Bohemians crowded round her in the store that day, when she gave Emil her candy? You remember those yellow sparks in her eyes?"

Alexandra sighed. "Yes. People couldn't help loving her. Poor Frank does, even now, I think; though he's got himself in such a tangle that for a long time his love has been bitterer than his hate. But if you saw there was anything wrong, you ought to have told me, Carl."

Carl took her hand and smiled patiently. "My dear, it

was something one felt in the air, as you feel the spring coming, or a storm in summer. I didn't *see* anything. Simply, when I was with those two young things, I felt my blood go quicker, I felt—how shall I say it?—an acceleration of life. After I got away, it was all too delicate, too intangible, to write about."

Alexandra looked at him mournfully. "I try to be more liberal about such things than I used to be. I try to realize that we are not all made alike. Only, why couldn't it have been Raoul Marcel, or Jan Smirka? Why did it have to be my boy?"

"Because he was the best there was, I suppose. They were both the best you had here."

The sun was dropping low in the west when the two friends rose and took the path again. The straw-stacks were throwing long shadows, the owls were flying home to the prairie-dog town. When they came to the corner where the pastures joined, Alexandra's twelve young colts were galloping in a drove over the brow of the hill.

"Carl," said Alexandra, "I should like to go up there with you in the spring. I haven't been on the water since we crossed the ocean, when I was a little girl. After we first came out here I used to dream sometimes about the shipyard where father worked, and a little sort of inlet, full of masts." Alexandra paused. After a moment's thought she said, "But you would never ask me to go away for good, would you?"

"Of course not, my dearest. I think I know how you feel about this country as well as you do yourself." Carl took her hand in both his own and pressed it tenderly.

"Yes, I still feel that way, though Emil is gone. When I was on the train this morning, and we got near Hanover, I felt something like I did when I drove back with Emil from the river that time, in the dry year. I was glad to come back to it. I've lived here a long time. There is great peace here, Carl, and freedom. . . . I thought when I came out of that prison, where poor Frank is, that I should never feel free again. But I do, here." Alexandra took a deep breath and looked off into the red west.

"You belong to the land," Carl murmured, "as you have always said. Now more than ever."

"Yes, now more than ever. You remember what you once said about the graveyard, and the old story writing itself over? Only it is we who write it, with the best we have."

They paused on the last ridge of the pasture, overlooking the house and the windmill and the stables that marked the site of John Bergson's homestead. On every side the brown waves of the earth rolled away to meet the sky.

"Lou and Oscar can't see those things," said Alexandra suddenly. "Suppose I do will my land to their children, what difference will that make? The land belongs to the future, Carl; that's the way it seems to me. How many of the names on the county clerk's plat will be there in fifty years? I might as well try to will the sunset over there to my brothers' children. We come and go, but the land is always here. And the people who love it and understand it are the people who own it—for a little while."

Carl looked at her wonderingly. She was still gazing into the west, and in her face there was that exalted serenity that sometimes came to her at moments of deep feeling. The level rays of the sinking sun shone in her clear eyes.

"Why are you thinking of such things now, Alexandra?"

"I had a dream before I went to Lincoln— But I will tell you about that afterward, after we are married. It will never come true, now, in the way I thought it might." She took Carl's arm and they walked toward the gate. "How many times we have walked this path together, Carl. How many times we will walk it again! Does it seem to you like coming back to your own place? Do you feel at peace with the world here? I think we shall be very happy. I haven't any fears. I think when friends marry, they are safe. We don't suffer like—those young ones." Alexandra ended with a sigh.

They had reached the gate. Before Carl opened it, he drew Alexandra to him and kissed her softly, on her lips and on her eyes.

She leaned heavily on his shoulder. "I am tired," she murmured. "I have been very lonely, Carl."

They went into the house together, leaving the Divide

behind them, under the evening star. Fortunate country, that is one day to receive hearts like Alexandra's into its bosom, to give them out again in the yellow wheat, in the rustling corn, in the shining eyes of youth!

Now, the complete [illegible]

[illegible]

Please allow [illegible]
Prices and availability [illegible]